Dead Certain

Dead Certain

J. LORIN

Presage Publishing * Idaho
2013 Presage Publishing Print Edition

Published in the United States by Presage Publishing

Idaho

Hard Cover ISBN: 978-0-9852713-0-5
Electronic ISBN: 978-0-9852713-2-9
Paperback ISBN: 978-0-9852713-7-4

Dedication

To the men and women of courage who will prevail as society melts down amid the flood of altruistic good intentions, brotherly love, sacrifice for the common good and social "compassion." You lived because you took the risk and refused to bow to the source of destruction.

Acknowledgments

Robert Laws: *Every writer needs a second set of eyes and another brain to shape and expand the vision. Your insights, comments, and provocations helped make this possible. Thanks, brother!*

Leilani Arenas: *Couldn't have gotten this far without your obsession for commas, periods, and a list of other details that I can barely remember.*

Champps Americana, Gameday Grille, TGIF, and Buffalo Wild Wings: *Thanks so much for letting me camp out with my laptop for hours, serving me copious amounts of Diet Coke, and letting me chat up the waitresses while I was taking a break. You guys are great!*

George A. Romero: *I don't think there would be a zombie genre without your creepifying vision. Everyone needs to thank you for the fun we've had.*

Max Brooks: *Thanks so much for expanding the genre and giving us a richer and more compelling milieu. You first taught us how to survive, and then you wrote the history, but as always what people remember years after the fact is rarely what really happened. And when the government finances the textbook . . . you can be dead certain it isn't the real story.*

The Nursing and Medical faculty at Lincoln: *Vincent Alexander, Lisa Deters, Cindy Campbell. Thanks for helping me understand R (naught) and the basics of Epidemiology and the rudiments of medical imaging. You only rolled your eyes a few times when I told you that I was writing the zombie apocalypse. I know you told me the right things, so I do hope I used the medical terminology correctly.*

1

Global Infection: ≤ 00.56251%

Incubation Stage: Infection begins when an intact virus enters a host cell and begins to replicate. During the latent period, the host has no symptoms nor is he infectious, because he hasn't yet started to shed virus.
— STAGES OF AN INFECTION

Washington, D.C.

Tess answered the hotel door wrapped in a sheet, wearing a smile. Ryan Sage was sure she wasn't wearing anything underneath. Tess stood on her tiptoes and kissed Ryan's cheek. He kissed her forehead and followed her into the premium suite at the Four Seasons on Pennsylvania Avenue, Washington, D.C.

Ryan said, "Nice. Nice. Not the penthouse, but beggars can't be choosers, right? A gift from his mommy and daddy?"

Tess rolled her eyes. "Good to see you, too." She wrestled with an earring while trying to hold up the sheet with her elbows. "And no, this is all Bexley. His parents have gone back to their house in Pittsburgh, and he wanted to celebrate tonight."

"Calling Bexley's parents' place a *house* is like calling the Great Wall a pile of rocks," Ryan said. "So, what are they doing back among the *hoi polloi*? Organizing another strike? Intimidating CEO children in their parents' house? Holding yet one more American business hostage to union demands?"

"Stop," Tess said. "They just want a break from the East Coast insanity." She disappeared into the bedroom.

"Yes, yes, the lifestyles of the rich and Marxist can be so very taxing," Ryan said, looking idly at some wall art. "And yes, the pun was intended."

"Where did you go?" Tess waved him toward the bedroom in her black bra and black thong,

"I was waiting on you to get dressed, goofy."

"Don't be a prude. I need you to zip me up."

"You have cooties."

Tess rolled her eyes again. "Just help me, okay?" She looked at her Rolex. "Shit! Selma was supposed to be back with the kids by now." She stepped into her black dress, shrugged into the delicate straps, pulled the dark blond hair up from the back of her neck and turned. "Come on, zip me up."

"Of *course*, you are running late." Ryan slid the zipper until it finished below her shoulder blades. "You talk to Lenna by chance?" he asked. "Did she tell you about her boys?"

"How do I look?" Tess said with a spin.

"Mehhh . . . pretty good." Tess was a nine on the male hotness scale, but Ryan would never tell her that. "Bexley is a very lucky man, considering that most women pork up after a couple of kids. What did he do? Chain you to a treadmill and put you on bio-identical endocrine therapy to optimize your metabolism?"

Tess punched him in the chest. "You are the one who needs the therapy, Mr. Lard Butt, and I'm surprised that BOHMeC hasn't chained *you* to a treadmill. I'm surprised they haven't levied a constraint."

"Break your hand if you hit me again," Ryan flexed his chest. "And some women like chubby."

"I don't want to know. And yes, I did talk to Lenna. The boys are not doing well. She said she asked you for money." Tess worked on her makeup in the mirror, her lower jaw dropping in proportion to where the eyeliner brush was on her eyelids.

"She did."

"You said no?"

"I did."

"Why?"

"Did she ask *you* for money?"

"It's not the same."

"Tess, it is never the same. Ever since you married Bexley you have assumed that somehow your life is exempt from the family and it's my respons—"

"Don't start with that".

"The one thing you defiantly got from Mom was the inability to see the cause and effect of your own involvement. And my point was that I refused to give her money for the same reasons that you refused."

"But it is Bexley's money."

"It is actually mommy and daddy's money, but it shouldn't matter. He is married to you. If he won't give you money because you asked, you can always shake your butt for him. It's not like you haven't shaken your moneymaker before—ow!"

"You are not the only martial artist in this family," Tess said, turning back to the mirror and continuing her makeup.

Ryan chuckled, but stepped out of arm's reach. "The one thing I admire about Bexley is that he dotes on you. But even if he didn't dote on you, Bexley shouldn't need a two for one in the Diamonds VIP." He raised his hands expansively as if to give the world a hug. "Aren't the poor and down-trodden the very people he is so eager to give money? Lenna is one of those poor and downtrodden."

"Lenna's money goes into Steve's bottle."

"And for once he and I agree."

"That isn't the only thing you and Bexley agree on."

"Did he suddenly become a free market capitalist, an advocate of limited government, and a constitutionalist?"

Tess backhanded Ryan in the chest again. "No, silly. You agree that I'm a great person."

"That depends on the minute," Ryan said, rubbing his man boob. "Ever notice how fast women resort to violence when they just *hear* something they don't like?"

Tess brushed past him into the bedroom. "Help me put this on." She handed him a dazzling diamond necklace.

"Always nice to see that the champions of the poor and destitute have a few dollars leftover for the finer things in life."

"Oh, we just rented this because Bexley is being honored at the Kennedy Center. He wanted me to look really nice."

"Like I said, he dotes on you." Ryan turned his sister to face him. Tess was stunning. "If Dad saw you now, he'd say . . ." His words trailed off as emotions rose in his throat

"That I don't need any damned rocks to make me look good," Tess finished, her eyes a little wet. "Damn you. I'm gonna have to touch up my mascara." She ran back to the bathroom looking for a tissue. "Did I tell you that we got invited to the ICES Accords? We leave for Beijing in two months. He is going to present a paper."

Ryan took a deep breath and leaned against the wall.

"No congratulations? No comment? Can't you just be happy for us, for me? Your sister is married to a man who is successful?"

Nothing good would come from what he really wanted to say about yet one more international conclave plotting international policy that did little more than fleece America and subjugate humanity in the name of the common good. He said, "It was so nice to find out you were in D.C. You say that Selma is bringing Xyla and Georgia soon?"

"There will be senators and congressmen," Tess continued. "and even a chief justice, and maybe the vice president, and heads of state, diplomats from all over the world, and representatives from every member of the United Nations will be at the ICES Accords. The invitation to present at the Accords is a big honor!"

"Is Xyla still growing like a weed?"

"You are not funny!"

"Do you want me to crack a joke about you being a Stepford wife? Tess Stepford! Funniest thing I ever said was at your wedding—"

"Shut up," Tess said with yet another patented eye roll. "The work Bexley has done is extraordinary!"

"How about this D.C. weather? Have the people here learned to drive in the snow? No? Some people believe in miracles."

"Oh, you *hate* talking about the weather. Listen, you know the Accords are important. The advances in health care technology?! The global initiatives to distribute the Eternity vaccine . . ."

"Tess, you really can't see me trying to avoid a fight?"

"I'm just saying . . ."

"You are just saying you do want a fight? First, Bexley hasn't worked as a doctor for what, five years? He isn't in research anymore, so there is no actual medical work being done. His claim to fame, Tess, is that he publishes papers for the sole purpose of advocating for population control. And he doesn't even write about medicine; he publishes moral diatribes in the name of medical science. What does that acronym ICES stand for?" Ryan snapped his fingers as if to remember. "Ignorant Collective for something, something Sterility?"

Tess puffed out her cheeks. "International Coalition for Ecological Stability. We are trying to save the planet—"

"By sterilizing free people?"

"We spay and neuter animals. How do we have the right to do that but not the responsibility for our own species? How can you not see how unfair it is that so many babies are born into such bad circumstances? The bad governments, the wars, the famines, the hardships? And then there is the ecological impact, the rise of climate change and how we are impacting wildlife?"

Ryan said, "If it is bad government causing the problems, how come it is never the government that people want to destroy? You will destroy the ability to make life, but not the institution that kills? Tess, do you even hear yourself?"

"Why do you think Israel declared its self-imposed national quarantine? It wants to limit population growth, too."

"What are you talking about? How do we get from world population control to Israel closing its borders?"

"Well, someone has to solve these problems!"

This was classic Tess: unabashed appeals to generalities and clichés without the slightest shame. Ryan said, "And the *something* is the monstrosity you propose? But of course . . . *you* are the great and wise philosopher king, and the *am ha'aretz* should bow to your great insight. The Gnosis was poured forth into *your* enlightened soul, so the *Untermenschen* should accept their predestined place. *You* have received special revelation from the gods, so the world should submit to your benevolent but forcible rule."

Tess stabbed the cap back on the mascara. "I didn't ask you to come here for one of your lectures on Plato or Augustine or Marx or Kant, or whatever other ancient thinker is in the business of plotting against humanity."

"I'd stop giving the lecture if you'd start listening."

"You just love undermining Bexley's achievements."

"Achievements?" Ryan said, "Bexley hasn't achieved anything, but merely repackages very old ideas for modern consumption. And he isn't very good at that."

"Why can't you, just this once, say a good thing about my husband?"

"You *know* me, Tess. Have I ever been different? Have I ever been shy about my opinion? Have I ever been willing to stand by quietly and watch something I think wrong go unchallenged?

"No," Tess said, "You've always been exactly the same pigheaded—"

"So, no, I can't just be happy for you. What Bexley is advocating—the rationale behind the whole ICES Accords—is an evil that I cannot abide, condone, or affirm in the name of family peace. We disagree on the princi- ple here, Tess. There is no compromise."

Tess rolled her eyes. "You just called my husband evil. At least Bexley is doing something besides *writing*."

"Your eyes will get stuck that way if you keep rolling them like that that."

"I'm serious!"

"No, you are Tess. I should talk to your kindergarten teachers."

"You are not funny! And you do a terrible imitation of Mom."

"I'm hilarious. And I do a great imitation of Mom. Want to see her look?"

Tess wagged her finger, her eyes suddenly wet. "No! Don't give me her look. Dammit! See what you did." She grabbed tissues, trying to stop the damage.

Even after the passage of years Tess struggled with grief. In moments like these, it was hard to look a sibling in the face and see the family legacy. "You are so aggravating."

"It is my sole purpose in life to torment my sister."

Tess dabbed at her eyes staring daggers into the mirror. The silence drew out like a blade over skin.

Then Tess said, "They have a file on you, Ryan. You are not safe."

2

Global Infection: ≤ 00.56252%

Prodromal stage: a period of generalized or mild symptoms of ill health.

—STAGES OF AN INFECTION

Washington, D.C.

A file? They? Safe?

And then things finally started to fall into place. Tess didn't look at the world like he did, but she wasn't stupid. She knew the ICES—Bexley's comments would start a fight. It was her way of warming up for something she didn't want to say.

And if he wasn't safe . . . that must mean . . .

Ryan walked to the bedroom window. His eyes moved to the lone granite spire rising from the ground like a defiant finger; its two-tone granite façade was washed in the color of embers from the deep red of the evening sun. "It looks like it's on fire."

Tess joined him at the window. "What does?"

"The Washington Monument. It is fitting, I suppose. I am dead certain that George is rolling in his grave. Or maybe after he heard what you just said, he's trying to crawl out of the ground."

"Are you talking to dead people now?" Tess said, as if she were speaking to someone with dementia.

"After a fashion. I am channeling dead men, or maybe speaking for the dead. Government is not reason; it is not eloquence—it is force! Like fire, it is a dangerous servant and a fearful master. Never for a moment should it be left to irresponsible action."

"You're mumbling."

"I was thinking of George Washington's words, or maybe it was Mary Baker Eddy's words. It doesn't matter who said it. The point is well-made. Government is fire. Government is dangerous. And the US government has been left alone in irresponsible action for far, far too long."

"This is serious, and you are quoting dead people."

"Yes, and let me quote this dead person, 'The man who would choose security over freedom deserves neither.'"

"Thomas Jefferson?" Tess asked, like she was a student in a classroom.

"At least you were listening sometimes. Tess, it is always serious when people stand over humanity, presuming they can fix human nature in the name of virtue. It is always serious when government rules the affairs of men with fear and intimidation by putting them on lists to threaten their lives."

Tess pulled him close, like the embrace of a lover. "Please. Listen to me. Homeland Security is investigating you. They are saying you are a national security threat."

"I'm a man without a gun who speaks about the constitution, and I'm a national security threat?" He leaned his forehead against the glass, suddenly feeling very tired. "We didn't start the fire. We didn't light it. But we tried to fight it."

"I really hate it when you talk to yourself." Tess said, "Who are you quoting now? Thomas Paine or John Locke?"

"Billy Joel."

"Who?"

"Kids today."

Tess punched him in the shoulder. "You are such a dork."

"Well, I guess it doesn't matter. We are all on lists, Tess. For my whole life, I've been on the BOHMeC list. Every baby born in America is subject to the whims of that debacle. They can harm me by merely issuing a constraint."

"But BOHMeC isn't like Homeland Security."

"Oh no, BOHMeC is far worse. But do you know how many other lists I'm on? You heard about the fatwa, right? Somehow my name has been whispered to the Caliphate. I've been getting death threats for two years since I pointed out that the Religion of Peace has been waging the same war in Europe since before Charlemagne repelled that same *peaceful* religion over a thousand years ago. Irony intended."

"But they are so far away. And you live here."

"Right. Fatwas never transcend borders. The Caliphate is so respectful of international sovereignty. You should probably mention that to Italy. I'm sure the Vatican will be pleased to hear it."

"Don't be an ass," Tess said.

"Or maybe there is the Neo-Calvinist zealots' list—the ones that can't seem to get enough of the word "heretic"? Or the Republican Party and my unrelenting criticism of their lack of political will to affect any law, or bring criminals within the government to justice? Or the rumblings from the Conference for Progressive Political Action? Of course, I'm on a list.

I'm on a lot of lists. And there is even a large list of readers that like what I have to say."

"But none of those people are big," Tess said, like she was talking to a five-year-old. "Them. The Big Them. Do you know they can RICO your assets? Bexley wanted me to tell you."

And suddenly Ryan knew they were getting to the nub of the issue.

The federal RICO statutes started out as a legal effort to undercut organized crime by nullifying the economic power gained from a criminal conspiracy. RICO was sold to the American public to level the legal playing field for those who hid behind the Constitution and civil rights. If gangsters couldn't use their ill-gotten gains to buy the best legal defense they wouldn't escape justice. But most people missed the singular fact: RICO was a government's end run around the Fourth Amendment. RICO granted the power to preemptively seize assets before a citizen was convicted of a crime.

By adding the concept of racketeering to the mix, the government could then cast the net of illegality as wide as they chose, creating guilt by the smallest association. Small fish at the very fringes of ethical lapse got caught up in weightier federal crimes that carried fully disproportional jail sentences and punishments. The small fish couldn't survive a day in a federal prison, let alone suffer asset liquidation, so they became informants—often manufacturing crimes on bigger fish until the authorities got their teeth into the sharks at the top of the food chain.

RICO was masterful in its paranoia-inspiring intentions, and it proved a brutal political weapon the likes of which the KGB had only dreamed. The early versions of the RICO statutes were aimed at the Al Capones of the world. But as all laws do, the statutes morphed into a lever to penetrate any organization that became the recipient of federal displeasure. Soon the law was used to threaten the Catholic Church, dozens of nonprofit charitable organizations, and then finally strengthened to apply to anyone the federal government saw as a threat. All the federal government had to do was tie an individual to the most marginal "criminal" activity and it gained the freedom to devour an individual's life with impunity, and civil liberties be damned.

When the Fairness Doctrine failed to shut down Talk Radio, RICO was the tool used to crush the industry. Federal authorities took random acts of violence committed by any average street thug, waved a magic wand to create a connection between the champions of free speech and immediately transformed multimillionaire talk show hosts and their sponsors into racketeers against American "public interest." The result was that most radio hosts languished in Guantanamo. A few broadcast Radio Free America from locations around the globe.

"Bexley wanted you to tell me this?" Ryan asked, "Why would he want to help a capitalist?"

"You turn everything he does into a joke. They are monitoring your blog after your latest articles about dissolving the government . . . what were you thinking writing such a thing?"

"No, I said that government, for the people and by the people, had already been dissolved. And that the Declaration of Independence provided the answer. You remember the document that was at the center of founding this country?"

"Don't patronize me," Tess said, "I had the same father you did. You are not going to survive—"

"Survive? Tess, the goal is to thrive, to beat back this disaster, and beat back the government forces that are at the root of the world's tyranny. The goal is to take back this planet from the endless tide of political tyrants. America was founded on the premise that governance is at the consent of the governed. I don't consent to ruling class despotism. I don't consent to the endless assault of government against my life, my liberty and my pursuit of happiness! I have watched the inexorable march of philosophical tyranny dismantle liberty. They have a file on me? I have a file on them. That file is huge, sitting on the Internet right now because I have been writing about this since you were running around in hot pants as a Duquesne coed and Bexley Mengele was robbing the cradle."

"Don't call him Mengele, and he wasn't robbing the cradle. I was plenty old enough to make my own decisions."

"Now that you mention it, you probably taught Johns Hopkins' medical superstar more about sex than he learned in med scho—"

Tess punched him hard.

"Ow!"

"You're a jerk!"

"No, I'm your brother. And your secret is safe with me. Well, secrets," Ryan said, emphasizing the plural. "I never told Mom about that time I found you in the basement with Rick and Regg—"

"You know I don't like it when you call him that." And now Tess had their mother's look. The similarity was chilling.

Ryan took a step out of arm's reach. "Facts are fact. Bexley is a doctor. He's advocating the advances of nanotechnology for noninvasive women's health or some such absurd euphemism for sterilization, at your Bejing conference, right?"

"It's just not that simple," Tess said, wagging her finger. "They are projecting that humans will live well past 150 years with our advances in nanomedicine, nanobiophysics, and stem cell therapy. We have to find a way to control population—"

Ryan shrugged. "Ergo, Mengele!"

Tess stomped away. "You did it again. I'm not going to talk about this."

"You are so like Mom."

"Fuck you!" Tess called from the bathroom.

"Bexley is my age, ergo, robbing the cradle," Ryan taunted as he followed.

"I have daddy issues! So, I needed an older man to teach me!"

"Eww, you do not! And don't talk about dad like that." Ryan leaned against the door frame and crossed his arms.

Tess primped in the mirror and said, "Won't you ever take me seriously?"

"The moment I get serious in a conversation you bail, so all we have is our witty banter. Besides, it's what makes me so adorable."

Tess sighed; her face softened. "You are adorable. And I do love you. I'm afraid for you."

"I'm afraid for you too Tess. I'm afraid that when you finally do wake up it will be too late."

"I called you here because I wanted to tell you that the government is looking at you hard. You have such a good job. Just stick with the computer work. Forget the writing. Forget the philosophy."

It was funny to hear Tess call his very successful business "computer work," but that was his sister. She never let details get in the way of her opinions.

"Tess, let me ask you this. Why is the government so nervous about a guy who writes and speaks?" He rubbed his paunch. "It's not like I am training for some militia. So why do they fear me?"

"I don't know."

"Tess, you need to pay attention. You are on the wrong side of this. The government wants a piece of me because the ideas I advocate undercut their tyranny."

"You can't keep talking like this. You have to stop."

"Again, you are not even hearing yourself. Did you lose sight of constitutional protections? That pesky Bill of Rights?"

"The Founding Fathers could never have understood how complex the world would get."

"Tess, the Founding Fathers were profoundly aware of how complex the justifications for government tyranny could get. For example, they were fully aware of the Augustinian justifications for despotism. They were fully aware of how dangerous it was for religious despots to acquire the power to compel other men."

"Bexley said you wouldn't heed the warning. He said you were too hard-headed to take the hint—"

"Uncle Ryan! Uncle Ryan!" Georgia and Xyla exploded into the bedroom and wrapped themselves around any limb they could find.

"Oh, slow down, girls!" Ryan said, scooping Georgia into his arms.

"Let's wrestle!" she said, grabbing his neck and giggling like a psyche ward patient.

"Me too! Me too!" Xyla shouted. "We can take you!" She monkey-climbed onto his other shoulder.

And for fifteen minutes the hotel bedroom was a whirling dervish of nine-year-old Georgia and eleven-year-old Xyla pandemonium that didn't end until they were both tied in bed covers laughing riotously under Ryan's tickling hands.

"Okay, enough!" Tess shouted. "Mommy has to finish getting ready. Xyla, Georgia, you heard me."

"Aw, Mom," Ryan sang out. "Do we have to?"

The girls giggled in the knot of covers. "Aw, Mom. Do we have to?"

Tess gave her mother stare. "You are not helping."

"I know," Ryan said with an ornery glint, pulling his nieces from under the sheet. "Okay, you heard your mom. Go find Selma and terrorize her."

The girls thundered from the room shouting about *tear-izing* until their noise faded into the suite's recesses. Ryan held the silence for a hard count of thirty and then said, "So Bexley asked you to talk to me? This summons was his idea?"

Tess nodded. "He knew you were speaking at George Mason this week. He has your best interest at heart."

And then Ryan put one last piece of the puzzle together. It was how his mind worked. "Oh Tess, bless your very, very naïve heart. *They* are watching *him*. And they sent the message for him to send a warning. I am an embarrassment. He isn't concerned for me. He is concerned for *his* reputation."

"You just can't see it when people care for you. This is exactly how you treated Mother."

Ryan sighed. This was a very old fight that went well past his personal boundaries. "Tess, as my younger sister, I tend to pull my punches when talking to you. But you are a big girl now, and my relationship with our mother isn't a card you are free to play."

"But she just wanted you to change a little bit. She just wanted you to not be so . . ." Tess' words faded into a tumble of colliding ideas.

"I'm so what? What is my unredeemable personality flaw? I'm direct? I think? I happen to know what I'm talking about?" Ryan shrugged. "Where is the sense of proportion? I'm not Lenna constantly making excuses for yet one more bad choice. I don't drink like Steve and terrorize my children. But all I ever hear is how sad it is that he doesn't use his potential and make excuses for his accident. I'm not filled with delusions of grandeur that makes me believe I can reengineer the human race, like Bexley, but somehow I'm not lovable unless I'm different? Everyone else gets a pass on their behavior, but somehow that benefit of the doubt isn't applied to me?"

"Well, that is why you are alone."

And this is where family conversations always went—they made it personal. The proof of their criticism was that since he was alone, it must mean that there was something wrong with everything he thought and believed and talked about. This was his mother's criticism over and over. And when Tess said it, the image of his mother moaned back from the grave like a ghost to the forefront of his mind.

Ryan started to snap off a reply when Xyla, his oldest niece, wandered into to the bedroom and leaned into his side for a hug.

"You would have made such a good father," Tess said, conciliatory.

Ryan mussed Xyla's hair. "All right, Tess, message delivered. But know this. Tell whoever sent the message, or whoever is listening to this conversation on hidden microphones, threats don't move me. They make me mad. I didn't start the fire. I didn't light it. But I will fight it. I won't quit. I won't stop. The colonists fought tyranny in the dead of winter without shoes and barely any food. I can't stand by and watch bad things happen and pretend that it doesn't matter just to secure a little safety."

Ryan paused as he lifted Xyla into his arms. She laid her head on his shoulder. "Tess, I do have a good job, because I have made a great business, but what does it profit a man to gain the world and lose his own soul? If the price of keeping my life is to buy it back from the extortion of thugs and despots by self-imposed blindness. What is the quality of that life?"

Tess kept biting on her knuckle and then said, "I don't know, Ryan. I don't know. These problems seem so big and I am so scared for you."

"Tess, the path you and Bexley are sprinting down makes me scared for Xyla," Ryan kissed his niece's cheek. "Government is fire, Tess, and the ICES Accords in Beijing are merely one more effort to stoke the blaze. Just remember that whatever you spark in Beijing will eventually burn your daughters."

Global Infection: ≤ 26.40123%

*Acute stage: the disease reaches its highest point of develop-
ment, shedding to secondary susceptibles without intervention.*
—STAGES OF AN INFECTION

Pittsburgh, Pennsylvania

Ryan Sage was tired, frustrated, angry and more than a little bit scared, but he really didn't like looters. Men don't get to steal just because the world is falling apart. And besides, he'd had a very bad day, and it wasn't even past eleven o'clock. So, when the skinny college student with a Penn State sweatshirt underneath a trench coat decided to rob the sub shop where Ryan sat, it was destined to go wrong.

Trench Coat leaned over the counter, flashed the hilt of a katana, said something about corporate greed keeping him in Pittsburgh and demanded the register money.

Ryan leaned back in his booth and said, "What moron steals from a restaurant before lunch?"

Trench Coat's head jerked around fumbling for the Japanese sword. "Stay out of this!"

The smell of body funk and alcohol rolled toward Ryan as he stepped out of the booth, rising to full height. "Get out. There is nothing here for you."

"I need the money, man! You don't know what it is like out there. Those airline bastards are price gouging, holding us hostage for our lives. We gotta get out while we can."

"Are you from here? Maybe you can answer this; do you think this city could have more hills and side streets and back alleys?"

Trench Coat just looked at him, wary and confused. He raised the katana.

"No hu? And how does corporate greed justify stealing from this woman now?"

"It's people like her that let it happen. She has to pay her share. You don't understand. You are just some rich white prick!"

Ryan looked from Trench Coat to the young Middle Eastern woman and back. "Okay, so you are an idiot, right? You are as white as me, and her ancestry is what, southern cracker?" He pulled his jean jacket off the bench seat. "I checked out of my hotel at five this morning with a room rate of about seventy-five dollars." He wound the jacket around his arm tight. "It was a great deal, but less than two hours later, I tried to rent the same room and I'd have to be Donald Trump to get back in. So, did I steal to get what I wanted? No. That is the way things go in a free market. When it was to *my* advantage, I accepted the laws of supply and demand."

"Those big corporations don't give a damn about people," Trench Coat said, as if they were bonding.

"My point is, people only bitch and moan about capitalism when they can't take care of themselves."

"What the hell are you—"

Ryan drove the katana away with his jean jacket clad arm and delivered a blow into Trench Coat's throat; He slumped to his knees clutching and gagging. The katana clattered to the floor.

Ryan unwrapped his arm, checked his coat. "No holes, that is good," he said. He picked it up the sword and wiggled the blade in its tang. "I thought this was a fake, but better safe than bleeding out in this sandwich shop. Anyway, funny story, I was probably twenty-one, and I did some MMA fighting, specialized in Brazilian jiu-jitsu. I even won a few bouts. I know, right? You look at a fat old man and think. what a pussy. Right? Truth be told, I sucked. I got knocked out and had some training injuries and decided I really don't like pain."

Trench Coat gasped and rolled to his back losing consciousness.

"Hey, listen to me!" Ryan thumped the flat of the blade off Trench Coat's forehead. "Here is the funny part. If you had stabbed me, I would have been useless to that pretty woman right there, and she would have had to come save me. And then where would we be?"

Trench Coat started to breathe, the blue leaving his lips, his body relaxing but Ryan put his foot on Trench Coat's throat. "You should leave now. If you come back, I'll stab you in the eye." He probably wouldn't, but it sounded fun to say.

And to think when he woke up at 5:00 a.m. Ryan's most pressing worry had been getting to the airport to catch a flight scheduled to leave at 8:54. He was standing at the concierge desk at five thirty for an airport shuttle. They said there were delays on the service, something about the shuttles being caught in the Fort Pitt tunnel. They recommended a taxi.

Three taxi drivers refused to take his fare, their English suddenly very poor, their explanation even poorer. He tried Uber and Lyft, but no one could get to him in time. Ryan called for a private car, and they took his charge card over the phone. It was going to cost a small fortune, but if he didn't get moving, he was going to miss his flight. Cell connection was inconsistent so while waiting he checked the airline app. The flight showed delayed. His brain finally clicked, something big was happening in the world.

He stepped into the hotel bar, and saw the local news broadcasts and found out that it wasn't just Pittsburgh. Airlines were delaying flights in New York, Washington, Miami, Chicago, and Los Angeles. Pilots were refusing to fly, and others had been relieved of duty. It was being described as a negotiating tactic from one of the unions. The halting service in these international hubs delayed everything else through the heartland.

The news told him exactly nothing important until he caught a lone local reporter on location, with an empty runway behind him, detailing that a terminal had been locked down and the authorities were looking into possible terrorist threats.

Terrorists in Pittsburgh? What the hell?

For weeks Ryan had been living in the bubble of family crisis. This was the first time in days that he was aware of the bigger world, a world spinning down a chaotic path. Before he was sucked into the black hole of family death and destruction, Ryan remembered that the Islamic Caliphate had taken credit for New York City uprisings. They said that Allah was creating an army in the heart of the Great Satan. Jihadists in New York were not hard to fathom, considering the last two mayors had been openly Muslim and instrumental in helping Imam Mohamed Hage-Ali establish sharia courts in New York. Religious unrest was becoming normal, but it seemed strange that jihad would have traveled to Pittsburgh in the interim.

He had been to Pittsburgh twice in recent months: the first time for the Bexley Stepford funeral, the second time for Tess. For the duration, Ryan let world affairs take care of themselves. But if the reports were true and the airport was part of a broader religious action, Ryan was likely stranded in the city with nowhere to sleep.

Get the room back.

At the hotel front desk, he explained the situation. They were unfailingly polite, but the management insisted they could not check him back in. They were, in fact, booked up.

How was that possible?

It was irrational, but when the manager declined his stay Ryan suddenly felt as if he were in a dream, unable to wake, unable to move, knowing that something was coming for him. The menace was faceless and the surroundings dark, like he could hear ominous distant footsteps echoed on marble floors.

Pock . . .
   Pock . . .
      Pock . . .

Ryan walked to a nearby hotel. They had a room—expensive but available—until they swiped his card and it came back declined. He had been living off that card for weeks, and the charge for the private car service had pre-authorized the account down barely enough for three meals. The deposit wouldn't correct for twenty-four to forty-eight hours.

Pock . . .
   Pock . . .
      Pock . . .

Ryan Sage was not poor. Far from it, but he needed help to get his money. Twelve months ago, standing in a premium suite at the Four Seasons, Tess Stepford, his sister, had warned him about a RICO investigation. He called his attorney, Jeff Steiden, before he exited the hotel lobby. It took Jeff two days of discrete inquiry to verify that indeed the Feds were trying to manufacture a racketeering case. Within a week they had developed a plan and put it in motion to combat the inevitable. The last year had been a flurry of preparation. Ryan sold his part of a lucrative information technology business, but stayed on as an employee in his own company. This arrangement kept money coming in for living expenses, but most of his salary was deposited into trust accounts managed by the law firm.

From the hotel lobby landlines, Ryan made the call.

"Jeff, I'm in a bind."

"How is Tess?"

"She isn't coming back to us, Jeff."

"I'm very sorry to hear that."

"Stuck in Pittsburgh. I need some money transferred into my working account."

"Will do, but it will take at least twenty-four hours to get the transfer done. If I spot you any capital, they might extend the RICO to me as well."

Pock . . .
   Pock . . .
      Pock . . .

Ryan had maybe enough cash for a dive hotel, but not a hotel and a cab to get into the suburbs. He only had to last a day. For almost three hours, he walked the streets rejecting rooms because they were scary or nasty or both. But when he found no good options and returned to beg any bed, everything was fully booked.

Pock . . .
   Pock . . .

Pock . . .

Desperate, he checked the local shelters, only to find they refused to take occupants until after six, but they told Ryan in terse terms that the space was for the disadvantaged. They were impatient with a misplaced tourist and very creative in communicating the general message: "Get lost."

He found one more shelter a short bus ride away. But while he waited, he witnessed three people assault someone on the street. One minute, all was peace and quiet; the next, it was violence and mayhem. The first two attacks were close but not imminent. The last attack happened right beside him. Two men faced off and suddenly started a savage beating that spread from person to person like a spaghetti western bar fight.

Ryan walked to Saint Joseph's Catholic Charities up some long, long, long hill past an old school that had *Connelly* written on the side. Halfway up and out of breath, Ryan paused. While he waited he tried calling Lenna, his youngest sister. Cell connection had been inconsistent all morning but this time it rang and rang. He was disappointed and worried but not surprised Lenna hadn't answered the phone or replied to an e-mail in weeks. She was pissed, but that was nothing new. Lenna lived to hate life and the world and it wasn't uncommon for her to drop family for months.

They had all been together—Ryan, Tess, and Lenna— for the funeral. It was a gray, rainy, cold, dismal affair in February as they watched four caskets lowered into the earth: three adult caskets and one casket sized for a child.

Mr. and Mrs. Stepford were laid to rest in ornate mahogany boxes with a silver S shining dully in the murk. Bexley's casket was an uninspired flat black box that was a testimony to the family hostility. Georgia's final resting place was a tiny white box; a last symbol of her innocence.

The extended Stepford family looked daggers at Tess while she sat in her wheelchair, oblivious—the throes of pain, painkillers and grief muting her mind. Afterward Lenna remained in Pittsburgh to help Tess and Xyla recover. Ryan returned home to work.

Tess and Lenna had never gotten along, so each of them calling to complain about general agitation didn't register as strange. To be sure, their mutual sniping seemed to mean that the world was slowly inching back to normal. Tess and Xyla convalesced. Lenna got paid to live at the sprawling Stepford estate. Lenna's husband Steve had money, so he could drink at home in his recliner, and Lenna's boys vanished into adolescent limbo. This seemed the standard life for the Sage extended family . . . until Ryan got a frantic call weeks later at 9:31 p.m. from a hysterical Lenna.

"Your bitch of a sister attacked me."
"What?"

*"I'm in Mercy getting nine inches of flesh fuzzed. These BOHMeC doctors
are a fucking joke. I had to wait for six hours to get treatment."*

"What are you talking about?"

*"This NanoMend itches like poison ivy and chicken pox combined. Tess
took a bite out of my arm."*

"She did what?"

Xyla was murdered. (Lenna left out that detail.) The Pittsburgh police
had Tess in custody at Mercy Hospital. (She left out that detail too.) Lenna
left Pittsburgh before Ryan could get there.

Pock . . .

   Pock . . .

      Pock . . .

Sixteen hours later, Ryan walked onto the high security ward at Mercy
Hospital. Tess had a broken arm, Taser burns, and endless blows to the
head and shoulders. It had taken four male police officers to subdue her,
proving that Ryan wasn't the only martial artist in the family. It was a
miracle she hadn't been shot on sight: she had maimed Lenna, the maid,
the Stepford family groundskeeper, and killed her own daughter.

When Ryan asked what happened the BOHMeC Doctors used words
like *psychotic break* and *Huntington's disease* as if they were describing
catching a common cold. He was allowed to see her; Tess was lucid and
pleasant, acting like her old nosy self, seemingly oblivious to her mayhems.
They talked about everything. They talked about nothing.

". . . Bexley hates sushi."

"Even I know he never eats it."

". . . but he did in Beijing."

"No one makes Bexley do what he doesn't want to do."

"Did you know that Bexley tried to cancel . . ."

"The trip to Beijing?"

"They insisted . . ."

But the small talk grated on his soul. Ryan needed to know what happened. How could she destroy her daughter . . . like that? What really
happed with Bexely? What really happened with the Stepford patriarch
and matriarch?

Ryan needed Tess to explain but instead . . .

". . . Can you believe they made us travel even though Georgia was sick?"
Ryan touched Tess's restrained hand. *"They made her fly with the flu?"*

*"They were going to revoke our visa if we remained in the country . . . and
try us as spies."*

"I didn't think it was legal to fly sick."

"Georgia will be okay. She'll be okay."

Georgia was dead. Bexley had shot her in the head, just like he shot his mother and father. The BOHMeC psychiatrist said it would take time for Tess' memory to come back, for her mind to heal from the trauma, but her mind didn't heal.

"Xyla got sick in Beijing, and I couldn't go to the final day ceremony," Tess was saying. *"I couldn't go."* She was rational, sane, and coherent, and in a blink swung to . . . not.

"Xyla got sick in Beijing, and I couldn't go. Can you believe she did that to me? Can you BELIEVE SHE DID THAT TO ME?!"

Tess almost broke Ryan's hand as she squeezed and thrashed in her restraints.

Pock . . .
    Pock . . .
        Pock . . .

The doctors watched real-time brain activity in an MEG scan, but could not diagnose the cause of the vast fluctuations between hemispheres. Early testing showed no physical problems but a week later, CAT scans showed the medial prefrontal cortex was full of holes, and the PET scans showed that the thalamus and hypothalamus were working at 43 percent higher capacity. The first part of the brain processed impulse control. The second part governed a broad list of tasks: consciousness, sleep regulation and hormone production, among many others. Per the doctors, Tess's condition was degenerative and five days later, the medial prefrontal cortex of Tess' brain looked like a sponge.

The BOHMeC doctors doubled the Maksimov therapy regimen. With the maturation of nanobiology combined with stem cell medical therapy, many degenerative brain diseases like Alzheimer's had been wiped from human experience like polio. And for two days, Tess became calm and lucid, and the holes in her brain tissue looked like it was regenerating.

"Bexley bit me. He hates raw meat, eats his steaks well done." That was Tess humor.

"How did he get the gun?" Ryan asked. *"He hates guns."*

"Membership has its privileges," Tess said, meaning that being part of a certain political class meant exceptions could be made. *"You can't imagine what Georgia did to Xyla . . ."*

"That is why he shot her? Because of what she did to Xyla?"

And that was the last sane conversation before the madness took over.

That evening Tess bit four nurses and a doctor. They strapped her down to her bed wearing a straitjacket and a muzzle, and the BOHMeC machine abandoned her care. In days, she had open sores from the restraints, and her hygiene was abysmal.

Pock . . .

   Pock . . .

      Pock . . .

Ryan fought to have her moved to another facility until the doctors cornered Ryan on the ward, flanked by two security guards and two orderlies. They told him that Tess would never recover. The disease was something new, something hereditary. The BOHMeC medical opinion being that hereditary ailments did not respond to the Maksimov Therapy and Eternity Vaccine regimens.

"Why then do they cure myopia and hyperopia and astigmatism?" The point was obvious to any first year medical student.

"Sir, we are the doctors." And their point was obvious to anyone suffering under socialized medicine. No one could question government doctors no matter how incompetent.

Pock . . .

   Pock . . .

      Pock . . .

Ninety percent of all doctors were members of the Bureau of Optimal Health and Medical Compliance (BOHMeC). These men were government functionaries, more concerned with Ryan's body mass index being out of regulation than trying to diagnose Tess' condition.

A few M.D. dinosaurs remained in the United States, but new, young, serious medical talent left America for Australia, New Zealand, Dubai, the Czech Republic, Mumbai, and the Delhi metropolitan region. The brain drain grew so dramatic that ten years prior U.S. emigration legislation was passed to forbid medical school graduates from leaving the country. Of course, that just meant that potential medical students left the country *before* they started medical school. The result was as predictable as it was tragic: all but twelve American medical schools closed, and the only people in attendance were international rejects only employable by a government agency whose goal had nothing to do with making people well.

BOHMeC doctors had stethoscopes and white coats, but that was all they shared with their Hippocratic forefathers. They were glorified technicians who could barely cling to the knees of the intellectual giants that gave them the Eternity Vaccine, Bio-Identical Endocrine Regeneration, or the Maksimov Therapy. They were like 1950 car mechanics who only knew how to use a wrench and hammer to fix cars manufactured in the twenty-first century. They were useless.

To cover their uselessness, they issued a constraint. The constraint had nothing to do with money; the Stepford fortune was more than enough to cover all expenses and Ryan had access to Tess' bank account.

With polite government euphemisms about comfort and well-being and quality of life, they declared Tess' treatment a social extravagance. There weren't enough resources to go around; some people needed to sacrifice for the greater good.

The BOHMeC doctors knew they were condemning Tess to a cell that would provide little more than life support until she withered away. Their show of force meant they expected a fight. The orderlies and security were prepared to take another "hereditary" manifestation of the disease into medical custody. Civil liberties died years ago with the passage of the PPACA. It was only the logical extension that doctors would be given police powers. Resisting BOHMeC arrest was a felony.

Ryan said, "Thank you, gentlemen," turned and walked from the hospital.

Ryan wanted nothing to do with the Stepford estate but with Bexley's parents, Bexley, and the girls dead, Tess was the sole surviving heir. Her lawyer said Ryan was named in the will. If she were declared incompetent, he would be the executor until she died, and then stood to inherit a huge portion of the estate. Of course, the will would be contested in court. Ryan was too numb to care, but that didn't stop lawyers on all sides of the Stepford estate battle from calling him to hint at reward or threaten retribution for failure to aid their interests. Such was the way of things when four hundred million dollars was at stake.

Tess was a ward of the State of Pennsylvania. The Pittsburgh police made it clear that if she recovered, Tess would either be one of the few women to receive the death penalty in the last few decades, or she would live out the rest of her life in a hospital for the criminally insane. Maybe it was a mercy that she wouldn't receive the death penalty. But Ryan had seen the pictures of Xyla without arms, her neck broken, and the rest of her body twisted and bent. Sister or not, family or not, there are some crimes that can only be reconciled with the death penalty and there are some maladies that make a person a threat to all humanity.

4

Global Infection: ≤ 26.40124%

Convalescence stage: recovery from illness as the body repairs itself and the patient is returned to normal.
—Stages of an infection

Pittsburgh, Pennsylvania

At Saint Joseph's Catholic Charities, Ryan spoke to a very polite lady named Shaniqua, but she said the same thing as the other shelters, but was much, much more pleasant. Out on the street with nowhere to go, Ryan dithered. "Where is a stable and a manger when you needed one?"

Walking and thinking and grieving make a man hungry so Ryan found a sandwich shop tucked into the ground floor of a row of buildings fronting Our Way, not far from Saint Joseph's. He felt absurd when he saw Mercy Hospital just across the valley; he had been walking in circles.

Pock . . .

   Pock . . .

      Pock . . .

The buildings on Our Way were like most historic Pittsburgh construction—a long line of eight stories of old red brick and granite; windows looking out over the street and fire escapes lining the back walls. The ground floor was sealed off from the upper living floors and used as retail space. Minute Mart Food Liner dominated half of the street level. The next retail space was called Firouz Hoagies. The remaining buildings were featureless and boarded over, except the last unit that had an overhang with large letters that spelled out

H-A-Y-E-K, a business banished from Pittsburgh long ago.

Ryan chimed through Firouz Hoagies just a few minutes after 10:00 a.m. "Let me have an Italian sandwich, no lettuce, and a touch extra mayo," he said. *The BOHMeC can shove its body mass index up its socialized medicine ass.*

"Lunch for breakfast?" said the young, very attractive Persian woman. She gave him a sly smile.

Ryan's heart skipped a beat. The smile framed by delicious lips was intoxicating. "It sounds good right now."

She stood tall, her shoulders back, head high, regal in bearing. "A man should eat what he wants to eat," she said, somehow managing to make the words sound vaguely erotic. "That is what I think. BOHMeC should stay out of our lives." She sliced the bread and went to work. "Can you believe what is happening in the city? It is crazy. I'm just happy to have a customer. The last few days have been pretty quiet. Do you want peppers?"

Ryan thought: *What is your name?* But the words never came out because he was fighting to keep his eyes from the cleavage pressing against her V-neck sweatshirt. She was younger than he by enough that it mattered and since American culture had decided that all men were buffoonish predators, he was certain to be called a perv for merely noticing. "I'm sorry, what?"

She smiled that same sly smile and seemed to stand up straighter as if to give a better look. "Peppers. Do you like things a little spicy?"

She was beautiful, and he was not. He couldn't think of a witty reply. "I do like hot stuff," he said smiling like an idiot. "I mean, I like peppers.'

"I just want to make sure you can handle it," she said, flipping meat slices onto the bread like a black jack dealer.

Ryan tried to hold eye contact but found his gaze drifting down and down. He felt creepy so looked left and saw a book. "*The Road to Suridon.* I thought they banned that."

"I found a copy tucked away in the library stacks. It didn't even have a barcode sticker. I think someone just hid it there. Not sure I agree with everything he says but it is an interesting book. Have you read it?"

"Yes, years ago. It was a staple in my father's mandatory reading list."

"If you want to eat this here, I wouldn't mind the company," she said, wrapping the sandwich. "Chips and a drink are on the house."

"Yes, that would be great. Thank you. Thank you," he said taking the sandwich, his mind told him to turn toward the booth, smooth and confident, but his eyes struggled to leave her face. She was the kind of beautiful that inspired a stab of pain in the male soul.

"You want some help with your bags?"

"What? Oh . . ." he stumbled over his backpack and almost dropped his sandwich. "I really am not this clumsy."

"Well, you made stumbling look graceful," she said, walking around the counter, sliding the backpack toward a seat. "And besides, you look a little stressed."

"It has been a long morning," Ryan said, setting down the sandwich, chips and laptop bag. He stepped to the soda fountain and filled the cup with ice and a beverage. "I'm feeling a little stuck and I need to get online and get a plan."

"You wanna use the WiFi here? The password is: 'itputsthelotioninthe-basket', all lower case all one word."

"Itputsthe . . ." Ryan paused, thinking. "Is that by any chance from—"

"Yes, that is me and my sister's idea of a joke. Here, give me your power cable; the plug is under the table. I'll be your hookup girl."

"You don't have to do that. I can crawl—"

"I need the exercise," she said, biting her lip and eyes sparkling. She was masterful in her coquetry. She bent over, and for ten glorious seconds her butt was perfectly outlined in her jeans and her sweatshirt rode up her back, revealing smooth, rich coffee-and-cream colored skin.

Ryan wasn't stupid, so he knew she was flirting, but as usual, his tongue was tied around his teeth, roping the endless string of wit and riposte inside his mouth. If history proved consistent, the moment he opened his mouth to say "Hello," her eyes would narrow as if he had just said, "Can I stick my hands down your pants?"

When she stood, dusting off her knees, wearing that same sly smile she said, "I got everything put into the right holes."

"Uh . . . yes. Uh . . . thank, you. You have been very kind," The idiot grin etched into his skin.

"Okay," she said, the smile fading and confusion growing. "If you need anything I'll be over there, reading." The woman went back to her stool and opened at the marked page and started twirling her black hair between long fingers.

She was a very nice distraction, but not enough for Ryan to pull his thoughts away from the last two months of dread and his current crisis. He had to find a way home and that required him to find out what was going on in the world. And he soon found out the world wasn't where he left it.

5

Global Infection: ≤ 26.40124%

For three years the Caliphate's European Peace Initiative dominated every media narrative. Domestic news agencies held an endless diatribe over the ineffectual nature of American military's ability to wage war. Fighting against the Arab Spring was a war against democracy, they said. America was hypocritical for sustaining the conflict. The Caliphate was justified in its self-defense against the Catholic West—the racist and extreme religious right's domination of world affairs. America was morally bound to withdraw and let the tide of Islam have its day; that was the appropriate conclusion of the evolutions of European democracy. Imams reminded everyone that the world would be at peace when they vanquished Allah's enemies. America's news agencies insisted that unless the world wanted to see the Caliphate's use of biological warfare, and child suicide bombers take over northern Italy, the only moral action was to withdraw immediately.

This was the narrative that Ryan expected to see when he finally plugged back in, but he found a new story: The outbreak of something called African Rabies. He vaguely remembered stories from roughly six months prior about an epidemic in unnamed locations with the standard voices issuing the standard statements about the ongoing global healthcare initiative.

Washington had been curiously cautious in its reaction to African Rabies, exercising an uncommon display of prudence, merely releasing standard warnings about contact with those suffering from this new infection. The Beltway mercifully limited the politicizing to denouncing private schools for failure to teach proper hygiene and giving lessons on the floor of the House of Representatives on how to cough into a sleeve.

Production for the Eternity Vaccine and the Maksimov Therapy was tripled by UN member nations. Certainly, this was sufficient to banish the disease into the annals of medical history.

But in the last six weeks, while Ryan was dealing with his own private horror story, African Rabies went from simmering in a pot to a full boil. Now the standard voices were issuing statements filled with hand-wringing panic. It seemed the public didn't take them seriously. Indeed, it was hard to take the media seriously after the ILBIG outbreak—an event portrayed as destined to wipe out the human race, but in the final analysis only killed 774 people in a total population of eight billion.

As Ryan brought himself back up to speed, he found a report featuring a senator from Kansas who derided private schools and all home schools for failure to maintain federal health guidelines. If they were compelled by law, then epidemics like African Rabies would never threaten humanity. A congressional investigation was underway.

Then Ryan found another report from two days later: A representative from California proposed legislation that doubled vaccination schedules for K through 12 and mandated doctor's visits within fourteen days for Eternity vaccination and Maksimov Therapy. Failure to comply tripled IRS penalties for refusing the federal PPACA mandates and further empowered BOHMeC's oversight. Washington's logic was simple. If the existing treatment wasn't holding the outbreak at bay, a double and triple dose should do the trick.

Doctors in the Czech Republic insisted that the Eternity Vaccine was not a universal cure for combatting viral diseases. Medicine should not be practiced from London, Paris, Washington and the UN, but by people who went to medical school. MSN-UNC and CNN-Jazeera led with stories denouncing the doctors as members of a fringe group, out of medical community consensus, who should be silenced for their fear mongering.

International news agencies insisted that African Rabies had been working its way around the globe for years. America was just late to the global suffering. As usual, the world was on fire while America was living beyond its means. The United Nations chastised the United States for its indifference, of course, ignoring that America was the originator and the third leading manufacturer—led by China and Australia—of the Eternity Vaccine and Maksimov Therapy.

The Pope condemned American materialism and then begged for that same material to help cure the outbreak. The Pope made no mention of the American lives spent to defend the Vatican against the Caliphate's European Peace Initiative.

Ryan sat in Firouz's sub shop finishing his sandwich and watching news outlets:

Dateline Today: The World Health Organization issued travel warnings for three countries.

Dateline Today: Social unrest had risen sharply in New York, around the United Nations, and in Washington, D.C. near Embassy Row and Georgetown University Hospital.

Dateline Today: Hospitals all over the East Coast, Chicago, and Los Angeles were begging for volunteers to help with the sudden increase of violence-related injuries.

Dateline Today: Police actions were executed in Miami, Jacksonville, Atlanta, Boston, Philadelphia, and Hoboken against angry mobs.

Dateline Today: Governors in West Virginia, Ohio, and Indiana were "considering" calling out the National Guard to keep the violence from spreading into their states.

Dateline Today: National news outlets were offering contradictory advice. Some said if you don't have to go out, stay home, and others encouraged mission-critical workers to get to work. And still other cities seemed to have no problem at all, issuing public statements that working was important to keep the economy and people's lives stable.

Dateline Today: The local news was walking back the earlier reports of terrorist threats at Pittsburgh International to merely a civil disturbance. Speculation was that Tea Party members are responsible for shutting down a single terminal. The police had taken four men and three women into custody. Sarah Connor was among those taken into custody. An investigative reporter did a web search and found the name Sarah Connor was also on Tea Party rosters in Ohio, Kentucky, and Tennessee. It could be that this Sarah Connor was also part of the Tea Party. Unconfirmed reports suggested that events at Pittsburgh International were most likely Tea Party terrorism.

Dateline Today: Pittsburgh officials insisted that local unrest was isolated and being addressed by authorities; Workers should carry on as normal. Government services relied on individual commitment to the greater good.

6

Global Infection: ≤ 26.40124%

*All human actions have one or more of these seven causes:
chance, nature, compulsions, habit, reason, passion, desire.*
— ARISTOTLE

Pittsburgh, Pennsylvania

Ryan was so engrossed in the state of the world that he forgot his intended mission—finding a way home—and started working on an article for his blog that addressed the United Nations Associated Press news feed, "Looting or Social Justice: Chicago on the Verge of the People's Republic."

He was taking notes and refining a rant in his mind—or at least Ryan thought it was in his mind—when he saw the beautiful Persian woman standing by his booth.

"You know you are talking to that thing, don't you?" she said with that wonderful sly smile. "I don't think I've ever seen someone talk to something that can't talk back but can't say three words to someone who can."

"What?" Ryan said. "Oh, I'm sorry. I . . . uh . . ."

"And you are blushing." Her dark eyes flashed pleasure.

"Well, you have done it to me now, player that I am," Ryan said, "Doing my Mr. Smooth imitation here."

"Well, Mr. Smooth, I might think you are a crazy person."

"Considering I've been unsocial and you have made the effort, I'd understand why you might think me crazy, but just think how much fun I am to watch TV with. I shout at the screen and give a running monologue. Have you seen the insanity on the cable news? Do you see how the hospital riots are portrayed in Chicago? Social justice? Who are they kidding? I'm about five minutes from writing an article."

"You are a writer?" she asked, her intrigue making her eyes darker.

She is so beautiful.

Ryan knew that a lecture on social justice would condemn all flirting to a quick, dry, flaccid demise. He had never mastered the modern language of seduction, a language in America that began and ended with the lubricant of romance: alcohol. Give a woman a thesaurus and she buttoned her coat up to her neck. Give her alcohol and she couldn't unbutton her skinny jeans fast enough. Ryan knew all of this, but couldn't seem to stop what he said next. "Morally justifying theft in the name of justice is a perversion of justice, and that destroys men's ability to actually have *justice*. That is what I was going to write about."

She dropped into the opposite booth, somehow managing to make the move look like it belonged on a magazine cover. She regarded Ryan with probing eyes. "So you are a political philosopher? That is very interesting. I would like to talk to—"

The door chimed. A college kid in a trench coat walked backwards through the door.

She flashed a dazzling smile and slid gracefully from the booth. Her last words were, "Hold that thought, Mr. Smooth. I want to talk to you some more."

A moment later Trench Coat said, "Give me all the money in the register and you won't get hurt."

And those words fanned the flames of a fuse that had been burning toward the TNT in Ryan's soul.

Bexley . . .

Tess . . .

Xyla and Georgia . . .

Lenna . . .

BOHMeC doctors . . .

Homeland Security . . .

No hotel . . .

No place to stay . . .

Walking, walking, and walking some more . . .

Trench Coat interrupting his conversation with a beautiful woman . . .

Trench Coat threatening that same beautiful woman.

Pock . . .

   Pock . . .

      Pock . . .

All things considered, Trench Coat was fortunate to crawl out of Firouz's sub shop only missing his katana.

The woman disappeared into the sub shop's recesses. Ryan sighed deep and put the fake katana on his table, fully expecting to be tossed out for causing a fight.

No good deed goes unpunished.

Ryan could be scary when he was angry; his family had told him that every time they picked a fight. The Persian woman was most likely scared. She wouldn't want any trouble. The reinforcements would politely but firmly ask Ryan to leave. He started getting his things collected when the woman rushed back into the shop, robo dialing a land line and looking at the phone like it was telling her dirty jokes. Looming large behind was a hard-looking Iranian man wielding a bat.

"This thing you do?" the man said. "Drive a thieving man from this my store?"

Ryan said, "Yes, I'm sorry. I didn't mean any harm."

"My daughter, you protecting?"

His *daughter*?

Somehow that made Ryan smile. "That was part of the deal, I guess," he said. "He had a sword and he interrupted our conversation."

Suddenly, the man broke into an expansive grin, opened his arms wide and hugged Ryan with gusto. A moment later, he was showering each cheek with kisses between bursts of Farsi.

"My father says thank you," the woman said, her dark brown eyes flashing. "His name is Firouz; mine is Ahou."

"Firouz. Ahou. Uh . . . you're welcome? Do you want me to leave?"

Again, Farsi went back and forth in a blaze of foreign gibberish.

"Leave? Oh no. There are no police coming. The line is busy all the time," Ahou said. "He wants to know if you will stay through lunch. I told him about what you said to the college kid that you had missed your flight and didn't have any place to stay. He says you can stay here for as long as you like. And he has another bat."

Ryan was being offered a job as a bouncer at a sandwich shop.

"I feed! I feed!" Firouz said.

"He'll let you eat what you want," Ahou said, "for as long as you want to stay." She flashed a very inviting smile.

"Uh . . . sure?"

Those words marked the beginning of his vigil. Ryan sat with the katana across the table and the bat leaning against the booth. Firouz was also the owner of the Minute Mart Food Liner, so he returned to the grocery to help his wife and other daughter. They were experiencing a run on milk and bread and eggs.

The lunch rush started, and he caught Ahou looking and smiling. She wore a tight gray Duquesne sweatshirt with a low neckline under her apron. On occasion, she caught him looking; a second too late, Ryan would glance away.

But as attractive as Ahou's sweatshirt was, Ryan's mind kept wandering back to conversations with Tess just before she descended into a permanent, mindless rage. Even the article on social justice lost its power of distraction. Something nagged at his attention like his dead mother.

"... Bexley hates sushi. The Chinese insisted ..."

Suddenly that line didn't sit right, as if his mind found a connection with something else. One thought inspired another thought that inspired a web search that demanded more research.

"... Can you believe they made us travel even though Georgia was sick?"

Working like a fiend between his iGlass and his laptop, Ryan picked at the threads and refined searches, but what he expected to find he could not locate.

"They were going to revoke our visa if we remained in the country ..."
"You can't imagine what Georgia did to Xyla ..."

His brain hit a dead end.

Ryan tried to watch the customers just in case they were about to hurt lovely Ahou. Mostly people regurgitated the latest cable news talking points: Allah was building an army in the Great Satan's very heart. The riots in New York City were the beginning of Allah's war to defeat His enemy. Tea Party members should be arrested for their racism.

Useless information ...

The police had been called to Mercy Hospital to restore peace.

Concerning information—the hospital was close ... Hospitals all over the East Coast called for police ...

Three customers talked about grabbing a sandwich before they fought their way out of downtown.

There is rioting in the suburbs ...

What?

Did the Steelers threaten to move their team to Cincinnati?

Then something clicked in Ryan's mind.

"You can't imagine what Georgia did to Xyla ..."

"They were going to revoke our visa if we remained in the country ..."

Within moments, Ryan was absorbed in research. And if a whole battalion of katana-wielding, trench-coat-wearing frat boys came into the sandwich shop, lovely dear Ahou's sweatshirt would have been in trouble.

7

Global Infection: ≤ 26.40125%

ZOONOSIS: a disease communicable from animals to humans under natural conditions.

—MERRIAM-WEBSTER

Pittsburgh, Pennsylvania

Ryan had lovers this close, but they had never smelled of coffee and cigarette breath. And they most certainly had never been sixty-something men in very expensive suits. Ryan's first thought was, *WTF? Didn't you ever hear of personal space?* So, he said, "I don't suppose you realize you are almost standing on top of me?"

The man in the suit gave a winsome smile and replied, "I've just never seen a data pad like that."

What did that have to do with being close enough to kiss my cheek?

He had always been direct, blunt even. He tried not to be rude, but for many people blunt was rude. Ryan saw a distinction, but apparently others didn't. His mother insisted this was the reason he wasn't married. Even from the grave her words lived on an endless tape in his mind, nagging him towards social acceptance. Some days the tape worked; other days, like today, the droning maternal appeal toward interpersonal development was filled with static.

In the last two hours, Ryan's nagging suspicions were slowly turning to certainty: there was something bigger, something monstrous behind what happened to Tess. And what had happened to her was the first ripples in the water preceded by a tsunami. The whole puzzle didn't make sense yet because he couldn't find some key pieces. But Ryan had found enough of the puzzle border and a few scattered center clusters to get a glimpse of the final picture. The peek made him yearn for a safe place to hold up and beg

God that his understanding was merely flights of paranoia. And now some man with bad breath was hanging on his shoulder like a high school crush.

Ryan had heard the comments about the iGlass dozens of times. The personal data pad could do about anything, and that included becoming a conversation starter. It was a thin strip of glass that weighed next to nothing and possessed no moving parts. Everything was performed by nano- and solid-state technology. The iGlass was powered on by a biometric scan of the owner's palm. Once open, the glass could be opaque on the back and clear on the front or fully see-through depending on the need. The commercials showed it being shot with a small caliber handgun without breaking or scratching. It was an impressive piece of technology and everyone wanted to talk about it, but in the last two hours, his statistical interest in talking to other people had dropped to zero.

"It's new," Ryan said.

"I keep up with these kinds of things, it must be very new."

Ryan was halfway through two related articles on infectious disease published fourteen months ago by a team of researchers working out of Nepal on the Tibetan border. They insisted they had discovered a new viral infection that seemed to be a non-zoonoitic strain within the Rhabdovirus family that traveled man's central nervous system just like its most common form, but affected the human brain much like Creutzfeldt–Jakob disease.

The authors expected the reader to understand prions and the implications of misfolded proteins and what they called "curious" RNA sequencing that created a virus that had never been seen before. The articles consistently referenced two researchers, Prusiner and Manuelidis, and the work they had done decades before for their various roles in identifying parts of the disease called *spongiform encephalopathies* There was some drama about what role prions played and if there was, in fact, a "viral type" cause to the disease. But the article insisted that— just as Manuelidis suggested—*this* manifestation of Creutzfeldt-Jakob was driven by a highly contagious viral infection and produced a brain tissue deterioration that showed ". . . a frightening resistance to the Eternity Vaccine . . ."

"This is a beta product," Ryan said. "I happened to know someone in the tech world."

"So how does the keyboard work?" the man said. He was tall and slender, somewhere north of sixty but weathering life very well. He reminded Ryan of a feckless presidential candidate from some years back, a Mormon or some such, who looked like he belonged on a magazine cover, but the candidate's name eluded him.

The voice of his mother rolled through his mind. *It never hurt to offer kindness.*

Ryan said, "It's an app that projects the keyboard onto smooth surfaces." He lifted the iGlass off its charging pad and held it away like a magician showing there were no wires. The keyboard disappeared from the tabletop. For all of America's familiarity with technology, it never failed that men looked like the first barbarians to discover fire when they saw something new. They oohed and aahed and readied to offer sacrifice.

"My granddaughter would love that," he said, finally standing up but still admiring.

"Yes, the keyboard gives me the ability to take notes and navigate better than my fat fingers." Ryan tapped the iGlass to find the notepad app and then used the keyboard to type out a brief note and illustrated a couple other functions. He had done this riff a few times, and it always impressed.

"How much did that set you back?"

Free. But Ryan said, "It's pricey . . ." He let his words drop with nothing else to say. Give him a conversation about the disaster of Kant's Categorical Imperative or Calvin's use of Pervasive Depravity as a tool for political subjugation and he couldn't shut up. Ask him to talk about the weather and Ryan died a quick social death.

"I'm Daniel Ryder," he said, as if he expected to be recognized and extended his hand.

"Ryan Sage."

Daniel appraised him for a moment and then said, "Firouz, could I change my mind? I'd like to get the sandwich with double pepperoni. They say the world is ending, and I'm tired of watching my cholesterol."

"Angry, Mrs. Ryder being?" called Firouz from back in the kitchen.

"If you won't tell her, I won't."

Firouz laughed, big and hearty. "Mayonnaise and oil, sandwich very good?"

"Yes, mayonnaise and oil. It is usually a veggie sandwich and some other tasteless something," Daniel said to Ryan conspiratorially. "It keeps my wife and BOHMeC happy, and I get to take a long walk from the office and sneak a cigarette, which doesn't make BOHMeC happy, but sometimes it helps with the stress, you know?" He motioned to the opposite seat in the booth. "Do you mind if I join you?"

"Sure," Ryan said, realizing Daniel Ryder was sitting down whether he wanted the company or not.

"I am sorry if I butted in."

"I'm thinking probably not," he said, the bluntness coming out before his mother's voice could play in his head.

As the man sat down, his suit jacket opened and the butt of a handgun peeked out of a holster. "You are correct. I did mean to butt in. I'm curious by nature and I'm really curious what has your attention more than a certain lovely brunette."

Ryan looked around, vaguely disappointed that Ahou was gone.

Firouz delivered Daniel's sandwich to the table with an expansive flourish. He paused. His eyes traveled back and forth between them. "They is son, yours?" He shook his head. "*He* is son, yours?" he said to Daniel, trying to correct his English.

"Richard?" Daniel said, shaking his head. "No."

"The word is, what? Intention. Uh . . ." Firouz growled as if to act out his vocabulary. "You, it is same."

Daniel frowned, "Firouz, you know Richard. He used to come in with me. Dark blond hair . . .?" Daniel Ryder prompted with a hand gesture, like that would jog Firouz's memory.

Firouz shook his head as if he was being told a fib. He tossed up his hands and walked back behind the counter.

"You don't have any stray mistresses out there, do you?" Ryan asked.

"No, no mistresses." Daniel's phone rang and after a brief glance he silenced the phone, tucked it back into his suit pocket. "My wife is not the sharing type, and besides, I never really wanted anyone else."

For as pushy as he had been, Daniel Ryder was easy to like. "Yeah, and I am my father's child. And my mother is not the sharing kind either. Funny story . . . she thought she saw my father pulling through the drive-thru ahead of her, and she honked. But he didn't respond. She got her order, then gunned her van to follow and get his attention. She got to the stoplight and honked again. Still no reaction. She was so mad she followed him all the way through town getting madder by the minute. Well, until the truck pulled into a strip mall parking lot and a perfect stranger got out of the truck saying, "Lady, what do you want?"

"What did she do?"

"I don't remember. My dad had never ignored my mother for five minutes since he met her at church when they were teenagers, let alone avoid her while driving across town. And that was after forty years of marriage. Can you imagine? That was because my dad didn't respond to her honk. She'd have dismembered him for a mistress. I just realized I'm eating alone."

"I'm fine. Firouz has been very kind to feed me."

"Firouz told me that you saved his daughter and that you drove out a looter."

"Yeah, I did."

"Why did you do that?"

"Do I need a reason to resist bad people doing bad things to innocent people?"

"No, it is just rare."

"Blessing to we he was this morning," Firouz shouted from the kitchen. "Sent him to my Ahou today from God."

"Now I am a blessing," Ryan said.

"He's an Iranian Christian. He was persecuted in his country. His wife was picked up by the police and interrogated for hours for showing a stray lock of hair. They snuck to Pakistan, to get visas to the U.S., then snuck back in and managed to smuggle themselves to Dubai. That is where I met him. He is a good man, a great businessman, and he makes a good sandwich no matter what BOHMeC says." Daniel's phone buzzed inside his suit coat. He looked, frowned, silenced the phone, and slid it back into the pocket. "Eventually, they came to America. In less than ten years here, he owned three sandwich shops. Then he sold those, bought the Mini Mart Food Liner at the end of the street and this restaurant, and he is going to be a partner in yet another larger grocery in downtown. They have a nice place just a couple of streets over."

"That is an impressive story."

"Yes, one that is repeated over and over by people not born into it."

"And almost never duplicated by people who *are* born into it," Ryan finished.

"You took my next sentence. Maybe you are my son. I actually wish my son thought the way you do." Then he shook his head and waved a thought away. "So, what were you studying so hard? Everyone else is wailing about the apocalypse and you are sitting in a sandwich shop reading medical documents."

"So, the iGlass and keyboard comment was just a ruse?"

8

Global Infection: ≤ 26.40126%

The research that has been conducted to date reveals a disturbing fact. Once the infection enters the body, it does not seem to give way to the convalescent stage. There doesn't seem to be a recovery.

—FOOTNOTE 378, NEPAL REPORT

Pittsburgh, Pennsylvania

Daniel Ryder let his CEO demeanor radiate, eating casually and Ryan felt no need to fill in the silence. Finally, Daniel said, "Not so much a ruse. More like a conversation starter. It is an interesting device. My granddaughter really would like one of those. Now that I've seen one; I'm surprised she hasn't asked grandpa to get her one." He took a swallow of his soda and wiped his mouth. "But now that you know I had a deeper motive, I would like to hear your answer. So much is happening around you and I never saw you look up. I happen to know that Ahou wanted to talk to you, and she is hard to ignore. Most men kill themselves trying to get her attention. Your focus was absolute. Very few men have that ability to focus in those circumstances. Things that interest me, I explore."

"Okay, fair enough. Ahou is beautiful, but I'm smart enough to know she's way out of my league, so a conversation with her—"

"You shouldn't sell yourself short. She is a sharp woman."

Ryan waved the thought away. "Look, I feel a rabbit trail coming on that I'm sure you will find tedious—"

"Take me down the rabbit trail."

"Really? I think we are being manipulated by the media, which isn't new, but something caught my attention about Desmolin Pharmaceuticals and its corporate plot to create this disease called African Rabies. Pretty much all national outlets are saying that they create a man-made disease so they can sell their new drug called Philaxix."

"And you don't think so?"

No, I don't think so, but I'm hoping you will think I'm a conspiracy nut and leave.

Ryan said, "Of course not. The news leaves out the facts: Desmolin Pharmaceuticals has been working on Philaxix for more than fifteen years. Its drug went to the FDA four years ago, was approved by BOHMeC, and in drugstores for over three years. They have recycled the standard evil corporation narrative about Desmolin at least three times over the last few years, if my memory serves. Why resurrect a myth that is easily refutable? The answer is the same as always; the media is deliberately trying to manipulate public opinion."

Daniel's phone buzzed again. He checked, frowned, and put it back. "Reports are that African Rabies is a real threat. Worse than the SARS outbreak back some years or the more recent ILBIG outbreak. This disease hit quick, so quick that the Federal Government closed international flights this morning out of JFK, O'Hare, Dulles, Miami, and Hawaii. You don't think there could be any truth to the story?"

Ryan felt himself getting pulled down his favorite path, but the moment he started pontificating he knew Daniel would tune out and then the conversation would die—

That's right! He'll tune out!

"Well, since you brought it up, monopolies are not a free market event. Monopolies require government intervention. But the media propaganda works because they leverage collective misunderstanding of free markets and government controlled markets. If the truth were known, they would lose their favorite villains: corporations. But government is the villain because government has the guns. When you must ask the guy with the gun for permission to buy or sell, someone always pays the guy with the gun for a competitive edge.

"Desmolin can't create a monopoly for any cure unless the FDA or BOHMeC is running interference."

Cue the exit warm up!

"But what if there are no competitors?" Daniel asked.

A follow-up question?

"You asked me for an example of manipulation. I pointed out that the reporting around Desmolin isn't right. Desmolin started working on a cure for AIDS ten years ago and it succeeded with Philaxix. As the first pharmaceutical to cure HIV/AIDS, it already had a monopoly. It doesn't need to manufacture another disease to corner market share."

Daniel Ryder had put down his sandwich. "What do you think is really going on?"

What the hell? A second follow-up question?

"People fail to understand this fundamental truth: government is merely force. So, if there is an omniscient evil mastermind manufacturing a doomsday bug, that goal can only be achieved by the force that comes with government." Ryan paused, as a stray thought went through his mind. He really wanted to get back to his research. "And as a side note, most likely a government committed to Hegelian philosophy."

Please be bored . . . please be bor—

"Hegel?" Daniel Ryder said with a wry smile. "That is the first time I've heard that name in conversation since my master's work decades ago. I can tell you are a well read, and expansive thinker. You really do fascinate me."

Damn! Damn!

Daniel said, "So how does our Hegel driven government fit into your conspiracy theory?"

Sorry, Mom. I must be blunt.

Ryan said, "Look, I'm sorry. The tragedy is if you had caught me on any other day, I would probably not shut up, but today I need to keep my conspiracy theories to myself. I really don't have the time to unravel the fundamentals of government and the implications of political philosophy. I know I sound like an ass, but I don't have the time to connect the dots on following a progression of thought or an argument."

"That was blunt," Daniel said. "I don't think I have ever been called an idiot like that before."

Ryan rubbed his forehead. "Yeah, it was blunt."

"But you weren't wrong. I wasn't listening to what you were saying. I am so used to hearing people blame America that I assumed that was where you were going. I am sensitive to the criticisms. Firouz is a prime example of the power of our government system."

"Firouz is an example of what happens when government gets out of people's way. The Founding Fathers were masterful in checking government force to prevent the inevitable encroachment into the lives of free men. They knew that government was fire. They knew that once kindled, it was almost impossible to extinguish."

"That was very well said."

"Well, I didn't say that. George Washington said it—the part about government as fire."

"You were direct so I'll will be direct. Why don't you have time to talk to me today? Ahou said you were having some trouble."

Ryan was unsure how to explain the list of woes: getting home, the leaps between Beijing, Bexley, Tess, social unrest and African Rabies. "Oh, I was just trying to satisfy some suspicions I have."

Daniel regarded him for a long minute. "Ryan, I am a very good judge of men. I caught just enough of what you were reading to know it was a paper on infectious disease. After having talked to you, I am positive you would not spend your time in a sandwich shop on a day like today to satisfy suspicions. What is it you are not saying?"

Behind his affable demeanor, easy smile, and wizened good looks Daniel had a powerfully quick mind and he was a shrewd judge.

"Here is what I'm not saying. I think the spreading violence is a symptom of a disease."

"What?"

"The media is reporting the violence in various cities and hospitals and the so called "African Rabies" as two separate events. Social justice riots fit their anti-capitalist template, although hospitals are run by the Bureau of Optimal Health and Medical Compliance—which means hospitals are really government installations. The media *wants* the violence to represent the archetypical class struggle finally coming to America, but I am convinced that the violence is a symptom of what is being called African Rabies."

"All violence? There is a lot of looting and social unrest," Daniel said, "Are you saying that everything is part of a disease?"

"No, there are, of course, opportunists resorting to looting and robbery because of the unrest. But here is what I noticed. The police action is in or around hospitals. Hospitals all over the East Coast are calling for any medical help they can get. Of course, while the police are working to pacify that emergency, bad guys scurry out of the shadows to pillage and prey in cities and towns. So, the specific cause of hospital violence gets buried under the cascading event of social unrest."

"So how do you get from the hospital violence to African Rabies?"

"There is no quick way to explain the last few months of my life, so I will summarize. My brother-in-law committed suicide after shooting his youngest daughter and his parents in the head. The incident was about ten weeks after returning from the ICES Accords in Beijing."

Daniel Ryder sat up. "Bexley Stepford was your brother-in-law?"

Ryan sighed. It was foolish to believe that a Pittsburgh native wouldn't have heard the story of the Stepford slaughter. Of course, the lifestyles of the rich and scandalous filled the papers for everyone to read. "Yes."

"Is it true that the younger daughter—Xyla—maimed her older sister?"

Ryan shut his eyes, willing himself not to see the images the police had shown him. "No, Xyla was the oldest. And please, I have no interest in discussing the details."

Daniel raised a conciliatory hand. "Yes, I'm sorry. How rude of me. So how do their deaths mean that the broader social violence is a symptom of a disease?"

"Bexley doted on my sister, and I know he would never harm her. But just before the suicide, there was a fight, and he bit her. Among many other injuries, he took a chunk out of Tess' shoulder. My sister is a fighter—a good one. To put a hurt on her would have required an uncontrollable rage. Just before their fight, Bexley's mother had a similar breakdown where she maimed her husband. The family spent a lot of money to keep it out of the press even though they ultimately failed. And then in between the parents' and Bexley's incident, Georgia maimed Xyla."

"And the murder-suicide? How does that fit?"

"The suicide is only relevant because Bexley realized he and Georgia and his parents were sick. Bexley was a talented medical research doctor. Well, he used to be before BOHMeC drove him out of medicine, but he still knew a few of the top people left in American medicine. He came back to Pittsburgh for help. Bexley knew the leading doctors in neurochemistry. One of them was a friend that somehow managed to remain in residence at Mercy.

"Around nine weeks after Beijing, Bexley arranged to get his mother and himself in to see the specialist. Of course, the days of average people calling up a specialist to get expert treatment are gone. As you know, waiting lists for specialists were booked, in some instances, years in advance. BOHMeC controlled those lists with ruthless determination, but money opens doors and lots of money moves bureaucracy like the Red Sea before Moses.

"The police told me that the Bexley incident happened right after his third appointment. Evidently, they had run extensive tests on the whole family. When the police finally got around to talking to the doctor two days after the murder-suicide, the neurological specialist was gone. He had been called away for an "emergency consultation." He hasn't been heard from since. They wanted to know if I knew where he was."

Daniel wrinkled his brow. "Why would the police ask you about the specialist?"

Ryan shrugged. "They were grasping at straws. Powerful political types wanted to make the Stepford scandal not be so scandalous. The Stepfords have serious connections to this administration. A murder-suicide by a crazy donor so close to home doesn't look good. Pressure was applied to the local police to find another 'solution.' They were desperate to find a different theory of the crime.

"Anyway, the only thing that makes sense is that Bexley knew something was wrong. I think he killed himself because he knew that he and his mother and his daughter were abnormally, dangerously, incurably violent."

"And you think something happened to them at the ICES Accords?" Daniel asked.

"Yes. They were all in Beijing. I think something was put into the food on the last day. Xyla got sick, and my sister couldn't be a part of the ceremonies. Bexley and his parents and Georgia participated. Tess only got sick after getting it from Bexley. I can only guess how she was infected."

"Do you have any proof?" Daniel said, his tone somewhere between compassion and patronizing. "I'm plugged into a lot of global government outlets. I haven't heard that China is having any problems like the rest of the world is. And the disease is called *African* Rabies."

Ryan nodded. "I am aware of how this sounds in context. You think this is some wishful delusion of a grieving man. I don't really care if you believe a word of what I'm saying. You asked what had my attention. I'm telling you. But my proof is in what is missing." Ryan gave a rueful smile. "Here is why I wasn't talking to Ahou. My goal was to find an invitation list to the ICES Accords and then see if I could identify any other participants that suffered the same symptoms, and then maybe try to collate their hospital locations with places where violence is happening. And guess what I found?"

"What?"

"I found nothing. Meaning, I can't find a list anywhere on the web. Even the people who were known to be in attendance do not appear in conjunction to the Accords—speakers, diplomats, heads of state. The web has been cleaned. I found some information in cached pages because someone forgot to get rid of those, but whoever is behind this has made a serious effort to remove that information from public consumption. Even my brother-in-law's name is gone.

"So, I started to look for other people who I *knew* attended the Accords to see if they were reporting sickness or symptoms and found virtual cyber silence. Many are public figures with public appearances published months in advance. But with consistency, their schedules were canceled indefinitely, or their itineraries pulled off the web entirely, their social media accounts very obviously silent or filled with trivialities. Old podcasts posted as current material. A striking number of them have disappeared from the public eye. And that includes the vice president."

That brought more hard wrinkles to Daniel's face as if something just clicked in his mind.

"So now let's talk about this thing called African Rabies," Ryan said. "Where did that name come from?"

"I assume it came from Africa," Daniel said.

"The reports are that African Rabies has been in existence for some years, lingering in the wilds of Africa, but I can find no reference to that name past six months ago.

"I checked the CDC and the WHO, and they don't have any record of any disease by any such name, which makes no sense if it is so dangerous. And what they do have about African Rabies on their website looks like it was taken from the press newsfeeds. All this screams misdirection and sends my government bullshit meter pinging off the charts.

"I found these two reports published by a research team working in Nepal near the Tibetan border. In case your geography is rusty, that is close enough to China that it matters."

Daniel said, "Could I read through that report?"

Ryan tapped his iGlass and handed it across the table. He said, "My sister named me on her HIPPA disclosure and granted me access to family medical records, so I have a full copy of her medical records and all family medical records in my iGlass. I found their reports by typing in the medical terms for my sister's symptoms. These reports deal exactly with my sister's symptoms, and Bexley's, and my niece's. I found out that that two of the four researchers who released this report are insane, which I think means they were infected. The other two are dead: one drowned and the other was killed in a car accident with her three kids in the car. I found this information in their hometown obituaries. I do not believe in that much coincidence. Only governments, maybe a lot of governments, can bring enough force to bear to squash knowledge."

Daniel Ryder's face was grave. "I keep reading about this R-naught factor. What does that mean?"

Ryan paused and waited for Daniel's eyes to meet his. "The R-naught factor is part of the mathematical equation that the CDC, and other infectious disease agencies around the world, use to help determine how virulent an outbreak might be."

"Can you understand the calculations in this report?"

"I'm not good at math, but I understand it by comparison to other infectious diseases. The factor for the common cold is one to less than one. One person will infect one other person, and mortality is effectively zero. For the flu, it is one to three or four. And with intervention, the mortality rate is very low. For say, smallpox, the R-naught factor is one to seven. For measles, it is one to ten. But the issue is not just infection but also the mortality rate. I was trying to compare this to the bubonic plague's R-naught factor because I know that disease was very deadly, but I've not been able to find that number."

"What is the R-naught factor for the disease in this report?" Daniel asked, as if he already suspected the answer.

"Assuming I read the report right, it is a factor of one to eight. But I'm confused on the mortality rate. I don't think they have figured out any means of intervention. And more disturbing, I'm not sure the infection kills the victim, which means they remain infectious and they keep seeking out new people to attack."

Sirens yowled in the distant streets and then there were gun shots and men yelling.

Finally, Daniel said, "That means that the human race . . ."

Ryan finished the sentence. "Is in real trouble."

9

Global Infection: ≤ 26.40127%

. . . for me, the imagination which so often kept me awake and in terror as a child has seen me through some terrible bouts of stark raving reality as an adult.
—STEPHEN KING, NIGHTMARES AND DREAMSCAPES

Firouz interrupted their conversation with an insistent call from the kitchen. Ryan and Daniel huddled around the TV listening to breaking news. The National Guard was mobilizing in New York and New Jersey. The video showed riot police facing off against an erratic mob, with troops dismounting from personnel carriers in riot gear and engaging with batons and shields. Then the report switched to politicians fielding a barrage of criticism from local mullahs who heralded the people's actions as freedom of religion and the sacred will of Allah. They insisted that the governors in both states were making a feeble attempt to fight against God by using force against an otherwise peaceful people.

Ryan's boredom meter filled after five minutes as the news anchor blathered on with endless speculation fueled by unnamed sources. Innuendo, rumor and gossip were not news; he had better things to do, so he excused himself to the bathroom.

When Ryan returned, Daniel was just hanging up his phone and put it in his coat pocket.

"How do you get such good reception on your cell?" Ryan asked. "My carrier circuits are overloaded."

"I have a very good carrier," Daniel said with a wave of indifference. "I need to get back to my office. Before I go, I want to tell you this has been an interesting, if not enlightening, conversation. You make me think. That doesn't happen often. And your suspicions, they seem a little extravagant. Maybe the social unrest is just that—social unrest?" He shrugged. "If it is, the authorities will get it under control. And since the papers you were reading don't call it African Rabies, maybe they really aren't talking about the same things. Maybe it isn't what you think?"

"Yes. Maybe," Ryan said without conviction. "That would make things less worrisome, I guess."

"Well, I don't know what to say. But could I get those articles you were reading? And if I want to get in touch later, how would I do it?"

"Let me flash you my information." Ryan tapped an app for information exchange between phones. "My main e-mail address is Ryan@rsagespeaks.com. If nothing else, you can leave a message on the blog, and I will see it there. And if you bear with me a second, I will send over the reports." Ryan worked on the iGlass to quickly attach the Nepal medical documents and sent them.

Daniel reviewed the information on his phone. "Good. I see the e-mail and the attachment. Wait, rsagespeaks.com? You are *that* Ryan Sage?"

"Uh . . . well, I guess it depends on who you think that is?" Ryan said with a nervous chuckle. He was always a touch unnerved when readers met him. His web traffic was high, and people spent a lot of time reading his articles, but he didn't think of himself as famous. And from the hate mail he got, Ryan never knew what a face-to-face reception would be.

"I have read a couple of your articles. They are intense, if not long."

"Well, that isn't quite an endorsement, but thanks for reading."

Daniel handed Ryan his business card and said, "I wish I could . . ." his voice faded as he considered his next words. "Look, keep this card in a safe place. You are an impressive young man. Maybe we will see each other again. Good luck." They shook hands.

The phone was already at his ear as Daniel pushed through the door. "Mora, I need you to get me Ellis ASAP. Get him out of a meeting. Get him off the toilet or out of the shower, whatever . . ." His voice faded as he started jogging into the cool spring afternoon.

"Firouz, could I use your landline to make some phone calls?" Ryan asked. "And do you have an old-fashioned telephone book?"

"Yes, yes, over there. It on the wall is. Telephone book? Is what?"

He wished Ahou were still here to fill in the language gap and it would give him an excuse to talk to her again. With his iGlass, he found phone listings. Ryan called the local shelters again, and this time they just laughed—everyone, except for Shaniqua. She remembered him and was unfailingly polite, talking for five full minutes like she had all the time in the world, her deep abiding compassion coming through the phone. But eventually, her voice broke and there was a hitch as she stifled a sob. They had filled the shelter well beyond capacity, and she implied that it might not be safe even if he did come. Some men were very angry and fighting.

They said their goodbyes and Ryan kept dialing until the campaign produced a room that he could swing for a night or two. If his geography was correct, there was a car rental place within a few miles of the motel.

Firouz fed him one last time and he waited about an hour in his bouncer capacity to pay for his food, Ryan finally said, "Firouz, you have been very kind to me. Thank you for letting me stay."

"You are leaving?"

"Yes, I need to get to a hotel over near the city called Duquesne; it is a few miles south of East Pittsburgh. It is a hike, but it was all I could find."

"You knowing what is this neighborhood?"

If Firouz's reaction implied that the area hotels were rented by the quarter hour, with condoms and farm animals supplied at the front desk.

"Driving I cannot. The store is guarding. My family to home after closing the store, but so must stay close for them."

"Oh no. I'm not asking for a ride but do you mind if I take the bat?"

"Bat? Is yes."

"Are you going to lock up now? Or wait through dinner?"

"Maybe no more evening today customers." Firouz shrugged. "My daughter and wife to close up the grocery. They're work is in the grocery. But maybe needing to guarding this place. My wife is to want me home. Women have fearing of such things, but should protecting this store if looters coming back in the night."

Ryan debated explaining his African Rabies theory to Firouz, but decided that the Farsi to English translation didn't make that possible. Maybe Daniel Ryder was right. It wasn't what he thought. Maybe Ryan's comments were a poor use of hyperbole, more reactionary than factual.

What did he really know about the spread of infectious disease?

The paper he read was dense with statistics interwoven with genetic theory and epidemiology. These subjects were hardly his forte. Certainly, people who worked with such things had methods to prevent an exponential explosion of infection. He had been on an emotional marathon since the suicide and the funeral and Tess. He had a total lack of support. He had been alone in his own head for a very long time, and there wasn't anyone to help balance the world. Maybe it was best to keep things simple.

"I'm sure it will be all right, Firouz. I'm sure you will be fine, but it is good to keep an eye on the store, maybe just for a couple of nights until the authorities get everything under control. It should be a nice evening for a walk, but I need to get moving before it gets too dark."

"Yes, it is good to be guarding. My wife will be to waiting to come home after working. You being safe on the street too. Yes?"

Ryan nodded and for a brief moment he was envious. Wife and family had eluded him for most of his adult life. His parents died in an accident four years ago. Being a decade older than Tess and fourteen years older than Lenna, he had not been particularly close to either of them. It didn't help that Bexley and Steve had little patience with his philosophical musings. Bexley leaned to the left of Stalin, and Steve leaned no farther than his Coors twelve pack. If—and this was a big if—all three men could stay focused on football, that conversation lasted a whopping fifteen minutes.

Christmas was fun.

Ryan said. "Thank you again. And good luck."

"Luck to be needing when I am having God. We will meeting again. Seeing you before again," Firouz said and gave his expansive hug and cheek kisses. "God with you is too. He watch you over."

Ryan smiled, waved and started to push the exit and stumbled over a young girl wearing a pink coat, jeans, and some brown Uggs.

"Look where you are going," the man behind her snapped.

"But he walked into me!" she said, indignant.

"I'm sorry. It was my fault." Ryan said, giving the girl an apologetic smile.

"She needs to learn," the man said, annoyed.

"No, really, I wasn't looking where I was going. My apologies," Ryan said again to the girl, and she gave the barest smile. And then he caught something in her eyes—an unspoken fear, an underlying cry for help. "It will be all right," Ryan said. "These are scary times, but I'm sure your dad will take care of you." Ryan touched her shoulder and smiled.

The girl said, "Could you he—"

"You hear that? Your dad will take care of you," the man said, pulling the girl by the back of her pink coat toward the sandwich counter.

"I'm hungry. Could I get something?"

"Are you gonna be good?" the man said.

"Yes," the girl said her face sullen. She flashed one last look at Ryan.

Ryan smiled bigger and waved, suddenly uneasy with leaving. The two went to the counter and Ryan caught one last look from the girl and the man pulled her close and flashed Ryan a hard look.

Ryan felt as though he'd encroached into something private and stepped into the late afternoon air, letting the family drama fade behind him. He wore a sweatshirt over a long-sleeved T-shirt, but he still needed to button up his denim jacket against the spring chill. He squared his shoulders, and walked into the tumultuous evening.

The trip to Pittsburgh had been a blur, catching a plane with no time to prepare. He had arrived with almost no clothes and spent his days in the hospital, his evenings in restaurants and his nights in the comfort of the hotel. He had not packed to endure the elements, but as unprepared as he was for the weather, Ryan was fully surprised by the noise. Not one sound separated itself above the general cacophony—car engines and sirens, squealing tires and detached shouting, voices on bullhorns, the crush of breaking glass, the infrequent distant *pop, pop, pop* that might have been an engine backfire, animal shrieks, and an occasional low moan that didn't register on any known experience.

To the left of Duquesne University by Mercy Hospital, the hillside festered with activity; emergency lighting bathed the building's east side, and it looked like the police were building a command center in the parking lot.

He started east down Fifth Avenue. Ryan had written out his route and kept trying to check it against his iGlass, but the GPS connection was inconsistent. Soon he was desperate for a good old-fashioned paper map. The main streets were clogged with abandoned cars as the Monday commuters made their futile dash out of downtown. The city streets were systematically backed up far into the distance. A few people made the effort to get their vehicles out of the way, pulling them onto side streets and sidewalks. Others shut the car off with the keys still in the ignition and left. Store owners were holding forth behind barricades on the sidewalk, defying looter and cop alike to violate their property. And this was just in the first mile-and-a-half.

Ryan sat in the sub shop long enough that at first walking felt good and cleared his worried mind. He was invigorated until he grew closer to a woman's hospital farther east with an almost identical scene to the one at Mercy: a police command center and barricades lining the exterior. Ryan cut a wide path around and found himself briefly lost in the turning roads and unfamiliar landscape. His iGlass was useless and now that he was off his written route, he found himself constantly needing to double back, every step increasing the hike.

It seemed that the nightmare was back sucking him under: the echoing footsteps of a faceless menace hounded the back of his mind.

Pock . . .
  Pock . . .
    Pock . . .

His endless morning walk finally caught up with him. His shins hurt, his calves were tight and he felt a knot in his hip. By the end of mile three, up and down hills, his backpack and laptop bag were cutting into his shoulders. By the end of mile four, he had seen five fights: two were minor scuffles between two neighbors and the other three looked like small gangs squaring off.

Pock . . .
  Pock . . .
    Pock . . .

Twice Ryan came around a car and had to shout, "Don't shoot." The mini militias patrolling their neighborhoods seemed to have only the barest restraint from squeezing the trigger.

Ryan lost track of how far he had walked. The enormous focus required to dodge between cars and constantly scan the street for trouble was sucking the last of his waning energy. And then reality crushed down on his shoulders. He had been wrong. He had made a catastrophic error. It was not a nice spring evening for a walk in the Pittsburgh suburbs but rather a gauntlet of terror. He was in a nightmare . . . and he could not wake up.

Pock . . .
  Pock . . .
    Pock . . .

10

Global Infection: ≤ 26.4013%

If ye love wealth greater than liberty, the tranquility of servitude greater than the animating contest for freedom, go home from us in peace. We seek not your counsel, nor your arms. Crouch down and lick the hand that feeds you; and may posterity forget that ye were our countrymen.

—SAMUEL ADAMS

L ike most Americans, Ryan Sage grew up with the expectation of mass civil peace. Despite the nightly news' endless determination to report a laundry list of violence and mayhem, large segments of the population lived safe and secure behind their—sometimes—locked doors. By contrast, in other countries, holdups, domestic violence, and the occasional mother who put her kid in a microwave loses its lead story appeal where the local despot might toss an entire village in a pit of flaming gas to entertain party guests.

Historically, America's momentary manifestations of cultural violence are aberrations, stray spots on a vast canvass of peaceable interaction, an extraordinary feat when measured against a population of near four hundred million people that shifts political power every four years.

By contrast, in most every culture throughout history, people lived with the expectation that any day someone might rape their wives, burn their daughters, mutilate their sons and wreck their livelihoods, merely because the tribal despot took offense at a stray look, or wanted territory, or decided the gods decreed it.

The campaign to portray America as morally inferior and guilty of human rights violations was relentless, but the truth was America's founding created an unprecedented social tranquility. When the Founding Fathers crafted the Constitution, they created a means to undermine tyrants and oppressive monarchies and tribal despots by destroying their power at its root. The Founding Fathers destroyed the tribe's death grip on human life by defending the individual against force and mysticism. They crafted a limited government whose sole function was to defend the individual. The result was that for the first time in human history, mass cultural peace became a reality. The Enlightenment was the first full intellectual challenge to ideas that held the world hostage to tribal dogma, and the Founding Fathers were the first men to put those ideas into political practice. And for generations the ideas they put into action produced a legacy of peace that American citizens enjoyed.

As heirs of the Enlightenment and the Founding Fathers' extraordinary vision, most Americans had the luxury of remaining at a distance from tribalism's penchant for institutional violence. The American people did not understand that mass cultural peace was the product of a very specific idea: the *individual* is sovereign. The individual is the sole possessor of his right to life, liberty and property. The use of government force is in service to defending that foundation . . . and nothing else. The moral foundation of social freedom is in the defense of the individual.

Unfortunately, man finds it very easy to backslide into primordial mindsets: If they look like *us*, act like *us*, and talk like *us*, they must be willing to defend *us*. In a casual stroke of fifth grade logic, the group, the collective, the gang, the tribe is elevated to the highest value. The tribe is everything and the individual, nothing. The tribe's will is good, and the individual's will is evil. Tribal identity is supreme, individual identity is insignificant. Barbarism grows and cultural chaos escalates as tribalism intensifies its war against individualism.

Fifth grade logic dies hard, so tribalism lurked at the fringes of western civilization waiting for a time to strike. As America strayed farther and farther from the Founding Fathers' vision, committing philosophical treason after philosophical treason, the segregation and internecine pressure gave rise to more and more tribes emerging in the social and political landscape. Their names are many—Bloods, or the Crypts, or the Latin Kings, or Democrat or Republican, or SEIU or Catholic, ISIS or Hezbollah, Nazis or Antifa—but they all elevated tribal identity above all other values.

To subordinate individuals to the collectives, the tribalists used their best weapon of choice: *self-sacrifice*.

By removing moral egoism from political freedom, the tribalists succeeded in condemning all resistance to the collective will. Or said more simply, by turning *self-interest* into a crime, they rendered all men impotent to resist tyranny.

Tribalism and Individualism are mortal enemies; it took scant generations to destroy American rugged individualism with altruism. The collective applauded its selflessness and social consciousness and giving back to the community. It looked in the mirror, mirror on the wall and the mirror confirmed that the collective was the fairest of them all. Never once did the people realize their moral narcissism eroded liberty at the root.

They never realized that their peaceful lives were an illusion based on the flimsiest fantasy—mass cultural peace as the birthright of morally superior tribal pacifists.

Ryan Sage was not a man prone to fear. But the farther he walked into the evening, the more he realized that the thin veneer of social stability was unraveling like a denim loom in reverse. The morally superior fantasy of collectivist tranquility was coming apart. And since state and federal governments had used every means to circumvent the Second Amendment, the streets looked like a reenactment of *Conan the Barbarian*—roving tribes armed with cudgels and knives fighting over turf and survival.

Anxiety hit Ryan like a war hammer to the chest. He longed for home, for a place to escape the madness behind locked doors. This was a new feeling, for home had always been a place to sleep and keep his stuff. He could live most anywhere, *had* lived most anywhere, with little concern for nostalgia or affection. Until recently, he had condos and lofts in six cities. They were modest places to lay his head when he was in town for business or pleasure, but they were never home.

As part of the plan to survive government persecution, Ryan sold all his properties and moved into a self-sufficient house to weather a federal investigation. But home was little more than walls and doors and climate control. Beyond the accumulated knickknacks of adult life and his books, there wasn't anything special about home.

But now, walking through a Pittsburgh, Pennsylvania, suburb, he lusted for familiar surroundings, the smell of his blankets, and the warmth of his bed. His mother had given him a comforter many years ago, and no matter how many times he washed it, the smell of that blanket was that of his parents' house. And with a desperation he had not known in many years, he wanted to bury his face in that blanket and just breathe.

Ryan stopped at an intersection, watching with dismay as the sun pushed farther and farther down to the horizon behind him. As he stood calculating the time before full dark he heard the screaming.

Throughout the hike, shouts and cries had been an inconsistent counter note, floating through the streets, distant echoes unreal in their ghostly remoteness like the droning soundtrack on a B-grade horror flick.

These weren't the screams of little kids frolicking in the backyard, or the screams of adolescent girls reacting to a fashion malfunction, or the scream of a hot coed showing off her engagement ring to her best girlfriends. This was sinister in its desperation, lilting and hideous, announcing to the world terror and panic and mortal pain. And it was very close.

Ryan dashed to the sound.

A man on all fours had his face buried in a woman's neck. The woman writhed, trying to pry his savaging mouth from her throat. Then her

keening turned to gurgling, and then the gurgling ceased and her body
went slack.

Pock . . .
   Pock . . .
      Pock . . .

Ryan had been desensitized by thousands of television images of destruction and carnage. Ryan had played hundreds of entertainment console
games featuring killing. He paid money for movies with homicidal hordes
hunched over a fresh human kill. But his mind would not wrap around
what he saw. He should be able to move, to act, to shout "Stop!" He should
be able to throw himself at the assailant and wrestle him away.

But he could not.

Pock . . .
   Pock . . .
      Pock . . .

His mind stuttered and seized like an engine refusing to fire. Memories
from the last few weeks popped into his mind like backfire.

When Ryan arrived in Pittsburgh for Bexley's funeral, the police asked
to speak with him. Confused and grieving, Ryan obliged. The Pittsburgh
PD manufactured a distant absurdity that Ryan was involved in Bexley's
death. That Tess and he conspired to kill the Stepfords for the inheritance.
That Ryan hated his brother-in-law and his political views. Ryan wanted
him dead. They were cruel and punishing in their inquisition. The detectives showed him crime scene pictures: the gore and carnage in Technicolor.

The bite marks on Xyla's face and hands and arms. . .

Slap, scraape . . .
   Slap, scraape . . .
      Slap, scraape . . .

*Little playful Georgia wrapped tight in her father's arms, her head tilted
forward, chin in chest, the right side of her face a crater made by a bullet
exit wound . . .*

Slap, scraaaaaaaape . . .

*Bexley's vacant eyes, his mouth frozen in a small O where the barrel of
the .38 special had been before the recoil ripped a tooth out by the front sight
and blew across the plush dining room . . .*

Slap, scraaaaape . . .

The savage destruction that Mrs. Stepford had visited on her husband of forty-eight years . . .

Slap, scraaaaaaaaaaaaaaaaape . . .

Instinct saved him. He felt the presence on his right before he saw . . . it. Ryan looked.

It was a young, blonde woman, maybe twenty years old, dressed in a hospital gown flapping immodestly off her body like broken bat's wings. Her chest looked like a paper target at a shooting range—holes in a scattered group from nipples to navel; dried blood, dark and gruesome in lines down to her knees. Her face was slack, eyes vacant but haunting in their intensity. She looked like she had bit into a dark red peach and the juices dripped down the jawline toward the top of her breasts. But there was no her; there was no woman, no person behind the eyes.

Ryan had seen those eyes before. He had seen that same look on Tess, watching *it* writhe against the restraints seething with rage and madness. Whatever animated the body was not his lovely sister that he so enjoyed tormenting. It was not the little girl that loved to get into his business since she was old enough to be nosy.

This creature had that same look. *It* came inexorably forward.

Slap, scraaaaape . . .

Its left shin bone was jutting through the skin like a spike, the leg buckling at angles with each slap of her foot.

Slap, scraaaaape . . .

It lunged.
Its hands were a wicked vise.
Adrenaline dumped into Ryan's body, and his brain kick-started.
Ryan got his forearm in front of his face.
It bit down like a pit bull, savage and merciless.
The rest was physics and terror.
Ryan bellowed and threw it off his denim-clad arm. It weighed a hundred pounds after a good meal. The body flipped in an arc, landing flat on its bare back. The horror multiplied as the creature righted itself without a reaction. No *ooofff!* No outcry of pain. No recognition that its bare back was filled with road rash or that its head bounced like a ball on a string. Ryan had dropped the woman with an MMA body slam, and it registered less than the bone driving out of her leg.

The man looked up, muzzle dripping with gore, and a mouthful of meat. They faced off. Then she dove for an arm. They fought over the kill like jackals, and the arm ripped from the shoulder with a wet *craaaack;* they fell apart feasting on the spoils.

Ryan dropped the bat and ran.

"Please, be there! Please, don't be locked! Please, defend the store!"

Horror fueled his flight for a half mile at full tilt, but his body betrayed him. His lungs were holes and his right hip threatened to seize from knotted muscles.

"Oh, God. Please, let him still be open. Please, let him," he begged, leaning against a car, frantically watching the streets as he caught his breath.

Pock . . .
   Pock . . .
     Pock . . .

Ryan raced the sun towards the horizon: a tour of agony and dread. He raced ahead of every invisible terror that lingered around buildings and down narrow, dark alleys. He raced the foreboding that the stores would be locked and dark. He raced the demons of his mind.

Ryan turned the corner, cutting hard around the edge of the pharmacy at Fifth and Pride, and saw that the gremlins of bad had beaten him to the finish line. The metal security door to Firouz's sandwich shop and grocery were drawn down. He slogged up the hill, hoping the metal gate sealing the shop was an illusion of malevolent spirits. He crashed into the metal like the despair that crashing into his soul: hard, fast, and savage.

Pock . . .
   Pock . . .
     Pock . . .

"Come on!" he shouted between gasps, scanning the streets for more of those shuffling, malicious creatures.

"Think! Think! Think!" he demanded between heaving breaths. Thinking is what separated man from the rest of creation. He had to control the terror that threatened to reduce his mind to goo.

Crawl into a car and lock the door.

What was that thing?

Find another open building.

Were those bullet holes all over her chest?

Run to Shaniqua's shelter. Beg for a spot somewhere.

Did I see a bone sticking out of her leg?

Find a corner in the top of the parking garage just down the street.

It should have been dead?

Climb to the H A Y E K overhang. Maybe there was a window open? Maybe he could find a dumpster.

Was that man eating her?

The ideas came fast and furious and ridiculous.

Pock . . .
  Pock . . .
    Pock . . .

"Come on!" Ryan said, again banging his hand against the door. "Think!"

"Go away," the voice said, muffled behind glass and metal. "Gun is here. In my hand. To kill if you coming."

"Firouz! Firouz! It is me, Ryan! Remember? I left a few hours ago. Firouz, please!!"

A key scrapped into the lock and the heavy metal gate rolled into the brick façade above. "Come to the inside. I knowing this! God would sending you back!"

11

Global Infection: ≤ 26.40132%

The Basic Epidemiological Model
S = Susceptible to disease
I = Infectious
R = Recovered (assumes immunity)
—Kermack-McKendrick 1927

Firouz was on the phone speaking Farsi; his demeanor had gone from benevolent to grave, then stern, and finally, resigned. He dropped the phone into the cradle. "My wife home is needing to me coming."

Ryan's heart sank.

Since Ryan's return to the shop, they had spoken little, mostly because the language barrier was too great. They exhausted common subjects in short order. Their longest conversation revolved around Ryan's charades account of the attack and Firouz's endless apologizing for not having a shower.

Exhausted and sweat-soaked, Ryan collapsed into a booth, desperate to stop shaking. Eventually, he peeled out of his sodden clothes, which lead Firouz to show him a washer and dryer in the sandwich shop utility space and a deep sink. It was the deep sink that brought the endless apology. It was the bruise on Ryan's arm that brought the charades.

Ryan shed his clothes into the wash and clung to the sink in his underwear, his legs convulsing like a toddler taking his first steps. He washed up with industrial soap and fresh bar rags. He was stepping into a fresh pair of jeans just as Firouz returned with a large bottle of water and some chicken noodle soup. That was when Firouz saw the teeth-shaped epicenter right below the elbow that radiated reddish blue toward Ryan's wrist and bicep. It was impossible to mistake the source.

The fact that Ryan had been bit by another human being was a scandal that Firouz could not fathom. He wanted details.

Two syllables, sounds like . . .

But explaining the woman's broken leg or bullet holes or the man feeding on soft tissue, or the two psychopaths wrestling the body until body parts snapped from sockets taxed Ryan's party skills. Besides, he still hadn't processed the attack, so he reduced the nightmare to being caught in a riot.

Two homicidal cannibals constituted a riot, right?

Mollified, Firouz tested the language barrier up against the most demanding conversation of all—the weather. This was a conversation that Ryan proved yet again incapable of sustaining, so they defaulted to amicable silence.

To pass the time, Firouz started mopping the grocery floor and Ryan helped. When they finished, there was little else to do but prowl between the sandwich shop—back through a hallway to the loading docks—to the grocery. Ryan walked the aisles of the grocery as if someone might have magically walked through the mini mart walls and found a place to hide under an endcap. They took turns walking the sentry posts while the other watched the news. Eventually, they both sat in the Mini Mart Food Liner manager's office, idly chewing on food that sat like a brick inside their knotting stomachs.

The time passed, tense and quiet.

The news story cycles rolled around every twenty minutes, the media news template having long since been written, the angles tailored to fit an agenda that had little to do with objective information. No one seemed to know what was going on. The details were merely trivia with an overarching analysis to shape opinion toward the inexorable rise of statism within the United States. Ryan and Firouz alternately smiled like idiots at something they had heard, or shook their heads in wonderment, or yawned with boredom until 12:21 a.m.

That was when a worried blonde female reporter spoke with gravity that research showed a link between a human bite and the spread of African Rabies. She finished the sentence and faltered. Her eyes dropped to the desk. She brushed a stray lock of hair behind her ear, recovered, and reread the sentence again. She was on the teleprompter, and this was news to her.

"Oh, dear Jesus," she said and ripped her blouse open to look at a wound on her right shoulder while on camera. "Call my husband! Call my husband!" she shouted, scrambling from behind the desk, wearing shorts and bunny loafers. The news set exploded in panic, and for two minutes that alarm was shown to the world. Then the feed went to colored bars.

Ryan and Firouz stared at the TV, silent and unmoving, each man trying to digest what he had just seen. Firouz broke first, suddenly, frantically working on papers at his office desk, casting sidelong glances.

The clock read 12:27 when the reality hit. *I've been bit.*

Ryan exploded from the manager's office, back to the deep sink. He scrubbed his arm until it was raw and then bent his arm in ways that didn't seem possible, looking for the smallest break in the skin.

For an hour, Firouz's suspicion hung like syrup in the air. Ryan showed him that the skin was unbroken, that the coat and sweatshirt had protected his arm, that he didn't think he was infected, that the incubation period was . . . well, who knew how long, but it wasn't immediate. But to no avail. The language barrier seemed too great to explain the details.

Ryan slumped into agonizing silence, aware that his arguments had fallen on a Farsi-speaking mind. And then, for no apparent reason, Firouz walked up to him and hugged him, kissed both cheeks and said, "Yes. Yes. You are good. You are good. God watching you over."

The landline rang. They both jumped. Firouz spoke for long minutes.

Firouz stood holding the receiver against his forehead, eyes shut. He replaced the phone and hung his head. Then he made his announcement. "My wife, home is needing to me coming."

Ryan's stomach lurched.

Firouz fidgeted with papers and keys on the desk. He sat for a moment and then stood and paced, then sat again.

"Wife needing me to coming home," he said again. "She is fearing for themselves in the house."

"I see," Ryan said. "I don't blame you." He couldn't take the suspense. There was little chance that Firouz would let a perfect stranger stay in his stores. "Uh, do you, uh, need me to leave?"

Firouz's eyes went wide. "No, no. Staying inside you are watching. My store will be safe. I have not words. You will helping me?" His tone made it sound like he thought Ryan would be doing him a favor. "I to be coming back tonight." He shrugged. "Maybe to morning. Wife and daughters, they will not be liking it alone."

"You want me to guard the store?" Ryan was relieved but mystified. It seemed strange that Firouz would want a perfect stranger to stay in his store. Certainly, he knew that Ryan could loot everything and be gone. "I don't know what to say. I, of course, will watch your store. But are you sure? That is very generous. But are you *sure*?"

"Please, a moment," Firouz said and dialed the phone, and a woman answered on speaker. There was a brief exchange in Farsi, and the phone changed hands.

Then Ahou was on the phone. *"Hi! Salem?"*

For a few minutes, she and Firouz spoke. Then she said, "Ryan?"

Ryan's heart sank a little from her tone. "Yes?"

"My father would like you to stay in the store. He wants you to be safe, but he does not want you to risk your life."

"Ahou, uh, I understand what he wants me to do, and I am glad to do it. And frankly, I would be terrified to be on the street alone, but he is asking a stranger to watch his store."

"Ryan, you are no stranger. You defended me today. My father, he wants to protect you for that. But he also believes God has told him to help you."

"Okay, I don't think I know what to say to that."

Ahou was quiet for a minute. "Ryan, is it true that you were bit by a woman?"

Ryan sighed, deep and long, the stress of the day reaching a breaking point. "Yes, my arm. She didn't break the skin. The human jaw is strong, but it really can't bite through heavy cloth like that. My arm hurts like a bad somebody, but I don't see how I could be infected."

"I see." And her tone said she did not see. "My father wanted to bring you home, but my mother is afraid. I told my mother that you would never hurt us, but she does not want you to come here. So, my father wants you to stay in the store, but he will come home."

"I understand. He doesn't want to be locked in with me through the night."

There was relief in her voice. "Yes, thank you for understanding." There was a slight hitch like she was crying. "And I'm sorry. It is probably not true, but that is what the news is saying. They spread panic like this. This is what they did with that ILBIG outbreak. They made something out of nothing. My mother called to tell my father to leave the store and come home when she saw that woman take off her clothes on camera. She thinks that everyone who loots will bite him. Then she learned you were there. She is very afraid of you being with him."

"Ahou, your mother is right to be afraid. This report I think is true."

"Really? But the news is always so wrong. How can you be sure?"

It made sense: the woman trying to bite him, Tess biting the nurses and doctors, Bexley biting Tess, Georgia biting Xyla. It was a wonder that it took this long to for the connection to be made. "Just trust me on this. This report is probably true."

Ahou was quiet. Then she said, "You are not mad that we are leaving you there?"

"Mad? No, surprised really that your father would even consider doing this. He is risking a lot to let me stay here."

"You have made an impression on my father. He really likes you. He is a good judge of men, and my father said you made an impression on Daniel Ryder today. That is very hard to do. I doubt they are both wrong."

"Well, Daniel Ryder made an impression on me today. And that is very hard to do."

Ahou laughed, deep and throaty. "You are funny. Too quiet but funny."

"Yes. Yes. Women like a man who can make them laugh, but no one ever wants to marry a comedian. So, what does your father need me to do? How do I lock this place down tight? Does he need help getting home? If it is not far, maybe I could walk with him."

"Oh, he will show you how to lock up."

"Yes. Yes. It will be good," Firouz said. "How you say? Easy pie? I showing you the locking."

"You should be safe," Ahou went on. "When we started selling some high-end electronics a couple years ago, data pads and phones to the Duquesne students, we had some break-ins. Once from the back of the store and two separate times someone just drove a car through the front. My father decided to have the back and front entrance built like a vault. There are concrete barriers so cars can't crash through, and we have had a sign outside for months that that tells everyone there is no pharmacy. So, no one should be trying to break in and steal Philaxix."

"Steal Philaxix?"

"Yes, crazy people believe the news that maybe Philaxix is a cure for the African Rabies, so they go to pharmacies and try and steal it."

"Ah, okay. That is good to know."

"Just lock the doors that connect the sandwich shop to the loading docks. You should be fine."

"All right. That sounds easy enough."

"Ryan, don't worry about trying to keep people out of the sandwich shop. Just be safe. Stay in the manager's office. My father can get home by himself. We live very close to the store, only a few streets over."

"Okay . . ."

"And Ryan?"

"Yes?" He really did like the way his name sounded in her mouth.

"I never did say thank you. For what you did."

"Well . . . you have now. You are welcome."

"Okay. Maybe we will talk later. Good night. And be safe."

Indeed, it was simple and secure. The grocery was much like Ahou had described. The rolling gate was embedded into the structural facade. When pulled down, it fastened into metal grates in the concrete walk. The street frontage windows also had exterior metal gates with wire reinforcement woven throughout. And even if someone managed to get past the first two obstacles, Firouz had installed a second mesh gate exactly like mall retail stores, roughly four feet inside the store. The grocery front was like a bank vault.

It took ten minutes of broken English and another ten minutes of charades to teach Ryan where all the important things were: lights, power, keys, and the appropriate locks. To Ryan's great pleasure, in an adjacent room to the manager's office was a cot with a thin mattress, blankets, and pillows. There was also a couch, if he preferred. Ryan was so tired he didn't care.

Firouz's car idled in the enclosed receiving area at the back of the store as the heavy metal gate lined by barbed wire trundled back in its track. They waved as he drove out. Ryan pressed the remote in his hand and watched the gate trundle closed and latch with a clang.

Inner city alleys are a study in siege warfare. Since cops can't patrol every nook and cranny, every side street and cul-de-sac, most buildings are fortified against vulnerabilities. Urban castle building was directly proportional to how far down the path of urban decay a city had tread; the harsher the environment, the more formidable the defense. And from where Ryan stood, Pittsburgh had suffered decades of decay.

Like many cities, Ryan suspected it had tried the standard revitalization initiatives of symbolic building projects: ball parks, restaurants and tourist attractions. And when those didn't work, the social engineers assumed that yet more taxes, more levies, more wealth redistribution, more K-12 school interventions would stem the tide of deterioration, never once realizing that their actions were the plague everyone fled to the suburbs to avoid.

Average homeowners did not want to live behind twelve locks and worry about their kids on the sidewalk. Average homeowners didn't want to pay the government overhead on an endless list of social engineering projects that were passed off as good deeds. Average homeowners didn't want to travel twenty miles out of the city to buy toilet paper and milk if they could live five minutes from a Walmart. Average homeowners didn't want to be handcuffed by building codes that demanded keeping ancient façades and archaic inefficient building materials in the name of historical preservation. Average parents didn't want to turn their kids' minds and souls over to the whims of an educational bureaucracy that assumed *they* are the problem. Those who could, those who had the skill, took initiative for a better life. Those who couldn't built castles to survive the predators that remained behind.

The back of Firouz's grocery, the bottom two floors of the surrounding courtyard, were lined with bars on windows and fences and grates built over AC units. Ryan was standing in a microcosm of city decline portrayed in architecture. And he was glad for decades of urban decay that demanded a castle. This small courtyard was a bastion against the night beyond the walls filled with the sounds of menace: sirens and fire engines and tumult.

Ryan locked himself in, checked, re-checked and then checked again every barrier he could find. Concerned that he would forget which key went to what, he made a cheat sheet that correlated key numbers and description, put the paper in his pocket and dictated the notes into his phone. Then put the important keys on his own car key ring.

He sat in the office watching a comedy special, trying to take his mind off the chaos. But sitting isolated made him paranoid that he would miss someone breaking down a door. Then he wandered between the grocery and the sandwich shop, keeping a vigil, and found himself jumping at every noise. Exhausted, he sat in the dim sandwich shop, fearing that if he turned on the lights it would leak through the cracks in the gate and attract looters. Ryan wasn't sure what else to do. As Ahou said, he should just lock himself in the grocery. But that seemed wrong. The reason Firouz left was because of him; he needed to watch the store as long as he could stay awake.

In the same booth from the day's vigil, he browsed the web on his iGlass and checked his e-mail every ten minutes, but what he read did not register. At 1:34 he heard something hammering on the sandwich shop gate. He froze, throttling the bat in his hands and crept close to the interior glass door.

"Come on, hurry up. If the cops come, we are in trouble."

"Shut up. This fucking thing is stronger than it looks."

The sandwich shop front was covered with a sturdy metal gate over the whole front facade.

"Come on. This is taking too long."

"Just give me a minute. Shit! The gate is locked into the concrete."

More banging and more rattling. The crowbar slipped and clanged to the sidewalk.

"Ow! God da—"

"Come on, dude! What are you doing?"

"Shit! Shit! Shit! Is that a cop car? Dude, we gotta go."

Ryan's heart pounded through his shirt. He stood there for a full five minutes. His nerve broke.

He moved quickly from sub shop, to the hallway, to the loading dock and into the grocery. He fastened every door he could find between himself and the manager's office. He locked that door too, turned off all but one light, pulled the blanket and pillow off the cot and lay on the couch.

Ryan Sage shut his eyes, exhausted. His mind spun down as if it were tossing useless thoughts into the trash to get rid of clutter before logging off. Suddenly it got stuck in a loop.

Scream!

Man bent down on all fours.

Slap, scraaaape!

Scream!

Man bent down on all fours.

Slap, scraaaape!

Like a bubbling cauldron, slow and malevolent, the images simmered at the edge of his mind—the bone poking out of the leg, the twitching, stumbling stride, the blood-ringed holes in the chest, the dull light behind the woman's eyes, the gurgling moan behind a mouth full of flesh.

Ryan understood what he had seen, but he couldn't make sense of the moment. The details added up like clear figures in a column, but the sum was a surreal nightmarish collage of variables. His mind worked and worked and worked at the math, trying to reject the useless, but couldn't seem to find the sum. Over and over, the calculator ran through the equation.

Scream!

Man bent down on all fours.

Slap, scraaaape!

Finally, somewhere between the eerie sounds of the woman's steps, Ryan's mind gave up on the calculus of horror and drifted into a blessed reprieve. He didn't remember the time that unconsciousness mercifully shrouded him in oblivion, but he was keenly aware that he was ripped from sleep at 6:47 a.m.

The roar of an engine.

The scream of tires on asphalt.

The rending of metal and glass.

And finally, the muted rushing clatter of settling debris.

12

Global Infection: ≤ 26.50000%

Democracy is two wolves and a lamb voting on what to have
for lunch. Liberty is a well-armed lamb contesting the vote!
— BENJAMIN FRANKLIN

Ryan was sure that someone drove through the Mini Mart Food Liner front door, and every person in Pittsburgh was pouring through the doors. He strained to hear beyond the walls, but the silence was complete. He struggled to rise, feeling the rebellion of his legs and stomach and shoulder muscles. He hadn't pushed himself so hard since his track and field career.

Ryan powered on the security monitor, only to find the store beyond a picture of serenity. He returned to the couch and shut his eyes trying to settle back to sleep.

His eyes flew open.

"The sub shop!"

He bolted upright and quick action ignited his sore body. Yesterday's boot camp of terror screamed derision in his ear like a cruel drill instructor, taunting him to do the simplest actions. Put on those pants, you fat puke! Bend over and get those shoes tied, maggot!

Finally dressed, Ryan made a heart-pounding trip to the sub shop, unlocked the door and slowly pulled it open.

All was quiet.

Confused, Ryan retreated through the hallway to the grocery loading docks to do a quick check of the courtyard.

All was secure.

What the heck made that sound?

And then it just didn't matter. He went back to the bed, expecting Firouz to return soon. Restaurant owners don't have the luxury of sleeping much past sunup; prep work started early. But Ryan woke again after ten and still no Iranians. Worried, he dialed *69 on the manager's office phone. He got a busy signal.

He had to have gotten home all right or Ahou would have called, and his wife would have come looking, right?

Worry made Ryan hungry, so he made breakfast and spent an hour answering e-mails from friends and co-workers. They were concerned about the Tess situation. He checked his bank account; the money had not been transferred yet. He dashed off an e-mail to Jeff asking for an ETA. He called his former business partner on every number he had and finally left a message on the home answering machine.

"Erik, it's Ryan. Just calling to see if you and Sarah and the kids are all right? I thought maybe we'd talk about the business. The stuff in the news isn't the whole story. My Spidey senses are tingling, and you know what that means. Maybe let the people go home. Give me a call when you get a minute. Wait. I can't remember the number where I am. I'll e-mail it to you. Talk to you soon."

When it became clear that the feds were going to try and RICO his assets, Ryan decided to sell his interest in his business to his partner, Erik. After twelve years they had built an information technology support company into a very lucrative enterprise. Fortunately, they had made some very wise business decisions, and despite the ongoing economic stagnation, the business was cash rich. Erik was motivated to help Ryan, so he was glad to buy him out. And Ryan was willing to sell for a price that was less than full market value, so at first it looked like everything was going to work out well. But over the following months, the pressure of inordinate government scrutiny got to Erik. And it didn't help that his and Sarah's marriage was struggling.

Ryan hadn't talked to Erik in a few months, partly because Erik's lawyer advised against contact, and it was hard for them both to remember that Ryan was just an employee. Tensions increased when Ryan—the employee—had been absent from work for almost two months and the company bereavement policy only allowed for two days. Ryan had long since burned through his vacation and personal time. Their last conversation had been when Erik suggested that Ryan formally go on family medical leave. It was an ugly ten minutes, but Ryan Sage never went on FMLA.

Ryan used some web-based tools to log into his home security system to make sure all was secure. It was an older country home that suburbia had grown out to meet. Ryan got the benefit of a well, septic tank, fireplace, wood-burning stove for heat, and land in case his thumb ever needed to turn green. And he got the benefit of city electric and chain restaurants in case he didn't. Ryan was a suburban boy, but he could live rustic if necessary. If the feds decided to put pressure on Erik to remove him from the payroll, he would learn to garden, can food and hunt deer with the best of them. If he had to weather a protracted legal battle, he figured a house like this, paid for by a corporate trust, was a good move.

He surveyed his security cameras and reviewed the online digital backups and found nothing amiss. All the unpacked boxes were still in place. The Ben Franklin stove sat cold in the living room. His writing desk, bookshelves and home network were the only things that were fully set up. When he got home, he would have a house warming party. Maybe he would invite that lovely blonde who worked in finance. He hadn't seen a ring on her finger.

Wait, that would be sexual harassment. Damn!

Ryan shifted mental focus and started reading comments on his blog. His readership wanted to know when he would post again. Two people gave their condolences about his family situation. He hadn't made an issue of it online, but many knew that he was Bexley Stepford's brother-in-law. No amount of effort was going to keep that juicy tidbit away from public consumption.

Ryan toyed with working on an article developed from yesterday's research, but being cooped up in the manager's office made him stir-crazy and his curiosity was getting the best of him. He needed to see what the bigger world looked like. He needed to see people. Ryan put on his sweatshirt and jean jacket, and exited the courtyard through the electronic gate clutching the bat like he would go to war.

The street behind the building ran left toward the shipping entrance—the sports arena where the Pittsburgh Penguins held their NHL dynasty. Directly across the road was the wooded hillside and manicured landscape of the Washington Plaza apartment building. A tall, heavy wrought iron fence ran unbroken around the property. He followed the fence to Pride Street and saw the mob at the intersection of Fifth. Hundreds of people stood around the pharmacy. Two cop cars were parked at angles in a small blockade and three uniformed PPD officers were trying to keep the people at bay as bullhorns blared demands for Philaxix.

Ryan walked past the minimart front doors wanting to speak to other people but then he realized that people were looking at him, pointing.

Shit! They saw me come out of the grocery loading dock!

Ryan made a show of checking his phone, and then casually turned back toward the street. When he was out of sight he ran to the gate, dashed into the courtyard and behind Firouz's catering truck, jamming the electric opener. If that mob realized there was a way into the minimart from the back, he wouldn't have a chance.

The heavy gate latched shut moments before half a dozen people banged against the heavy bars, testing its strength.

"One of them dirty Muslims shouldn't be able to keep his shit," one of them shouted, "when the Caliphate is causing problems."

The crowd echoed the sentiment.

"Climb over!" someone said.

"That's razor wire, you moron!"

"Get one of those cars started; we'll crash the gate!"

"Shit! Cops!"

The mob ran.

"Oh, this is getting better and better," Ryan said.

Needing to see what was happening in the world beyond he climbed the catering truck, jumped the small gap to the fire escape and worked his way to the roof.

Six brick buildings were built so close together as to make one structure that ran from Pride to Stevenson. Ryan made his way to the farthest point east to look down into the valley beyond. Pittsburgh's Hillside area was well named. A long ridge started where the old Mellon Arena stood for over fifty years and ran like a spine toward the east. The slice of land between Colwell Street and Our Way was halfway down the south side of the spine. From eight floors up, the view south, east and west was unobstructed.

Sticking through the chain pharmacy front window was a green Ford F150. Blue emergency lights flashed atop two police cruisers parked in a wedge as if they were the last line of defense. The mob pressed in.

Fifth Avenue, a major artery running east and west, was glutted with vehicles and barricades built out of tables and dumpsters and pallets. Store owners openly sported weapons in defiance of gun control. Three police officers were trying to get the owners to surrender their weapons.

"That isn't going to go well," Ryan said.

A SWAT truck was stopped a hundred yards west, waiting as four tow trucks worked to open a path so they could back up their brothers in blue. The crew moved the vehicles in Stevenson Street and dropped the abandoned cars right in front of the minimart doors.

Ryan was offended on Firouz's behalf. "Hey idiot! You can't block the store!" Not that words would do any good from eight floors above.

On the opposite side of the street from the pharmacy, private security dressed in dark blue military gear circled the Banco Federal property and held positions on the roof. Ryan counted fourteen men with assault rifles cradled in their arms. They were letting customers inside the bank and keeping the growing crowd at bay. Twice people tried to rush the bank doors and were repelled by violence. The crowd thought the security people were breaking the law. The cops didn't move.

A woman broke past the police around the truck and started to crawl into the pharmacy. The PPD officers subdued her, slapped plastic restraints on and sat her on the sidewalk.

The mob jeered. Now they thought the cops were the criminals.

The pharmacy manager came outside and stood on the hood of the truck with a bullhorn. "Please. Listen to me! There is no Philaxix on site!"

"Liar!"

"No, I am telling the truth. There is no Philaxix. And it does not cure African Rabies!"

"Prove it! Prove it! Prove it!" the throng chanted.

A fight started on the back of the mob for no apparent reason and rippled around the outer edge; the mass of humanity ebbed and flowed around the cruisers.

Then about a half a block east, someone threw a trash can into the Starbucks plate glass window. The baristas came to the street, dismayed. And for a while no one moved until one by one, people crawled through the window and emerged with something in their hands. The surge was on; people pouring in, fighting over whatever they could wrestle away and then disappearing into the street. Two men hauled an espresso machine out the door, trying to tote it down the sidewalk as the employees fled. The cops moved toward the coffee shop.

The mob surged toward the pharmacy.

13

Global Infection: ≤ 26.50001%

*The basic premise of the Founding Fathers was man's right
to his own life, to his own liberty, to the pursuit of his own
happiness—which means: man's right to exist for his own
sake, neither sacrificing himself to others nor sacrificing
others to himself; and that the political implementation of
this right is a society where men deal with one another as
traders, by voluntary exchange to mutual benefit.*

—AYN RAND

The pink coat caught Ryan's eye, but he focused when he saw the swift backhand to the teenage boy's head. The father's blow was quick and harsh, and made the boy buckle to the ground. The girl in the pink coat pushed between them, hands outstretched as if to hold back the tides. She was the blond girl Ryan had almost stepped on yesterday.

The father, one young man about college age, the teenage boy, and the girl swirled in their own family drama as the mob pushed over the truck bed, leaking around the corners, driving the remaining police officers and the pharmacy manager with them. The father yelled, the girl yelled back, the boy on the ground said something, and the father took a swing. The girl pushed the boy out of the way, then pushed the father. Throughout the drama, a college kid leaned against a car fender, arms crossed like he was too cool for school. Finally, the girl wagged a finger as if she were telling a dog to stay and dashed into the pharmacy. The dad loomed over the teenager, defying to him rise.

"What the hell is going on?" Ryan asked.

The minutes passed and then a blaze of pink coat crawled over the bed of the truck, carrying two bags. She showed their contents. The father nodded, ruffled her hair.

"He sent *her* to loot?"

The scene below was at the tipping point. The longer the cops did nothing, the bolder the mob became until finally, a SWAT truck came charging down Crawford and rammed through cars, slamming to a stop at the pharmacy. The force dismounted to the street, wearing riot gear. They dispersed the crowd with beanbag shotguns, Tasers, and batons. Before it was over, twelve people had joined the woman in restraints.

And then Ryan saw the mob move toward the mini mart. He climbed down the fire escape, to the truck to the ground to the sub shop. He could hear people banging against the metal gate, talking excitedly, demanding to open the door. Then he heard the telltale sounds of someone prying at the gate.

Ryan saw nothing to barricade the door so he ran back to the loading dock looking for options. His mind took inventory, looking for something big and heavy and roughly the shop dimensions. Ryan was good at Tetris, so in minutes he had a plan.

And that was when he heard the phone ring.

"Firouz!" he said, sprinting to the manager's office.

"Hello?"

"Is you all open today?"

"Open? Uh, no."

"Your hours are posted. You have to open so I can get some batteries for my camera."

"We are not opening today."

"Let me speak to your manager."

"Ma'am, he is not in."

"Don't ma'am me. Put your manager on the phone. I know he there. Put him on or I'm calling the police and tell them—"

Ryan hung up. "Call the police because she couldn't buy batteries?"

The phone rang.

"Hello."

"Don't you dare hang up on me. Get your manager now! I'm gonna make sure you get fired."

Ryan laughed.

"Did you just laugh at me? Oh no, you din'it. Oh no, you din'it. Tell me your name. I want to know your name. I'm gonna call my lawyer and have him talk to your—"

"Woman, do you know how many retail jobs I've had where it was expected that I take shit off of people?"

"What?"

"You heard me. And now I speak for every person who has ever had a retail job and listened to some insane, utterly ridiculous human being threaten our jobs. You are useless. And no, we don't want your money. Don't come back to the store. If I ever see you in this store again, I will throw you out the front door. Do we understand each other?"

Silence. Then, "So I can't come get my batteries?"

Ryan hung up. Maybe she would figure out later that he had no idea who she was. Then it occurred to Ryan that Firouz could be calling, and he had been outside. Ryan clipped the cordless handset to his hip and ran back to the stock room. Ryan disassembled an industrial-grade shelf. He was laying the last pieces on a cart when the phone rang again.

"Hello?"

"Are you all gonna be open today?" It was a man.

"No, we are not open today."

"How about tonight?"

Something about the way this was asked sent a chill down Ryan's spine. Then an idea hit him. "Sir, we are investigating a crime. Do you come to this store often?"

"What?"

"Sir, I have your number on the caller ID. You wouldn't happen to know the victims, would you?"

"I, uh . . ." The phone went dead.

He pushed the cart into the shop and started building. The more he worked inside the shop, the more the people outside banged on the gate, demanding to be let in. He slid two sheets of plywood between the shelving and the windows, and he started stacking the leftover winter stock of rock salt on the shelf. Two skids filled with fifty-pound bags firmly pinning the plywood against the windows. If the mob outside got past the metal gate they were not easily coming inside.

The phone rang.

"Hello," Ryan rasped.

"So, when are you guys gonna be ope—"

"Oh my God! Oh my God!" he said whispering and excited. "I'm so glad you called. Something is in—wait, hang on. Don't talk, please." He pulled the phone to his chest and groaned deep and unintelligible. "Hello? Are you there?" Ryan whispered. "They're in the store. You gotta help—"

Click.

The phone rang.

"Who is speaking? We are investigating a crime. Do you come to this store often?"

"What?"

"Ma'am I have your number on the caller ID. You wouldn't happen to know the victims, would you?"

The phone went dead.

The phone rang.

"Shit! Shit! Shit! Those crazy people are in the story you gotta help me!"

Click.

Ryan watched the phone waiting for the next call.

Silence.

Ryan clipped the wireless to his hip and went back to the stockroom, to break down the last two salt pallets.

That final piece of his Tetris puzzle required putting a third sheet of plywood against the glass door and wedging it in place with salt pallets. He pushed the pallet jack into place, pressed the lever and the load settled to the floor. Ryan was almost disappointed when he realized the crowd outside was gone. He grabbed a bottle of water and collapsed in the manager's office, idly watching the cable news crawler along the bottom of a mute television.

> New York: Wall Stock Exchange ransacked . . .

> New York: Wall Street burning . . .

He was tired. Ryan hadn't done this kind of physical labor since he got his first A+ certification and started on a helpdesk.

> Pennsylvania: Governor calls National Guard . . .

> Governor Celebreeze: NG to deploy in Philadelphia . . .

Ryan picked at the blister forming along his thumb from swinging the hammer to pull the shelving apart.

> New Jersey: Governor demands New York State deal with spreading violence . . .

> Florida: Miami, Jacksonville Hospitals calling for volunteers . . .

> Cuba: Fidel Castro III refuses South Florida refugees . . .

> Pittsburgh's Mayor news conference: He stood in the convention center a curfew of 6:00 p.m . . .

"Got it! Six p.m.," Ryan said with a salute of his water bottle. "I'll be inside. Just keep the bad guys out of the store." He drained the bottle and wished it didn't require moving to get another.

The phone rang. Ryan pulled it off his belt. "Hello?"

"I was just wondering," said a male voice, "when—"

"Oh my God! They're here. You gotta help me. They're—"

Click.

The phone rang. "Hello?" Ryan said still whispering.

"I was just wondering if you have . . . uh, why are you whispering?"

It was a woman. She sounded sexy. Bored, Ryan decided to change it up. "So, what are you wearing?"

"What?"

He breathed heavy into the phone.

The woman was quiet for a minute, then said, "Firouz, is that you?"

What? Firouz?

"Wait, Firouz would never ask that question. And your English is too good. Who is this? What have you done to Firouz?"

"Um, nothing," Ryan said. "I'm just a friend who was asked to watch the store while he checks on Ahou and his wife and other daughter."

"I see," she said. "Ahou is very pretty. But what if I were even better looking than her?" her voice changing to smoldering. "I don't have to be wearing anything."

"Uh . . ."

"It is the end of the world, right? I'm open to anything."

Ryan's mind went blank. "I think I have the wrong number." he put the phone back in its charging base.

Being propositioned made him hungry, so Ryan decided to fend for himself. The grocery had suffered a run on basics but was still stocked with frozen, packaged, and canned goods. Nothing struck his fancy, so he went to the sub shop and found the walk-ins with plenty of food. He made a sandwich, grabbed some chips, two bottled sodas, put everything in his laptop bag and climbed the fire escape.

The roofline was in fact the collection of many buildings erected over dozens of years, each within five feet of each other and with a small amount of climbing could be traveled end to end. Some rooftops were empty, except for the standard vents and antennas and satellite TV dishes and the small rooftop maintenance access common to all such buildings. But the two roofs farthest west had been transformed into a garden. Ryan had seen the mini oasis on his first trip: it was surrounded with a four-foot half wall and lined with planters that bloomed spring flowers. Ten massive pots held budding trees. A vine-covered, six-foot trellis offered privacy to the north. A sturdy gazebo stood tall with a string of softly glowing white lights tracing its edges. Two brick outbuildings—a service elevator and a workshop—had been crafted into the oasis, with strategically placed plants and shrubs.

From eight floors above Ryan checked the streets; the mob was gone. The wrecker crew had stacked up the vehicles thick and deep around the minimart; Our Way was shut off at Pride and Colwell. A construction crew removed the truck from the pharmacy and was building a sturdy temporary wall. Banco Federal security remained around the building, guarding the money and a slow trickle of customers.

He tried the rooftop outbuilding doors. They were locked. The service elevator required a key to power on and was secured by a metal gate. Ryan sat under the gazebo, spread out his food, plugged into the outlet that powered the string of lights and started working between iGlass and laptop. The sub shop Wi-Fi was not strong enough on the roof, but he did find "Bobsboys," unsecured Internet connection.

The money still hadn't been transferred into his account—the private car charge had not reversed—and Jeff had not responded with an ETA. The first two were not surprising; Ryan was being impatient. The third was concerning. Jeff was notoriously prompt. Ryan dialed Jeff's law office number, and it went to voice mail.

Where is his secretary?

"Jeff, Ryan Sage here. Trapped in the big city. Need to get out of the madness. Not sure how much longer I can stay here. Home sweet home is sounding better and better. Give me a heads-up on the transfer, please."

Ryan called Lenna, and it also went to voice mail. He didn't leave a message. He dialed work to talk to the woman filling in while he was away. Technically, his title was Chief Information Officer even though everyone still treated him like a part owner. She had taken over his duties and was doing a great job, which was probably why Erik was fussy about Ryan going on leave. They wanted to pay the woman what she was worth in that role and Ryan was still getting his paycheck.

The phone rang once and then disconnected. He dialed back only to get a busy circuit message. Eleven people directly reported to Ryan; he tried three of their numbers. Sometimes calls went to voice mail, but most of the time the circuits were busy. He was looking for anyone who might have a suggestion on how to get home.

Finally, Ryan sent an e-mail to a distribution list telling them he was trying to get home. Two e-mails came back almost immediately. One said they missed him but couldn't help; the other merely said, "Big Brother is looking for you. Run, Forrest! Run!"

Ryan laughed. That was Dean. It was not a surprise that Dean had missed the request for help. He had the communication skills of an IT guy and a conspiracy nut who couldn't get enough of hearing about the potential RICO investigation.

Ryan made a point of taking his case public. His first article on the legal atrocity that was subsumed in federal law appeared within two weeks of Tess' warning. Ever since then Dean kept tabs on the issue like he was a doctor checking for a pulse.

Ryan was a mouse click from logging off e-mail when a third message pinged for his attention. Stephanie was a recently hired young desktop support technician. She was good and the message proved very clever.

Mr. Sage,

Call the local crop dusters and see if any of them will take you. It is late spring. If they were planting, they are most likely done. Their planes are sitting in the barns, and dusters love to fly. As long as they have the range, they will get you home.

Great Idea!

Ryan started a web search for crop dusting in the greater Pittsburgh area. There was nothing close. He would have to travel a hundred miles toward Ohio, but he found two men who would gladly make the trip. The price was steep but doable when the money transfer finalized. He hung up from negotiating the details and wondered how he was going to drive to the landing strip.

Ryan made the convoluted trip down the fire escape thinking there had to be a better way. He dropped his bag on the desk, his backside into a chair in the manager's office. He snapped on the television. He caught a breathless reporter crouching behind a bullet-riddled car mid sentence. She vamped into the camera with a report that could have been summarized in two sentences. She paused as the network rolled the footage from the President yesterday morning:

". . . *and of the necessity to restore social order in the streets, I have ordered the Marine 'Corpse' [sic] 2nd Infantry Division into New York City to help with the social unrest . . ."*

Her report continued: "And about seven hours after the President's forces entered New York City, a firefight broke out between gun extremists and American militia groups when the military tried to seize weapons on the banned armaments list."

She paused as if to weigh what was going to come out of her mouth next. And then it became clear why she paused: she went way off script. "I must apologize. They were not militia groups, but average citizens trying to defend themselves from roving bands homicidal maniacs. Thousands of civilians lie dead on the streets of New York." She used too many adjectives—massacre, atrocity, and murder.

"Shut her down!" someone bellowed off camera. Something heavy struck the cameraman. He sounded like wet laundry as he fell to the ground. The camera tilted, then clattered to the street. In the last few seconds of broadcast, the viewers could hear the *crack* of a rifle and see the side of the blonde reporter's blonde head blow out.

Ryan stared at the TV, watching a screen full of electronic snow and all he could think about was *Posse Comitatus*, and the tyranny that was on the horizon.

14

Global Infection: ≤ 26.60003%

SEC. 15. *From and after the passage of this act it shall not be lawful to employ any part of the Army of the United States as a posse comitatus or otherwise, for the purpose of executing the laws, except in such cases and under such circumstances as such employment of said force may be expressly authorized by the Constitution, or by act of Congress and no money appropriated by this act shall be used to pay any of the expenses incurred in the employment of any troops in violation of this section, and any person willfully violating the provisions of this section shall be deemed guilty of a misdemeanor and on conviction thereof shall be punished by fine not exceeding ten thousand dollars, or imprisonment not exceeding two years or by both such fine and imprisonment*

—SECTION 15 OF CHAPTER 263 OF THE
ACTS OF THE 2ND SESSION OF THE
45TH CONGRESS

Latin: Posse . . . Picture, if you will, the wild wild West six-shooter-toting, ten-gallon-hat-wearing, mustang-riding band of cowboys with shiny new deputy badges glistening from leather vests. They are circled around an oak tree that has suddenly sprouted hemp knotted into three nooses. At the end of each noose sits a man facing backwards, hands tied behind his back. . .

Now add the word *comitatus* to the thought experiment and notice how it changes the picture. The word comes from Latin, meaning retinue, the king's special guard, his inner circle of friends, his companions who guard him and share in the spoils of war.

Now the men with badges and ten-gallon hats are wearing suits of mail and sit astride destriers, war horses, and they dress the banner of their sovereign. The captives are no longer seated on horses but stand atop gallows that grow hemp that is knotted into a noose.

What have the men on horseback done? What have the men standing on the gallows done? What is their crime?

What does it matter? The sovereign ruler is able to use his men-at-arms not only to wage war, but he is also able to use them as the police. The King has his posse, and when kings have their own private retinue there are no such things as civil liberties.

Thus went the beginning of an article titled "The Hangin' Tree" that Ryan wrote nineteen months prior in response to the president signing into law the Insurgency and Domestic Insurrection Obstruction and Terrorism Statute. The new law all but eliminated *Posse Comitatus* and strengthened the Insurrection Act to the point of dictatorship.

The article continued with these words:

In the early part of the twenty-first century, the executive branch had the bright idea that the War on Terror and natural disasters were sufficient excuses to roll back "separation of powers" to little more than polite suggestions. And just like their predecessors, who pushed the door of federal domination open wider and wider, they passed the law out of "necessity." They sold it to the public that it was for the protection of civil liberties. What greater necessity could there be?

"Necessity is the plea for every infringement of human freedom. It is the argument of tyrants; it is the creed of slaves," said William Pitt the Younger.

"Necessity is what everyone else is responsible for, but no individual wants to prepare for," said Ryan Sage the one and only.

Not long after the War on Terror started and the implications of the laws passed to fight that ill named war on American soil started to become clear, the elected representatives realized that they had vested enormous power in the hands of one man. In a rare fit of Washington sanity, they repealed the additions, but they never closed the door, leaving the original law in all its exception-riddled glory, wide open to the broadest interpretation.

Posse Comitatus started out as an 1878 appropriations bill that became a political compromise with the states in the reconstructionist South. The agreement was reached to suspend the use of U.S. Army, the Department of War, from being used as a police force against civilians.

It matters not the caveats and addendums built into the law to confine federal use of military might against citizens. It matters not the bromides uttered in lip service to Constitutional restraint in defense of citizens. These inhibitors have proved as thin as the momentary political pressures. When it has been "necessary," the executive branch has used military power against citizens. So it was only a matter of time before "necessity" was once again the reason for presidential use of military force. It was only a matter of time before the exception became the rule.

As in all arguments over principle, the moment one concedes the premise, the only conversation left is, "How much?" If "necessity" is the justification in *some* instance, what prevents "necessity" from being the justification in *every* instance?

If the president can be commander in chief *and* constable in chief for five minutes, why not ten minutes?

If terror-ism is reason for the president to take over police action, why isn't emotional-ism a reason for sustaining a police state?

If an incompetent governor cannot execute his oath of office for the citizens of his state, how does that same incompetent governor remove a militarily superior tyrannical power from his borders?

If the president holds the power to declare all national disasters and deploys his posse out of "necessity," then what prevents him from declaring an unending disaster?

People pretend that the president will never use the Armed Forces on American soil against American citizens. Certainly no president could be so crass. Certainly such fear is the product of conspiratorial delusions by unstable minds. This is America, for God's sake. We are the freest people on the planet, right?

But the reality that no one wants to face is that America is already under federal military occupation, and not one governor in decades has lifted a finger to resist the onslaught against state sovereignty by removing federal agencies from operating with impunity inside state boarders.

The president already has a posse, and he uses it with ruthless precision against the law-abiding and the criminal with equal measure, depending on the political tides of the moment. Their names are alcohol, tobacco, and firearms, Federal Bureau of Investigation, U.S. Marshals, Drug Enforcement Agency, Department of Homeland Security, and IRS and a list of other acronyms that are little more than paramilitary organizations with police powers.

(And as an aside, notice that all of these organizations were created out of 'necessity.')

If you doubt the equation, take a quick look at a Delta Force operator and DEA agent and notice their loadout is almost identical. The agents train in the same schools, learn the same tactics and deploy the same armaments. The only difference is the rules of engagement. Delta Force has to grant *American* civil liberties to Islamic combatants. The DEA gets to shoot first and ignore civil liberties later if the judge happens to throw their case out of court.

Does this observation hit to close to home?

Does this reality make the stomach turn queasy?

Does it seem better to act like the governor of a state and live in denial?

Then let's continue to ignore the obvious and return to the fantasy world where American citizens have only to worry about the President deploying the Armed Forces against free citizens. Let us now revisit our picture of the tree (or the gallows), surrounded by a posse. Ignore the men with ATF, DEA and DHS insignia standing in full tactical gear and digital camouflage, surrounding our desperados at the end of a noose. Ignore the IRS and BOHMeC agents armed with guns and the power to seize anyone's property or body in a fit of bureaucratic autocracy. When the "good will" ends and the "necessity" demands, the Armed Forces will be wearing the same digital camouflage as the rest of the president's posse. But they will stand virtually invisible underneath their Nano Mirage Skins; they will be mounted on personnel carriers, holding the latest advance in carbine technology. Encircling that platoon is a company and outside that circle is a mechanized battalion and around that is the full might of the Air Force and around them is the Coast Guard, and then the Navy. This is the picture of *posse comitatus*.

The reconstructionist South understood what was behind the gate they tried to close. But the door was left propped open and the inexorable pressure of "necessity" has repeatedly pushed the door wide open. Now, a hundred plus years later, the Insurgency and Domestic Insurrection Obstruction and Terrorism Statute gives the president the power to deploy his personal police force, and let them roam the lands restrained by little more than Good Will.

Good Will—so fleeting an emotion tasked with so great a charge: the responsibility of protecting free men's liberty.

The future is already foretold. The date is just not set. But Good Will ... will surely die under the strangling power of political expediency in a noose made of necessity. Maybe it will be tomorrow, or next year, or the year after. Maybe it will be this president or the next (if he ever abdicates his office), but the executive branch will surely claim that it should have greater authority to send its *posse of friends* to police the several states. As always, it will be done in the name of the common good, civil liberties, natural disasters, terror-ism, emotional-ism, someone got offended, someone got afraid, someone said forbidden words, someone sneezed, the president had a tooth ache, or the president thought it was Allah's will. And on that day, he will send his tribal warriors to do his bidding and the specific justification won't matter, because you can be dead certain it will be a "necessity."

What then of the restraining force of our great and mighty Good Will?

Shall we bolster that robust power with wishes upon a star and the tooth fairy and rainbows and cosmic happy thoughts to mount resistance when the Representative Republic of the United States is subsumed into the whims of Caesar?

The political powers inhabiting Washington got excited when Ryan closed the article with these words:

> Congress, in the great tradition of statesmanship handed down for the last few decades, "deemed and passed" yet another law. Why waste a thought on men who cringe from the arduous task of casting a vote? Why waste cyber ink on self-declared irrelevancies?
>
> The Senate passed the Insurgency and Domestic Insurrection Obstruction and Terrorism Statute into law with handshakes and hugs, celebrating their forethought and foresight. But will it be so embracing when Caligula demands its members hand over their wives so he can rate their sexual performance?
>
> And you cowardly governors who have shirked your responsibility to repel federal invasion of sovereign states and abetted the exploitation of the free people you swore an oath to defend—you can kiss your ass goodbye when Caesar's *posse* circles around the hanging tree. No free citizen will lift a finger to cut you down, because there won't be any free citizens.

Ryan felt as dirty inside as he was on the outside. He needed to wash the dirt and sweat off his skin. He desperately hoped the water would soothe his soul. He shed his dirty clothes into the washer and started a cycle. Ryan was about to take another sink bath—clean or not—but bar rags were hardly ideal, and he didn't want to smell like industrial cleaner. He walked back through the hall to the loading dock to the minimart naked. He wandered the aisles looking for shower gel, shampoo, towels, and washcloth. It wasn't quite the vast selection of Walmart, but the grocery was designed to save shoppers the runaround where they could find everything they needed.

Ryan was heading back to the manager's office to grab some underwear out of his bag when the phone rang.

"Hello?" he said whispering.

"Ryan?" Ahou said. "Why are you whispering?"

"Oh, Ahou?" Ryan said, putting the bass back in his voice. "I was . . . uh, long story. Wow, finally someone called. I was worried, but I wasn't able to get in touch."

"Yes?" she said, starting to giggle. "We didn't call early because we wanted to let you sleep."

"Sleep? That was like hours ago. Almost a whole day has gone by. Did Firouz declare a day off? And oh, did you know that someone crashed a truck into the pharmacy just down the street?"

"Yes, we saw that on the television." Ahou's voice was light and playful. "It is *amazing* what one can see on video. I called you earlier a couple of times, but you didn't pick up."

"Well, I've had the phone with me most of the afternoon," Ryan said, a little fussed. Ahou didn't seem to be taking his frustration seriously. "You must have called when I was outside. So what happened to Firouz? I guess I shouldn't be worried, but I was. And it seems like he would want to make sure I didn't steal the store."

"He got a call early this morning from Mr. Ryder. I don't know what about, but I know it changed his mind about going to the grocery. After the call, he and my mother started arguing. Then he spent most of the afternoon on the phone. My father banished me and my sister to our rooms while he and my mother argued and talked on the phone." Ahou puffed her exasperation into the phone. "Being sent to my room is one of the downsides of living with parents well into adulthood. They still think I'm twelve."

"Oh, parents never stop thinking you are twelve," Ryan said, "even when you don't live with them."

"Anyway, they stopped arguing, but they have been in their office all morning and afternoon. My father called you, and when you did not answer, he was worried you had left," Ahou said, "But then I could see that you were building that thing across the windows and doors, so I told him you were still there."

"Oh no, I haven't left. I took the liberty to redecorate. It took some effort, but I think a few thousand pounds of rock salt will slow looters down . . ." And then her words clicked into place. "Wait. Uh . . . you could *see* that I'm still here?"

"Yes," she said, trying to hold down her giggles.

Ryan's stomach knotted, and his face flushed. He looked around the manager's office for a camera and saw one that had a full view of the wall safe. There was nowhere to hide. "Oh my."

Ahou could not hold back her laughter.

"So you can monitor the store cameras from home?" Ryan said, pinching the bridge of his nose. He had remote audio/video monitoring of his house. It was only logical that Firouz's security system let him monitor from anywhere.

"Yes, I have been monitoring your very cute butt for a while now," she said laughing, deep and rich.

"Ahhh. Thank you, I guess."

"Oh no, thank *you.*"

"It really is mean to laugh at a guy when he's naked," Ryan said testy.

Ahou composed herself. "Oh, you have *nothing* to be ashamed of, and the man-scaping is much appreciated. Tell you what. I'll be nice to you. I will call you again when you are finished getting cleaned up. And Ryan?"

"Yes?"

"I promise not to peek."

15

Global Infection: ≤ 26.679999%

*It is incident to physicians, I am afraid, beyond all other
men, to mistake subsequence for consequence.*

—S<small>AMUEL</small> J<small>OHNSON</small>

*It is an event of the politicians who dabble in the economic
affairs of men to obscure subsequence for consequence. Or
said more simply, they love to wreck cause and effect.*

—R<small>YAN</small> S<small>AGE</small>

"I think that makes the second time I've made you blush."
Two security cameras gave a shot toward Ryan's sink bath. He taped a sign
in front of each that said, "No Peeking." He was flattered that Ahou wanted to
peek but not nearly so enthusiastic that Firouz had seen him wandering around
the store. "Men don't blush," Ryan said into the phone trying to sound manly.

"Liar, if you are not blushing, Skype with me and prove it!"

"Skype with you? Uh . . . err . . . I think the camera on my laptop is broken."

"You're funny. Turn on the office computer. I'd rather talk to you face
to face."

The office computer was already on but locked. "What are the login
credentials?"

"Camellia should already be the username, and the same name plus
1111 is the password. And after you launch Skype, the account should say
Orwell, and the password should be 198419841984."

Ryan laughed, typing in the last of the digits to the video conferencing,
watching it ring and connect.

"Oh, there you are. And you shaved!" Ahou said with a wave and a smile.
"Oh, let me see your arm. I could see it before on the security cameras but
not close-up."

Ryan held up his arm for inspection. "She didn't break the skin."

"It doesn't look too bad. And the bruise looks like it is fading already."

"Hmm . . . I hadn't really noticed. One of the advantages of the Eternity Vaccine—everything heals faster."

"So, you are not going to go crazy on me or anything?"

Ryan raised a brow. "The night is young, my dear!"

"I read 1984 when I was in high school. And when the government passed the legislation that gave them the power to monitor all Internet communications. That was my attempt at protest."

"Clever," Ryan said as he adjusted the screen settings. The camera loved Ahou, and his little picture in the bottom right corner confirmed—for the thousandth time—that it didn't love him.

Ahou leaned in close like she was studying him under a microscope.

"What are you doing?" Ryan said, looking over his shoulder and looking around the room. "Do I have something on me?"

"No, I'm trying to see if you are still blushing."

"Funny girl. The blushing is a side effect of being out of BOHMeC compliance. I haven't been able to pose in an Abercrombie photo shoot for about ten years."

Ahou flashed a winning smile and leaned back, showing her white designer T-shirt that had *SHAKIN'* printed on the front in swooping letters. "You look just fine. Maybe it is your butt that Abercrombie should be shooting."

Ahou was being polite. "Thank you. So, are you the only one who got a show, or does your whole family now know my secrets?"

"Oh, I called my sister and mother to come watch immediately."

"Oh, you are just evil."

"My mom said you have a nice butt."

Ryan pinched the bridge of his nose. "You are never going to let up, are you?"

"No."

"All right. All right. Just as long as your father doesn't come after me with a bat."

"My mother learned long ago not to tell my father everything about his daughters."

"I'm thinking I might need to have a conversation with your mom."

"But you don't speak Farsi."

"I'll buy my own unbiased, *honest* translator."

Ahou blanched as much as her complexion would allow and said, "She wouldn't tell you anything anyway."

Ryan leaned in close and studied Ahou. He was quiet, taking in all her details until she started to fidget.

"What are you doing?"

"I'm reading your thoughts," Ryan said with his best serious voice. "So, I know that your mom would tell the truth about you. And . . . what is this?

Oh, isn't that interesting? I need to ask her about that thing in high school. And oh my, what in the world did you do in college?"

Ahou bit her lower lip. "You can't know about that," she said, her turn to blush.

And it was true. Ryan couldn't know any of "that." He was just being outrageous. Who doesn't have something from high school and a scandalous story from college that they don't want anyone to know about? "That is okay. Your secrets will be safe with me."

"I don't have any secrets."

"Liar, liar, pants on fire. Hang your shorts from a telephone wire."

"Where did you get that from?"

"At playground growing up?"

"Are you still in grade school?"

"I don't want to grow up," Ryan sang. "I'm a Toys "R" Us kid."

Ahou put her head on her desk laughing until another girl cracked her door. The mic filled with Farsi for a minute, and Ahou shooed the girl way with the back of her hand. "That was my sister, Asalam. She is very pretty, isn't she?"

"Yes, she is very pretty."

"What about me? Do you not think I'm pretty?" Ahou said, suddenly girlish and insecure.

She was fishing for a compliment. Ryan decided to make it a real one. He paused, letting his eyes linger, appreciative. She pulled her dark hair around to the right shoulder, self-conscious. "Yes, Ahou, you are very beautiful. I happen to really like your neckline."

Ahou demure, her eyes dropped. "I was beginning to think you didn't find me attractive. You hardly talk to me."

Ryan nodded. "Yes, I suspect that doesn't happen to you too often, particularly when you want a man to talk to you." Not the smoothest line, but it is what came out of his mouth.

"You make me sound so conceited."

"No, I just pointed out what no one says out loud. Beautiful women aren't supposed to know they are beautiful, and they aren't supposed to be treated differently than the rest of us average folk, but everyone indulges the polite lie."

"So, you didn't talk to me because you thought I was a snob or something."

"No, I didn't talk to you because I am a terribly insecure dork when it comes to meeting beautiful women. I was terrified because I don't do social banter well, as I am sure you have already noticed. And in some small, teensy-weensy defense of my social incompetence, when I came into the shop I was very, very preoccupied."

"What were you preoccupied about? Do you have a wife? Or lots of girlfriends?"

Ryan smiled. It was refreshing on so many levels to have a woman this interested, asking probing and leading questions. "No. Never been married. No girlfriends . . . my harem is depleted just now."

"Oh, he has a harem?"

"That would be comedy and really funny if I do say so."

Ahou leaned back in her chair. The woman had returned, confident and considering. She looked like she was trying to solve a riddle. "You are not like I expected."

"Well, since I'm not sure what you did expect . . ."

"You were so intense in the shop yesterday. Well, you were scary when you were dealing with that robber," Ahou said, her eyes sparkling with the memory. "And then you were so focused, but now you joke and make fun." She paused, thinking. "You are right. Rarely do men ignore me. I saw you looking like most men, so I knew you were not gay."

"Yes, right. The only reason a man ignores a beautiful woman is because he *must* be gay."

"That didn't sound good, did it?"

"Not really."

Ahou shook her hands like she was trying to air dry them. "You make me so . . . so . . . I meant to say . . ." Ahou shook her hands again.

"I know what you meant."

"Oh, you do?" Ahou crossed her arms. "So why don't you tell me what I meant to say?"

"I was trying to be amicable . . ."

"Amicable? So, you were trying to let me off the hook?" Ahou said coquettishly. "So, you think you can read my mind?"

"Is this one of those female conversations where it doesn't matter what I say?"

"So, you are perceptive too."

"That is me, Mr. Perceptive."

"First, you were Mr. Smooth. Now you are Mr. Perceptive." Ahou was enjoying herself. "Ha! A man who is perceptive. I don't believe you."

"You are a feisty one."

"Can you handle it?" Ahou had turned on the sexual charm up a few watts. "I double dog dare you to show me your perceptivity, Mr. Perceptive."

"Well now, a double dog dare. How can a kid back down from that?" Ryan paused for a long moment, looking deep into Ahou's eyes until she fidgeted. "Just remember, you asked."

Before she could respond, Ryan said, "Here is what you were thinking. You couldn't believe that a man would ignore you because you are smoking hot and know it. You wanted me to talk to you. You gave me all the subtle signals that make men fawn all over you, but none of them got the reaction you wanted, which made you obsess on how a man could ignore your charms. Gay was off the table because you saw me repeatedly check out your chest and your backside. You took notice of my left hand and saw no ring and no tan line, so that meant that I probably was not married.

"You came over to my table trying to understand the mystery and expected me to focus on your boobs while uttering adorably desperate pickup lines, but instead heard political philosophy. Since you were reading *The Road to Serfdom*, political philosophy was on your mind, which increased your intrigue.

"The Katana Boy comes through the door and you watch me take on an armed man; you watched me face danger. Men who face danger bring out three potential reactions in women: fear, awe, or inspiration. Your reaction was awe and inspiration.

"I still didn't fall all over myself to get back to you, and now your confidence was wavering, so you didn't have the nerve to interrupt me. You saw me demonstrate a focus you rarely see in men when you are around. All of this further intrigued you because you are just about old enough to realize that the cool frat boy riff is a relational dead end. You have begun to realize that after the orgasms are over, the Captain and Coke drinking grad school boys bore you to death. They might be your age, but you don't consider them your equals, because you can manipulate them at will. You've tried some of your standard ploys with me and find me refreshingly immune. Now you are flustered with what to say and do. You feel like a schoolgirl tripping over her tongue and feet.

"That is what you were thinking, but you couldn't say any of that. So that is why the words wouldn't come."

Ryan's words faded down to silence. And the longer the silence went, the more he was certain that she would end the Skype. He should have kept his big blab mouth shut and played like the average mute male idiot. He had lost count how many times he had demonstrated this level of insight to a woman, and it never went well.

Ahou squirmed in her chair, scrunched her shoulders up around her neck like she was trying to disappear. She ran her fingers through her hair and finally settled on twirling a lock of black hair around her fingers. Then her lips curled into a half smile. She said, "Well yeah," like it was the most obvious thing in the world, "I wouldn't have said it that way, but yes. That is ... uh ... that is what I was thinking I can't decide if I find that kind of insight terrifying or refreshing." Ahou studied Ryan like he was a whole new, unprecedented experience. "So, you are a defender of silly Persian girls, a political philosopher, *and* a psychic?

"I'm a man of many talents."

Ahou's eyes flashed. She bit her lip and cleared her throat. "You said you write about politics. Are you a college professor?"

"Why do you ask?"

"The only people I've ever met who talk about political philosophy are college professors. I'm getting my master's in political science at Duquesne. I don't ever hear what you said anywhere else. I've never heard anyone say what you said. If theft is justice, then that destroys the concept of justice. And that destroys man."

"Wow, you were listening."

"You didn't expect that because I'm a silly, conceited Persian girl?"

"Ahou, you are hardly a silly girl. I see a blazing fast mind behind those eyes. My cynicism comes from years and years of talking and people promptly ignoring me. But philosophy is everywhere. Man can't escape it, though he tries desperately to do just that. As far as I am concerned, the only place to really have these discussions is on the street. But we have almost outlawed free speech."

"Philosophy is everywhere?" Skepticism dripped off her words.

"Turn on your television."

"Oh, you said you were fun to watch TV with. Are you going to yell at it?"

"I reserve the right."

"Okay, Mr. Smarty Philosopher, I'm on Channel 7. Show me the big ideas."

Ryan powered on the TV and changed the channel just in time to hear a congressman continue his news conference:

> ". . . ever-newer waters flow on those who step into the same rivers . . . though some try to compel the river to stand still with their constant, greed-driven assault as they try to gouge the hardworking common man in his hour of dire need.
>
> "My colleague from Florida, in his misguided attempt to defend small business, has succumbed to the thinking inspired by the corruption of big business interests. It is not his fault that he has fallen victim to this type of thinking. It is likely he does not even know the source of his error. Such is the way of cultural indoctrination of the rich on a society. It is not the consciousness of men that determines their being, but on the contrary, their social being determines their consciousness. And my colleague from Florida has been corrupted by the corporate social consciousness.
>
> "He would like us to believe the force behind profits is merely harsh economic realities. He would like us to believe that prices are determined by strict, harsh, inhuman economic laws. But I say, why must providing for the needy be an either-or decision? I say that those who tell us these either-or choices have been corrupted by corporate greed. I say that there are no strict laws, particularly when it is human compassion that should rule all our hearts. Reality is merely the ongoing change from state to state, and today we must protect the children from the ruthless efforts of those who would take from those who are suffering misfortune. There is no contradiction between economic costs and the cost to demonstrate our commitment to the least of all people in our midst. Indeed, the sum of injustice and inequality is in that a few benefit from the sweat of the many. The concept of profit at the expense of those who sweat and suffer is a stain on all that is moral. To be an American in this new age is to submit the *I*, to the *thou*. To be a patriotic American is to sacrifice the Individual to the nation in this time of need.

"In light of the disturbing developments by those businessmen determined to price-gouge, I have called for the House to start an emergency session to investigate what may be a criminal conspiracy. And I will put a bill before Congress to save the free market. Indeed, **we have abandoned free market principles to save the free market system so people in need can receive life-giving necessities.** When people come to understand how much is happening, they will understand why we had to act as—"

"All right," Ryan said, turning his volume down, "I've heard enough. Uhhhh, where to begin?" As he collected his thoughts, he noticed the news ticker scrolling across the bottom of the screen.

The President: It is time for people to remain calm, but we should always remember to make sacrifices for the common good . . .
Russia: The dead are walking . . .
Pastor Alfonse Meller: Demons walk the earth, end times fulfilled . . .

Russia: The dead are walking??

"Well, why don't you begin at the beginning?"
She was so playful. Ryan found it irresistible.
"What is it? You look worried. Can't find your philosophy?"
"No, something I saw on the television. A news update that said the dead were walking."
"I saw the report a few hours ago. Come on, Mr. Logical, you can't tell me you think those reports are true."
"It is just that I had a something fit together in my mind . . ."

16

Global Infection: ≤ 26.7341%

We develop new principles for the world out of the world's own principles. We do not say to the world: Cease your struggles, they are foolish; we will give you the true slogan of struggle. We merely show the world what it is really fighting for, and consciousness is something that it has to acquire, even if it does not want to.

—KARL MARX, LETTER FROM THE
DEUTSCH-FRANZÖSISCHE JAHRBÜCHER TO ARNOLD RUGE

Ryan's mind churned through the details: the attack, the blonde woman, the man eating . . .

The dead walking . . .

But they weren't dead, not in the walking corpse, necrotizing flesh, Halloween kind of sense. Take away the macabre images and the man on all fours and the woman that bit him, and those two people could have been taking a walk on the streets.

So, what does that mean . . .?

But whatever insight he thought was imminent wouldn't coalesce.

"Did you see a ghost? Or are you just stalling?" Ahou drummed her fingers dramatically on her desk.

"You know, they have this thing called patience."

"Stalling . . ."

"All right, you asked for it. The most obvious manifestation of philosophy is man's commitment to Heraclitus and the practical outworking of dialectic materialism."

"Heraclitus?" Ahou said, "You just made that name up didn't you?"

Of course, the chance that she had ever heard of Heraclitus and his theory of endless change was slim, but it was time for him to push back.

"Right, I say the name of a historic figure and I'm the one who made it up. No, Heraclitus is a real person. One of the first Western philosophers as a matter of fact. Since you are taking political philosophy, you've probably heard of dialectic materialism?"

Ahou scrunched her neck down. Her body language that signaled she was unsure. "Dialectic what?"

"Okay, not knowing Heraclitus is understandable, but your course work hasn't discussed dialectic materialism?"

"Umm . . . no."

"And you are how far through your master's?"

"I have one more semester, if I didn't work full-time, but with as much as I work it will probably take me two."

"If you are halfway through and they haven't covered dialectic materialism, you need to get your money back. You know who Karl Marx is, of course, yes?"

"Yes. Of course I do. I'm not that stupid."

"Ahou, I didn't say you were stupid. And I wouldn't even be talking to you if I thought you were. My comment about the master's degree is because there is no way a political science degree can be comprehensive without a full introduction to Marxist ideology in general and dialectic materialism, since it is dominating the global social political landscape.

"Anyway, I was trying to figure out what you knew and what you didn't, so I know where to start."

"I over-reacted. I knew you weren't being mean, but I'm not used to feeling out of control. Feeling like I need to . . ." She rolled her hands like that finished the sentence.

"Okay, so do you want me to go on?"

Her eyes sparkled. "Yes. And you warned me, didn't you?"

"Yes, I did."

Ahou stuck out her tongue.

"Regressing, are we?" Ryan said, "The philosophy underneath the congressman's comments start with Heraclitus' metaphysical assertion that the only thing that exists is change. He is generalizing the nature of existence so he can appeal to what Marx called dialectical materialism to make a moral judgment: specifically, that capitalism is evil. His logic then says, that because capitalism is evil it is moral for him to use government power to end price gouging."

"Is it okay if I admit I don't know what you just said?"

Ryan nodded, patient. "I'm glad you did. Just don't let your brain go tilt and I'll be glad to explain."

"I promise not to let my brain go tilt."

"Okay, the congressman's first sentence is a reference to Heraclitus. The river metaphor is famous, because it concisely illustrates the metaphysical world-view that everything is in a constant state of change. Because the world is constantly changing, there are no absolutes. The congressman needs to reject absolutes so he can reject what he calls 'inhuman economic laws.' Laws are constants. If there is a measurable causality, then there is a right answer. If there is *no* constant, then the right answer is whatever he wants. He is laying the foundation for contradictions to exist. The loose logic is if everything is changing, then there is no such thing as formal logic, because even logic changes. Therefore, there is no such thing as a contradiction. And since there is no formal logic, there is no real formal economic science: there is no causality for money and markets.

"In the Marxist world, logic is the byproduct of economic environment that people are born into. Human thinking is shaped by cultural forces beyond their ability to master, or even be aware of. For example, the congressman in Florida has been corrupted by corporate thinking."

"I wondered why he kept talking about big business thinking," Ahou said.

"Yes, he is saying that man's selfish capitalistic tendencies are the result of social conditioning. Objective arguments about the laws of economics are just latent capitalist bourgeois corruption. People are born into the corruption and cannot help themselves. As an aside, this is why all communist dictatorships have reeducation camps: because the state must force people to think correctly."

Ahou looked sideways into the camera. "You got all of that out of listening to the congressman for two minutes?"

"If you know what you are looking for, it is a simple exercise. I told you, philosophy is everywhere."

"But maybe you are reading into what the congressman said. People don't really talk like this."

Ryan said, "Actually, people spout philosophical sayings all the time. The fact that they don't know that is what they are doing is irrelevant. As for reading into the congressman's words, make no mistake, he is being intentionally ideological. I just recognized the shorthand reference to the elaborate philosophical system and the political outcome."

"What is the outcome?" Ahou asked.

Ryan shrugged. "The same as all Marxist governments. Dictatorial power."

Ahou frowned. "He didn't say that."

"Buried underneath the words, is the real goal. The congressman presents himself as the savior who protects the poor as the champion of economic justice. He will use government force to compel evil greedy capitalists to do the moral thing."

"Okay," Ahou interjected, "I guess I have heard of Marx's famous line: 'To each according to his need. From each according to his ability,' but not all socialist governments become tyrannies. What about Sweden? It has a free market and the people are socialists."

Ryan chuckled. "Everyone thinks Sweden is a socialist utopia, but it isn't. The reality is you can't have a free market and socialism. Do you remember when the congressman said this: 'We have abandoned free market principles to save the free market system. When people come to understand how much is happening, people in need can receive life-giving necessities. They will understand why we had to act as we did.'"

Ahou nodded.

"This is like saying we need to abandon oxygen to save breathing. This is a contradiction. Right?"

"Yes?"

"To abandon a free market to save a free market is also a contradiction. To say you are abandoning something that is *free*, you can only mean that what comes next is slavery. The opposite of a free market is an enslaved market. And an enslaved market is a contradiction. Markets are merely the willing peaceful trading actions of individuals. If trade isn't *willing* or *peaceful*, the exchange must be caused by fraud, extortion or theft. If we have an enslaved market, we are really talking about slaves compelled to exchange values at the point of a gun."

"So, wait," Ahou said, "Maybe I'm missing something. What is philosophy then?"

"Oh, good catch. I didn't define it. Brief definition: philosophy is how man organizes and integrates his ideas into action. So, what man believes about existence determines what he knows, which shapes the moral framework for the kind of government man creates. So, if there are no absolutes, man can't know anything, which means Man needs a government to compel him to right action."

Ahou said, "But government shouldn't legislate morality. I ask my father all the time if his Christian values should be turned into law. And he gets uncomfortable when I say that the government shouldn't be legislating morality."

Ryan said. "I don't want to get too far into the weeds, but at the most basic level, all government action is the legislation of morality. And in the congressman's case, his definition of morality is saying that 'profit' is immoral. Price gouging should be punishable by law."

Ahou tapped her chin. "Okay, I think I get it. His morality goes basically like this: instead of stoning homosexuals because they violate God's law, he wants to stone price gougers because they violate Marxist law."

"Yes, something like that."

Ahou started writing in her notebook. When she stopped, she said, "But what about price gouging? I mean, it is a bad thing to take advantage of people."

Ryan said, "Let me take this out of a discussion on economics, because it is too easy to tangle economics with good intentions and people get twitchy when their good intentions don't square with the laws of economics.

"Man stands unique within existence. Nature gives man nothing. Man is the one creature who, to *live*, must choose his actions to achieve values in his environment. Man is the only creature on earth that must change his environment to live. If he fails, he dies."

"Wait," Ahou said with a pausing hand. "What if it is all predetermined? What if it is Allah's will? Or if you believe in the Christian God, like my father, what if it is God's will?"

Ryan smiled and sat back in his chair.

"What? Can't I ask questions?"

"No, I'm waiting because I am pretty sure you are smart enough to see what you just did."

"All I said was maybe man's actions are predeterm—" Ahou stopped; her eyes tracking fast like she was watching the ideas in her mind. "Oh, I see. I just asked a philosophical question. My counterargument was . . ." she shook her hand as if that would make the words come.

"You made a metaphysical counterargument. You implicitly understand that the root of human existence determines how man understands his existence. That is why I said that philosophy is everywhere. Man can't get away from it."

She picked up a pen and started writing in her notebook again.

"What are you writing?"

"None of your beeswax," Ahou said with a wink and kept writing. "So, keep going about price gouging."

"I'm still waiting for you to apologize for doubting me."

Ahou tapped the pen against the camera. "You are insufferable, Mr. Sage. I can't get away with anything with you."

"Why would you want to?"

"Fine! I'm sorry I doubted you. Now out with it."

"You are wonderful," Ryan said, enjoying himself for the first time in ages. "Anyway, the axiom of human life is that man must choose to shape his environment to sustain life. Individuals must seek values to live. Failure to obtain the right values means death.

"Well, not always," Ahou said. "People do bad things all the time and nothing happens to them."

"I'm not talking about karma. I'm not talking about balancing the scales of justice. I am talking about an accumulation of choices that produce an inescapable outcome." Ryan paused, considering how to illustrate his point. "For instance, what are the foundations of a good marital relationship? Mutual respect, shared values, sexual interest and fidelity?"

"That sounds about what it takes to have a good relationship. My parents have a good marriage and they have all of that."

"Can you forfeit the principles of a good relationship to save the relationship? Can you abandon fidelity to save fidelity? Can you abandon mutual respect? Shared values? To save a marriage?"

"I see what you are saying," Ahou said, her eyes shining into the camera. "You can choose bad actions, but eventually those bad choices will accumulate and destroy what you have."

"Yes."

Ahou picked up her pen and started writing fast. For the next five minutes, she was all focus and intensity, and Ryan was mesmerized with her every feature as she poured herself out on the paper.

Finally, she leaned back in her chair, her fingers brushing through her hair over and over. She picked up a pen again, making more notes, then laced her fingers and rested her chin. She smiled. "By the way, I have not had a conversation with a man who used the word *axiom*."

"Do you need a dictionary?"

She grabbed a small stuffed rabbit off the edge of her desk and tossed it playfully at the computer screen. "That would have hit you if you were here."

"If I were there, you would have punched me."

"That is not all I would do to you," Ahou mumbled.

"What did you just say?"

"Nothing!" she said, her eyes refusing to look back at the camera. "Now look what you made me do to my rabbit," Ahou said, petting the stuffed animal. "I got this when I was a little girl. I was in Tehran, and I had this friend. Her name was Dajinna, and her family was poor, but she got me this for my birthday when I was nine. Of course, I liked it. I didn't have many toys like this. I don't remember how I found out, but I learned that this stuffed rabbit was expensive, particularly since her family was poor. She had saved money for a while to get it for me. I was going to get her something really nice for her birthday. And just before I was going to give it to her, her family was taken away by the government. I never got to give her my present. I remember her every time I see this. I will keep it forever."

"I am sorry that I made you do that to your rabbit."

"Thank you," Ahou said. "And no, I didn't need a dictionary." She stuck out her tongue again. "So, you never answered my question about the price gouging. Do you think the anti-gouging legislation is a good idea? Isn't he really saying that to make sure people have money to spend, that it is good to keep prices down?"

"Oh no . . . It is a terrible idea and here is why I said people get twitchy when their good intentions don't square with the laws of economics. They tend to presume that public policy should be the result of good intentions. People want to be thought of as nice, and it sounds mean to let something like economic casualty stand in the way of their good intentions.

"They want to live in a world where any whim is fulfilled and they can never be held responsible for real world outcomes. They want to be able to blame everything else *but* the ideology for economic failures, so contradictions as a matter of philosophic principle make it possible for them to explain away the outcome of things like price controls."

"What is the outcome?"

"Price controls are a subtle form of tyranny. The guy with the gun tells people how much and when something can be sold. The effort required to produce; the knowledge required to create; the resources needed to make the product are irrelevant. So, the public policy is divorced from reality. This guarantees that the stuff people desperately need won't get to the people who need it."

"But it isn't right that people should have to spend all their money on basic necessities."

"Ah yes . . . necessity. Necessity is what everyone else has to provide, but no individual wants to be responsible for."

"That was a good line," Ahou said, writing in her notebook. "Who said that?"

Ryan shrugged. "Just some guy writing on a blog."

Ahou started typing on her laptop. "I'll look it up."

17

Global Infection: ≤ 26.78119%

The essence of all slavery consists in taking the product of another's labor by force. It is immaterial whether this force be founded upon ownership of the slave or ownership of the money that he must get to live.

—LEO NIKOLAEVICH TOLSTOY

"Wait, *you* said that," Ahou said. "Is this your blog? Wait, you are *that* Ryan Sage? I've heard about you in the news."

"Flattering stuff, I'm sure."

"Wow! Holy shit, I feel like such an idiot."

Ryan frowned. "Why would you? What difference does that make?"

"I'm just feeling—"

"You want me to do a search on you and find something—"

"No, don't you dare!" Ahou said, her face flushing. "You just stay right there. I need to make some notes." Ahou wrote in her notebook, occasionally stopping to smile into the camera. Finally, she leaned back, arms crossed, pen tapping against her cheek. "If it is a necessity, then you are saying people should be responsible to provide that at all costs?"

"At all *individual* cost would be action consistent with the definition of a necessity."

"That seems cold. What about the people who can't do that?"

"Well, let us not drop the context. It only seems cold because you are dodging the real monstrosity."

"Monstrosity?" Ahou said. "That sounds a little dramatic."

"Slavery is monstrous."

"Slavery?" Ahou said. "I don't understand."

"Yes," Ryan said, "most people think of slavery as black people in cotton fields driven to harvest by a man with a bullwhip. They don't see themselves as part of slavery when they tolerate laws that allow the government to take someone's property. Particularly when the government says they are taking that property for the common good. The only difference between them and the southern slave owner is that people make the government use the whip to force the doctor to treat patients, or the drug company to give away their drugs, or the manufacturer to make widgets, or the private citizen to pay his taxes. In each instance, people are forced to work and have their property taken to avoid the bullwhip of government aggression. That is slavery. And that is monstrous. Expecting people to supply the necessities of their own life is positively angelic."

Ahou took notes. The amicable silence dragged on until she put down her pen. "So, what do you think you will do when this is all over? Go home?"

"Home?" And in a moment unbidden, the image scampered out of the briar patch to the forefront of Ryan's mind.

Russia: The dead walking . . .

Scream!

Man bent down on all fours.

Slap, scraaaape!

"What is it?" Ahou said, reaching out to the screen with affection. "That is the second time you have looked like you saw a ghost or something?"

Ryan sighed. "Ahou, I'm just not sure what *over* means exactly. I've been working on a plan to get home all day. I don't see how I can stay in the city like this. The streets are dangerous. And I'm good with guarding the store, but Ahou, I really won't be able to hold off a mob. Your father has been very generous to let me stay here, but I really don't have the means to defend his store."

"Oh, he doesn't want you to get hurt," Ahou said, "I asked them four times to let you come here, but they were both firm that you couldn't come to the house."

Ryan was disappointed. "I guess I understand." He paused. "Well, I really don't, but that is all right. As soon as I have some money in my bank account, I've lined up a crop duster that will fly me home. I just have to figure out how to drive about a hundred miles." He sighed. "I'm just desperate enough that I thought about stealing one of the cars that got dumped on the street in front of the mini mart."

"You would steal a car?"

Ryan laughed mirthlessly. "No, I'm just being ridiculous. But I did notice that some cars that have keys in the ignition. If it gets too crazy out there . . ." He shrugged. "Not sure what I'm going to do. I will probably see if I can find some car to buy, assuming I can find one within walking distance."

"How about rentals?"

"I made calls earlier. *If* the rental offices were open, they were less than enthusiastic about renting a car for a one-way trip."

"Oh," Ahou said, her face falling. "How far away is home?"

"Much farther than I can walk. But I only have to travel about a hundred miles."

"Would you be safe at home? Maybe I could—"

"Safe?" Ryan said. "Sorry, I didn't mean to interrupt you. Do you know what I talked to Daniel Ryder about?"

"I know that you talked to him, of course. I know that you really, really made an impression on him. I know that doesn't mean much to you, but that is only because you don't know who he is. But I don't know what you talked about."

Ryan really didn't want to relive the story again. He didn't want to ruin the pleasant conversation with his nagging fears, and Tess' madness and Bexley and the girls and the disease. "Well, I'm trying to not be morbid. I was just enjoying—"

"You don't want to ruin the mood, right?"

"Yes, exactly."

"So, you are not telling me everything you think right now?"

"Yes."

"Because you don't think I can handle it?" Ahou sounded a touch hurt.

"No, because I don't think I can."

"Oh," Ahou said, her dark eyes suddenly wet. "I've been insensitive. I didn't really understand how much you have been through. I'm sorry. Maybe I could help you get home."

"Help me? How?"

"That is my car parked beside the catering truck. We leave a set of keys for the family cars at the store in case we have a delivery and the cars are in the way. Check the key box on the wall. One set should have Mickey Mouse attached to the ring."

Ryan rolled to the key box and looked inside. "Yes, they are here." He rolled back.

"Maybe you could borrow that to drive to the crop duster."

"You would do that?"

"Surely there is someone waiting for you at home. So, you must get there, right?" A tear leaked down her cheek. "Yes. Maybe. I don't know. It might be safer for you to just wait. Maybe this will all settle down. And then we could . . ." Ahou shook her hand in frustration.

"Ahou, I hate to be a pessimist, but my fear is that we are merely watching the tide going out just before the tsunami hits." Ryan sighed deeply. "And no, Ahou, there isn't anyone at home. My parents are gone. I have one sister, but I am concerned that she is gone as well." The tears started to well up as the reality that he was alone started gnawing into the center of his soul.

Ahou smiled through wet eyes. "If it is that dangerous, maybe we should all get out of the city. How big is this plane?"

"I think he said it was a four-seater."

"We can strap my sister to the top."

Was she really asking to leave the city with him?

"Spoken like an older sister."

Now Ahou was crying. "I don't understand why a woman hasn't snapped you up."

"A woman? What are those?" He laughed as he thumbed away his own tears. He recovered. "But that question goes to you too. I am presuming that you are not attached, no fiancé or significant other lingering out there."

Ahou's eyes were still wet, and worry lines had deepened around her eyes. "I have dated a lot, of course. And I have been asked to marry four times, but they weren't right for me. I was seeing a man for a while. He is a lawyer. Well, he recently passed the bar and is working in Washington, D.C. My mother loves him. She tells me I can't do much better."

"But something is missing?"

"Yes, something is missing." Ahou struck that pose again: fingers interlaced, her chin resting on her hands. It made her dark eyes seem bigger in the camera. They were the kind of eyes that a man could get lost in.

They both just looked until finally, Ryan broke the spell. "Would you be here when I get back? I need to go to go to the little boy's room."

"Yes, I will be here. I don't want you to be alone tonight. I will be here as long as you like."

Ryan made a pit stop and then a tour around the building, put his clothes in the dryer and then returned to the office. And Ahou was good to her word.

They talked about anything and lapsed into silence that dragged on for minutes at a time. They ate dinner together and talked. After dinner, they slumped into amicable silence watching the same comedy on pay per view. Ryan yelled at the TV, and Ahou shushed him and then laughed. It was the silence that Ryan found remarkable. As a conversationalist, he had no trouble engaging for hours, but he didn't entertain well. After four hours, he never once felt the need to hunt down her attention. But eventually, the yawns came and sleep pushed them toward their beds. Ahou said she would leave her connection open. If he needed anything, he could just call out. Ryan said that was very nice, but unnecessary.

"Well, just in case," she said. She smiled and waved goodbye, stood and walked out of the camera view. Ryan pushed his chair out of camera range, wanting to catch a glimpse of her. In all the time they talked, he had never seen her from the waist down. As she walked away, he saw long legs coming out of jean shorts. He heard her rustling and then saw her move out her bedroom door and close it behind her.

The mic picked up nothing but silence.

Ryan went to the bathroom, brushed his teeth, and took care of business. Bat in hand, he took one trip around the store, checking for bad guys in all the places that cameras don't reach.

When he came back into the manager's office, he changed into shorts and got the couch arranged for sleeping. He heard Ahou moving around and then saw her move in and out of camera view. He stood to the side watching. She was wearing men's boxers and a loose white T-shirt, getting ready for bed. Ahou's movement was mesmerizing, graceful like a dancer. The minutes passed as her ritual unfolded. Ryan crossed his arms leaning against the wall, enjoying, his heart occasionally beating faster as he caught an appealing pose.

Finally, she paused fully in the camera view. She moved to the door and locked it. Then with a finger on her chin, she stood with her back to him like she was considering something. Then slowly, Ahou pulled her shirt over her head inch by inch, revealing rich, smooth skin, the round swell of her left breast and delicate shoulders. She raised her arms, sensual and patient, over her head and let the lines of her body draw out long and lean, then let her right arm bend behind her head to sweep her dark hair from her neck.

Then with splendid timing, she let her hands slide down her hips, hook a thumb into the boxers' waistband and drop them off her hips. Ahou's hips were narrow, and the small of her back was lined with muscle. Each cheek of her backside was dimpled and her legs muscular. She let her body sway gently side to side for many beats of her heart.

Ryan could see the pulse in her neck.

Slowly, Ahou turned to face the camera, first revealing a profile, then her front. She looked into the computer screen and saw that Ryan was not on camera. She started to cover her chest, suddenly self-conscious performing for no one.

Ryan sat in the chair and slid into camera view, chin cradled in hand appraising, smiling, enjoying.

Ahou forced her arms to relax, standing open and revealed.

Ryan nodded, appreciating the art that was before him, a masterpiece of poetry in flesh. "Exquisite!" he whispered.

The apprehension evaporated out of Ahou's eyes, replaced with a smile like she had just been given the greatest gift. She took two rolling strides toward the camera. "Thank you."

Ahou walked to the light switch, turned one last time for a final look. "Good night," she said. And the lights went out, followed by the sound of her crawling into the sheets. Long minutes passed until Ryan heard Ahou's breathing even out, signaling that she was sleeping.

Ryan crawled onto the couch. And for the first time in longer than he could remember, he didn't dream about death and destruction.

18

Global Infection: ≤ 26.9999%

In great affairs, we ought to apply ourselves less to creating chances than to profiting from those that offer.
—F. DE LA ROCHEFOUCAULD

The office digital clock flashed 12:00 over and over and over. Ryan rolled to his other side and pulled the blankets around his shoulders. Eventually, the slumbering part of his mind realized the store had suffered a power outage. He had fallen asleep to Ahou's rhythmic breathing and the ambient glow of security and computer monitors, but now the office was dark. Rubbing the sleep from his eyes, he groped his way to the adjacent room and flipped on the wall switch, squinting against the invasion of light spilling through the door. Waking to absolute dark always disoriented Ryan, somehow separating him from the internal clock that connected him to the broader world.

From his cell phone, he learned that it was almost nine thirty and was mildly surprised that he had not heard from Ahou. Ryan checked the minimart landline and heard a dial tone. He found Ahou's number in the call log and hit the redial button but got a busy signal.

Their conversation last night ended on a note that seemed to imply a future, but he couldn't fathom what that future might be, or how it could materialize, or even if what they had shared wasn't merely a mirage.

He had met plenty of women where the initial contact was intense and intoxicating only to see the interaction dissolve into waves of heat the closer he tried to walk toward it. Experience made him suspicious, but every time it happened, he felt that delicious tug at the edge of his heart, the possibility of a broader, firmer connection.

It took a few minutes to get the security system back online; the battery backup had run out, so the system had shut down entirely. That meant power had been out for at least three hours while he slept. The login to the security system was Camellia, just like the office PC, and within minutes the rest of the grocery and the sub shop cameras lit in neat rows across the monitor.

He logged into the Skype account, but the connection would not complete. It took him five minutes to realize the grocery switch had frozen and was not passing DHCP to the computer. Ryan reset the device and tried the call again, but Ahou did not pick up.

Maybe their electric is out?

The feeling of being in a cave was fraying his nerves, so Ryan armed himself for the outside. He grabbed Ahou's car keys and went to the courtyard. The sun was bright, the breeze was cool, and the sounds of crickets and birds and distant dogs barking filled his ears, but Ryan didn't hear the telltale sounds of chaos that filled the air yesterday.

The quite seemed much more foreboding.

He saw people pressed against their windows again along the higher floors of the Washington Plaza apartments. They ducked behind curtains and blinds when they saw him look.

He crawled into the late model Acura, liking the smell of Ahou within its confines. He started the car and checked the gas gauge: three quarters of a tank, plenty of fuel to get to the crop duster.

Ryan retrieved his clothes from the sub shop dryer, returned to the manager's office, and started getting his stuff together. While he packed, he fretted over bringing Ahou with him, the logistics and the implications. There was little doubt that she was asking to leave with him. It was such a spontaneous, impulsive thing to consider.

What are Farouz and his wife going to do? Would they really leave Pittsburgh?

That was unlikely, but if this is as bad as it seemed it would be better for the whole Derakhshan family to run. It would be snug in his house: a smaller country house with three bedrooms and two bathrooms, but it would certainly be away from the crush of mobs and the rolling bands of looting that was sure to come.

But if they all went maybe the pilot had a bigger plane. He went back to the manager's office, called the pilot and confirmed that a six-seater was available: a bit more expensive, but it would work. Ryan said he would be in touch shortly.

He logged on to his bank account to see if the funds had been reversed and the money transfer complete. His heart soared when he saw the private car funds returned to the account, but his stomach dropped when he saw the bank's notation.

He pounded out Jeff's number on the manager's office phone. "Pick up! Pick UP!"

One ring. "Stapleton, Young & Steiden," the secretary said, "How may I help you?"

"Lisa, this is Ryan Sage. Jeff Steiden, please. He is expecting my call."

"Yes, Mr. Sage. He is expecting you. And Mr. Sage . . ."

"Yes?"

"I'm very sorry."

Sorry? She must be talking about Tess. "Well, thank you, Lisa."

"It's just not right what they've done," she whispered.

What they've done? Ryan was confused but didn't have the time to spend. "I'm sure it will all work out."

"You are so strong," Lisa said. "I admire that. I'll put you through now."

"Jeff Steiden speaking."

"Jeff, what in the hell is going on? My account is frozen." He had known this day was coming. It seemed absurd to ask, but it still felt surreal.

"Ryan, I'm so glad you called. They came yesterday, Ryan. I spent the whole day in court."

"And you couldn't have given me a heads-up?"

"I apologize for that, but . . . the circuits were busy. Things burned up in the heat of the moment. You know how that goes in some parts of the country. You should check the local Internet accounts."

Something in Jeff's tone said there was a message to be understood. "I see," Ryan said, even though he didn't exactly. "So, what 'conspiracy' did they decide that I was the mastermind of?"

"Among other things, they are attributing the violence in four cities to your articles."

"Really? My writing is at the root of an epidemic of violence?"

"It is bogus, of course, but we left the law and justice a long time ago. This isn't about sane. This is about closing you down, just like every other public voice. They have just been waiting to find any stray public action to pin to your coattails. We knew this was coming."

"We did. But the freezing of my bank account puts me in a world of hurt. How am I going to get—"

"Ryan, before you say anything else, as your attorney, I'm required to tell you that you are officially a fugitive from justice and are being sought on a federal racketeering charge. You need to turn yourself in."

"What? Fugitive? How did we get there?"

"They served a warrant at your home, Ryan. You were not there."

"No shit! I'm—"

"Again, before you say anything else," Jeff said, "it is important that as your lawyer, I counsel you to turn yourself. Maybe meet at your house?"

Meet at my house? What was Jeff saying? It was clear that Jeff assumed the phone conversation was monitored. So much for attorney-client privilege.

"I know you were going to take that trip, but some plans just go up in smoke."

And then he got it. Ryan's heart dropped out of his soul. He called up his home monitoring service and logged into his live cameras. Only one exterior camera that had been hidden in the back of his mailbox was still working. His mailbox was built into a stone enclosure near the road. The camera had been embedded in the brick. The camera had a full view of the smoldering ruins of his house.

It's just not right what they've done.

"Motherf—"

"The phones are not working because, as you know, the cell reception has been terrible for the last week. If the phones are not working when you get home," Jeff said, "just call me on a pay phone. I will meet you, and we will go together."

Ryan pinched his nose. He knew exactly what Jeff was saying. "Yes, of course. The Constitution being such a protector of civil liberties, I'm sure the authorities will respect my Fifth Amendment rights."

"And Ryan, this is what we prepared for. We will prevail."

"Very well. Well, let me get organized. I'm sure you will be contacted shortly."

"Talk to you soon."

Ryan hung up without another word. Angry, he fished around his pants for his iPhone, touched a security app called Power Down, verified its settings, and powered the phone off. He looked around the manager's office for a place to put the phone and noticed the wall safe. It seemed a small miracle that the safe opened with a slight tug, considering there was a lot of cash inside. Firouz had not gone to the bank, and yesterday's cash drawers were within. And that was just what Ryan could see at a glance. He saw two other bank bags tucked underneath the drawers.

He shut the door, careful not to lock the safe, and rolled back to the desk. Ryan called up the audio/video recordings from the previous day and found the feeds at 6:43 p.m. A storm of authorities drove into his yard, lights flashing, circling the house. They bashed down the door, weapons drawn. Men in jackets emblazed with big, gold letters stood around ransacking his personal items, or boxing things with no apparent rhyme or reason.

They joked and mocked, not realizing they were on video, and their conversations were being recorded. This was exactly why Ryan had invested in this monitoring service. He wanted proof of all civil liberties violations. Ryan found the last recordings before the cameras went blank to see how the fire started. Three agents stood in his living room talking. The microphones had trouble picking up the whole conversation, but Ryan did hear. "People don't get to hide behind loopholes. . ." They were referring to the fact that the property could not be seized. They were angry that Ryan had a place to live not subject to government tyranny.

"Of course, legal protections are loopholes," Ryan said sardonically. "Next, they will be giving traffic tickets for the *loophole* of going under the speed limit."

One agent popped open the Ben Franklin stove, started a fire, took a bottle of tequila from Ryan's cupboard sloshed it across the open door, and down to the floor and across to boxes full of papers. He exited his web account as soon as the flames sprouted from the box. Ryan knew the end of the story. He sat in the chair, the injustice grated on his soul like he had been dragged through lava rocks. He had never felt so exposed, so alone, so isolated, so violated.

The phone rang. It was a local number. He didn't recognize it.

Then again.

And again.

In a fit of paranoia, Ryan wondered if the call to Jeff had been traced and the government was calling.

The phone fell silent.

Ryan just stared into space.

The phone rang again. It was the Derakhshan home number.

"Ahou?!"

"Is not Ahou. This is Firouz. I am just to be calling from office phone."

Something in Firouz's tone had Ryan's attention. "What is it? Is everyone all right?"

"Yes. Yes. Everyone okay here. I to be apologizing for not talking more to you. Ahou is good with the talking, but I am not so much good with the English. I am thanking you for watching my store. So very important to me. I see the building you doing. I am thanking you."

"I needed a place to stay so I could get home," the word *home* hung in his mouth like a piece of unchewed meat. "Well, it has worked out for the both of us."

"You cannot be going home in this. You must be staying to the store. Do not go out. It is too very bad outside. Very dangerous. You must be building over the doors and blocking the windows. Very dangerous. Yes. Yes. I, uh—" Firouz was interrupted by a burst of Farsi. It sounded like Ahou in the background. "Are you good? Hurt? Ahou is talking to ask if you are doing safe."

"No, I'm fine. Of course, you know about the looting down on Fifth Avenue. The bank had security. At least they did yesterday. I suspect that is keeping the looters away from the grocery. That, plus some idiots with tow trucks parked a bunch of cars around your store to clear up Fifth Avenue, so it is kind of my dumb luck that everything is blocked off."

But Firouz was distracted by the Farsi in the background. Ahou was arguing with her mother. She sounded as furious as Ryan felt.

"Yes. Yes. That is good. Do not open doors. Very bad. Very bad. I, uh, I . . ." He stumbled over his own words. "I not to coming back to the store."

"Well, it has been two days. And it would be nice to have some company." Ryan wanted human contact like he wanted air. "I really don't think I'm infected. But I understand that you want to be safe. I won't lie to you though. I would really like some company. Ahou has been kind enough to talk to me, but it would be nice to actually be around people."

"No. My wife, she is fine. So are my girls. Very much thank you." Firouz fell silent. "They are not being worried about the biting. They know that God is watching you over. You will not be being sick."

Ryan felt the bottom falling out of his body. He could tell that Firouz was desperately trying to say something. "Firouz, what is going on? What is happening? Why—"

Firouz shouted in Farsi, then he said, "The news. The TV. You see?"

"When you say you won't be coming back to the store, what do you mean?

"It is very bad. Much bad, yes?"

The silence dragged on, and for a minute it sounded like Firouz was crying softly. Finally, Firouz said, "You have store and sandwich shop now, and my home."

"I don't understand."

"I to be giving you the store. Everything. My family, we are leaving. Cannot say where. Cannot tell you." He started to weep. "God watch you over." He was sobbing now. "You have my store and my home. Will not be back, coming to there."

"You are not coming back to the store? Ever?" Ryan could not wrap his mind around what he heard. "Where are you going?"

"Cannot tell you. We leaving now. Should not call you. Was told no one to be telling. It is much bad. It is like you tell Daniel Ry—"

Camellia's Farsi was rapid, stern.

Firouz replied the same way.

"Must be going now, but I leaving you all the papers in my home. Address to be writing."

"Firouz, where are you going?" Ryan said feeling desperation. "If it is safe, can I not come with you? Please? Firouz?! Please, I'm not infected. Please, let me come with you. I don't have anywhere to go. . .."

Firouz wept. "I am so very much sorry. God is watching you over. I'm sorry. I must be to packing. You must get this from my home. The home is on Arthur Street. You to be writing this address to paper!" He paused and then said the address again, then again.

Ryan scribbled it on the desk calendar.

"You having the house keys there. It having a pink rabbit attached. The rabbit will let you in the backdoor. The store is to you. I give money to the peoples so there is not creditors. You do what you want. I must go. God bless you. I see you before again."

The phone went dead.

19

Global Infection: ≤ 27.3751%

I know no safe depository of the ultimate powers of the society but the people themselves; and if we think them not enlightened enough to exercise their control with a wholesome discretion, the remedy is not to take it from them but to inform their discretion by education. This is the true corrective of abuses of Constitutional power.

—THOMAS JEFFERSON

Ryan wandered the minimart, looking at everything but not seeing anything. He moved past the canned goods, down the aisle with boxes of dried foods, past the shoe displays and clothing racks. He passed the aisle that looked like it had been transplanted from Lowe's, the games and model cars, a small glass case with four different brands of data pads, prepaid cell phones and low-end cameras, the candy and confection, the magazine and bookshelves and two continuous aisles of health and beauty. He finally found himself dithering around an end cap filled with gardening paraphernalia and seeds for the perfect intercity garden.

"Leaving? Forever?" Ryan said. "What the hell?"

There was no way that after last night, Ahou was willing to part without a word. Suddenly he wanted to hear the words to his face. He would look in Ahou's eyes and see the truth. If they were going to leave without him, if Firouz could call him friend and insist that God was watching over him, then Firouz was damned sure going to explain.

You must get this from my home. The house is on Arthur Street . . .

The words rolled though Ryan's mind.

It having a pink rabbit attached. The rabbit will let you in the backdoor.

And suddenly, Ryan was a blur of motion, sprinting to the manager's office, digging through drawers like a madman. He found the rabbit on a key ring hanging in the key box. He grabbed the bat, Ahou's car keys and the gate opener, and his iGlass. He dictated the address and got the location in seconds. The Derakhshan family lived just off Center Avenue a few streets away. He hit the courtyard at a sprint, the gate already trundling open. He pulled the car to the exit and slammed the brakes. Colwell looked too tight: vehicles all but closed off passage. He jammed the car back into its parking spot and started jogging.

It hadn't been chaotic near the store. But within a block, the sounds of social disorder rippled around him: shouts and fighting, and the occasional gunfire. Three times people ran past telling him to run. It took ten minutes to jog to the house.

The windows were dark. Ryan tried the front door but even though the locked turned the door didn't budge. He moved between the neighbor's side lawn into the Derakhshan backyard. He heard the shouting first and then he saw two men burst onto the street six houses away.

Four police officers followed, weapons drawn, "Stop! Stop!"

Ryan dashed through the wood gate and shut it behind him.

"Police! We said *stop!*"

Two white men in jeans and sweatshirts sprinted past bags clutched in their hands.

Two gunshots slapped off the houses.

The trailing man spun like he had been hit with a bat, the bag spilled forward, milk and food scattered.

Two more shots and the second man sprawled face first, his bag bouncing and coming to a stop. They lay on the street writhing and moaning.

Ryan dropped down, watching through a crack. The four officers circled the men, their voices low and indistinct. Finally, one cop nodded at his three buddies and they nodded back. He pointed his handgun.

"What the fuck?" one man said.

"This is for what you did to the mother," the cop said.

The report slapped off the houses. He aimed at the second man. "This is for the girl!"

"We didn't—"

All four cops waited as the echoes faded to silence. "Get the stuff," one cop said, "and move the bodies over there."

Ryan slunk to the patio, fumbled with the key and stepped through the door, locked it behind and froze in the kitchen.

Summary execution?! Shit!

Ryan tiptoed to the front window: the bottom half boarded over and the shades drawn down. He found a crack between boards and shades and watched three cops in the street.

Where is number four?

A shadow passed across the patio door. The fourth cop was silhouetted against the glass; his left hand was on the door knob, his right hand on his weapon.

Ryan had read somewhere that men in military or law enforcement develop a sense of when they are being watched. He turned his eyes. And then he saw the mirror that reflected toward the patio. The cop's face was pressed against the glass, and his hand was coming up over his eyes to shade against the glare.

Ryan dropped to the floor, trying to turn into a hole in the universe. The door handle wiggled and then the cop knocked.

"Open up!"

Another door handle wiggle and another knock.

And then all was quiet.

Ryan crawled to the stairs and climbed to the second floor. He stood deep in the master bedroom looking down on the street. The three cops were now spaced apart watching the street until the fourth joined them. They huddled and pointed at Firouz' home.

Was this what the people warned him about? Is this why they told him to run?

Answering these questions was useless speculation—terrifying but useless—and there wasn't anything to do but wait them out. The cops couldn't stay on the street forever, and he could stay in this house all night if he needed—

Did I shut the gate to the courtyard?

Fuck me!

Ryan sighed and suddenly he had to relieve himself. He went to the master bathroom and sat down.

Why did the cops kill those guys?

It was the uncertainty that was so chilling. Hunting down people for their food? Summary execution? If they were doing summary execution did they really need a reason to kill him?

When Ryan stepped back into the bedroom the cops were gone and he could finally notice his surroundings. The digital clock on the nightstand flashed 12:00. The Derakhshan's had packed in a hurry, clothes scattered like a grenade had blasted the room. He snooped around the second floor, feeling the voyeur's rush. He studied the haunting chronicle of pictures that lined the walls: a family from the beginnings to adulthood.

The Derakhshans were beautiful people.

He found Ahou's room and looked out the windows that gave view to the neighborhood's adjoining backyards. The houses were dark, the yards in the early stages of overgrown and the swing sets were still.

He turned his attention inside, studying, trying to get a sense of Ahou. The room was half little girl, half older woman, the dolls and posters of a teenager holding space alongside the sophisticated decorations of a woman. Half a closet full of scanty dresses and three-inch heels worn to twenty-something clubs hanging beside the Ralph Lauren and Gucci professional attire for the fashionable female executive.

Ryan inhaled, noting the smell that lingered behind. He had never been close enough to know what she was like, but now he could catch the faint scent that remained in everything. He picked up her pillow and breathed deep, suddenly desperate for even the most fleeting human connection, anxious for something to anchor him inside the chaos. For a long minute, Ryan shut his eyes and just let the smell of Ahou's perfume and shampoo act as a balm on his soul.

Eventually, he returned to reality. Ahou's laptop was still on her desk. He opened the lid and pressed the power button. The machine woke up in a few seconds and showed a web browser opened to the remote security interface at the minimart

"You won't peek, huh?" Ryan said with a half-smile.

Pictures were secured in frames that adorned two walls and a shelf: family, girlfriends, and three with a young blond man. He looked like he belonged on a European fashion magazine with the rugged, chiseled look that was perennially GQ chic. His Scandinavian heritage seemed to clash against her Persian beauty, but it was easy to look past the disharmony and only see two beautiful people captured in smiles.

Ryan wondered if he was the lawyer. Ahou had never spoken his name, and she had made their relationship seem to be an afterthought. However, the pictures on the wall showed a relationship that was anything but trivial.

He found three albums on the shelf. Such photographic collections were almost a relic of history. Most people took digital images and posted them to the World Wide Web, or banished them to the recesses of a hard drive. When the power went out on the world, billions of memories would be wiped out of digital existence. He flipped through page after page, seeing the little girl become a woman.

Ryan noticed a gap between bookends where it looked like a few notebooks had once stood beside a diary and two self-help books. Then he saw another notebook sprawling unceremoniously under her chair. He flipped to the last page and saw that it was her notes from last night. Then he saw the rabbit sitting on her desk. It was blue and frayed and worn, with small buttons for eyes. One button had been replaced sometime during its long life with the loving, patient stitching of a young, unskilled hand.

Ahou left the rabbit? And she left the notebook?

The rabbit had enormous emotional value and the way she poured herself into writing it didn't seem right that she would abandon these.

Suddenly sure he would see Ahou again, Ryan grabbed a large duffel from her closet and put the albums, the notebook, her rabbit, and her laptop and charger inside. He looked around the room for anything else he might want. In the last instant, he stuffed her pillow inside and made his way through the rest of the house.

Firouz had been busy boarding up lower floor windows and making barricades of furniture over the front door. But beyond the siege preparation it was a very nice home. In the kitchen, just where Firouz said, was a large box filled with papers: legal documents of all types, a zippered bank pouch with more money than he cared to count, and an envelope addressed to him. The handwriting looked like a woman's penmanship. He had a suspicion that it was Ahou's writing; he didn't have the nerve to open it.

Four sets of car keys were in a basket by the garage door. It was easy to tell whose car belonged to whom. Ryan already knew Firouz's car. The minivan in the garage most likely belonged to Camellia. Asalam's Toyota Camry parked at the curb.

He reconned the street one more time from the second floor, patiently checking to see if the police were waiting. Seeing nothing, Ryan returned to the kitchen, consolidated the car keys and the front door keys together on a ring and stood spinning the keys around a finger, trying to decide if there was something else he should take with him. Nothing leapt to mind.

"Well, this is the way of things," he said to himself. "Suck it up."

Ryan pressed the garage door opener and boldly walked down the driveway, unlocked the Toyota and started the engine. He only scraped the paint twice getting the Toyota down Colwell Street. He *had* left the gate open and the receiving area door unlocked. Ryan was feeling reckless. He grabbed the bat, ready to do battle. He moved through the grocery, every step of the way thinking about the bodies unceremoniously dumped on a pile of garbage. Maybe the dead men were villains; maybe they were not—their crimes and offenses uncertain. But this truth was dead certain: the men with the best weapons make the rules, and this was the reason the Founding Fathers crafted the Second Amendment. As Ryan cleared the minimart and sub shop, Ryan kept thinking he needed to find a way to keep and bear arms.

20

Global Infection: ≤ 27.37598%

The mean number of secondary infections generated from one single infected in a susceptible population.
—DEFINITION OF R0 (R-NAUGHT)

He was vaguely hungry, but nothing caught his attention. All he could think about while standing in the sub shop walk-in was . . . *I'll never eat it all.* The pre-sliced tomatoes and onions and the unsealed meats—the roast beef and turkey and chicken—would spoil in days.

Ryan thought of opening the front door and giving it away, but that was doomed to fail. The moment people came inside, he would never to stop the tide. And that assumed the front doors would survive another night. All it would take is some determined looters, time, and no police. Or after what he had seen, who knows, maybe the police would lead the charge.

A good portion of the beef and turkey was vacuum-sealed, and that would last as long as there was refrigeration. If it was bad enough that Firouz thought he was never coming back, how long could electricity last?

He walked to the manager's office and channel-surfed. The news rolled footage of suburban homes near Philadelphia put under quarantine; the bio-contamination sign plastered all over doors and windows. Then came the ubiquitous footage of spray-painted placards with Bible verses and some wild-eyed street preacher heralding the end of the world. Then the news showed footage of houses in Gaithersburg, Maryland, a street sign read Waxmyrtle Way, and the voice-over said authorities cleared out the infected. The homes' windows were boarded over, and the front walls were spray-painted with huge circles and a large AR with smaller lines pointing to smaller circles. They were the common markings used after a natural disaster to represent the total number of dead humans and dead animals.

He willed his mind to focus on taking action. He took out a pad of paper and started with the notes.

> Guns?
> Barricade?
> Ground level?
> Items to cache?
> Cell phone?
> Power shut down?
> Generator?
> Pay bills?
> Food spoil?

On a whim, Ryan dialed Firouz's home phone. It rang and rang then went to voice mail. Ahou's voice said, "Hi. This is the Derakhshan family. Please leave a message."

Ryan hung up, haunted that no one would ever hear that message again: Fearful that *he* would never hear that voice again.

Ryan started writing again.

> Give food away?
> How to transport?

The phone rang. *Please, let this be Firouz.* "Hello?"

"Hello? Is there any way I could come get some stuff from—"

"Oh my God! Oh my God! They're in the store. They are in the store—" Click.

Ryan said, "Someone is going to eventually come check the store—" A thought intruded on the sentence.

Ryan went to minimart front and hit the electric lock. The exterior metal gate slowly clacked into its housing and he saw what he hoped to see. He shut the gate, walked to the small electronics counter, and broke open a prepaid cell phone package. In the manager's office he typed in the provider's activation URL and then entered the activation code, the SIM card serial number and the phone serial number. He dialed the grocery and the phone connected two of the three times Ryan tested the circuits.

In the sub shop Ryan filled bags with enough food to feed twenty men, grabbed a small cart from the loading dock, and loaded up for a short trip. With the pallet jack, Ryan slid the rock salt away from the door and moved the plywood, then opened the door, and finally raised the metal gate. He pushed the cart down the hill to Banco Federal and asked the first guard to point him toward a commander. He got a grunt and a thumb over the shoulder.

"They feeding you?" Ryan asked the squat man with hooded eyes sitting in the bank manager's office.

"What's it to you?" he replied, leaning back in his chair.

"Thought you might be hungry," Ryan said, unloading the bags on the desk.

The commander raised a brow and said, "What do you want from me?"

"To be scary like you are right now."

If it were possible, the man's hooded eyes became more hooded. He read the front of the bag, then looked inside. "The sub shop. You don't want people to get inside?"

"That is what I want."

The commander picked up a handheld. "Tanner, pass the word to keep an eye on the sub shop. And tell the boys we have food for them."

"Thank you," Ryan said. He held up the cell phone. "You mind if I call if I have any trouble?"

The commander gave a brief nod. "You can call," he said fishing out a business card.

Ryan punched in the number on the card and waited for the commander's phone to ring. Ryan nodded and turned.

"The next shift comes at six," the commander said. "I'll call you if we need anything before then."

"Got it."

Ryan Sage was living in a sub shop. Locked back inside the shop, he reviewed his to-do list.

> **People check store?**
> **Put clothes in dryer**
> **Check on Lenna and Erik**

And so he did. Ryan called up his e-mail. Lenna had not replied, but he couldn't be angry. Deep down inside, Ryan was sure Lenna was amongst the diseased. Tess had bit her and the odds were she was in the throes of the disease. They had never been close, but Lenna wouldn't blow him off unless she was gone. She was too needy to survive the apocalypse by herself.

Erik, his business partner, was another concern. He still hadn't gotten back and that was a real worry. The last few months were very tense, but they had never ignored each other. Ryan dialed Erik's number from the land line; it went to voice mail.

"Come on man, give me a call. I'm worried. The stuff that is happening is serious. I think it is more serious than anything ever before. Send the people home. Lock the doors and get out of town. If nothing else get Sarah and the kids to the ranch. Anyway, love you, brother. Call me." He gave the new cell number and hung up.

Ryan walked by the sub shop freezer strategizing what to do with the good food. Feeding the Banco Federal security was only the beginning, and there were people out there that would need it, people like Shaniqua—

Saint Joseph's was just a few streets away . . .

Ryan took two hours to get the food ready to transport and the Toyota backseat and trunk loaded. It should have been a nerve-wracking trip, venturing beyond the confines of safety. He should have felt the hair on the back of his neck stand on end with every sound, every scream, every gunshot, and every distant siren. He should have been paranoid that the cops might be on the prowl. But he didn't, and he wasn't. Ryan's recklessness hadn't worn off. He felt angry. And when he wasn't on the edge of outrage, he could only manage . . . indifference.

He turned past a church built of large rust stone and navigated the mostly empty backstreets through the Hillside. Less than three streets from Firouz's upper middle-class home, the neighborhood deteriorated to inner city stagnant: a ghost town, garbage piling up on the roadside for a pickup that would never come, packs of stray dogs rooting through the white kitchen liner bags and dodging warily between houses at any movement.

Ryan considered driving to Saint Joseph's door and dropping the food off, but checked the thought. The people would want to know where it all came from, and one act of desperation could lead to another. As he rolled past, the shelter looked forted up. A chain-link fence surrounded the property; a crude barricade had been built over the driveway. Then, out of the corner of his eye, Ryan caught sight of two bodies lying on the side street, their heads smashed on the asphalt with what looked like dark oil spilling around them. Ryan goosed the gas to hurry on past.

He drove down Bedford and turned right onto a side street that dead-ended in front of a red brick elementary school. It was an old building, built very early in the nineteenth century that lay moldering in the heart of Pittsburgh. *NO TRESPASSING* was posted near the bomb shelter sign, a memory from the Cold War days long past. The windows had long since been covered with metal bars like the outside of a prison. To the left of the school was a parking lot surrounded by a leaning, rusty chain-link fence. The school entrance was ensconced above a granite landing. The barren flagpole sat in the front corner of a tiny courtyard. A four-sided bench surrounding a weed-choked planter was nestled behind a heavy wrought iron fence.

Ryan called Saint Joseph's but got a circuits busy message. The next time he called, it rang and rang. He dialed constantly for the next half hour alternating between ringing and the busy circuit. Daylight was getting short, so he made the choice to unpack the car and put the food behind the iron fence, deep in a shaded corner. The temperature was cool. The food would keep for a while.

He didn't want to go directly back to the store, so he drove the back-streets, seeing two roads closed from piles of tires and cars and furniture. He explored down another street. A bullet whacked off the Toyota bumper.

"Right, got it. You don't want any company," Ryan said, punching the gas.

The bullet ended his sightseeing and he sped back to the minimart, managing yet again to sideswipe two cars getting down Colwell. Back behind the security gate and the locked doors, tired from the stress of being on the streets, Ryan slumped into the manager's office chair fretting about a thousand details.

He dialed Shaniqua again. It rang and rang and rang.

"That was anticlimactic," he said, snapping the phone down into its base. But somehow that lack of a problem seemed ominous. It was like he described to Ahou the night before. He felt like he was standing in receding water just before the tsunami hit.

21

Global Infection: ≤ 27.38029%

If R0 > 1, an epidemic occurs in the absence of intervention.
If R0 < 1, the disease dies out.
—CONDITIONS FOR AN EPIDEMIC

"... *of the State of Pennsylvania a curfew is in effect* ..." The public address system was distant and muffled. Ryan moved through the grocery trying to catch more details.

"... *from 6:00 p.m. until 7:00 a.m. All people found on the street will be detained. Any aggression toward authorities will* ..." The broadcast seemed to be fading. "... *is in effect.* .... *immediately be met with force. By order of the mayor of Pittsburgh and by the governor of the State of Pennsylvania, a curfew is* ..."

"The curfew! Six p.m.?" He checked a clock: 5:45. "Dangit!"

The next group of bank guards would be coming any minute. He brewed coffee and put it in a gallon cardboard portable tote. He loaded two bags that had Firouz Hoagies emblazoned in swooping letters with sandwich fixings and headed out to the bank just in time to see three armored cars pull down the street. Banco Federal's lights were off; the door stood wide open, and the vault in the back looked like a yawning silver mouth.

"Oh, come on!" Ryan rasped, standing on the sidewalk just outside the bank at the intersection of Fifth and Pride. The street was blessedly empty and silent. But just to the south he could hear shouts coming from deep within the warrens of Duquesne. To the north toward the Allegheny River he could hear the rumble of heavy machinery. Far to the west, he could hear the squawk of emergency vehicles.

Ryan dithered, concerned about leaving the food on a car. The bags would give away where the food came from, but it made no sense to take it back. He laid the food on an abandoned car and stuffed sandwich shop bags in his pocket. Someone would find the food and maybe it wouldn't be too obvious where it came from.

Technically, he was now out past curfew, but he had to do something with the sub shop exterior. The only obstacle to the door was the slope of the street; the sidewalk was six feet above the asphalt.

How many nights could the doors survive?

The clutter of cars in front of the minimart inspired a plan. Ryan found one car with a shattered rear window and the keys still in the ignition. The battery was dead, but he was able to aim the wheels down the sidewalk toward the shop. Steering the car with no power but sweat and muscle took him until dark, but he managed to park the car where he wanted. It was far from perfect barricade; there was still a gap that allowed access to the gate.

Ryan was checking other cars to drive into place when he heard movement by the bank. And there she was, her pink coat spotlighted by the streetlights, sitting cross-legged on top of the car roof, drinking a soda and eating, her pink coat standing out against the gloom. The little girl was all alone. She watched the streets with the calm vigilance of a hawk. Between bites, she organized the extra food into plastic bags.

"Little girl," Ryan said, waving, "Are you okay? Up here on the street! Do you need help?"

Her head snapped around and saw him walking down the hill. In a blink she slid off the car roof, bags in hand.

"No, wait!" Ryan said, jogging toward her. "Do you need help? Is your dad okay—"

He heard the rumble of engines coming from the west along Fifth Avenue.

"_. . . of Pennsylvania a curfew is in effect. . . ._"

The Humvee headlights and the spotlights sweeping side to side, burrowing into the black depths of buildings lining the streets.

"_. . . All people found on the street will be detained. Any aggression toward authorities will . . ._"

Ryan sprinted to the sub shop. He wouldn't make it.

He dove into the clutter of cars as the searchlights chased at his heels lingering over his location. He held his breath.

The spotlights shifted to the bank.

He peeked above the window sill to see a Humvee inch past Pride Street, a soldier standing inside a turret, swinging the muzzle of a mounted machine gun back and forth. A second Humvee followed, which was followed by a third: each vehicle probing Fifth Avenue with spotlights and machine guns alike.

"Just keep going . . ." Ryan said. But they didn't. They turned up Stevenson. "Shit!"

He low crawled toward the car parked in front of the door and dropping behind the rear wheel as a spotlight washed over; Ryan was pinned on the wrong side of the car.

When the floodlight swung away, Ryan slowly opened the rear door and slid into the backseat. The door closed just as the light swept back. The light stayed.

"Possible violation," a man shouted.

"I don't see anything," said another.

"You there, come out with your hands up!"

Ryan lay still.

How far down the path of street justice had everyone traveled?

The best Ryan could hope was to be carted off to some central holding area. But the fastest way to make sure the infection spread through the population was to centralize the people. And the worst thing was that pesky federal warrant. Ryan had no idea how to handle that hurdle, but entering a corrupt federal system as that system was suffering collapse was a recipe to be locked up for a really long time. It wasn't impossible that they would shoot him on general principle. He hadn't heard the words *martial law* uttered, but the governor's warning promised the use of force. And when the president's posse came calling, the game changed.

"Someone dismount and go check out the street."

"With all due respect, Sergeant, I'm not getting out of this Humvee."

"If you don't come out, we will be forced to fire," another voice said on a P.A.

"Corporal, there is nothing there," the sergeant said. "Keep your finger off that trigger. Isn't this the address for the reported Article 86?"

"*Which* Article 86 would that be?" said another.

Someone laughed.

"What do you expect from those National Guard pukes!"

"Secure that shit," said the sergeant. "Is this the address or not?"

"Yes, Sergeant. It should be one of them apartments up above, but it don't look like there's anyone home."

"Let me have the handheld" the sergeant said. "Test. Test. Test. Turn the volume up."

"Copy that," someone responded. "Try it now."

"Test," the sergeant's voice boomed over the P.A. "Sergeant Dietz, if you are in there, you *will* report back to your post. If you return by no later than 1600 hours tomorrow, command will not proceed with court martial. We need you in the field, soldier."

After a long pause, someone said, "We gonna go find him?"

"No, we are gonna do our job. We have two more stops to make. Let's move out."

"Streets blocked," someone called from the Colwell Street side of the building.

"Turn this parade around," the sergeant said, spinning his finger.

The Humvees started down Stevenson. The first Humvee hit its brakes. "What is that there?"

The spotlight spun farther down the street.

"You! Halt!"

Then Ryan heard a low and menacing moan, first one, then two, then more floating up the hillside.

"It's one of the infected."

"It's just a kid!"

"Oh Jesus. There's three of them. They are running. Shoot!"

"But they haven't done anything. You can't shoot civilians."

"Halt!"

"Shoot! They don't understand.

"It is a goddamned civilian!"

"Fucking shoot! They will be on us in a second!"

"Hold your fire!" the sergeant shouted.

"We gotta kill them. They are gonna be on us."

"Try to restra—"

"He's on Geno! He's on Geno!

"Fucking shoot!"

Ryan didn't wait. He opened the car door and tumbled toward the sub shop gate. He pushed it up and rolled through the front door. He locked the gate back in place huddling, gasping, listening.

"Get him off! Get him off!"

Automatic gun fire ripped through the night.

"Hold your fire!"

"Fucking shoot!"

"Beat him down!"

"They are coming!!"

"More coming down the hill!"

The ripping, chugging rattle of the Humvee's machine gun filled the dark world with sound.

"Fuck! Me!'

"They are still moving."

"Drive! Drive! They are still coming!"

"Man down! Man down!"

"How's Geno? Geno?!"

"Shoot!"

"How can they still be alive?"

"Shoot! God dammit!"

There was a long rip of gunfire and then silence.

Ryan stripped out of his sweat-soaked clothes and dropped them in the washer, shaking like he had the palsy. He struggled to turn the dial and start the cycle.

He stood naked, holding the sides of the washer until the shaking passed. He washed up in the deep sink again, toweled of, and plodded back to the grocery and found the clothing aisle for fresh socks, underwear, long-sleeved T-shirt, and a nice Russell sweat top and bottom.

The moment he sat in the chair, the shakes returned. He dialed the phone. "Come on, if you don't pick up, girl, you will never get that food." The phone rang once, twice, three times.

"Hello?"

"Shaniqua? This is Ryan Sage."

"Yes. Hello."

"We spoke a day ago about staying at the shelter."

"Oh yes, Ryan. How are you? Did you find a place?"

"Yes, I did. How are things there?"

"Well, as good as can be expected, I suppose. It is crazy here. We've had some fights. There were two men outside this morning that just kept trying to pick a fight. It was like they were crazy. Four of the men here in the shelter went out and tried to tell them to leave. It was awful what happened. It made me ill. I had to go home." Her voice was full of stress and fear. "The cops never came, even though we called. The bodies are still out there.

"Did you say four of the men went outside and fought?"

"Yes."

"Were any of them bit?"

"No, the men here have had pretty rough lives, some of them, and can fight real good. They had lots of blood on them, but I don't think any of them were bit."

Ryan wasn't sure what to make of that. For a minute he thought Shaniqua was in danger, but now he wasn't so sure. So he said, "How are you all doing for food over there?"

"Oh, we don't have any to give you. We will barely have enough for ourselves." She was so used to hearing people ask her for stuff that she couldn't think any other way.

"No, I don't want your food. But it turns out that I might be able to help. You were so nice to me that I thought of you."

"Why, thank you. What do you have?"

"Do you know where the elementary school is?"

"Yes, of course. That is almost our backyard."

"Send a few men to the school, not on Bedford but other side where Cliff Street dead-ends. You will see food behind the fence. There will be a lot to carry. It should help you for a couple of days."

"But how?"

"Don't worry about that right now. Hurry before it is gone. There are packs of dogs out."

"I don't know what to say about the food."

"Thank you is fine," Ryan said.

Shaniqua laughed. "Well, I do thank you."

They promised to stay in touch and said goodbye. Ryan made dinner and donned a pair of jeans and his jacket over top the sweats. He found some gloves and hat on a clearance rack and a Snuggie in one of the aisles. Then he grabbed Ahou's pillow, climbed to the fire escape and walked to the gazebo twinkling under strands of soft white Christmas lights.

In his earlier visits to the roof, Ryan had not noticed the dozens of photoelectric walkway lights that circled the oasis, but now they offered their soft glow to drive back the bogeyman that lurked in the darkness. Ryan just didn't want the stress of every sound, real or imaginary, on ground level. He probably couldn't stay here all night, but if even for just a little while he didn't want to feel the threat lurking just beyond some flimsy metal that would fold if someone breathed hard.

Ryan grabbed a new blue plastic tarp out of the pile by the workshop to use over top of his Snuggie. He lay on a recliner crafted from treated decking. They were heavy and smooth and covered with thick outdoor pads and surprisingly comfortable. He held Ahou's pillow under his chin, liking the smell that lingered. Ryan stared into the night sky, his eyes immediately traveling to the UPMC building towering over the city, then to the Pittsburgh Plate Glass buildings to its left. The Pittsburgh skyline was an impressive testimony to human vision.

Ryan hadn't realized he had fallen asleep until he felt the shotgun probing the side of his head.

22

Global Infection: ≤ 27.42113%

*Classes of the Basic Model, (adapted) Susceptible (S) Zombie
(Z) Removed (R)*

—MUNZ, HUDEA, IMAD, ET AL

S hotgun barrels are cold and itch and smell bad.

"And I thought the streets would be dangerous," Ryan mumbled, staring into the barrel of the gun with sleepy eyes. "Could you shoot me after I finish sleeping, please?"

Ryan was never one to wake up quick or well, so he thought it was a dream. Later, when he was fully awake, he realized that his life depended on what came out of his mouth when he was half asleep. It was a fun thought.

Fortunately, the building supervisor had a sense of humor and thought asking to sleep with a shotgun to the head hilarious.

"And everybody knows them looters don't make jokes," he said, like it was a universal fact.

Ryan understood this to mean that he couldn't be a looter because of the comedy. It didn't seem like the right time to argue logic.

Ryan noticed the sergeant stripes on the sleeve and the last name Dietz sewn into the uniform. But the man introduced himself as Bob, the building super. He was a builder. Builder Bob he called himself and laughed every time he did. The gazebo was his creation, as were the planters, and the whole oasis eight stories above Pittsburgh's hustle. It was a perk for being the building maintenance; a perk that the landlord didn't know about because the "Rich Prick" never came to the property.

The price of the nap was a night of helping Bob build a barricade for the eighth floor stairwell landing and fastening plywood to the staircase.

Builder Bob had a theory. He had been places and seen things, so he had come home "for just a few minutes to help his family." When asked exactly what he had seen, Builder Bob said, "These African lunatics, they're mean as shit and act like ants, but they don't have a queen bee."

Ryan thought that was an obvious statement since ants were not bees, but Builder Bob still had the shotgun. So as usual, Aristotelian logic was going to take a beating at the point of a weapon.

"Them lunatics, they just keep coming and coming just like them ants in Africa. Must be why they call it the African Rabies. Am I right?"

"Sounds like a compelling rationale to me."

"That is what I thought when I saw them. It was like them ants on those geographic shows that build bridges out of ant bodies. Ant bodies, antibodies . . . get it? Get it?"

"Haha! Sure." *Not really. . . .*

"So they just keep coming and neither love nor money can stop them. But then I notice that they can't talk and chew gum at the same time."

Ryan understood that this was a metaphor, but that didn't stop Builder Bob from saying, "That's whatcha call a meta four," drawing it out in two distinct words.

Since the Army came looking for Sergeant Dietz, Ryan also gathered that he had seen those "African lunatics" while deployed. When Ryan tried to press for details, the typically wordy Builder Bob got quiet and looked into the distance. He was remembering something that was fully unpleasant. And then as if Ryan had asked another question. "These African lunatics might hammer through doors and walls, but the infected didn't perform complex tasks over and over."

How do they not break their bones?

"A few hundred might push against a fire truck and flip it into a ditch."

Terrifying if true.

"They might pile up like ants and stumble over cars or Jersey walls. They might pile up like rats against a barrier and finally spill over to the other side."

Who could be safe if they piled up to the second floor windows? Or the third?

"But them 'African lunatics' were stymied by ladders and trees and," Builder Bob was sure, "they would not be able to climb up slippery, plywood covered stairs. They would have to fill up the whole stairwell to pile over the upper floor, and by then no more could get in from the bottom, because the hole was plugged." His only fear was that a person with the "African bug" could navigate the obstacles, get behind, and then "do that African madness." His master plan included chain-link fence in the hallways.

Ryan was dubious until he tried to walk up Builder Bob's proof of concept leading up to the eighth floor landing. Then he thought maybe Bob was onto something. Ryan would defy anyone over the age sixteen to walk up sawdust-covered, smooth plywood at a forty-degree angle without breaking a bone. And if the infected managed to claw their way to the top, they wouldn't be able to bring leverage against the barricade. Builder Bob had a design improvement on the standard barricade building: a wedge like the prow of a ship that anchored into the stairwell structure. Pushing on the wall was like pushing on the building.

Between Builder Bob and his two teenage sons and Ryan, they finished the seventh floor barricade and plywood covering by 1:00 a.m. Ryan asked why the neighbors hadn't complained about the noise. To which Bob replied, "'Cause I haven't seen 'em."

Beyond that dazzling logic, Bob went on to explain that the neighbors didn't complain, because there weren't any people left in the building. The building wasn't even half-rented in spite of them "rich pricks" trying to make money. Or maybe it was because they were trying to make money. Builder Bob was vague on how the "rich pricks" were the cause and the effect of the building's emptiness.

Ryan did eventually learn that most of the building tenants were hospital workers or police officers or graduate students.

It made sense that they weren't home, Ryan assumed. They were probably out on the street trying to keep order, or at the hospital trying to heal people. That was the logical assumption, all information considered. But who knows what use graduate students were in a crisis?

Of course, Bob's wife had her theory. She was a mousy, nervous creature who spent her time fretting over every sound, every bang, every threat, real or fictional, that crept into her mind . . . out loud.

She said that people didn't rent here because they had all gone to "them saved places." It was clear that in the Builder Bob household, logic was a prized commodity. And after an hour of hearing the commodity exchange between husband and wife, Ryan was sure that they could have built a barricade around the entire block if she had shut up.

Ryan tried to keep up with Bob's tireless energy, but that was a feat not to be duplicated by ten men. But it was achieved by one woman. She seemed able to talk as long as Bob hammered. He kept saying that he was home "just for a few minutes," so he had to keep working. He wanted his family safe while he was gone. "Good old Uncle Sam might miss Builder Bob," he said, laughing every time he did.

Mercifully, Builder Bob offered Ryan keys to the apartment beside his, where Ryan could sleep. The apartment was rented by a fastidious woman who must have cleaned every surface and changed her bed sheets every day. Within minutes, Ryan was fast asleep in the master bedroom.

The indentured servitude continued the next day at 9:00 a.m. sharp, with breakfast and the missus in full broadcast mode. Builder Bob's supplies were dwindling, so the morning was spent moving building materials from four large storage containers permanently parked in the parking garage that sat between Fifth and Our Way. The parking garage was built for the sports arena events but the "Rich Prick" pulled some strings and got him the space on the top floor of the garage. It was nerve-wracking work to tote the supplies down four parking levels to the Our Way pedestrian exit and around to the back of the building. The actual distance was measured in feet between the garage and the apartment building service elevator, but each trip threatened to take off years of Ryan's life. The streets south and east seemed to teem with rolling bands of chaos. It seemed every minute exposed on the streets invited disaster to rain down on them, but Builder Bob seemed unmoved, presiding over the resupply dressed in fatigues and a rifle in a harness. On the second trip, Ryan asked for his own weapon, to which Builder Bob promptly said, "Don't want my best helper to shoot his own foot off now, do I?" It was an insulting response, but maybe not too far from the truth. What Ryan knew about firearms could be written on fortune cookie paper.

Ryan offered to supply food for lunch and dinner, mostly because the missus made twenty comments within the space of ten minutes about having an extra mouth to feed. The fact that Ryan showed up with bags of food didn't seem to register, nor did anyone inquire about their source. It was as if the groceries were a metaphysical given, just as Ryan's current incarnation to help with the building was an ontological certainty.

By midafternoon, Builder Bob's wife started talking about "going north." This was the new wisdom coming over the airwaves. Rumor had it that the African Rabies could not survive freezing temperatures, so people should head for cold climates. Since it was rumor, it must be newsworthy. Why else would media outlets offer it for public consumption? When Bob's wife wasn't talking about going north, she was discussing the merits of "them saved places." And then she combined the two—going north and them saved places—together and came up with her very own: "them saved places in the north."

They had a brief reprieve from Bob's wife while they fortified the elevator access on the lower floors, because she was "keeping an eye on the news." Ryan trembled because that meant she was just reloading with more ammunition. As Builder Bob had it figured, chain-link fence over the elevator shaft would keep "them African lunatics" out of the building.

"Yeah," Ryan said, "we wouldn't want any of them African lunatics in the building." Irony was not Builder Bob's strength.

The indentured servitude pushed well past dinner on the second night. Twice Ryan asked Builder Bob to add his skills to the task of securing the sub shop. And twice Bob replied, "Why would I do such a thing like that?" But he wasn't really asking for an explanation. The question was merely a reflection of the narrow nature of Bob's world.

Bob was midway through the barricade for the sixth floor landing when the wife came and told him that the governor was making people go to "them saved places in the north." Bob assured her that the building was a "saved" zone. He just needed a few more minutes and they would be fine. Then he could go back and work for Uncle Sam. Ryan was pretty sure that 1600 was already past, and a court martial was awaiting him, but Builder Bob didn't seem to be worried.

Bob's wife had radar for trouble. She had long since gone to bed, but she materialized out of the air saying that the news was reporting something bad in the big city. "Them African nuts had gone crazy in the streets."

Hadn't these two ever heard about political correctness?

Bob kept working on the stairs, and she disappeared back to the apartment only to return five minutes later with a handful of sass in one hand and a full bucket of "I told you so" in the other. And for good measure she left again, then came back five minutes later with a wheelbarrow full of "we have to get to them saved places."

Builder Bob and wife began yet another display of tireless energy. The second argument in as many days started and threatened to never stop. Ryan didn't bother to say good night. Builder Bob and wife were a lot like babies: Ryan's existence was only perceived when he was standing before their eyes.

Ryan was an IT guy. And when he wasn't fixing networks, or managing his IT business, he was writing. Physical labor was in his past, back during college and on and off the decade after when he wasn't training for track and field. He was exhausted. He slept hard and oblivious. He woke to silence and streaming sunlight. The clock said 10:30. Scrambling from bed and to Builder Bob's apartment, he found the door closed but not locked. On the kitchen table lay all the building keys beside a note.

It's yours unless the rich prick wants it back. Good luck!

"You have *got* to be kidding me! What? Do I smell?!" He flopped down into a chair, feeling a wave of rejection.

Isolation was a powerful human motivator, so powerful that Ryan had worked happily long into the morning for two days. It was nice to have another person standing near you to help fend off the demons that haunted the darkness. Isolation was powerful, driving Ryan to tolerate that woman's incessant nattering. Isolation was so powerful that he had planned on tolerating her broadcast mode well into the foreseeable future.

"Bob," Ryan said, "you will surely be safe. That woman will nag every enemy you have to death."

Ryan decided he did smell. He took a real shower. While the hot water rained down on his sore body, Ryan began to think that maybe, just maybe, he could make a go of it here. With some work, he could stock the apartments with the grocery resources and fort up inside. For the first time in days, a vague ray of hope shone in the darkness.

Builder Bob and family had packed quick and light so there were plenty of cloths. Between the teenage sons and Bob, Ryan was able to find something to wear so he didn't have to climb back down to the grocery naked. The only exception was that Ryan decided he wasn't far enough into apocalypse to wear another man's underwear.

He searched the apartment for weapons. Bob had taken his rifle, and there were no other guns around. Ryan prowled through each apartment on the top floor, and then the seventh, and then the sixth. To Ryan's great pleasure he found a revolver under a pillow, and a Glock with the number 17 etched into its slide occupying a holster lying atop a nightstand. There was a badge in the drawer. In the same apartment he found two boxes of ammunition. Another apartment had a handgun with a big CF carved into a rosewood handle and Model 1911-22 stenciled in white along the slide and a 550 round box of .22 LR ammunition. He also found a rifle that said Winchester that looked like it should be in a cowboy western, but no ammunition. He found one double-barreled shotgun in a gun rack. He found another shotgun that had M590A1 stenciled into the metal and ten boxes of shotgun shells. He also found some cheap binoculars and tallied about four hundred rounds of mostly .22 ammunition. The rest was divided between 9mm Parabellum (that is what the box said, and he wasn't sure what Parabellum meant) .38, and shotgun shells.

He walked out of one apartment on the fifth floor, thumbed through the key ring for the master to open the next apartment, when he noticed a door at the end of the hall boarded up.

There was a note on the cross braces. The note said, "African lunatic inside. Keep out!"

"What the hell?" That hadn't been there all day yesterday. And that hadn't been there last night when they were working.

Ryan heard the low thumping, thrashing, banging, and moaning.

A twist slithered down Ryan's spine. He sprinted to the stairs and climbed the plywood incline to each floor

and locked himself into Builder Bob's apartment.

"Oh my God!" Ryan leaned against the door. How had an infected gotten into the building?

And when did Builder Bob find the African lunatic? And why didn't he just shoot it?

"And then he left and didn't tell me?"

Ryan paced the apartment until he was too unnerved to remain. He took his bag full of guns and ammunition to the roof and sat down, inspecting each in turn.

Ryan didn't know guns much past which end was which. The Glock wasn't loaded, so he jammed nine rounds into the magazine, but didn't have the thumb strength to push in any more bullets. His hands were on fire from swinging a hammer, and his forearms were worn out. Loading the Chiappa 1911 was easy. Ryan didn't think a .22 round would do much damage, but it was better than nothing.

He walked the roof parameter thinking about the uninvited guest, but he couldn't get past the commotion that spun on the streets below. Two nights ago, the streets were normal, eerie maybe, but calm. Today everything was violence. From Duquesne University toward downtown was a hornet's nest. Armed bands moved openly down Forbes Avenue, some with guns, but most held bats, or axes, or wrenches. They attacked lone people or looted stores. Humvees rolled up to the destruction and soldiers dismounted. The command to disburse filtered dimly over the valley, but no one did. The military dropped tear gas into their midst, and then fired shotguns into the frontline with bean bag rounds.

Ryan shifted his focus and found people on Fifth Avenue carrying mirrors and computers and chairs towards the suburbs to the east.

"Apparently, not everyone is motivated to get to one of them 'saved places.' Just think what you are missing, Bob."

Then Ryan saw a man toting a very large flat panel TV on his back like it was his very own cross.

"It is the apocalypse. I need that HD TV."

He pulled the binoculars from his eyes to get a bigger picture and then he saw a flash of pink coat. The binoculars came up. "There you are again?!"

Ryan adjusted the focus. She was a cute thing, even with her face streaked with dirt. He could see a tear in the arm of the coat, her jeans were stained, and her Uggs had seen better days. The blonde girl was darting from car to car, opening doors, climbing inside for a few minutes. She pawed under seats, pulled out floor mats, but he couldn't figure out her purpose.

She snuck across the street and looked into a store front with its plate glass windows shattered out. She took a step inside, froze, and then sprinted Ryan's direction.

Shotgun in hand, Ryan ran to the fire escape at the rear of Builder Bob's oasis and descended to the second floor landing. He stepped onto the ladder rungs, and the counterweight released and dropped to Colwell Street. He jogged down Stevenson to Fifth, scanning the streets for pink.

Then he spotted her crawling out of the backseat of a car a half block away. "Hey! In the pink coat!" Ryan waved and jumped. "Here! I can help you!"

She paused briefly in front of Ace's & Deuce's Lounge looking around, glancing everywhere but toward Ryan.

He took three strides and froze. Ryan started patting himself down for the minimart gate opener and keys but no matter how much he felt around he wasn't going to find them. He was wearing Bob's clothes, and the keys and opener were lying on the dresser in the fastidious woman's apartment.

"Oh, you have got to be kidding!

23

Global Infection: ≤ 27.42122%

This model is slightly more complicated than the basic SIR models, because this model has two mass-action transmissions, which lead to having more than one nonlinear term in the model. Mass-action incidence specifies that an average member of the population makes contact sufficient to transmit infection with βN others per unit time, where N is the total population without infection. In this case, the infection is zombification. The probability that a random contact by a zombie is made with a susceptible is S/N; thus, the number of new zombies through this transmission process in unit time per zombie is:

$$(\beta N)(S/N)Z = \beta SZ$$

—Munz, Hudea, Imad, et. al.

The groan came long and hard. Ryan was browsing the minimart aisles, feeling real pain. He needed disinfectant and Skin Mend—the over-the-counter version of the hospital grade skin fuser. The barbed wire poked holes in places that threatened fatherhood, but it served him right. A ten second lapse in thinking at the edge of the apocalypse and the world only got more interesting.

Ryan stood in the intersection like a stone, the river of chaos flowing around him. Everyone noticed and washed wide left and right out of respect. A large, pissed off man with a scowl and a shotgun inspired distance.

Ryan walked around the whole building twice, looking for a way in. The fire escape to Builder Bob's oasis was too high to grab without some kind of hook. All doors were sealed and he didn't want to destroy his own fortifications. The only option was climbing the gate that blocked off Firouz's loading dock courtyard. He pulled two floor mats from an unlocked car, threw them over the circles of barbed wire, and proceeded to climb. Scaling the gate was deceptively hard. The spaces in the wire were narrow and the metal was layered with a slippery plastic coating. Two feet above the gate's top edge was a wide steel plate that ran from wall to wall with a sign that said *Clearance 14.* To get over the gate, a person had to squeeze under that beam, which required them to crawl *through* the barbed wire.

Shaking from exhaustion, he flopped over the gate like newborn calf and slammed into the asphalt. Then Ryan had to climb back to the oasis—nursing puncture wounds, sucking the blood off his hands, and feeling it run inside his pants—to get the keys, then back down to the minimart for first aid.

He patched up cuts and scrapes and punctures in the manager's office. He had ripped the hell out of Builder Bob's pants, and thinking about the girl alone on the street ripped the hell out of his heart. He couldn't imagine a mother or father leaving their daughter on the street. That probably meant there was no mother or father.

Ryan leaned back in the chair thinking. He had two choices. Figure out how to remove the infected from the building, or abandon the building. Boarding over the door really wasn't a solution. He could not imagine sleeping another night with something like that so near. And if one could get in, what stopped others?

He had to get the infected out or remain in the grocery. But the street level was nerve-wracking. When those marauding bands turned their attention on this building, there would be nowhere to go.

Since they had spent hours on the sixth floor, the only reasonable alternative entrance was from the fire escape; someone—somehow—had managed to do what Ryan couldn't, trigger the counterweight and climb the ladder. But Ryan had seen no broken windows on the way down, and he knew from experience that the fire escape ladder was twenty feet above the ground. That only left one real explanation: someone had indeed gotten into the building before they got that "African madness."

Ryan used a screw gun to remove the fasteners that held boards over the door. Armored with two pairs of jeans, heavy contractor boots, jean jacket over the thick sweatshirt, and leather gloves, Ryan almost felt ready to do battle. He retrieved a football helmet from an apartment on seven—from a shelf display, a memento of past high school heroism—and pulled out some pads to make it fit. The helmet jabbed at his skull in all the wrong places and tended to swim into his vision. But if Tess' death grip and the hundred-pound blonde woman were any measure, fighting the infected was a contact sport.

Ryan had no confidence using handguns, so his only choice was which shotgun. Ryan's friend, Rob, always raved: "Just point and shoot. Just point and shoot. The shotgun will do the rest."

Six shots were better than two, but the pump action made him nervous. Could he rack the slide fast enough for all six shots?

In the end he chose the two-shot weapon. His logic was simple: fewer moving parts meant fewer ways to screw up. Ryan broke open the action, added shells, closed it, and put the weapon on safe.

"Point and shoot. Point and shoot." He crawled over the barriers and slid down the plywood. He used Builder Bob's keys to unlock the door and he slammed it back, expecting the creature to leap out like some horror flick monster.

Nothing.

"Here kitty, kitty, kitty," Ryan said as he began his search. It took fifteen minutes of inch by inch, agonizing, heart-pounding anxiety to work through the apartment to verify the only threat was the banging coming from a locked bedroom. The door was splintered and cracking, but still holding back whoever was inside.

"Hello? I don't suppose you can talk and are just mad that you got locked in?"

The banging increased, followed by moans and guttural shrieks that grated on the nerves like chewing on Styrofoam. Those sounds couldn't come from a sane human being.

Ryan's plan was simple: kick the door so hard that it flew off its hinges and knock the creature back, point and shoot. But plans never survive battle. Ryan's foot went through the door. Suddenly he was wedged, straddling the door bottom.

"Idiot!"

Frantic, Ryan kicked and connected with something solid, but then he felt pawing, grabbing, clutching followed by teeth pushing through the jeans and socks at his ankle. Panic shot into his chest and down Ryan's spine like a bucket of spiders.

The creature savaged his leg.

Ryan heaved and fell on his back, the shotgun tumbling down the hall, the helmet rolling over his eyes.

The infected crashed against the door, its head spearing through the hole.

Ryan scrambled for the shotgun, spun, and the helmet rolled into his vision as he pulled the trigger.

Nothing.

"What the hell?"

The infected pushed farther through the splintered door.

Terror clawed at Ryan's throat, throttling his breath like a malevolent asthma attack. Ryan pulled again and again. He swiveled the face guard out of his eyes.

"Safety! Safety!"

The safety made a snapping sound and a ring of red showed. He rose to a knee, pulling the weapon to his shoulder. "Point and shoot. Point and shoot!"

The helmet twisted as he pulled the trigger. Thunder slapped against Ryan's head twice.

He righted the helmet and saw a nice hole in the wall and the breach in the bedroom door was larger. One shot had peppered the rugby shirt with holes. It plowed through the ragged gap.

Ryan bolted from the apartment and paused at the stairs to see if it was coming. He could hear more banging and scraping and moaning, but nothing emerged. Holding the shotgun butt forward, Ryan peeked around the hallway corner; in one last push the door gave birth to a snapping, writhing predator.

Ryan made eye contact. And he saw into *those* eyes: the blonde woman's eyes—Tess's eyes. It was the same lack of self. It was the same eerie, narrow awareness that had only one goal: violence.

Ryan stood mesmerized as it gathered to all fours, then moved like it was in a yoga pose with palms and feet on the floor, then toddled to standing. And then it turned its whole body to Ryan.

It lunged.

Ryan ran.

"Too stupid to live. Too stupid to live," he said over and over as he ran to the landing, sure that the creature's mouth was an inch from his neck.

Halfway up the incline his foot slipped and he dropped the shotgun as he grabbed for the banister. The creature shambled along, well behind, but Ryan would not get to the weapon before the creature got to the stairs.

Ryan used the banister to reach the top.

The infected stepped its right foot on plywood, then the left, the right, and then . . .

It was a wonderfully beautiful face plant, chin bouncing and teeth shattering. It slid to the bottom and lay still. Minutes ticked by. Ryan thought the blow to the face had killed it. He started to crawl to the bottom, but then it got up and tried again. Over and over and over, the creature righted itself, took a step, then two, and then three, only to crash face first, pulverizing its head splintering bone, and crushing eye sockets.

Ryan made his way behind the barricade and checked his legs, fearing that by an evil stroke of fate he had been bit. All he found was a bruised ankle. Two layers of jeans was a good strategy. The human jaw could create enormous force, but it didn't have the biting power of a hyena.

Nerves shot and exhausted, Ryan locked himself into Bob's apartment and collapsed into a recliner intending to sit for a minute. He was terrified when the banging woke him two hours later. Panicked rushed to the door, looked into the hall to find it empty. Ryan moved down to the barricade and saw it: its face was flattened, its teeth were tiny, ragged chips behind smashed lips.

The human body cannot absorb that kind of . . .

And then Ryan had the craziest thought: this is what people meant when they thought of the walking dead.

Slap, scraaaape!

The image rushed back, unbidden and vicious—the bullet holes, the bone sticking out of her leg, the indifference to pain as her head bounced off concrete.

Slap, scraaaape!

This was the ancient horror story of zombies; this was the sick, twisted world of console entertainment in Technicolor authenticity.

Slap, scraaaape!

This is what the people were talking about when Ahou mocked the stories; monsters existed and zombies were real.

Slap, scraaaape!

This was every George A. Romero geek's zombie apocalypse wet dream.

That meant there was only one way to kill this thing.

From the top of the stair, Ryan tried shooting the head with the Glock. His effort confirmed two things. First, the characters in those television shows who snapped off headshots from a hundred feet away with every shot were a flat-out fiction. Second, Ryan Sage had no skill with the weapon.

He had to get much closer and this time he armed himself with a 2x4. From the Oasis he used the fire escape to get to the right floor, entered the adjacent apartment through an unlatched window and slowly opened front door.

The creature slipped and slammed face first.

Ryan covered the distance in ten strides, planted a boot in the back, and swung the two-by-four like he was going to drive it though the floor. The skull cracked deep and wet, spraying gray matter. The zombie went still like someone let air out of a blowup doll.

Ryan stood, shaking, his breath coming in ragged heaves, waiting for the horror to reanimate. That is what always happened in the movies.

The zombie was a kid, a boy, maybe sixteen. Ryan could see now that he had been muzzled with a heavy towel secured by duct tape. There were rope burns on his arms and wrists that looked matted over from healing over and over again. And then he saw the stake sticking out of the back off his shirt. Ryan tore the fabric and saw the tip of a stake buried under matted, regenerated flesh. Someone had tried to kill the boy, but he didn't die. So they gagged and tied him down. And that was how they kept him from disturbing the building. But the endless biting and straining with no thought for pain destroyed the restraints and loosed him on the world. If not for unrelenting persistence, this kid would have remained in that room until he rotted away.

Or not?

This creature didn't look rotted like normal zombies. The skin looked dehydrated and maybe a little thin, like he hadn't eaten but the skin looked surprisingly smooth like the boy had recently come from the salon and gotten a body buff.

Then like the jarring crush of a car wreck, the next thought plowed into the intersection of his mind. This was a *kid*. He wasn't hospital staff, he wasn't law enforcement, and yet he was diseased.

Ryan's one small abiding hope was that the sickness was limited to the hospital, but this boy implied that it had spread much farther, festering in locked rooms away from public knowledge. How many more boys and girls, and wives and husbands were just like this? Their contagious menace tied down to a bed, or a post, or in a cage, the family too full of grief, too confused to take action.

Bexley!

This is what Bexley had known! This is what he had tried to save his family from!

Ryan opposed his brother-in-law on so many fundamental issues that they shared no real affection. He'd come to—grudgingly—admire Bexley, his determination and courage and devotion to Tess when the police forced him to read the suicide note. Sitting in the interrogation room, the detectives mocking the missive left for Tess, insisting it was a forgery. Ryan had been too caught up in the moment to see the bigger picture the method behind Bexley's madness: the fate of this young boy was every parent's worst nightmare and exactly why Bexley put a gun to his own daughter's head.

But Ryan could never have seen it then—they had shoved its blood and brain splattered existence under his nose, taunting him to confess his crimes. Ryan read the long, soulful declaration of Bexley's love for Tess— the endless revelations of his devotion—jealous that he had never been able to say these things so unabashedly, with such vulnerability to a woman. Ryan read the letter and was proud that his sister had married a man filled with such utter devotion.

Ryan wept as he copied the letter onto a pad of paper.

As a kid, Ryan suffered the mockery of his fifth grade teacher, and every subsequent educator, over his penmanship, grammar and spelling So it never crossed his mind that such disability would absolutely exonerate him of conspiracy to commit murder.

He spun the pad toward the detectives and said, "You, sirs, are cruel human beings, not worthy of the badges you wear."

He walked out of the police station.

24

Global Infection: ≤ 27.43008%

The bourgeoisie is many times stronger than we. To give it the weapon of freedom of the press is to ease the enemy's cause, to help the class enemy. We do not desire to end in suicide, so we will not do this.

—Vladimir Ilyich Lenin

Ryan tried to clear his vision; staring made the corpse move even though it didn't. Paranoia drove Ryan to beat the skull until a mash of gore hung off the tip of the spine.

He puked.

Then Ryan checked lower floor apartments to confirm they were empty and then checked the entrance. Long ago, the street level was built as retail space and sealed off from the upper floors. Ryan walked down to the ground level by a wide, well-lit stairwell. The tenants shared a small courtyard tucked safely behind a fifteen-foot brick wall covered in ivy. The renovators were going for that old time European look, locking the living space behind decorative barriers for the quaint enclave feel. The egress to the world beyond was handled by two interlocking wrought iron gates; if the first was open, the second was locked. To sell these locations, the real estate people knew that they had to impress residents with security. They had the right idea. The courtyard was filled with nice landscaping, a picnic table, a small child's jungle gym, and post office mailboxes. It was homey, if a bit isolated and small.

The second floor was a common area with game room and meeting room and kitchenette. Three of the front windows were thick semi-opaque glass brick that let through natural light but made it impossible to see through. The fourth window to the far right, tucked into a corner, was a standard double-pane glass. Rusty bars fastened to the brick outside many years ago blocked entrance. Ryan could see down Our Way to the left, but the view to the right was obscured by a red brick column, the top of the portico overhang, and the darkened Hayek sign. With work someone might be able to break in, but it seemed unlikely.

He confirmed that the public elevator was turned off and then found service elevator down the hall, which was turned off as well. Ryan regretted every cheeseburger and French fry with every step up the stairs.

Ryan found some bleach, a water bottle, rubber gloves, trash bags, broom, dustpan and some duct tape. He turned the service elevator on and headed down to start cleanup. With bleach water he sprayed down the body and gore, wrapped the top of the body in a bag, taped it tight, and swept up the bits of brain and bone.

 He hauled the body to the service elevator and then to the roof. He did a fireman's carry to the sub shop and took off the plastic bag.

"Bring out your dead. Bring out your dead," he said, and dropped the body over the edge. It wasn't perfect, but the body sort of landed behind the car blocking the metal gate.

He paused, letting the stress fade, noticing the world beyond. Sirens and horns clashed, fires dotted the skyline to the east and south across the river along the mountain ridge. Some were full-on conflagrations; others were car fires in the street. Far down Fifth Avenue, Ryan could see abandoned fire trucks with lights still flashing beside cop cars pulled into crude blockades.

He turned to leave. The gunfire made him turn back.

The police had built a temporary command center to the left of Mercy Hospital and now they were shooting. A mob was running from the building, but under the temporary lights the surging, writhing mass of people would not be stopped. One by one by one, the lights slammed to the ground and went dark. The gunfire subsided to the occasional quick bark of a single gun and finally stopped.

Ryan waited and waited and waited to see if cars and lights and the crackle of radios would burst back to life. But the ridgeline from Duquesne University well past the hospital parking lot was dark, shapes shifting and moving like snakes under a blanket.

Securing everything he could think to lock, Ryan retreated to Builder Bob's—his—apartment, shed his clothes into the wash, took a shower, ate some food and stared at the walls listening to his heart beat until he couldn't handle the isolation.

He changed the linens in the master bedroom, grabbed Ahou's pillow and photo albums, and sat on the bed. Within minutes of mindless browsing, he started arranging the best pictures into one book: her as a pimply teenager, gawky and awkward; high school poses with friends flashing ridiculous gang signs; jaw-dropping pictures of her dressed to kill at college parties and clubs; a dozen prints from a fashion portfolio and twenty nudes with photographer watermarks that made him jealous and aroused.

Then Ryan found his favorite pictures tucked into the back of one album. They hadn't made Ahou's cut, banished to confinement within a yellowing envelope. The first four were of Ahou sleeping, the sleek lines of her long legs out from underneath the sheets, her coffee and cream complexion mixing nicely with the floral blue print. Others showed Ahou looking barely awake, her back and sides to the camera silhouetted against a window, stretching naked. Then she was walking around an apartment with tousled hair in a loose T-shirt and boy short panties, looking at something off camera, puffing out her cheeks, grimacing and snarling, and half smiling. She wasn't posing. She wasn't mugging for the camera. Ryan had the feeling she didn't even know she was being photographed. She was radiant. It made him smile.

These pictures were the last images before falling asleep.

In the morning he lay in bed, occasionally watching the time pass, occasionally looking at the closed photo album on the nightstand. Last night, he had felt so much pleasure looking through the chronicle of Ahou's life. But this morning it seemed to only inspire isolation. At 10:32 he looked at the 9 millimeter on the nightstand.

It's loaded.

It could be over in a second?

"Cut that out! Get up!"

Ten minutes later Ryan was dressed, drinking some orange juice and listening to cable news. He searched for a local report about last night's firefight but there wasn't any local news. He did find the usual national talking heads droning on about the authorities pushing back the "horde" in Washington, D.C. But they didn't look like their usual touched-up, refined selves. The male anchors had five o'clock shadows and the female anchors seemed to have missed their last three Botox treatments.

Evidently the military was working overtime to fortify the government triangle, but Ryan could see the boats and ships on the Potomac. They were shuttling important people out as fast as they could load them. A senator from Massachusetts was doing press conference dressed in fatigues, declaring his determination to stand fast in defense of God and country and not take the easy way out, implying that the exodus into the Potomac, just in the background, was the height of cowardice.

A sudden burst of gunfire somewhere off camera interrupted the press conference. The senator grabbed a female staffer—dressed in a business pantsuit—and used her as a shield.

"Priceless!"

Between news reports he called Erik and got a circuit's busy message for the cell carrier. He called from the land line to encourage Erik to shut down the business, take Sarah and the kids and get to their ranch in Wyoming.

Erik's mail box was full and so was Sarah's. He called their home and got no answer.

"Where the hell are you guys?"

For the duration of their relationship Ryan had been the visionary, the one to look ahead and see what was coming. Erik was the detail guy, relentless in his ability to make sure everything was done to capitalize on the moment. They had been a great team and Erik respected Ryan's passion for political philosophy and encouraged his efforts to impact public opinion. But when the government started its investigation into the business Erik changed.

He returned his attention to the network news broadcasts.

> Dateline Baghdad: Caliphate backtracks from claiming that Allah has raised an army. "Allah's Army" has descended on Baghdad. Caliphate declares they have been deceived. The creatures are the Great Satan's befouling demons.

> Dateline Japan: The average Tokyo native lives in a four-hundred-square-foot home, built with materials no thicker than bamboo. With a population of 16,790,000, Tokyo was a biohazard deathtrap. The prime minister and the National Diet order the evacuation of Japan.

> Dateline China: Reports from China . . . well, no one was sure what was happening in China. Suddenly, the media had decided that news from a communist country couldn't really be relied on. Such governments use propaganda and are therefore unreliable sources.

Ryan threw a wad of paper at the TV. "You are just now figuring this out?!"

> Dateline New York: Yesterday, Yonkers. The 2nd Marine Division 10th Regiment, the 3rd Infantry Division, and the Army's 3rd Infantry Division 64th Armor Division were deployed and conducted a successful campaign to restore social order. The armed forces met with brief resistance but prevailed against social agitators.

The footage showed the military in force and in charge. Then a long shot of people in the distance, coming from the city.

Ryan squinted. *Are they sprinting?*

The feed cut to a reporter with beads of sweat on his brow, "As you can see, operation Peaceful Resolution is going to be a success . . ."

Ryan believed about three words from the government news networks on a good day, but this report screamed phony. He did a quick web search and found dozens of independently posted videos.

By the internet's technological nature, it was almost impossible for the U.S. government to keep the truth fully suppressed. Hackers took delight in keeping the Homeland Security censors chasing their tails. Within seconds of watching the tilting, swirling, jolting camera work, it was apparent why the reporter was sweating bullets.

The government footage showed soldiers forted behind sandbag bunkers, decked out in full battle kit, from I87 to I95, from Yonkers to New Rochelle, and mechanized units were positioned tight on the roads like they were at a border checkpoint.

To a sane enemy, an enemy that values self preservation, it looked like a formidable force.

A helicopter video chronicled what the government feed suppressed. Loudspeakers blared warnings to cease and desist over and over and over.

The horde blitzed through the street heedless of pain or caution, smashing, swarming and sliding, over, through or around any obstacle.

This was what Builder Bob described: like a mad march of ants using the carcasses of the fallen to ford a river. The infected in the front mutilated themselves against metal and concrete, glass and bullets; the horde behind writhed ever forward, trampling them underfoot, mounds and mounds of undead heaping up before barriers to spill across to the other side, like an endless tide of rats. The horde flowed down Saw Mill River Parkway, over cars and Jersey walls and around buses like a river of teaming carnivorous rodents fully indifferent, fully heedless, fully without restraint.

Humans rely on some form of restraint in most every social interaction. So when one person ventures into unrestricted mayhem, people scatter. Even in combat where the point is death and destruction, enemies rely on some form of survival instinct to temper the action. The reason that suppressive fire is a military tactic is because the soldier on the other side of that hailstorm of bullets wants to get out of the way. But that combat method vanishes when the enemy doesn't give a fuck.

The hoard seemed almost superhuman, by sheer speed, ferocity and destruction.

The front checkpoints initiated a devastating spray of lead. The Marines reinforced the checkpoint, seeking to stem the tide, but a second mob descended from New Rochelle, swallowing outposts one by one by one, stranding them like desert islands. The Marines and the Army were cut in half. Army ground troops were pinned between their own impotent mechanized units and the leading edge of the human wave.

The combined strength of a Marine regiment and an Army brigade— roughly five thousand men—no matter how well armored, were no match for a zombie population of millions.

The helicopter videographer closed with a statistical breakdown and commentary. The Marines refused to leave anyone and lost 90 percent of their total force. The Army's forces rolled into Yonkers at noon. They were overrun by nightfall, having lost 60 percent of their personnel and 90 percent of their mechanized units.

What the hell did I just see?

Ryan couldn't make the images square with his experience. The girl had dragged toward him, methodic but slow. The boy moved like he was drunk, lurching without coordination, like the zombies of old horror flicks. But the people on the videos looked fresh and nimble as they ran through the puddles in the streets and the dismal spring shower that fell on the New York suburbs.

Was it a different infection?

He dove into research. The government was trying to suppress their own broadcast. The administration had been televising the event, ready to take credit for the victory that would inspire confidence across the country. Someone forgot to pull the plug when it went to shit. The public had been exposed to eleven minutes and forty-one seconds of homicidal destruction. And now the administration was working overtime on damage control, trying to spin what happened into yet one more problem with the First Amendment. This chaos was really caused by a reprehensible video published by a fringe producer. Everyone should stay calm. It was all right. Most of what was seen was special effects. Stay indoors and shelter in place. The government of the United States of America will take care of you. Just don't take matters into your own hands. Such action would be reckless and foolish. Individual action is wrong. Act only for the common good and do what authorities tell you.

But it was already too late. The Builder Bobs of the world were abandoning the common good in favor of survival. Bob knew how the infected acted, how they could boil and climb like ants overcoming obstacles.

And then it made sense. The nattering wife must have dragged Bob to the TV to see the New York video, and he knew that no stairwell was high enough to stop an inner-city population. Bob likely took the missus and the kids to open spaces where the zombies couldn't accumulate. They left at night, because the darkness offered protection from prying government eyes.

This video also explained why the talking heads started offering alternate solutions for survival. Head north seemed positively sane by comparison to standing against the tsunami of the un-killable mobs breaking over the East Coast landscape.

With a new perspective Ryan started watching network and cable news. Broadcasters typically read from scripts filled with endless anti-capitalist rants and idle storylines, advancing political agendas crafted by government pressure. For weeks they had been repeating the talking points handed to them to shape the news to favor underlying agendas.

But now they were on location near the moaning, snarling horde and there was panic behind their eyes. They were face-to-face with a reality that did not square with the talking points. Their problem was apparent: the truth was before them, but they didn't have the courage to say it. That wasn't surprising. Journalists spent years in school to learn how to be soulless. They had been indoctrinated to believe that truth was relative, news was spin and moral equivalency meant everyone had a selfish agenda. So what did an objective reality mean anyway?

Ryan gave a few of the reporters credit for struggling to lie. Somewhere in their soul was a conflict that implied a moral compass. But that was not true of every reporter. There were those journalists who remained oblivious to truth. They squared their shoulders, strapped on their million dollar smiles and told whatever tale was on their teleprompter.

A pert blue-eyed blonde, still young enough to be beautiful without TV makeup, stood beside Interstate 70 with the sign saying *Breezewood* blazing behind her in the morning sun. ". . . many Midwestern cities are peaceful and we are being told that people from the east coast can find refuge in Pittsburgh, Zanesville and Columbus. Government sources say that these cities have a very small infection rate and authorities are working around the clock to monitor their safe zones."

"What?"

Incensed, Ryan went to his blog, posting a brief, harsh rebuttal article, and fully uncaring if the feds were monitoring. He looked for other places to post the truth but many of the major blogs had been closed for comment. The news outlets were not taking information and some of the pages were down. In a fit of exasperation, he decided to spam all his friends. He clicked on the mail client and new mail pounded down from the servers. He idly read subject lines until she saw: **Daniel Ryder. Safety! Offer expires today at 12:15. Bring NO ONE with you**.

Ryan saw the clock. His heart flipped.

25

Global Infection: ≤ 27.6008%

The means of defense against foreign danger historically
have become the instruments of tyranny at home.
—JAMES MADISON

The thing people call a "smartphone" that lives in their pockets like a friendly pixie giving them any information desired, making suggestions and magically paying bills is really a gremlin of evil. Smartphones are just like when AllSpark hits a machine and turns it into an agent for Megatron, an eternal slave for the Decepticon plot against the galaxy. The United States government can and does use cell phones to keep detailed tabs on its citizens.

People pay almost no attention to the amount of information government agencies are privy to, because they forget how much information smart-phones refine for individual use. With location services, police powers were expanded exponentially by the endless data mining of buying habits purchase locations, bank account totals, website browsing history, when people sleep, and how much coffee they buy at Starbucks when they wake up. With GPS, it is easy to tell if someone drinks copious amounts of alcohol, cheats on his gay lover, works out at a gym, goes to a hospital, or attends church eight times a month. Social media web portals compile enormous amounts of self-disclosed information that is subsequently used as a filter to map out requests via voice recognition software within the smartphones. And all this information is simply handed over to the government merely because it asks.

Ryan wrote an article called "Tap and Rap" that detailed, among other things, how often law enforcement accesses smartphone information . . . via casual request to cell phone providers. In ten years of Ryan's adult life, statistics detailed that cell phone carriers responded over eighty *million* times to law enforcement requests for data. These requests were not made with a subpoena or a warrant. Law enforcement asked, and the carriers obliged.

Surely this practice must be a violation of the Fourth Amendment and Fourteenth Amendment, right? Information compiled by a private device, for private use, by contractual agreement is private property, right?

Never mind the odious impact that the fourteenth amendment historically had on the separation of powers. A few lone voices warned the American people, but no one listened. But it's not like the Constitution matters anyway, when it can be interpreted to justify a tax on refusing to purchase a federally mandated product. If the government can penalize actions that people do *not* commit, then listening to conversations and tracking the details of citizen life *at will* is a trivial step farther down the path of American despotism.

In the world of smartphones, the legal logic says that citizens do not have a "reasonable expectation of privacy" when cell phone data is being broadcast to whomever has the *ability* to listen. This subordinates the Fourth Amendment and Fourteenth Amendment to the sweeping generalization of government "ability."

And, of course, American citizens tolerate the encroachment on civil liberties because *if* they think about what is really being done, they generalize technologies together into a massive scientific black hole that is more akin to magic. So certainly, paying attention to the details of cell phone wizardry isn't something that mere mortals should bother with.

After all, magic sounds come out of a magic box called a radio that gets magic music out of the "public" air space. How could tapping into a cell phone broadcast be any different? It is also a magic box that gets magic sounds out of the magical "public" air space.

The barbarian mind has a hard time grasping how to make fire, so it really struggles to grasp an important conceptual distinction. The issue is not the *means* of the magic, but who *owns* the magic. By the same barbarian logic, mailboxes—that magically fill up with messages from pixies—stand in that magical place called a "public" street. If the government has the *ability* pry open the magic box, it is therefore legally justified in reading the mail. The barbarian logic can be applied to that magic building called a house where meals are cooked by pixies who also sprinkle dust that makes people sleep. Houses have front doors that line that magical place called a "public" street. And if the government has the *ability* to turn the knob—or break down the door—to enter a home, citizens better be careful about what magical things they do in their bedrooms.

It is by the wizardry of government "ability" that the Fourth and Fourteenth Amendment have been banished to the lower planes of hell. And just like the ancient philistines bowing in submission before the man who can make fire, modern barbarians have been enslaved to the tribal shaman. The barbarian logic goes like this: the shaman has the magic, so he must be in charge. If the shaman is in charge, then he must own everything. (That is what the shaman says anyway, so we must believe him, because he makes fire.) And if the shaman owns everything, then who needs the

Fourth and Fourteenth amendment? There is no such thing as private property, so there certainly isn't a need for due process.

Of course, without *private* property, there is no freedom . . . pericd. But the American people lost sight of this fundamental truth. So, by the time lawmakers passed legislation that required manufacturers to build a remote *On* switch into every cell phone—to be exploited at government request—the Bill of Rights had long since begun to rot like a corpse, and the Fourth and Fourteenth Amendment could barely pass the smell test.

Ryan pulled his iPhone out of the manager's office safe. His phone was still off. The app Power Down was designed to force a shutdown in four seconds if an access code was not entered. The safe offered interference from cellular carrier efforts to engage the phone, and the app prevented the phone from being remote-started and used as a self-inflicted bug. He powered the phone on, knowing full well that as soon as the phone reported to the network, the feds—if they were looking for such things—would know where he was within the broadcast range of a cell tower. But it couldn't be helped. The prepaid phone didn't give him nearly the automated abilities of his iPhone. He needed to make calls and he needed the GPS and mapping functions because Ryan Sage needed to run through the streets of Pittsburgh and he wasn't sure where he was going.

Three e-mails waited in his inbox. Ryan read them in turn. The first, sent a day-and-a-half ago, had been a simple message:

Mr. Sage:

   Daniel Ryder asks that you call him as soon as possible. He is trying to reach you on a very urgent matter.

Mora
724-555-5555

The second e-mail with a time stamp ten hours later said:

Ryan,

   This is Daniel Ryder. We met at Firouz's sandwich shop. I need you to call or e-mail me as soon as you can. I would

*like to talk to you about the future. We called your cell phone
and it goes to voice mail. We posted messages on your blog
hoping that someone will direct your attention.*

724-555-5555
412-555-5556
987-555-5557

Daniel Ryder

P.S. *You were right.*

And the last message had a time stamp of 11:21 p.m. last night. It came just about the time Ryan was arranging the photo album.

Ryan,

*I pray that you are all right. I am worried. I am very
sorry that I could not have reached out to you sooner. You
must respond by no later than today. Time has run out. Call
me or come directly to Smithfield Street. The tower is impossible to miss on the south side of the city.*

*You **must** be here no later than 12:15 today. This is a life-
and-death-matter, most likely your life and your death. Come
prepared to leave forever. You can bring NO ONE else with
you. If you show up with anyone else, I will retract the offer.*

Please, son, come or call as soon as you can.
Daniel Ryder

The question that haunted Ryan every minute that he took trying to get organized to travel the streets was "which *today* was today?" When Daniel sent the message, *today* was a quarter past midnight. He prayed to God that Daniel Ryder just got confused. Hopefully, Daniel didn't want him to travel at night. Unfortunately, Ryan didn't think that man was ever confused about much of anything.

And now he was a blur in the manager's office, arranging his stuff for transport while he waited for the phone to boot up to the home screen. He sent an e-mail from the apartment, but he was determined to speak to Daniel in person. He snapped the office phone off the base and dialed the numbers on the e-mail—three numbers, two no answers, one busy. This was the same result he had gotten since he started dialing in Builder Bob's place.

Ryan's phone finally found the network and promptly started notifying of messages and e-mail. He tapped through the apps for Daniel's contact information and verified that he had all relevant numbers. He dictated the address and engaged the mapping function and it took forever for the GPS to show his location.

"Leaving forever. Leaving forever," Ryan said, trying to think of anything he'd missed on his list. He was missing a pair of jeans, but didn't have time to look for them. Then he saw the letter lying atop Firouz's box of papers and the money pouch.

Do I need money?

He stuffed Firouz money bag deep into his laptop bag beside Ahou's notebook. He placed the envelope into a Ziploc along with Ahou's pillow case. He put the Glock on his right hip. Then he put all of that in the duffel with the guns and ammunition. He loaded his jean jacket pockets with shotgun shells and fastened Builder Bob's key ring clamp to his belt.

With shotgun and Toyota car keys in hand, Ryan moved out of the minimart, locking doors as he went. While the gate trundled open, Ryan set up Daniel Ryder's numbers for speed dial and then studied the street map on his phone. He memorized a route and hit the gas, making sure the gate trundled closed in the rearview mirror.

From Stevenson to Fifth to Diamond Street, Ryan sped, refusing to slow down for anything, scraping past cars, bouncing over curbs, breaking off parking meters. Twice, people dashed out of his way, and then he ran out of road. He hit the intersection of Shingiss and Diamond and halted in front of a tangle of cars and trucks piled in metal mayhem. Cars and trucks had slammed over the concrete barrier from the Crosstown Boulevard overhead and stacked on the streets below like a junkyard.

The streets around were tight, narrow chokepoints of destruction underneath an overpass. Ryan could see figures dashing this way and that through the tight warrens. He turned the car back the way he came, studying the map looking for a way around.

The most direct route was straight down Diamond to Forbes to Ross. The streets and ways of Downtown Pittsburgh were a maze. He could drive around the city, endlessly trying to find a way to punch through.

And then he saw ten people shambling behind him. He did a double take and then a triple take—there was something off about their gait, the manner of their walk.

Slap, scraaaaape . . .

They were horrifying in their unanimity.

Slap, scraaaaape . . .

Ryan killed the engine, grabbed his bags, and shotgun, and locked the doors. He ran.

The acrid smell of smoke hung in the air, pricking the nose and eyes with a thousand small pins. Horns and sirens and bells and car alarms blared into the morning, an orchestra of clashing chords. It was like the gods of pandemonium were doing a tap dance on everyone's head.

He sprinted until his lungs couldn't breathe. Ryan huddled behind a car at the intersection of Forbes and Diamond watching the bedlam. Soldiers and cops were beating down a small mob of Duquesne coeds. They fought until the unruly pack lay on the street, unmoving. Then they headed toward some looters carting away whatever wasn't nailed down. Ryan was about ready to move when he saw the coeds stir, then gathered to all fours, then moved like it was in a yoga pose with palms and feet on the floor, then toddled to standing. Some had broken arms, some had shoulders that hung at odd angles, some that couldn't stand on fractured legs, some that had jaws crushed to one side.

They lurched after the soldiers.

Ryan pressed his back against a massive rust-colored stone wall of a building that looked like a castle. He readjusted his bags and verify that the Glock was secure in the holster. He managed to get eleven rounds into the weapon before his fingers were too sore to press. He knew he couldn't shoot for shit, but at least it was loaded. He figured that he could hit something close, like inside of ten feet close.

He moved and something poked him. He dropped to his knees to readjust a strap on the duffel when a bullet struck the stone above his head.

"Really? Do I look like one of *them*?" he shouted.

Not that it was easy to tell between *us* and *them*, between threats and allies. He scrambled to a car's front wheel looking for the source. A bullet whacked off the windshield. "Cut it out!" Ryan shouted. Once was a stray bullet. Twice was attempted murder.

Frantic, Ryan tried to get himself organized, cinching the straps tighter. He draped the bags around his shoulders and back. He crept from car to car moving down Forbes. He peeked over the trunk of a blue Mercedes, looking for a gunman. And that was when he saw her. The girl in the pink coat and brown Uggs was a mesmerizing contrast to the turmoil. She darted between cars, occasionally patting down a body that lay unmoving in the streets. She dug through a fallen cop's pockets, and then stood for a moment counting something in her hand. She was counting coins. She rummaged through a back pocked, pulled out a wallet and grabbed a few bills. A twenty fluttered away. And then the pieces of the puzzle fell into place. She's living out of vending machines. "Hey!" Ryan said, waving a hand. "Hey, over here!"

She turned, looked, gave him a sly smile of recognition, waved like it was a normal day at school, and snuck toward a restaurant that boasted famous corned beef.

"... *no one else can come* ..."

Even a lone girl on the streets?

Ryan checked the time on his phone.

Tick ...

Tick ...

Tick ...

"*. . . Your life and your death . . .*"
And her life and her death.
"*. . . Come prepared to leave forever . . .*"
Last chance to help her.
"*. . . Safety . . .*"

"If I wanted safe, I would have quit writing when Tess warned me about the feds," Ryan said to himself, "Screw it! If he tells me to go home, I go home." He ran after the pink coat.

26

Global Infection: ≤ 27.62000%

There is a huge difference between government compulsion and individual compassion. They are both taking action motivated by the deepest character, but only one of them is acting out of benevolence.

—RYAN SAGE, MORAL ROPE-A-DOPE

He was too late.

Ryan dashed into the broken out windows of the shop front. "Hey, you in the coat!" he rasped. "I'm Ryan Sa—"

A handgun fired. Bullets hit the ragged glass to his right. He dropped and rolled. "Cut it out!" he shouted. "I'm just looking for a girl." He scrambled to a stone planter box with a tree and flowers growing inside circled by marble bench.

"Get out of my store!"

"I'm already out!" Ryan shouted, throttling the shotgun. "Is she in there?!"

"Ain't no women here! I drove out a little thief every day for the last two days. She ain't coming back. If she stole from you, you can catch her later. But now, put that shotgun on the ground, and I'll let you leave!"

"You were the one trying to kill me for my gun?"

"Survival of the fittest! Now leave the shotgun and any ammunition you have, and you can leave."

"Survival of the fittest," Ryan mumbled. "Thanks, Darwin." He looked around. He wasn't pinned exactly, but if he were going to run, he had to move with a gun pointing at him. Two shots, and two misses however, even a blind squirrel does something important occasionally. A plan formed: *Shoot twice into the store. Bad guy ducks. Bad guy can't shoot. Run behind those cars.*

"Good plan," Ryan said, getting his feet under him while snapping the safety off.

"Last chance before I put a bullet in your head."

"I've already seen you shoot!"

"Fuck you!"

"Good comeback!"

The handgun barked, and the round struck the concrete two feet to Ryan's left. Ryan cringed feeling watery inside.

"Give me the shotgun. Now!"

"No can do!" Ryan shouted, rising over the planter, butt stock on shoulder, check on stock. He was a heartbeat from squeezing off a round when he saw her. She was a ball of pink, leaned against a trashcan just inside the broken-out glass, sipping a soda and eating a bag of chips. She looked like she was at home slouching on the couch watching TV. She smiled, raised a finger to her lips for quiet, and dumped the last of the chips into her mouth.

"What the heck are you—"

Crack!

Ryan never knew where the round hit, but the sound made his stomach drop out between his knees. He flopped back down behind the planter. Ryan poked his nose under the bench seat that surrounded the planter. She waved and tilted her head toward where the shooter stood. She drained her soda and then tossed it in the opposite direction.

"Who's there?" the shooter shouted.

Crack! Crack!

She bolted out the window giggling like a prankster.

Ryan bolted to his feet and cracked the back of his head hard against the underside of the bench. "Fuck me!" he shouted, grabbing his head, crushing his eyes shut against the pain.

Crack!

Stone sprayed in his face. Ryan rolled back, hugging the ground. He saw her dashing down Forbes into the city. He rolled to his feet, aimed toward the grocery.

Blam! Rack. *Blam!* Rack.

"Shit!" the shooter shouted.

Ryan sprinted after the girl.

She paused, briefly looking north down Ross, and then in a blink dashed south.

"Let me help!" Ryan shouted, sucking wind, his bags beating mercilessly against his body. He hit the intersection and knew immediately why she took off. The big castle was a municipal building that was being overrun by the diseased. Police cars, emergency vehicles and National Guard trucks were drawn into a crude barricade from curb to curb. It was like a scene out of Braveheart: bloody hand-to-hand medieval combat.

Then a few creatures on the back edge saw Ryan.

In the movies zombie infections are portrayed as rotting, decaying, animated corpses dragging toward their prey. The good guys and the bad guys were obvious: if it looked like death and smelled like death, it probably should be shot in the head. But that wasn't what this apocalypse looked like. The diseased looked exactly like the businessmen they had been in life, or they looked like cops, or firefighters, or school kids, or moms in skinny jeans with the complexion to match. And it was so easy to think they were just lost and needed direction . . . until they started toward you with those singularly deadly eyes.

They staggered toward him, the faster creatures immediately separating themselves. Fast movers didn't exactly sprint, but they moved quicker than a brisk walk. Behind them were the walkers, and bringing up the rear of the ghoul train were the draggers, creatures that seemed to have some hitch in their step, some flaw in motor skills.

Ryan ran, adjusting the duffel and bags, terrified they were going to fly off his shoulders. He passed a church on the left and a sign that asked, *Need bail?*

He sagged against a car, sucking wind, looking around for the coat. *Yes! Yes! Bail me out! Bail me out!*

The fast movers closed the distance.

At the intersection of Third Street and Ross, he paused scanning. "Where did you go?"

He heard the footfalls like the sounds from his nightmare . . .

Pock . . .

　Pock . . .

　　Pock . . .

Only these were the sounds of Florsheim shoe leather slapping asphalt. The first four fast movers were thirty feet away.

Ryan saw that pink blur toward Second Street, sneaking between cars. "God, girl! How are you so fast?!" He huffed and started running, dashing between the cars and trucks that clotted the street, and the girl was nowhere to be found.

He dropped behind a truck, measuring the distance to the infected and realized they had lost him in the clutter. He duck-walked to a mural of baseball players, trying to catch his breath. He pressed his back tight against the wall and tucked himself into a corner created by a car that had jumped the curb and smashed into the wall. He fished into his jean jacket pocket and pulled out two shotgun shells and slid them into the port. Then he dug for his iPhone, praying that the GPS was working. Miracles do happen: he found himself in a moment and realized his goal was a straight shot down Boulevard of the Allies. He was sitting *under* Boulevard of the Allies, and he was maybe two blocks away.

He rose to full height straining to see, scrutinizing between cars. This girl seemed particularly sneaky and he spotted her under a truck. He took a step—

The fast movers hit the car in the front quarter panel, rocking it like a hobby horse, snapped their knees backwards as they flipped over the hood.

Two more slammed the passenger side windows with faces and hands and chests, howling menace.

"*. . . They are mean as shit!*" Builder Bob had said.

No shit!

Ryan jumped to the hood and then the roof. The car rocked and tilted. Ryan swung the butt of the shotgun and connected with a ghoul clawing across the hood. Another gripped his calf like a clamp.

He raised the shotgun but paused.

They looked so normal. So, average. Until he made eye contact.

Blam! Rack.

A businessman in a grease-stained Armani suit lost his head.

Blam! Rack

A businessman in a pressed JC Penny's suit followed him into oblivion.

Blam! Rack.

Heads vaporized.

Blam! Rack.

The shotgun hammered into Ryan's shoulder. His bags shifted, pulling his body down, tilting him toward the street. His finger hit the trigger. The recoil sent the gun butt into his cheek.

It felt like he had caught a punch from Emmanuel Pacquiao III. He staggered. The duffel fell to the ground Ryan fall to the opposite side. A ghoul flipped over the hood, legs snapping, and landed on the sidewalk at his feet, clawing unmercifully at Ryan's shins.

Blam! Rack.

Another ghoul speared through the passenger window and thrashed through the car, its face flattening into a bloody pulp in the driver's side window.

Ryan's hands shook, and he dropped shells on the ground. He fumbled two shells into the port. Four zombies surged around the trunk.

Point blank: *Blam!* Rack. *Blam!* Rack.

Bodies vaporized from the shoulders up.

The weapon ran dry, chamber empty and smoking.

He scrambled for the shells on the curb and fed them into the port.

A zombie hit him like a rugby center. The shotgun clattered away.

Ryan's training took over.

His words to Trench Coat were accurate: he didn't like the pain after taking a beating, but the brilliance of the Brazilian jiu-jitsu system developed by Hélio Gracie is in its simplicity and physical economy. Most fights go to grappling and then to ground within seconds. Hélio developed the system to compensate for his physical weakness by maximizing leverage, which meant even though Ryan was far out of BOHMeC compliance and hadn't entered a dojo in years, he could execute the techniques.

Ryan let the collision roll him to his back, getting his feet on the zombie's hips like he was going to play airplane with Xyla, then he braced his forearms under its throat. At the peak of the roll, Ryan kicked hard using the momentum to send the man flying. The man flipped high and crashed butt first into a windshield. Ryan finished the back somersault and rolled hard into the knees of the next ghoul like he was doing a forbidden football roll block, dropping it to the ground.

Ryan drew the Glock holster, planted a foot hard into zombie's chest, and pulled the trigger; brain matter splattered at the mural baseball player's feet.

An infected teenager tore around the trunk. Ryan took a hard step, kicked him into the rear door and punched the Glock at the forehead and pulled the trigger.

Ryan rummaged at his hip to get the Glock back into its holster and spun for the shotgun. Adrenaline made his muscles thrum like a high-tension wire as he dug through his jean jacket for the last of his shotgun shells.

He slammed his back against the mural, muzzle forward, ready to put metal on meat. The street was silent, but his heart roared in his chest and blood thumped in his ears.

And there she was, her blonde hair glinted off a small sliver of sunlight, then slashed down into the gloom under the overpass superstructure. She had been watching the whole time.

Then she turned and ran.

"Hey! Come back!" Ryan shouted.

She was running from a roving band of thugs dressed in orange jumpers out to plunder and kill. They had been drawn to the gunfire. They were coming toward Ryan. They were shooting.

Ryan crouched.

". . . *no one else can come . . .*"

Ryan checked the time on his phone—12:18.

". . . *Your life and your death . . .*"

And her life and her death.

". . . *Come prepared to leave forever . . .*"

Then he saw the third wave trundling forward. They weren't moving as fast, but their numbers were greater than the average football team.

"I'm so sorry. Be safe." He scooted across the car hood, grabbed his bag from the ground, and sprinted west down Court Place past an ivy-grown wall with a picture of a baseball jersey with the number 409. He hit speed dial for one each number in turn. On the third call he got voice mail. "Daniel Ryder, this is Ryan Sage. If you get this, I'm coming! I'm coming!"

27

Global Infection: ≤ 27.62099%

Remember; no matter how desperate the situation seems,
time spent thinking clearly is never time wasted.
> —MAX BROOKS,
> THE ZOMBIE SURVIVAL GUIDE

He was standing in front of a tower at the south edge of the city, and it felt like he was standing at the edge of the world. Now that he was at the right address Ryan realized he had walked past the location a few times during his extended stay in Pittsburgh. The tower was impossible to miss, rising on south side of the city like a sparkling jewel, ensconced above the street level on four levels of beautiful granite terracing, lined with planters and trees and covered pavilions. City buses had a pull through and a premium bus stop right on Smithfield. It was big and beautiful and almost homey. Inside looked safe and inviting.

There was only one problem. The building was closed. Not just locked but fully dark with premium metal security gates drawn down tight like it had been abandoned for the apocalypse. Ryan circled the south and west sides of the building, dashing between cars and hiding behind trucks trying to find a way to the interior.

The south Fort Pitt Boulevard side of the building was nothing but smooth granite façade three stories high. The west Wood Street side was the same monolithic stone construction. The north side sign said First Avenue to mark the passage that led behind the building, but the street looked like an alley—narrow, cramped and hunkering under the tower's forbidding bulk. He saw access to a parking garage, loading docks and rear security doors, but Ryan heard movement: a furtive skittering in the shadows that he was powerfully motivated to avoid.

He retraced his steps through the endless clutter of cars and garbage to Smithfield and pressed his face against the tinted glass, trying to look deep into the complex. On one side he could make out a security desk and a bank of elevators. On the other side was a wide mezzanine that held two retail levels. The bottom floor had a sign for a chain grocery. A plywood barrier with the chain's fashionable mural still firmly covered the entrance that said, "Coming Soon."

Not a living soul anywhere.

"Okay, that was a bad joke," Ryan mumbled.

His detour to help the girl had cost him. It was 12:36 when he got to the tower. And it was looking like 12:15 meant 12:15 today.

"Am I sure this is the right address?"

He verified the building number one more time.

He checked the e-mail for the fifth time and then scanned the streets looking for infected or the roving gangs that might decide to shoot him on general principle.

Nope . . . I'm in the right spot.

"Well, late was late," Ryan said to himself. The calls and the e-mails that he was coming, notwithstanding, the time frame said 12:15. He had gambled and lost. Ryan ran his hands through his hair, pulling tight.

First Avenue didn't look any more inviting from the east side. The corner of Smithfield and Boulevard of the Allies was a high-rise construction site surrounded by Alaska barriers—twenty-foot-tall Jersey walls—and on the First Avenue side barricaded off behind contractor trailers and oceangoing shipping containers. The job site looked like a lot of places for bad things to lurk in.

"Damn it!"

The only doors—other than the front entrance—were far down First Avenue among the haphazardly parked cars.

"I do not want to go down there."

He hid behind a massive round stone column—one of four—that supported the front façade. Knocking was an absurd exercise, but he did it anyway. He might as well have been hitting a bank vault.

Ryan's anxiety rose. He was going to have to return to the minimart. He was going to have to fight his way back.

The distance was a mere mile-and-a-half, but it might as well have been across a state. He calculated how long he could sustain a run. He could make it to the Toyota, maybe.

Ryan adjusted his bags; ammunition and guns were heavy. He fiddled with the holster on his hip. The Glock chaffed miserably at his side. He wondered how cops managed it. He wasn't even that fond of donuts, but his muffin top was resenting the constant prodding.

He topped off the magazine and maxed out the shotgun, psyching himself up for the trip back. Then Ryan spied the intercom to the far left of the entrance. He moved between columns like he was the Grinch stealing Christmas in Whoville until he got to the door. Ideally, there would be a security person on the other end of the com. But when he tried the door to enter the vestibule, it was locked.

"What good is a com system if no one can get to the button?"

He heard a sound and his head snapped around. Ryan scanned Smith-field between the cars and trucks; then his attention shifted toward the Monongahela River to the sounds of fighting. To the south, beyond the rail-road tracks, past a train station that had been converted into a strip mall, people were in a pitched battle: shooting and screams rolled over the water and the fighting looked to be coming across the Smithfield Bridge.

It was time to go.

He took a step and stopped: a zombie trundling around the corner at Fort Pitt Boulevard turned toward him.

Shit!

He dropped behind a large stone planter filled with evergreen bushes.

He tried to thumb a shell into the shotgun and then realized he'd already loaded it. The zombie climbed up the terrace's first level, stumbling through the maze of abandoned cars.

"Fuck it!" Ryan rose, jammed the stock into his shoulder, making a point to weld his cheek to the butt stock. He pulled the trigger. The head vapor-ized, the body dropped. Ryan thumbed a shell into the port and retreated back behind the stone planters.

"Okay, one trip down the alley," Ryan said, still trying to get motivated. He did his Grinch imitation again from pillar to pillar. He was about to jump down a terrace level when he heard a voice.

"*Amigo! Amigo!* Ryan Sage *es tu?*" The speaker was a rangy South American, tall by those standards, with the patrician look of Spanish conquistadores. He was holding the business end of an AK-47 in Ryan's general direction. He bristled guns like a porcupine—his rifle clipped into a harness at his shoulder, a handgun on each thigh strapped into a tactical holster, another handgun in a cross draw holster at his left hip and the butt of shotgun visible over his shoulder.

It was just a hunch, but Ryan was sure this man could use all of them very well.

"Yes, I'm here to find Daniel Ryder."

"That bag? What *es* in?"

"Well, pretty much what you have all over you—guns and some personal stuff. I wasn't sure what would happen today. I didn't want to get caught out here without a way to fight back."

"Did you?"

"Did I what?"

"Fight to get here." He pointed his chin towards the blood spatter on his pant leg.

Ryan saw more zombies coming. They had been drawn by the shotgun blast. "Uh . . . this is not really a good place for chitchat, but yeah, I killed one just at the bottom of the terrace and a couple of them a couple blocks away. And I expect that is the bunch that was chasing me. Could we do this inside?"

"Have you the bite?"

"Uh, no, I'm not. And since you are holding that big gun, I'm guessing you will be able to look all you want. And if I am bit, you can kill me. But could you maybe kill me inside?"

The man's eyes focused to hard points, and he raised his rifle to his shoulder. "Don't move!" the man said, then he hunched, walking in a crouch. He advanced.

"Hey, I'm not bit. I'm not—" Ryan froze, unnerved as the man shot at him. *Crack, crack . . . crack, crack, crack, crack.*

The reports crashed off the stone exterior and echoed around the street like thunder, the weapon's overpressure rippling past Ryan's head in waves. Ryan turned in time to see the two heads explode and mangled ghoul bodies toppled to the asphalt. South American Rambo took three more strides and made eight more shots. Satisfied with his handiwork, in that same hunched bent-knee walk, he backpedaled to the door.

Ryan stood rooted to the ground. There are two fears that are said to be built deep into man's bones: fear of falling and fear of very loud noises. And at the moment, the loud noise startled Ryan down to his toes. His legs shook from the power of the muzzle blast ripping by his body.

"Si *vamos rápido! Inside!*" he said.

Ryan's panic gave way to anger. "Look, don't do that shit again. I get it. You are the guy with the gun, but that wasn't right. I need more than 'don't move' when bullets start coming my direction." Ryan turned and looked. The man had dropped all the zombies coming up the terrace. "And on the more pleasant side, Good shooting."

"*De nada!*" the man said with a wry smile. "Safe your weapon."

"Safe my weapon?" Ryan asked, confused.

The man raised a brow. "Put your weapon on safe."

"Oh right." Ryan fumbled with the button but eventually clicked it home and moved through the door.

The door closing was the sound of security, the sound of safety, the sound of being able to relax. In an instant, Ryan felt days of stress flood out of his body.

South American Rambo flashed a badge and the electric locks engaged, followed by a metal gate that rolled down until it locked into the floor. "Stand there," he said, pointing with his weapon about twenty feet away. "And lay your bags down. Start taking off your shirt and pants."

"And you haven't even bought me dinner."

South American Rambo smirked.

"Do you have a name?" Ryan asked as he shed sweat-soaked clothes.

"Raphael."

"Well, Raphael, this is all of me." He spun in a circle standing in his undies.

"Yes. Good. Get dressed." Raphael walked over to the security desk looking at the console. "You did not fill your drawers today fighting the demons?"

"Oh, I did," Ryan said, digging through his backpack. He didn't want to put on his sweaty clothes again. And suddenly he felt like someone opened up a faucet and drained all his energy out. "I just changed in the phone booth on the corner before I came to the door."

Raphael gave a sardonic smile as he watched something on the security monitors. "Did you fight one of the demons with your fists?"

"What? No." Ryan shrugged into a dry shirt.

He pointed with his chin again. "You have bruises all over your hands."

"Oh. Yeah, I have been building for the last few days. It has been a while since I have built a castle."

"And what happened to your face," Raphael said, nodding toward Ryan's cheek.

"I got in a fight with a shotgun."

Raphael looked up from the monitors, his brow wrinkled hard. "*Que?*"

"Butt stock, trigger, recoil. *Bang!*" Ryan said, pointing to his cheek like it was obvious.

Raphael smiled like he was listening to a toddler. "*Es tu loco,*" he said, glancing back down to the monitors. "So you are a carpenter?"

"When I was younger, on and off for about a decade I was in construction." He stepped into a pair of jeans, fussing that he had not been able to find that third pair. He might only have a few pairs for the rest of his life. Maybe it would have been important to find them.

"What did you build?"

"Oh, everything from homes to high-rise towers. Well, I did the metal framing and drywall and cabling for data."

"You built one of these?" he said, waving expansively.

"No, I just worked on jobsites that happened to be high-rises."

"I see," Raphael said like he had just caught him in a lie. "It is not so easy to build something like this."

"That must mean that you did build this. I thought you were security."

"Why did you think I was security?" he said, motioning for Ryan to get on the elevator.

Ryan gave him a shit-for-brains look. "Maybe it was the El Cid imitation," nodding at the arsenal draped around his body.

"You know of El Cid? That *es* good. Do I make a good El Cid?"

28

Global Infection: ≤ 27.6301%

I always thought of the zombies as being about revolution, one generation consuming the next.

—George A. Romero

"Mr. Sage? Mr. Sage?" the secretary said. "Mr. Ryder will see you now." Ryan was slouched on a couch, his bags piled around him in an outside room that was acting as a receptionist area. He vaguely remembered the secretary's name was Mora, but the other details escaped him. When Ryan fell asleep, it always took his mind forever to reattach.

Slowly the details resurfaced: the brisk elevator ride to the penthouse, yawning to adjust for air pressure, Raphael leading him into the penthouse vestibule and seeing the massive chandelier that hung high above. He remembered seeing a half-dozen unfamiliar faces as he was led through endless rooms, including Mora's pleasant smile, like a grandmother who is glad to see one of her brood come home safe.

Ryan got his feet under him, grunting under the weight of the bags, feeling afresh the ongoing burning sensation of taxed muscles. He paused just inside Daniel's office door. "So this is how a greedy capitalist pig lives," Ryan said, trying for irony, but it came out like he was stoned. He moved into the room, and his bags slid awkwardly off his shoulder. He struggled to get them lowered into a chair. "Sorry. You said come as if I was leaving forever."

"Yes. Yes, of course, welcome," Daniel said, rising from behind an L-shaped, wide gray, laminate desk. He came around and shook Ryan's spare hand. "We were worried when we couldn't get ahold of you, but when we saw the e-mail . . ." He raised his hands expansively. "So what do you think?"

Ryan looked around the office, nodding his appreciation.

The penthouse beyond the office was a statement of opulence—the chandelier hanging high in the foyer's vaulted ceiling probably cost as much as a house and museum-quality paintings lining the walls. But Daniel Ryder's office was a testimony to executive functionality and almost Spartan in its utilitarian contrast. In place of lavish decoration, the office walls were lined with high definition monitors constantly feeding images from across the globe. The tickers of sixty-one of the world's stock exchanges slid across two screens, over half read closed. Silent newscasts from continents thousands of miles distant showed roving bands of attacking, rioting mobs. Four screens showed nothing but snow, their signals killed at the source.

"Impressive," Ryan said, "I'm sorry I'm not more eloquent, but my brain isn't back online. I fell asleep in the outer office."

"I'm glad you could be so comfortable." He returned to his ergonomic chair and slid from one fax machine and then another to gather incoming transmissions, and then back to his central position behind the desk. He looked like the captain of a starship surrounded by displays and conference phone carousel, as well as a video camera for conferencing. "Raphael said you fought to get here. Was it bad out there?"

Ryan laid his shotgun on the far side of the desk near some covered boxes and untangled the rest of his bags. His shoulder was throbbing from the relentless beating of the shotgun's kick. "Sorry, didn't mean to intrude. Just wasn't sure where to put the gun. And yes, it is bad out there."

"Well, I'm also sorry that I couldn't get to you sooner."

"I guess it worked out. It sure does feel a lot safer in here. I can't tell you how good that feels."

"And to answer your question, no," Daniel said with a smile.

Ryan shook his head, hoping the last of the molasses would finally loosen up between his ears. "I'm sorry. What? My question?"

"The penthouse is my son's idea of how the greedy capitalist pigs live. He is a student of Che Guevara."

"Oh, I was hoping you hadn't heard that. I was going for satire, but I thought my timing was off."

"Yes, I got the satire," Daniel said. All three fax machines were spitting out more documents, phones trilled quietly, and computers chimed an electronic alert every few seconds. "My son, Richard, handed an interior designer his checkbook, and this was how they thought the rich live. So how do you think they did?"

"How to explain? It is beautiful. But honestly, I'd rather have that desk than that chandelier out front."

"How do you think this desk got in here?" Daniel laughed. "Maybe Firouz was right. You are my son."

"Speaking of Firouz, do you know where he and his family went? I'm worried. They left in a rush. I went to their house and no one is there."

"He and his family are here in the tower. They are staying in one of the apartments on the lower floors. They are safe."

"Here? Really? That is great."

"It broke his heart to tell you goodbye. He wanted to tell you where he was going, but I forbid any discussion for anyone coming here, even though I understand he did call you." Daniel shrugged. "Well, he has a big heart. And he didn't tell you exactly where he was going, so there was no real harm. It would have broken my heart to refuse him and his family if they had not heeded my warnings. Speaking of which, I am glad you showed up by yourself. I was serious in my e-mail. Had you shown up with anyone else, I would have not let you in the door."

"Yeah. Well, I guess it worked out. There was this young girl on the street I was going to help but . . . she's gone."

"She died while you were coming?"

Ryan shook his head. "No, I don't know. It doesn't matter now. I guess there really is no way to help her."

"No, no, there isn't," Daniel said firmly. "But you should know that Ahou has not let me rest, asking to bring you here. Actually, if I had known how much of an impression you made on her, I wouldn't have—" He stopped himself. "There is limited space, so I have to be very selective about whom I invite."

"But this place is huge. What could one more person matter?"

"No, we are not staying here."

Ryan's brain was finally firing on all cylinders. "I see. So someone recently lost their spot and that made room for me?"

"Yes, that is correct."

"Who was it?"

"You wouldn't know him." Daniel's eyes started to mist over. "Anyway, Firouz is sure that God is watching over you and He must be. You survived what is going on out there by yourself."

"God is watching you over," Ryan corrected with a fair imitation of Firouz's Middle Eastern lilt. "But I don't know what to say. Mostly because I don't know what this is all about."

"Ryan Sage," Daniel said very sober, "this is about the end of the world."

"Oh, that's all?"

"That was a bit dramatic, but it was not an overstatement. Tell you what. You haven't had a tour. Why don't I show you around while we talk? Not too many more humans are going to get the privilege of seeing this building. I am sad about that, because it is impressive. At least what we tried to do, but now . . ." he shrugged, the melancholy suddenly resting on his shoulders.

"What *we* tried to do? Who is we?"

Daniel stood and regarded Ryan. "This was one of the things that caught my attention the other day in the shop. Not just that you didn't know who I was, but that you didn't care to know. Anonymity is very rare for me, particularly locally. And I have given out thousands and thousands of business cards in my lifetime, but you are the only one in recent memory who never used that card to call me for a favor."

"Ahou mentioned that you were someone important."

"She told me what you said." Daniel laughed. "Truly classic. I have met few men so sure of their own value."

"Celebrity doesn't impress me."

"Have you heard of the Molitor Group?"

Ryan's eyes went up to the right, considering. "Oh, I guess I heard about the company some years ago. What was it? It was some massive construction project in Myanmar, and American contractors were captured by a local despot. I vaguely remember it was an international incident. I don't remember the outcome. Something about the contractor's rescue is significant, but I can't remember what. Are you saying you are part of the Molitor Group?"

"I own it."

Ryan's eyes narrowed. "Didn't the Molitor Group work with Elf Aquitaine to expand the Panama Canal?"

Daniel started walking through the outer offices. "Yes, that is correct. Elf is, of course, an oil company. But it chose to expand its operations to the recovery of rare earth elements. There are some similarities between deep sea oil recovery and the collection of these elements. The Pacific Ocean is full of rare earth elements. To decrease production costs, Elf decided to approach the Panama government for a joint venture to build a new canal that would allow for the passage of the largest oceangoing vessels. We were the general contractor."

Ryan rubbed his chin. He was starting to get the picture. This man, who had hung on Ryan's shoulder like a clingy lover ogling his iGlass, was very, very rich. "So you build canals?"

"The Molitor Group builds everything everywhere, but our focus is on energy production. We are competitors to Halliburton-Cheliston, Exxon Mobil, and dozens of others, but we are partners to most all the world's energy producers in development projects."

"You really are a greedy capitalist pig," Ryan laughed. "I guess I'm glad you have a good sense of humor. Not a great way to insult a multimillionaire."

"I passed the millionaire stage over thirty years ago. If I were worried about being called names for how much money I had, I would have taken the insurance job my father wanted me to take."

The number past a million started with a B. Ryan raised a brow. "Okay, so I called a very rich man who has been very successful an idiot."

"Would it have made a difference if you knew?" Daniel said, scrutinizing.

"Knowing about the money wouldn't have mattered. The Stepfords had millions, and I was still fond of calling them idiots. And Bexley . . . well, he loved my sister, and that is why I tolerated him, but that hardly stopped me from writing scathing reviews of the insanity he proposed. I was commenting on the success. The Stepfords did not produce. They were merely rich enough that the money was able to overcome their idiocy. You produce. Your success in production is simply measured by a ledger sheet, but that wealth is just a representation of how much of an idiot you are *not*."

"Yes, good answer. But I wasn't being deprecating in Firouz's shop. I *was* being an idiot."

"Okay. So I am totally outclassed here. What could I possibly have that you want?"

"I have paid men to call me an idiot when I'm being one. But after I find the talent and pay them for a while, somehow that skill magically vanishes."

"You are offering me a job, on the eve of the apocalypse, to tell you that the emperor doesn't have any clothes?"

Daniel laughed, spontaneous and hard. "My wife already has that job, and she is much, much prettier than you."

"But grey hair is so adorable," Ryan said, tossing his hair and smiling.

"I'm not that kinda guy, sailor."

"So, what *can* I do for you?"

Daniel stepped into a room with more world class paintings and wing back chairs. "No, this is about what you have already done. I am not sure there are words for what you have done."

A man dressed in the tactical gear like SWAT knocked softly at the door. He had an automatic weapon snapped into a sling, a vest full of ammunition and a gun tied down to his right leg. "Dan? Mora said you walked this way." he said. "You have a second?"

"Yes, Rick."

"I really hate to ask you about this, but what's her name . . ." he shook his head, trying to remember. "The good-looking Middle Eastern woman; her fiancé is driving everyone nuts looking for her."

"Do you mean Ahou?"

"Yes, her fiancé insists that she has left the building. He's demanding that we go back out on the street and look for her."

Ahou has a fiancé? Waves of emotion rolled through Ryan's soul, and the first shimmering ripples of cold air blew across the mirage.

Daniel wrinkled his brow. "I do not understand what that girl saw in him," he muttered as he walked to the wall and jabbed three buttons on the speakerphone. "Raphael, are you close?"

"Yes."

"Could you come to my office in five minutes, please?"

"*Un momento.*"

Daniel started backtracking through the penthouse. "Rick, she didn't go back outside. The tower is locked down tight."

"I told him she was probably just around somewhere. The tower is huge, lots of places she could be hiding. But he is a royal pain in the ass. And we don't really have time to deal with the drama."

"Speaking of more important things," Daniel said, striding back into his office. "Have you heard from the ground team? They are clear about hitchhikers, right? They understand that our numbers are exact."

Rick checked his watch. "They should be arriving shortly. But they did mention a potential problem."

"A proble—"

"Daniel," Raphael said, striding into the room, still decked out in his array of weapons. He smiled at Rick then nodded at Ryan.

"You know Sven, yes?" Daniel replied.

Raphael let his eyes narrow and his mouth turned down.

"He is looking for Ahou."

"Again?" Raphael said. "How does a man lose his woman so much?"

"Needs to put a leash on her," said Rick.

"Raphael, is it possible that she has exited the tower?"

Raphael let his mouth turn down again and shook his head. "Everything *es* locked down. She *es* not on the street. But I think I know where she went. She asked me for pass card to the roof this morning. She said she wanted to see the sun."

"Why not just go out to the tenant escape?" Daniel asked with an edge.

Raphael's brow raised in a sardonic arch. "She *es* wanting to be *alone*."

"Oh right. What am I even saying?" Daniel said, "Rick, would you be so kind to take a look on the roof, please? And once you find her, make sure that she and Sven know this is the last time my security team spends one more second playing hide and seek."

"I'll give her a medal if she went up there to jump and get away from this guy," said Rick. He turned and put his hand on Raphael's shoulder. "Raff, by the way, I heard about Leona. She is the best. I'm sure she will be all right."

Raphael gave a grim smile, nodded, and checked his watch. "The helicopter *es* still two hours out?"

"Bret will call on the satellite phone if there is a problem," Daniel said.

Rick punched Raphael's shoulder in the universal sign of brotherly solidarity. "Bret is the best. He got us all in and out of Paraguay. He can certainly handle a cold extraction from Perry, Florida."

"Yes, Bret *es* an excellent pilot," Raphael said, "and she has Timoteo and Lucas with her."

Rick gave a knowing smile. "Your boy can shoot. The infected do not have a chance."

"Yes, thank you."

"All right, I'm off to play cupid," Rick said.

"And Rick," said Daniel, "When the ground team gets here, make sure they use the underground dock. Let's not leave the Strykers on the street. I don't want someone using them to blow a hole in this building after we're gone.'

"Already done, Dan."

"And that problem the ground team mentioned?"

Rick just raised a brow.

Daniel paused, chewing the inside of his lip. "The problem's name isn't Richard, is it?"

29

Global Infection: ≤ 27.63226%

A scrutiny so minute as to bring an object under an untrue angle of vision is a poorer guide to a man's judgment than a sweeping glance which sees things in their true proportion.
—A.W. Kinglake

"Sorry you had to be a part of that," Daniel said, "It is a stressful time for everyone. Did you know that Ahou had a fiancé?"

Ryan shook his head. "Uh . . . no, but I'm not sure I knew Ahou all that well."

Daniel appraised Ryan and then gave a magnanimous nod. "Let's get out of this office so we can hide and talk. Mora is a great watchdog, but she is a bit overwhelmed right now. Raphael, you want to come on the tour with us? You know this building better than I."

Raphael hesitated.

"You don't have anything else to do," Daniel prompted.

"I have a few things to check still," Raphael said with a smile, but his eyes were haunted. "I meet you in the restaurant? You love showing it. You will be there for a while." With a nod of his head, Raphael turned and left.

Daniel said, "Leona would hurt him if she knew he was worrying."

"Leona, is his wife? And she would be mad if her husband was worried? You realize that to the average person what you just said sounds backwards?"

"Yes, I suppose it does. How to describe Leona Paguero? Do you remember that actress from some years ago? What was her name? Catherine something?"

"The woman who played in those old Zorro movies?"

"Yes. Picture her, and then blend that with a Navy SEAL."

"Are you talking about a comic book character?"

Daniel laughed. "A comic book heroine who actually kills all the villains."

Ryan raised a brow. He still didn't get how that affected Raphael's worry for his wife, but it didn't matter.

Ahou has a fiancé. Bullshit!

The woman he Skyped with just a couple of days ago was no more planning to marry a man than Ryan would be. Plus, they had connected in a way that Ryan rarely experienced. He felt cheated. Ryan said, "So Raphael's wife is caught out in the insanity?"

"Yes, Leona has . . . well, had a brother who was in a hospital in Miami. She has their two remaining sons with her, Timoteo and Lucas. They used to live here in Pittsburgh, of course, but her brother had to remain in the Miami hospital. There was some family drama, so she decided to take her two boys with her for school. The school system was better in Florida. Raphael stayed with me here to finish up this project."

"Remaining sons? What happened to the other two?"

"Marco, their oldest, was in the Army. He is no longer with us. And a month or so ago, their son, Simone, was bit by someone who went crazy at school. Well, I should say there was some drama between Leona and Simone. And to keep his mother from killing him, he got shipped back to Pittsburgh to stay with Raphael. Simone is Raphael's wild child, and after he got bit at school, he had it in his head that it was the zombie apocalypse. Simone decided that he was sure he would turn into a zombie and bite his father. He ran away from home and hasn't been seen since."

"What made him think of that? The relationship between biting and the outbreak and the violence only came out recently. You were there the day I put part of that equation together. How did he get that idea?"

"Yes, I was there when you put that together. Actually, Simone's circumstance is one of the reasons I thought there was something to what you said. Like I said, Simone is a real hellion. Hard-headed kid, really smart, capable, resourceful, but can't seem to act with any sense, and a total smartass. Who knows why he thought that? No one took it seriously when he first started talking about zombies. Anyone who heard him just thought it was one more event in a long list of crazy behavior. And when he ran away, Raphael about lost his mind trying to find him." Daniel shrugged, "No one knew what to do about it. The terrible part of it is . . . he was right. After I talked to you, I made inquiries about the person that bit Simone. And he had fallen into a full-fledged case of African Rabies."

"Two sons dead?"

"Yes," Daniel said, "and it gets worse. We tried to make arrangements to pull Leona and his sons out of Miami. But we had to push it back. Private jet travel is impossible into Florida. Actually, it is almost impossible all over the East Coast. The Molitor Group's air fleet is large and has been running almost nonstop for the last three days. It is a huge logistical undertaking to get everyone to safety. Fortunately, most of the logistics in the

United States is being done in the heartland. I had to send ground teams in Strykers to get my family in the Northeast. Leona is trying to sprint out of Florida before she gets locked in with ocean on all three sides and the infected everywhere else."

"Why was her brother in the hospital?"

"Her brother was a political prisoner in Paraguay. They used him to get to her; to silence her political comments about the dictatorship of Gaspar José de Francia. They tortured him—"

The office phone started to ring.

Daniel sighed. "Anyway, we have to move, or I'll never get out of here." He pointed to an adjacent doorway and officially began his tour in a world-class security and communications room. It was obvious he had given the spiel before, and it was obvious that he was proud. Daniel called the offices "makeshift" because he had taken over a sub-suite of five rooms that had formerly been living quarters for guests. He had "thrown something together" so he could work out of the Renaissance Tower.

But Daniel Ryder's definition of "throwing something together" was an integrated security system with displays and monitoring systems that fed to this central location from all over the world. From this security office, Daniel could talk to anyone anywhere on the planet. It was as good as being in his office in the Republic of Texas or its counterpart in Dubai. It was all connected by redundant systems on the ground and via satellite uplink—a satellite he owned.

Ryan chuckled as he looked around at the monitors showing images from all over the Renaissance Tower and from dozens of cameras from buildings scattered around six countries. It was an endless stream of blinking information on state-of-the-art displays.

"What is funny?" Daniel asked.

"I have a good carrier?'" Ryan said with a fair imitation of Daniel's dismissal in the sandwich shop. "That was masterful understatement."

"How am I supposed to explain that I own my own communications satellite?"

"Just pointing out the irony."

The tour continued out through the security room's secondary door— an exit that did not require interrupting Daniel in his office—and moved through the penthouse. Two floors had been built within the whole thirtieth floor shell. It was big and bigger and then bigger still. The lower floor was living suites and kitchens and formal dining rooms, family dining rooms, housekeeping utility rooms, game areas and entertainment rooms, and lounges and spas, two fully stocked bars and a list of rooms with names that only belong in a thesaurus. The second floor was more suites and more of the same for the three full families that might choose to remain in the privacy of their own areas.

The penthouse was what one would expect of something called a penthouse and decorated by someone interested in a magazine cover. And there *was* a periodical with a full spread pictorial. The magazine was dedicated to capturing the lifestyles of the rich and fabulous.

The publication described the kitchens as ". . . able to handle the most demanding culinary needs while supplying the wholesome closeness of a family eating their morning breakfast in the quaint family kitchen." This was like calling Tutankhamun's tomb quaint because it didn't have the panache of the Great Pyramid.

The view from the living room and the bedrooms—and one other room that had a fancy name for *yet more space*—was breathtaking, even though it was merely overlooking a Midwestern city. The visibility to the south and west extended for miles. But today Ryan and Daniel's attention was drawn back to the streets below like a train wreck on TV, a distant disaster from which it was almost impossible to look away.

"So Strykers? Did I hear that right?" Ryan said, breaking the silence. "You mentioned using them to get your family out of the Northeast. Like as in those machines the military uses?"

"Yes, the combat personnel carriers," Daniel said, leading the way out of the penthouse to the elevators. "They are armored troop transport vehicles," He placed his hand over a biometric scanner on the elevator reader. He punched the eighth floor. "Just a little something I was able to pick up," he said, his tone contrite.

"Did you just apologize for being able to buy Stryker's?"

"That is how that sounded, didn't it?"

"If it were me, I'd be on the radio talking about how awesome it was to be able to save my family."

"It is a habit cultivated in a lifetime of public conciliation. Rich people are not supposed to let on that they are rich."

"Yeah, I get it. And maybe it isn't a good idea to tell everyone," Ryan said, feeling the elevator bounce softly to a stop, "but I'd stop apologizing for a good thing. You've earned it."

"I knew there was a reason I liked you," Daniel said, as he led the way from the penthouse express elevator to the general building elevators, placed his palm on the bio scanner and pressed 29. "Yes, many people who are near and dear to me will live out the month and very likely all of their natural lives because of my success. I think I'm done pretending that isn't a good thing." They exited the elevator into a dim hallway, but in two steps the motion detectors triggered the lights.

"Did you have to get a permit or something to buy those vehicles?"

"No, not the vehicles. I did have to be creative to obtain the weapons systems that go with each Stryker, but the vehicles were available to anyone with the money. I bought the infantry carrier vehicles and the engineering version, and the command version for my overseas operations to defend against whatever Marxist guerrillas were trying to wage a revolution at the moment."

"I'm not familiar enough with the variations to recognize the distinctions."

"The personnel carriers are just what they sound like. They carry people. The engineering version is built heavier and it looks like it has a plow blade on the front, and it is designed for tearing down barricades and dealing with bombs. The command vehicle has communications. Anyway, when I heard the drumbeat of Marxist revolution growing within the U.S. borders some years ago, and since I knew that this drumbeat would most likely become the song of the People's Revolution, I bought a fleet and stationed them here.

"I have been in four countries that have fallen into Marxist revolution and two that fell into Islamic revolution. Each time, I used the vehicles to get my people out in the midst of the fighting. I thought it foolish to assume both of those militant movements couldn't start hostilities within U.S. borders. That preparation from years ago is how I am getting my family to safety today."

The restaurant was called *Mon Pierre's*. Daniel used a badge to unlock the doors then spoke into his phone. "Restaurant. Lights." A moment later, recessed LED lights came on in the walking areas. "My son has affection for French food," Daniel said, nodding at the sign, "but the restaurant is American bistro. The idea was to provide concierge dining to all building residents and business tenants. The restaurant was, well, it is stocked for just about anything one could want. Give them a recipe and they will make it. They were staffed 24/7. Even with the building only about one quarter rented, both residential and commercial, the restaurant already had a staff of forty. The food was very good, reasonably priced, and the reputation was growing. We gave the public an express elevator to protect the privacy of the residential tenants and made the restaurant open to the public for lunch and dinner. After hours, all tenants of the building could come here and hang out all night if they chose."

"Impressive, but a little dark. How come we can't see out of the windows?"

"One second," Daniel said with a sly smile and spoke into his phone again. "Restaurant, dining room windows—open." Immediately, the dining room began to glow pleasantly. Then shutters slid down the windows, letting crisp spring sunlight spill within. The restaurant was built with a triple tier of tables like a sports stadium where every customer had a brilliant view of the southern skyline.

"You can control this whole tower from that phone?"

Daniel smiled and nodded. "It's a proprietary app created for the standard smartphone. The phones are connected via a cell tower on top of the building and then authenticated against the building network. The app is graphic interface or voice command. Once you understand the command structure, all automated functions can be done by smartphone."

"Sounds like a recipe for a security breach."

"Trust me. We have done this before," Daniel said, and then continued his tour. "Many people came to eat, loved it, and then want to come live in the tower. This restaurant was our leading marketing effort. The Renaissance Tower was not officially open for leasing, but we were making exceptions as a trial run for building function, testing, and the thousand and one punch list details that a building of this size inevitably has. Raphael, the South American man that you met, the one who brought you up from the streets, I've known him and his wife for over twenty years, since they escaped the jungles of Paraguay. He has been my right-hand man for over a decade and is overseeing the final stages of this project.

"I thought he was security at first. He wears guns like they are grafted into his body."

"You should see him in combat. But no, he has a master's in mechanical and electrical engineering and is an exceptional project manager. We had some problems with this venture, and we both had to step in and get things done."

"So you put storm shutters over the restaurant windows? Did you have problems with the window leaking or something?"

Daniel laughed. "Sort of. That glass is almost stronger than steel and a joint product between my design team and Pittsburgh Plate Glass. PPG are those buildings made of all glass a couple blocks over. You have seen the campus I expect?"

Ryan shrugged. "My trips to Pittsburgh have been very short on sightseeing. I think I actually noticed the buildings two nights ago in the skyline."

"We were leaking, but not water. We were leaking money. The Renaissance Tower building is a serious experiment in energy conservation and alternative energy production: solar and wind. The goal was to be able to identify all energy leaks and then manage all systems to the ampere. The secondary goal was building sustainable energy production into the structure. The shutters are a combination of insulation and photoelectric conversion panel."

"Really? A building run off of solar power?"

Daniel shook his head. "Oh no, not even close. The energy business is tied to what is called the Four Imperatives: power density, energy density, cost, and scale. No matter everyone's love affair with alternative energy, realities are what they are. Physics is physics. And people often misunderstand the difference between energy and power. How did you do in high school physics?"

"Dare I admit I didn't take it?"

"You are like most graduates of the government education system. And poor education is largely the reason we have so much social conflict over alternative energy solutions and totally erroneous public policy. But even if you didn't take high school physics, I am sure you will understand some basic physics. Energy is the ability to do work. Power is rate of production. So, to do work, one must deliver power. The kind of work you want to do determines the power demand. If the work is carrying a sock to the dresser, the delivery of power is a rather simple engineering problem where the power density is your body mass index, the energy density is a Snickers bar, and the cost is two dollars at the vending machine, and the scale is once a month."

Ryan smiled. "That is pretty clever. I'm guessing you have been talking to sixth graders."

"Well, grandpa has to answer his granddaughters when they ask, 'What do you do?' But in actual fact, I had to give that same speech to my middle granddaughter's high school science teacher. That idiot couldn't fathom that the world didn't magically run off the sun."

"So I'm guessing that energy density is the hurdle for powering this building?"

"Well, I'm trying to explain some complex relationships between energy and power and the factors that impact something we take for granted, like turning on the lights.

"First, we have to harness a power source. Power density is the measure of harnessed energy from a given area or mass. For instance, the average nuclear power plant is roughly the size of a bathroom. But even if we add the footprint of the containment structures, we are still talking about a space of maybe a square kilometer, and it generates 10,500 gigawatts of electricity a year.

"This isn't an exact comparison, because there are so many variables that affect photovoltaic production. But for example, the Nellis Solar Power Plant in Nevada uses 140 acres and 72,000 solar panels to produce 1.4 gigawatts a year. One square kilometer equals about 250 acres. Even if we doubled the numbers to equal the same square kilometer nuclear power footprint to 144,000 solar panels and 2.8 gigawatts, to get the same power production of a nuclear power plant would require over 200 square kilometers and almost 29 million solar panels. The cost to produce the panels alone is hideously expensive. And even with the recent advances in technology that boost photovoltaic production to over 24 percent from roughly 18 percent, solar panels are still very inefficient.

"So, when compared to actual energy needs for just one building, the picture gets very clear. For example, office buildings use about 17 kilowatt hours of electricity and 32 cubic feet of natural gas per square foot per year. The Renaissance Tower has a little over 300,000 square feet of office space alone. At full capacity, we would need roughly 5 million kilowatt hours or 5 gigawatts a year, plus almost 10 million cubic feet of natural gas. And this does not cover the residential energy requirements that make up the other two-thirds of the building or core systems.

"With these measurements in mind, you can understand the scope of the energy production equation and why we cannot build buildings that are independent of carbon fuels. With the energy density necessary to generate sufficient power, to run this tower alone would require an enormous swath of land dedicated to solar panels. That large amount of land dedicated to solar production would represent the power density required to do the work. And that embodies vast ecological impact. So, green isn't really all that *green* when you consider the resources necessary to build such an energy plant.

Ryan nodded. "So you are on the grid, right?"

Daniel let out a mirthless chuckle. "The fights we had over this very issue . . ." His voice faded and then he said, "Long story, and not a very pleasant memory. This building is still firmly connected to the electric, natural gas, and water systems, although the tower has its own well because it is one of the most energy-efficient ways to heat and cool a building of this size."

"I bet that saves on city water for drinking water," said Ryan.

"Oh, you could drink that water, but I wouldn't recommend it. When was the last time you drank from a well? We did install a water capture system that stores and filters rain water into cisterns for the aquaponics system that was going to stock the fish and vegetable section of the grocery. . ." Daniel's voice faded, and his mind moved deep into another thought.

"What?" Ryan asked, looking around for what took his attention. "What is it?"

Daniel shook himself back to the moment. "Oh, I guess it doesn't matter now. Nothing can be done. We never emptied the system. It wasn't like we were just going to throw the fish into the streets. Anyway, I have too many other things to worry about. Where was I? Uh, oh yes. Theoretically, the water capture system will ease the need for city water and maximize water conservation, but it is far from a full solution."

"So this building really is an experiment."

"Well, I've said 'we,' but this started as my son Richard's vision. He wanted to do a proof of concept that would merge modern living standards with alternative energy sources. And for once, he was willing to put his money where his mouth was, but . . ." Daniel shrugged, "the farther into the project he got, the more reality worked against both him and the political powers that wanted this project to be the ultimate environmentally friendly building.

"The politicians wanted a show piece to validate their bad public policy. When it became apparent that was never going to be possible, things got ugly. When I took over the project, I decided to make an honest attempt to fulfill the original vision. We added the installation of super high-density batteries and a list of other technologies to capture energy that is historically lost, and we do have natural gas generators on site for core systems, but it is just not possible to live at modern living standards apart from the energy densities of coal, petrol, natural gas, and nuclear power. Well, not unless one is willing to live at the level of a thousand years ago."

"And no one wants to do that," Ryan said.

"Well, there are some who push for what amounts to a total blackout, but no sane person wants to go back to the days of hearth taxes, cooking food over cow dung and chopping down the king's forest in the name of a fictitious creature called zero carbon foot print."

30

Global Infection: ≤ 27.63778%

and hence $S + Z + R = \pi$ *as* $t \to \infty$, $\pi \neq 0$. *Clearly* $S \not\to \infty$ *so this results in a "doomsday" scenario: an outbreak of zombies will lead to the collapse of civilisation, as large numbers of people are either zombified or dead.*

—MUNZ, HUDEA, IMAD, ET AL

"You hungry?" Daniel asked, walking toward the restaurant kitchen. "Your e-mail pretty much killed breakfast. Speaking of which, how close did I come to missing this train? Did today really mean tomorrow? Your e-mail from last night was sent before twelve. I was terrified that you wanted me to come during the night."

Daniel wrinkled his brow. "Oh no. Today meant today. Had you not responded, I was presuming that you were in fact gone. I was going to offer the last spot to someone else." He started rummaging around the kitchen and then into a walk-in. "So much food that will just spoil. Such a waste. See what you can find."

Ryan found a large white container labeled lobster bisque. "When was this made? Do you suppose it is any good?"

"Oh yes, that was made maybe a day ago. It is fantastic." Daniel grabbed some roast beef wrapped in plastic, cheese, tomatoes, and onions and moved back out to the prep area. "This bread is fabulous. They make it here." He dropped his head, suddenly overcome, tears welling in his eyes.

Ryan put the soup in the microwave and started it heating. "What is wrong?"

"It just kills me to see this go to waste, but there was no way to get it out to the street without it causing real problems. You saw the videos of how masses of those things swarm over a building? My security team is keeping a close watch on the outside to make sure that the infected can't mass. If we had a bunch of uninfected standing outside, it would be moments before the infected swarmed."

"All I passed by that municipal building and the infected hounded me until . . . until I shot them."

Daniel nodded solemnly. "So, you see the dilemma."

"I had the same fear about opening the sandwich shop doors. What did you do with all the tenants?"

"Two families are longtime family friends and are going with me. About half of the business tenants—and there weren't many—closed about weeks ago. Those that saw the unrest asked to be bought out or have their leases canceled, presumably to flee the city. The others, we don't know what happened to them. We tried very hard. We expect that they have gone to the safe zones that the governor was demanding people move to. They put one of the safe zones in the convention center, one at Heinz field, and one at Banco Federal Park." Daniel shook his head, his jaw grinding. "Hail always was a fool."

"Hail?"

"You probably know him as Celebreeze, the governor of Pennsylvania. We've known each other for years," Daniel said, starting to make a second sandwich. The microwave pinged. "I would like some of that lobster bisque as well, please."

Ryan found two bowls. "The tower is locked down. What if the people you couldn't get ahold of wanted to come back in? Would you let them?"

"I wouldn't recommend that course of action, but yes, I guess I would have to let them in."

An idea niggled at the back of Ryan's mind. "They could survive, right? I mean, all this food and the energy of the solar panels? No whistles and bells but just bare bones, how much of this tower could be energy-independent?"

Daniel shrugged. "I've never had to calculate that. We have been net metering since we turned on the solar array, which means we sell power to the electric company during production days and buy it back as needed. But with no grid power, I haven't run the numbers, but the tower could sustain maybe a handful of people with some creature comforts. With core systems managed to the ampere, maybe fifty people very, very conscious of their energy use could survive. But I am talking about mere survival. As long as the well pumps, had power and could continue pulling groundwater into the chillers, the system could conceivably keep people from freezing to death. However, the fifty-seven degrees of Pennsylvania groundwater is not balmy by any definition. Why do you ask?"

Ryan poured healthy helpings into smaller mixing bowls, and scooted one toward Daniel. "I don't know. Like you said, it seems like such a waste. That girl I mentioned to you, I'm guessing she is eleven or maybe twelve. It is hard to tell. Anyway, I've seen her scrambling for change, so she could get something to eat out of vending machines. I really did almost violate your rule while coming here. If I hadn't been attacked by the infected. I probably would have shown up with her in tow, or I might have missed getting here, because I took her back to the sub shop. I was just thinking about her and others like her."

"Yes, I understand. I get the compassion. But a twelve-year-old girl would have little chance of lasting long, even in this tower." Daniel tested the soup, with the tip of his tongue, blew on it, then took a sip out of the side of the mixing bowl. "She couldn't hope to understand the systems in the building. And all it would take is an open door. Or maybe not even that. You have seen those videos. You've seen how they smash through windows to get to their goals. It is truly frightening."

"Yeah, true."

Daniel took a sip of his soup. "But this is the very problem we knew we would have. We knew that in a disaster, the compassion factor would sink the boat."

"You say *we* a lot."

"Okay, *my* toughest days are six months from now when I have to look myself in the mirror and answer the question, could I have saved one more person?" Daniel took a bite of sandwich and then a pull off a beer.

"So what problem do *we* have?" Ryan said and took a bite of his sandwich.

"The problem of the *Titanic* lifeboat." Daniel said, "say I have a boat that maybe could take five more people. Do you row toward the drowning mass?"

"Yes. If you get too close, they swamp the boat," Ryan said, taking a sip of soup. "Outstanding soup, by the way."

"I told you, the chef is amazing. I should probably start at the beginning. Ten years ago, four friends and I were sitting around a table bullshitting about doomsday scenarios. If you will remember, ten years ago, the Middle East was on fire with Islam's endless internecine war between the Sunni and the Shia as they duked it out for who would emerge as the Caliphate. Israel was hitting back hard against all attacks on its national sovereignty. It was the lone island of sanity and had everyone very cautious about their willingness to use nuclear weapons.

"We were half drunk, but talking about how we would handle nuclear holocaust since Iran finally had a nuclear arsenal and was making threats at Pakistan. Everyone was on pins and needles that after they stopped killing each other, the Islamic world would unite under the Caliphate and turn once again to world domination. We knew that history would be repeated, and there would be no limit to their tools of war—nuclear, conventional, biological, or slingshots. It wouldn't matter which they chose because with history as our measure, once they focus on killing their enemies, only superior force stops them."

Ryan nodded. "And you had no confidence that America would be that force?"

Daniel snorted. "American political leadership has never understood this adversary. My friends and I had no expectation that our political class would figure it out, ever. Anyway, it started as a thought experiment, but it ended with us creating our escape plan. We called them our summer homes, but they are really vaults or arks. We built twenty of them worldwide with a capacity to house almost eighty thousand people.

Among the list of problems to solve for self-sustaining arks that could be sealed against any and every known threat, we had to solve the Titanic life-boat problem. We knew that at the last minute, the drive to save as many as possible would be almost too overwhelming to resist. And no matter how you planned who would be saved, in the last few minutes before the doors were shut, many people would already be dead, so the list would constantly evolve. The solution had to have an absolute threshold with utter fluid adaptability. Plus, we had to have internal integrity. What prevented one of the five men from locking everyone out at the last minute?"

"Yeah, that sounds like an important detail."

"So, we created a biometric lock that allocates a total number of people to each man. No one can be locked out, because it requires that we all remain alive to close all of the ark doors."

"What if one of you is blown up?"

Daniel's eyes narrowed. In that moment, the imposing personality that was able to shape a global enterprise showed forth. "All the more reason to make sure each of the principals remains alive."

"I see," Ryan said, even though the question hadn't really been answered. Not that it mattered. It wasn't his concern.

"Each of us must authorize everyone he has invited to the ark. The population threshold is based on hard numbers for existing resources. Taking into account basics and population growth over the course of years, the starting population threshold is absolute."

Ryan finished half of his sandwich and took a drink of the beer. "I see; so that is why you said the offer would be retracted if I showed with someone else. The best way to control swamping the boat is to make the swimmer responsible for the safety of the boat."

"Yes, something like that." Daniel took a long drink, his eyes focused into the middle distance, his face troubled. "Anyway, we have protocols in place that will lock us in and the world out. The reports I've read suggest that the virus cannot survive outside the human body and within twenty years will have been destroyed."

Ryan's head tilted. "What if the body isn't gone in twenty years?"

"What?" Daniel said.

"I'm not sure what it all means. I've encountered a few of the infected that by all rights should be dead. Zombies. The walking dead?"

Daniel laughed. "Zombies sounds a bit fantastic, even if Simone thought this was the zombie apocalypse. The human body is still a machine whose engine has to work to remain animate. I'm in the energy business. The laws of thermal dynamics make it impossible for these creatures to last that long."

Ryan shrugged. "I wouldn't put this in the realm of belief, like I'm engaging in fairy tales. They don't look dead or like rotting, walking corpses. Actually, they look normal, except maybe for the stake in the chest, or the row after row of bullet holes, or the limb that has been severed, or that rather mindless light that is in their eyes." He shrugged away the thought. "I was mostly just talking out loud. I don't understand it. I just had a bizarre thought that maybe these creatures would still be walking around in twenty-five years. That is my paranoia getting the best of me. It isn't possible they could remain alive that long. Like you said, the second or third law of thermal dynamics crushes that possibility. Anyway, so you are going to lock yourself in for the next fifty years, just to be safe?"

Daniel sipped his soup out of the bowl. Then he said, "Each ark is designed to be self-sufficient for one hundred years with aquaponics, animal stock, water purification systems, and nuclear power plants. At normal birth rates, we will outgrow the resources in the third generation. Well, three generations before the BOHMeC mandates for the Eternity Vaccine and the Maksimov Therapy. We were calculating life spans of roughly eighty years but the new projected life spans of one hundred and fifty years throws us a curve ball."

"Your arks will be able to keep out this infection?"

"Remember, these were designed with nuclear holocaust or even a killer asteroid's nuclear winter in mind. We also have a contingency for the subsequent generations. There are beta sites that can be populated, but they are merely shells that would need to be built out. Anyway, assuming we thrive, our birth rate will make us outgrow in that time."

"So how big is the ark you are going to? What is the population?"

"The one we are going to, our starting population is 2,231."

"Why that number?"

Daniel shrugged. "That was the maximum starting number based on our calculations for food, water, and habitable space. These locations have an initial stockpile for survival, but we will have to become a productive group in short order to sustain our survival."

"It doesn't seem like one more person would matter that much in the grand scheme."

"Of course not," Daniel said with a little too much heat. This was obviously a topic that was wearing close to the surface. "Just one more in the lifeboat never seems like it will matter that much, but how about two, or three, or even five more? Where does the experiment stop?

"Of course, I don't know," Ryan said.

"And neither does anyone else. What we came to understand was each new person affects the balance of the boat and the other passengers in a rippling effect. With each live body comes a whole range of motion and action that requires endless adjustment that is not immediately seen as damaging.

"So, while adding one or two or even three more people seems trivial in calm seas, the additions become certain death in five-foot swells. I understand that one more person seems trivial, but that is because people do not grasp the hard numbers around things like the production and consumption of potable water, food production, and sewage for what amounts to two military battalions. Trust me, we tapped into every expert we could find on the design, and then we committed to using the boat as it was designed."

"Yes, I guess it is hard to grasp the whole logistical picture," Ryan conceded. "So, if I understand this right, I'm here because someone previously on your list is in fact dead."

Daniel nodded, his eyes dropping to the kitchen floor.

"*Si Senior*," Raphael said from the corner of the kitchen. He was sitting on a pile of potato sacks, his weapon resting easily over his knee.

"Jeezes!" Ryan exclaimed, startled. "Do I even want to know how long you have been sitting there?"

Raphael just smiled, but there was sadness in his eyes and worry etched into his face.

"You sent for Raphael's family in Miami," Ryan said as the pieces of the puzzle fell into place. "That must mean it was one of your family?" he said to Raphael. "I am so sorry."

Raphael was moved by the condolence as he tried to push a wave of emotion down deeper into his soul. "*Es* okay," he said. "Miguel my brother-in-law *es* a good man," he said. "It was his time to go. He wanted to be in heaven. It *es* better this way."

"He is not one of the diseased?" Ryan asked.

"No, he was very sick," Raphael said. "His body was broken. He wanted to move on."

Daniel finished his soup and wiped his mouth on a clean kitchen towel. "The looting of our jobsites started getting out of hand about four weeks ago," he said. "I have three other building projects here in the city that I got saddled with completing. The construction site at the corner of Boulevard of the Allies and Smithfield is actually part of the legal contract that made it possible to put up this tower. The city required we build their civic building *pro bono*, and the—" Daniel stopped himself. "Anyway, the details don't matter. On the other locations, I had crews secure their jobsites to keep them from being cleaned out. Like most people, I assumed the unrest was just general social turmoil and we would ride out the storm. I spent most of the last three weeks pacifying labor unions, but for the most part assumed that when peace was restored, we would go back to work and start the painstaking process of getting the economy going."

"Okay," Ryan said, not quite following.

"I said all of that so you would have a sense of proportion for what I'm about to say. I want you to understand how much impact our conversation had.

"Ryan, after I spoke to you," Daniel said, "I spent the next twelve hours of my life on the phone. That wasn't the abnormal part. What was abnormal was I called in every favor I had and bribed anyone I could find to get the information I needed. And I have never given bribes my whole building career. By the end of hour four, I knew that we would never go back to work. By the eighth hour, we knew that humanity was fighting for its very existence. Within twelve hours, my partners and I executed the first phase of our extraction plan. And it became clear that we were five of the one hundred people on the planet that knew how big this problem really was."

"Only a hundred people know?" Ryan said.

"Yes. Well, the hundred that I know about. And you are the one who saved me and my family's life, and those of all of my friends and their families, and thousands of other people who may never know your name. After we decided to start our evacuation plan, I wanted to offer you a place on the ark, but my personal allocation was full. We didn't know about Raphael's brother-in-law's passing until late two days ago. You are the last spot."

"So this really is the end?"

Daniel nodded. "The pointy heads think this infection is the catalyst event that kills humanity. They think that roughly 20 percent of the populace is immune. The R-naught value you spoke of . . . you said that if the value was one to eight that it was serious. The actual value was one to fourteen."

"Almost most twice the original number? Oh shit!"

"Yes, but eventually, according to math I don't begin to understand, the exponential growth starts to decline. The growth curve has a potential threshold that eventually rises past the number of people available to be infected and starts to die out. The good news is that they think another roughly 30 percent of the world population will not be infected by this specific disease, because it will never come in contact with it."

Ryan nodded. "So, I'm not good with math, but that seems like a good portion of the population."

Daniel shrugged. "The bad news is the bulk of the survivors will die of infections that have been all but wiped out with modern medicine. They have calculated that 11.71 percent will die within the first twenty-four months from a pantheon of disease that modern medicine has been able to control, in addition to starvation and dehydration, and exposure. The actual surviving population of the earth will be roughly 3 percent."

"So that is what? Three hundred million people will survive? Worldwide?"

Daniel nodded. "Survival, if you could call it that. The places where the infection does not reach are very remote and tend to be apart from civilization and the knowledge that drives modern culture. The Wizards of Smart believe humanity will lose 97 percent of its total knowledge, mostly because whoever survives will have to relearn pretty much every advance man has made in the last four hundred years. The endgame strategists have decided that at the very least, humanity will suffer five hundred years of dark ages."

Ryan sighed. "Most people have no understanding of the utter barbarity of the Dark Ages. Unbelievable. Those statistics can only mean that very smart people have known about this for a while."

"Yes, they have known about this since before the ICES Accords," Daniel replied. "You remember telling me that the current outbreak in fact started in China. It did. The government created a virus, believing they had built in a genetically engineered immunity. They tested delivery methods on the Tibetan people expecting that they were sufficiently genetically different. Airborne delivery wasn't sustainable as a weapon and tended to inoculate the population, or at least make them more resilient to infection. They were finally successful, but lost control. They expected the geography of Tibet to work in their favor, but the infection spread throughout the region and into the nearby provinces of Xinjiang and Qinghai, and then into Nepal and the boarders of India. This represents about forty five million people. The entire area had gone dark before the ICES Accords occurred. You were right. It was government that was at the heart of the problem. As near as I can tell, you were right about every speculation you made."

"So China created this plague?" Ryan asked, "How did they figure they would be exempt?

Daniel said, "Governments get so used to lying to themselves about themselves that they forget that reality is a force all its own."

31

Global Infection: ≤ 27.6400%

Perhaps our greatest distinction as a species is our capacity,
unique among animals, to make counter-evolutionary choices.
—JARED DIAMOND WHY IS SEX FUN?
THE EVOLUTION OF HUMAN
SEXUALITY

L unch ended with a call from Mora who said there were issues that needed
Daniel's specific attention. Ryan offered to stay behind to clean up the kitchen. He said that the building should be clean for the apocalypse, but really, he wanted the time to think. Daniel seemed to understand, handed him the penthouse access card, explained the circuitous elevator path back to the penthouse and left with Raphael.

Ryan cleaned and then spent time wandering around the restaurant, looking at the food and feeling vaguely ill that the girl in the pink coat would probably starve to death after the vending machines ran empty. He found a couple of day-old, jelly-filled donuts and took his time eating them while watching the city below. The military cleared streets: tow trucks worked constantly to pack abandoned cars into a vast parking lot where the old Mellon Arena stood. He saw a line of Port Authority buses—escorted by a Humvee coming from outlying neighborhoods—travel the cleared roads toward to the Convention Center safe zone.

He'd seen enough. He'd dawdled as long as he could justify. Evidently riding the public elevators down to the eighth floor to connect with the penthouse express elevator was a security measure. Whether true or not, the indirect route was a pain in the ass, and he wondered why the stairs to the top floor were sealed behind at least three security gates.

Ryan stepped onto the penthouse landing, walked past a long line of statues and walls adorned with socialist realism art, and badged through the front door. The interior was a cacophony of voices; animated conversations flooded the residence. Voices meant people and Ryan thought it wise to avoid them; he was praying he wouldn't run into Ahou.

Ryan poked his nose into Daniel's office and found him wielding three phones simultaneously: a landline, satellite phone, and the conference phone. He and two other men were knee-deep in negotiations, and Mora sat off to the side running a stenography machine. One of the aides saw Ryan and acted as if he had just violated the sanctity of the Sistine Chapel, but without hesitation, Daniel paused the phone call, waved Ryan to a seat off to the side, pushed the box toward him, and said, "For your reading pleasure."

The meeting continued without a hitch except for the dirty look that both aides flashed Ryan's direction. Mora smiled politely and continued her recording. Ryan eased into the box while trying to keep up with who was asking for two hundred million dollars, but soon the reports in the box proved infinitely more interesting. The contents detailed the greatest scandal in human history.

It was a testimony to the reach that Daniel possessed. He had sources all over the world at the highest levels, many of them willing to commit treason to give him information. Apparently, that charge lost its power when every government known to man would be gone in six months.

He read twenty-three e-mails from the President of the United States detailing the deterioration of the vice president into madness. The VP assaulted his security team and staff. They isolated him, but his family was also compromised. The issue was resolved with an email from the president confirming the decision to terminate the VP and his family,

Holy shit! Was he trying to get caught?

Presidents don't use e-mail; they hardly put any communication in writing, period, because the Presidential Records Act makes all of it available for public review.

Not that this President had ever ruled as if he feared being held criminally responsible. The Republican Party had long since demonstrated its timid ineptitude in upholding constitutional law. So it came as little surprise that when the Middle East boiled over in endless violence, the executive branch used a little known executive order to suspend elections until the House and Senate passed a law that effectively set aside the Twenty-second Amendment. If the congress could pass laws that directly undermined the first and second Amendment what was the big deal about invalidating one more civil protection?

The states were the last line of constitutional defense, but in the early stages of what amounted to a coup, they were sued into submission with an endless list of civil rights violations, EPA infractions and charges of fiscal fraud. The Federal branch used its endless supply of tax dollars as the hammer and a complicit Supreme Court as the anvil. Between the two, the last barriers protecting states' rights were forged into the executive branch juggernaut of tyranny when all fifty-six states cast a unanimous vote to repeal the Twenty-second Amendment.

The days of free elections were over, but people still went to the polls. All tyrannies at least try to sustain the illusion of self-governance.

Ryan moved on to the Eyes Only and Top Secret files from three different governments: special sessions of Congress, senatorial oversight committees, internal British Parliament documents, Israel's Knesset and Mossad reports. Each account detailed some government's involvement with the outbreak. The president and the Senate Intelligence Committee was briefed that China was developing a biological weapon months before the ICES Accords, but refused to act.

Movies and television often portray outbreaks as quick-striking contagions that burn like wildfire through a populace. It makes for good television to watch an Ebola infection incubate in mere hours, and days later the leading lady is bleeding to death from every orifice. But Hollywood drama leaves out the epidemiological reality: Ebola-type infections have little time to spread to a large group, *because* it kills off the hosts. It can't penetrate a populous far enough to become a pandemic.

The Chinese understood that a successful pandemic requires a lengthy incubation period during which a carrier is infected but shows no signs of sickness. To this end, they created the pathogen RVCJ-2091 with an incubation period between eight and twelve weeks. It presents with little more than mild headaches, insomnia and irritability. Of course, the headaches cause the irritability, and the irritability is thought to be the product of sleeplessness. No one suspects a pathogen.

By creating a weapon that seemed harmless in the early stages, RVCJ-2091 was able to pass from person to person with little hindrance via bodily fluids. The writers could not seem to agree if that included sexual transmission and kissing. But certainly a bite and transfusion was a vector. The pathogen's function was to damage parts of the brain that regulate behavior: in particular, impulse control and rage. In its last stages the RVCJ-2091 virus produces irreparable, unrestrained violence.

The Chinese started seeding the pathogen into the global population and testing delivery methods nineteen months ago. Their *coup de grace* was to use the ICES Accords to infect heads of state across the globe. Ninety percent of the world's nations were represented at the Accords, sending as much as 30 percent of their top officeholders. The host nation made it a point to make it practical for every member to bring his or her family and even extended family. Then they fed them lavish banquets of contaminated food, namely raw fish. Sushi had the best temperature to hold the live cultures of RVCJ-2091 for the longest time.

And now Ryan understood why Bexley ate sushi and why they were forced to fly while Xyla was sick. The Chinese knew that everyone at the Accords was teeming with the infection, and they wanted to make sure the heads of state returned to their homeland to complete the last part of the plan. An infected national leadership would be fully reluctant to reveal the truth of the condition. And by the time the leadership fell into irreparable insanity, the government would be destabilized from the top. The world was not caught unaware by a lightning-fast viral infection; the world was caught by a slow, patient, deadly plot to corrupt the world from the top.

The weapon's purpose was total cultural and governmental destabilization to set the stage for global invasion. The Chinese government's plan accounted for three potential scenarios:

1. The national government would be caught *unaware*, and the populace would kill itself.

2. The national government would be *aware* and be forced to purge the populace.

3. Survivors would starve within twelve months and would be eradicated with secondary biological agents, or offer little resistance to a military invasion.

The Chinese government projected that a genetically pure people would possess 89.3 percent of global resources within thirty-seven months.

The Israelis uncovered the details. For whatever reason, they had gotten the original Nepal report—the same one that Ryan found in cached web pages—but also found something called the Tekhiya Narrative. Ryan found two copies of the Tekhiya Narrative in the box: one in English and one in Hebrew. It read like a long list of ghost stories from the Tibetan people that made little sense until Ryan realized that *Tekhiya* was the Hebrew word for resurrection. According to the Tibetan people, the Resurrection always occurred after the infected went mad. And the people only went mad after they had been stolen away by the state police and taken to a secret mountain facility.

The Tibetans were telling walking dead stories for almost a year and a half, and the only intelligence service to take it seriously was the Israelis. It seemed that the universal threat of annihilation made a people willing to believe anything that threatened their extinction, no matter how outlandish. Or maybe it wasn't that strange. This was a people that credited their existence to the parting of the Red Sea. Maybe it was genetic.

No wonder the Israelis built a wall around their country. A month after the ICES Accords, the Israelis declared a self-imposed international quarantine. The rest of the world cried bloody murder when the Israeli defense ministry bulldozed entire settlements to complete walls. The rest of the world cried even louder when they said they retreated behind those walls. The world went silent when Israel offered to let anyone emigrate without question. The world watched the long lines and the endless maze of dogs, but could offer no substantive criticism beyond the general outrage that some people had been discriminated against and forcibly removed from the entrance lines. Then they closed their gates and killed anything that came within four hundred meters no warnings, no exceptions.

When the Israel drama unfolded, Ryan had ignored it. Like most, Ryan thought it a means to fend off the inevitable Caliphate attack, but in flawless hindsight, the Israelis were way ahead of everyone. Israel had made forceful overtures to America and Britain about the threat, but the reports were rebuffed as absurd and then rebuffed because they were true.

Eventually, Ryan picked up a two inch thick dark red folder. Each page was a government document with a big, red stamp over the picture: deceased. Each person was a doctor or a member of the medical field or a journalist that had been labeled political dissident. "Does this signature belong to who I think it does?"

Daniel Ryder finished signing a document that one of his staff had laid before him. He was like an orchestra conductor, constantly organizing people and outcomes. His staff filtered in an endless stream, putting papers before him to sign or offer a brief update on one of twenty projects in various locations that were being shut down for all time. Who knew there was so much work to do for the end of the world?

"Yes, that is exactly who you think it is."

Ryan held out one of the sheets of paper. "This means that the President of the United States was in the business of assassinating American citizens to keep the truth of this infection away from the public."

"That is exactly what that means."

Ryan had written about the fully unconstitutional power of Executive Order assassination and been called a nut for his troubles. "So this is how they kept the details quiet? This is how the whole world has been kept in the dark."

Daniel said, "I couldn't get over how much you pieced together from so little information. Actually, you were so accurate that I had you checked out. I thought maybe you were an intelligence operative. I realized later that if you were, you were the worst one at recruitment ever. I'd never met someone so determined to tell me to get lost. Later I thought maybe you were the shrewdest judge of character the Agency had ever sent into the field because you got to me by saying nothing. Anyway, I've been approached a few times, so I did some digging just to be sure."

Ryan's heart sank. "I see. So you know about the federal investigation."

"Of course."

"And you asked me here anyway?"

"Ryan, if I shied away from men who were under investigation from tyrannical political powers, I would have quit doing business long ago. You know I'm a man of resources. I was able to learn about the RICO investigation. I know the details. I know they are going to use this as a show trial to slow roll you into oblivion to silence your writing.

"I remember the first time I read that article "Tap and Rap." I laughed myself silly with the joke about the All Spark and Megatron. I grew up on the Transformers and then, of course, I thought you were crazy for suggesting that government representatives who violate the constitution should be hung for treason."

Ryan smiled at the memories. "Most people thought that was crazy."

"Only it isn't crazy when compared to mandatory minimum drug laws," Daniel said soberly. "How did you put it? One pot seed equals one plant equals ten years in prison. And—"

"And one illegal search and seizure equals one case tossed out on a technicality and a paycheck on Friday," Ryan continued the quote from his own article. "There is no criminal penalty when government violates the constitution. You can go to jail for horticulture but get a promotion for treason."

Daniel nodded. "There is something wrong with that picture. I went back and read through some of your work on my breaks. Your writing represents one of the few voices advocating liberty and freedom within the United States. They want that voice silenced."

"Did you know they served the warrant to my home yesterday? Or wait was it the day before. I've lost time. Whatever, it doesn't matter?" Ryan said. "I guess I should tell you I am officially a fugitive."

"No, I didn't know that. And thank you for telling me. But that doesn't change my mind. First, because I know this is total legal fraud. And had the end of the world not come, I would have gotten behind your defense. The legal precedent set by RICO law has gone the only way it can—expanded into ever increasing circles of guilt and criminality. The legal standard has evolved to the point that the federal government can engage in the judicial version of the butterfly effect: it can find anyone guilty of any crime committed by someone who sneezed on the other side of the globe. All it has to do is draw a tenuous line from specious event to specious event and call the progression a conspiracy. Second, there isn't going to be a federal government. There isn't going to be any government anywhere."

Ryan looked far into the distance. "They burned my house down."

"What?"

"My house. Through my attorney, I purchased a place that they could not seize and put the pressure on me by driving me to the streets. They burned it down."

Anger flashed through Daniel Ryder's normally affable face. "How do you know?"

"I had the house wired with cameras that were attached to a secure remote monitoring service. It was all caught in high definition with full audio."

"I almost wish we weren't retreating. That is something I would have relished bringing out in public. That is the kind of truth that does damage to tyranny."

"Yeah, truth," Ryan said, his mind focusing out to things he had not let himself consider for a while. "I've been trying to tell the truth forever. I tried to tell Bexley Stepford the truth. I tried to tell my sister the truth. She didn't want to listen."

With the documents here in this office, his deepest instincts were confirmed. Bexley dragged Tess across the ocean to deliver some truly evil speech and fed her into the mouth of the beast. It was no consolation that he died from his own cause. Ryan balled his hands into fists. He thumped the desk in a rage that flashed white and hot. "Damn him for killing my sister!"

The staff bolted through the door. "It's all right, gentlemen," Daniel said. "Mora, would you be so kind and get Mr. Sage some Sprite, please?"

"Forgive me. I shouldn't have done that here."

"It is quite all right, young man. You have learned about the true force behind your sister's death. But I think you need to know something."

"Know what?"

"Bexley Stepford tried to save his wife, and he saved you." Daniel pulled a thick folder out from another cardboard box. "I know you didn't like him very much. And since I know who he is and what he advocated, I understand. But I was told by a very reliable source that he refused to betray you."

Ryan took the file, opened his mouth—

"Just read," Daniel said. He grabbed his cigarettes and walked out of the office.

32

Global Infection: ≤ 27.6761%

"*D*id you know that Bexley tried to cancel . . ."
"The trip to Beijing?"
". . . . They insisted . . ."

It was inconceivable that Bexley would refuse the speaking opportunity in Beijing. Bexley was not a man to be forced into any action, and he had enough resources to fend off most compulsions. When Ryan heard Tess say this in the hospital, he thought it was part of her sickness, dismissing the comment as a stray inconsistency in the broader chaos.

The file was filled with contact reports from Bexley's political handlers. From the transcripts, it was apparent that at first, Bexley thought he was working with sympathetic political ideologues toward the common goal of ecological sustainability and the corollary goal of human reengineering. And then it became apparent that he had seen behind the curtain. Something set Bexley at odds with his handlers, but the specific catalyst was unclear in the parts of the report that Ryan read. But it didn't surprise Ryan that it happened; eventually, people see behind the benevolent mask of global Marxism's brotherly love and high-minded compassion to see the true homicidal menace underneath.

Ryan found his name scattered throughout the reports, typically surfacing close to dates of a recently published article or speaking engagement.

From the transcripts, it was apparent that Bexley remained vehemently opposed to Ryan's philosophical musings, but at no point would he say anything personally defamatory.

Some of Ryan's hardest hitting articles were published right after the Tess conversation, and the pressure on Bexley increased proportionally. But "The Hangin' Tree" article is what caused the feces to hit the air-moving apparatus. They wanted Ryan's head on a pike. Ryan's heart stopped in his chest when he read the following:

> ". . . *Patriot Stepford has refused our counsel that he should turn in his brother-in-law for vaginal and anal intercourse with the daughters Xyla Stepford and Georgia Stepford. It is the humble opinion of these faithful servants of the common good that a review board should be assembled to evaluate the fitness of the Stepfords . . . the children should be given to the custody of the State until these sexual charges can be properly pursued and a pervert can be brought to justice . . .*"

And then Ryan found a follow-up report filed four days later. Bexley had taken his daughters to the doctor and validated his daughter's virginity and had the medical results entered into a sworn affidavit by four separate BOHMeC doctors. How Bexley used this as leverage to preempt his handlers was unclear, but they knew that the pedophile charge as an avenue to destroy Ryan was gone. Ryan let the names listed on the reports burn into his memory.

Oh Georgia! Oh Xyla! What you went through for me!

Ryan wept as his resolve turned into iron will. Somehow, someday there would be a reckoning for this tyranny.

Then Ryan read the write-up that chronicled Bexley's refusal to attend the ICES Accords. The report was terse:

> ". . . *these humble servants of the common good are pleased to communicate that the situation has been remedied. Patriot Stepford will be attending and speaking as scheduled.*"

"I've not seen that look in many men's faces," Daniel said. "That is the look of a man who is about to get himself killed."

"Oh, my rashness will pass, and I will focus down to outcomes," Ryan said, "Hideous barbaric unrelenting outcomes."

"I suspect that is true, son. I hope you don't mind that I call you that."

"No, that is fine," Ryan said, thumbing a tear out of his eye. "Comforting, actually. My father is gone. Everyone is gone . . ." his voice faded down to silence.

Compassion filled Daniels face. "I didn't read it all, but I read enough. From the look on your face, it is a horror story."

"Oh, there are people who will die," Ryan said, trying to push the emotion to the background. "Someday, somehow it *will* warrant bloodshed. But that is not today. I have a question for you."

"Please ask."

"People are committing treason and breaking dozens of laws to get you this information. How are you doing that? Or maybe I should say, why are they doing that? I can't imagine money means anything to these people. They know it is useless paper, or soon will be."

"Guilt," Daniel said without a pause, "mixed with a desperate desire to finally speak the truth. Most of the people can only lie for so long before it corrupts them. When I started asking the right questions they were relieved to unburden their souls. They were waiting for someone, anyone to give them the opportunity. Once they started talking, the information came like a flood. My fax machines have been running nonstop." As if on cue, two of the three machines started spitting out documents. "I had the IT guys set up a secure FTP site for digital uploads. There is a terabyte of related video on the servers filled with incriminating evidence, and I have a proxy e-mail address that has over two hundred gigabytes of unread e-mail with attachments and documents, many of them with biometric encryption to validate their source."

"Impressive. Once you get the info, what do they say when you talk to them?"

It was Daniel's turn to close his eyes tight. "I don't. I did a video conference with two of my sources to confirm I'd gotten the information and to clarify a question. They put a gun in their mouths before I could stop the feed."

"Shit!"

"I said something else, but the sentiment is the same," Daniel said. "After the second time, I just decided that I didn't need to confirm."

"That is the coward's way out, considering these people are complicit in the destruction of the human race."

"What were they going to do?" Daniel said. "Write about it?"

The *déjà vu* hit again; Tess mocking him for merely writing about philosophy. As if ideas were insufficient to affecting a real outcome. "I don't know," Ryan said. "The thought of putting a bullet in my head crossed my mind for about three seconds, so I get the temptation. But the reason America has fallen into global statist clutches is because people have become cowards. They quit. They refuse to fight. We will not survive as a species if we put a bullet in our mouths to opt out of the chaos. To prevent the coming dark ages, men must choose to prevail over the forces that are bent towards total subjugation."

"Agreed," Daniel said. "I understand the—"

An aide laid some papers on the desk.

"Thanks, Tim," he said. "I'm sorry. This needs to be done. Go ahead and sell the Levi's Corporation." Tim left the office wiping tears from his eyes.

"What can be done to prevent the dark ages?" Daniel asked.

"The same thing that drove back the Dark Ages in 1200 AD: Aristotle." Ryan paused, waiting for Daniel's reaction.

"You will have to explain that with more than a word," Daniel said. "I know who he is, of course."

"Most people have heard of him, but they have no grasp of the power of his ideas. The collapse of the Roman Empire had many causes, but the central underlying factor was the deliberate abandonment of critical thinking and the return to man's age-old preoccupation with mysticism combined with government force. The Dark Ages were ruled by a religious political correctness. For almost a thousand years, man was compelled to defer his thinking to religious authorities preoccupied with a world that was beyond human grasp. The result was a dogmatic darkness or a doctrine-driven anti-rationalism that shaped all human attitudes.

"Man was compelled to bow down to that darkness until Saint Thomas Aquinas reintroduced Aristotle back into the minds of men. In less than three hundred years, man went from churches lined with gargoyles to chase away the demons, believing that the earth was flat and he would fall off the edge if he explored too far, and living with the ever present threat of war that wiped out half the populace because Church and King lusted for conquest to fill their coffers, to developing a civilization that understood science, explored the world to unlock its secrets, learned to feed the world, healed man's diseases, and figured out that the ultimate function of government was to defend the individual against all forms of oppression."

Daniel chuckled. "You must be a blast at parties."

"I have my charms," Ryan said. "So, what are you working so hard on? It is the end of the world. It isn't like it is going to matter."

"It does matter. If nothing else, it matters to me. Among other things, I am trying to make sure that people who will need resources, people who might survive will have them. The currency hasn't collapsed just yet. And until it does, I will work with what I have to make sure people can get to liquid resources. And I'm working on finalizing all debt against this building. It is ridiculous maybe, but I've spent the last two years of my life cleaning up a mess. And now that it is clean, no infection will taint it, no looter or bank will take from it. It will be here when my great-great-grandkids are ready to come out."

"Cleaning up a mess?"

Yet another aide came into the office offering him something to sign.

Daniel wrote with a flair then leaned back in his chair, considering. "I told you this was my son Richard's idea, an ill-advised idea, right?"

"Yes."

"He worked for me over the years and had real aptitude for planning and building, but he has no passion for the business. His passion is saving the world. His passion is the environmental cause of the moment. His passion is the dismantling of the 'Imperialistic Industrial Military Complex,'"

Daniel said, using the quote fingers. "His passion is . . . other less noble life pursuits."

Ryan wrinkled his brow. "Less noble?"

"Women."

"Ah yes, they are easy to be passionate about, but some of them are noble." Ryan's mind floated down the shimmering sand toward the image of Ahou.

"Yes, some women are noble. I married one. I have two daughters that are noble. But Richard, his taste in women runs toward the ones who are not. Richard is a man of frenetic action . . . action for the sake of itself, or what most people call activism. His motto is *someone must do something,* but a specific course of action attached to economic or ecological realities is a nuisance. He spent almost a decade in the jewel cities of South America living like a king, but preaching the equality of the masses.

"The press in Argentina and Peru loved to portray us, our relationship, as a familial David versus Saul, a ridiculous comparison considering I'm not a king and the Molitor Group was responsible for employing almost seven thousand people within those countries for almost a decade."

"That had to be brutal to endure."

Daniel shrugged. "By this point in our relationship, it was more a matter of fact. Anyway, I'm not sure what happened, but Richard decided to leave yet one more People's Revolution in South America, put aside hobnobbing with despots and dictators, and turned his attention toward building ecologically friendly buildings. He didn't even come to me to fund his experiment, but instead put his money behind his mouth. His goal was to build an ecologically friendly, self-sufficient, modern building. I had never seen him so focused. For almost four years, he buried himself in the development of this project. He made a real effort to integrate all the pet technologies the environmentalists would like to pretend will transform the world. That was his dream."

"I hear a 'but' coming."

"It is a pipe dream. The numbers are what they are, but people will look at the equations and insist the equations are wrong . . ." Daniel's voice faded down to a shrug of futility.

"Separate man from his mind and his mind from reality long enough," Ryan said, nodding his understanding, "and all sorts of fairy tales become real."

"It sounds like a grand theory to convert sunlight and wind into usable energy. And maybe the day will come when we can convert sunlight with the efficiency of plants, but people seem to forget that even plants convert energy over the course of years. That kind of power density will never get a plane off the ground."

"Maybe after the dark ages, physics will be different," Ryan said, his attempt at light irony coming out as harsh, bitter sarcasm. "Anyway, you were saying . . . poorly conceived?"

"Richard's vision, however poorly conceived," Daniel continued, "played very well with the city planners. The sales pitch was mostly fantasy, but the planners loved what was presented, because they want to find a magical fix to renewing the city. I've been working on urban renewal projects for twenty years. The failure of urban renewal is no one wants to live where it is dangerous, a hassle to get toilet paper and bread, pay to park their car, and be taxed into poverty. No one wants to travel to the suburbs to get groceries when they could just live in the suburbs and have their own garage, and the property taxes are mostly a nuisance."

Ryan nodded. "Yes, I have written a couple articles about that very thing."

Daniel chuckled. "Actually, I was quoting you. Like I said, I reread a number of your articles. I was hoping you would notice. And as you know, if you solve these problems, cities renew. Anyway, before I get sidetracked, let me get back to this building. To fulfill the goal of safety and sundries, we built a grocery store on the bottom two floors. To keep residents safe, we built a running track around the outside of the building on the eighth floor with a nice sized outdoor promenade where kids could play.

"We converted the parking garage roof to what we call the Tenant Escape. It is an isolated recreation area accessed via skywalk that was to be decorated with gazebos and planters with trees and flowers. And last, there was a secure switchback that gave access to a green space on the street level behind tall, ivy-covered walls like the European enclaves.

"To accommodate public parking and private parking, we segregated the garage and designated the first three garage floors exclusive access from Boulevard of the Allies through a dedicated skywalk. The tenants' parking never mixes with public parking." Daniel stopped himself. "I'm raving. Sorry, back to my son's part of this project. For all of his denunciation of sweetheart deals, government kickbacks, the good ol' boy network and corporate welfare, he is a master of graft and payoff. He greased so many palms that this building should have slid from the earth by itself."

Daniel shook his head trying to will away a bad memory. "And he had the nerve to call me a hypocrite. I'm sorry. I shouldn't have said that. He is my son."

"He did a great job. It is beautiful."

"Yes. Well, like all committed disciples of Che and Mao and Marx that live very well off the people's money if they can, they will live off their own if they must. This penthouse was his permanent residence, but he lost interest in the grand experiment just about twenty months ago. He was never going to live in the Midwest. He's a Monte Carlo, French Riviera, Hampton's man."

"And *you* are the evil bourgeoisie?" Ryan laughed at the irony. "I'm sorry. He is your son. I shouldn't make light."

Daniel snorted. "You have earned the right to make the comment, considering he will probably live because of your observations."

"You are very gracious."

"The building project faltered. It was too close to completion to abandon, but too far from completion to sell off. The city had granted this building project because my name was attached to it. I had other properties here in Pittsburgh scheduled for development. I believe in urban renewal. There is no reason for cities to die a slow death. I made the choice to step in and finish.'

"A Marxist needing a bailout?"

"That is great irony," Daniel laughed. "Well, to Richard's credit, he footed the bill. Granted, he went deep into his principle to do it, but he did. In effect, my team—Raphael, and you've seen Tim, Dave and Mora, and a list of others that you haven't met—stepped in and finished the project. I've pretty much lived here for the last two years."

"Well, it is pretty comfortable digs. It isn't too much of a hardship."

"This is *his* property, so I rented the space like all good fathers do when their kids own something. In fact, he has made an effort to buy a fair amount of property in Pittsburgh. Richard was hedging his bets that I would succeed. He would then recoup his losses for this building. He wanted to be able to charge lots of money when the rich bourgeoisie live in the city."

At that moment a man, who looked very much like Daniel Ryder but twenty years younger, breezed into the room. "My ears were burning."

Global Infection: ≤ 27.6981%

One of the greatest perils which threatens us now is the tendency to centralization, the absorption of the rights of the States, and the concentration of all power in the General Government. When that shall be accomplished, if ever, the days of the Republic are numbered.
—ORVILLE HICKMAN BROWNING

"Richard, you're here!" Daniel said, rising from the desk, relief washed across his face. He hugged his son, but there was a formality between them. "Did you see Mother in the main rooms? She had been keeping a vigil on the news since we got the call for your location."

"Yes, of course, she is in the living room with Sara and Chrystal and Neal. All of the kids are here. The twins thought riding in the Stryker was a blast. Your captain let them ride near him so they could see out."

"Betty and Mark?"

"Yes, we are all here," said Richard. "They are all in the living room hugging and crying. They told me to say thank you. It is madness out there, far worse than anyone could have known."

"Oh, they knew," said Daniel. "It would chill your bones if you knew half of what they knew."

"Well, what can you expect from corporations more interested in making money than the good of the people?"

Ryan couldn't contain himself. "People's Republic and the beloved Chairman Mao Zedong III cooked up this bug." He held up a folder attesting.

Richard turned and looked Ryan from feet to eyes as if he just piddled on the carpet. "Father, I would like you to meet someone. Rachel, please come in."

A tall woman, a beautiful blonde in her twenties, smiled shyly as she walked into the room. "Hello, Mr. Ryder. It is nice to finally meet you." She extended her hand.

Daniel stiffened but returned the shake. Then he said, "Richard, I was very specific. No one else could come. No one! There is no more room."

"There is always more room. Pay more to whomever you bribed to get us this far."

Daniel Ryder straightened himself while his jaws ground his rage down to manageable levels. This was the bearing he used when addressing heads of state and other men of station. It was strong and indomitable. "Richard, mind your tone. And mind your accusations. I have no more patience for either. Not only did I bring you into the world, I'm about to save the rest of your life."

"Spare me the drama. It can be done. Bribes are the way of rich men. Pay whomever you have to pay to get her into wherever we are going."

Daniel let the silence drag on for a long, uncomfortable time. Finally, he said, "No."

Of all the responses Richard had been prepared for, he hadn't expected this one. "No? That's it? No, I don't love you, son? No, I hate you for being a man of principle? No, you're a loser and I can't stand the sight of you?"

Daniel's jaws continued to grind, but he did not respond.

Richard's face started to drain of color. "I don't understand. Why won't you help me? Why won't you talk to me?" Suddenly, he looked very scared.

Silence.

Ryan knew he was caught in the middle of a family fight, but he was stuck behind the edge of the desk, so he tried to sit very small.

"She is pregnant. She is carrying my child." Richard's words were wielded like a bat, with force and aggression, a defiant declaration.

Daniel continued his silence, trying to wade through the emotion and the attitude. Then with a nod he said, "Of course, she is. And so were the half a dozen other women that you are currently paying child support to. Richard, this crisis has been brewing for a while, and never once did I hear from you about them. I might have understood if you came here with Marisa, or Cherry, or what was that Asian woman's name?"

"Mia?"

"Yes, I have six grandchildren that I never see."

"You never see them because you are in Dubai—"

Daniel raised a pausing hand that brooked no defiance. "Miss, would you mind stepping out, please? I need to have a conversation with my son."

"Whatever you have to say to Richard you can say to me."

Richard gave a sly smile to his father and hugged Rachel close. "She can hear whatever you have to say, father."

"Okay, if you can hear it, then I will be blunt. Young lady, do you under-stand how many women my son has brought to me hanging off his arm? Do you understand that he changes women about once a week? A new flavor of the week does not make me take any of this seriously." Rachel blanched and let out a small yelp.

"Well, young lady, you asked to stay and hear a conversation I would have preferred in private. Maybe you are a fine person. But I know my son.

And his taste in women tends to run to strippers and money-seekers. Less than a month ago, it was Cheryl. Where did she dance? What was the name of the club?" Then with a wave of his hand he dismissed the question. And for a long moment Daniel looked at Rachel. Finally he said, "Now that I think about it you look like Cheryl," he said to Rachel, "You are taller, but still. You could be her sister."

Rachel blushed and dropped her eyes. "My younger sister is—"

Richard cleared his throat, a signal to be quiet and then looked away.

"Wait, you are Cheryl's sister?" Daniel looked hard at Richard. "This is her *sister*? This is the sister of the same woman you talked about planning a wedding with? The same one who you said would make me a grandfather . . . again? Did you ever get that paternity test? Oh, what am I asking?" Daniel clamped his mouth tight as he worked hard to cut through the threads binding the conflict together. "Is she really pregnant? Or is this a lie you told to manipulate me into relenting."

"I'm really pregnant," Rachel said.

"And is it really yours, Richard?" Daniel demanded.

"Hey!" said Rachel.

Daniel raises a commanding hand again. "No, you don't get to be indignant here. Not now."

"Yes, Father, it is mine. I was with both of them . . . together. They were both pregnant."

"What?!" he shouted. Then he got himself under control. He noticed that Raphael was standing at the door studying his fingernails. Raphael had walked in with Richard but had not made a sound. "Raphael, please pull the door shut. I don't want Lisa to hear this." Daniel moved back to the desk, sat down rubbing the bridge of his nose.

"There is no need to protect Mom; she already knows. I told her before I came in to see you. And put your puritanical judgments away. It just happen—"

"Two women at once does not 'just happen.' And it is not my judgment that is—"

"Cheryl is not here because she is dead," Richard plowed on. "She was in New York. I lost contact with her over three weeks ago. So this is the family I have left—Rachel, myself, and your grandchild. Besides, we both know that all bourgeois retreats, everyone will have space and enough champagne and cavia—"

"Stop! I will not tolerate this here and now. Your presumption knows no bounds. I made arrangements for an exact number of people. Here is the choice before you. One of you can go. Or you can both remain in *your* tower."

"But we cannot just leave her here by herself?"

"Who is we? There is no *we*. There is you. And *you* are welcome to stay here with her and *your* child. I am not the villain here. You have made a choice to disregard the standards I set. That is fine. You are free to do that, but the consequence of that choice is you will have to solve the problem of your own creation, with your own resources. The aquaponics system for

the grocery could sustain you for a while with the technology in the building . . . you could maybe survive for years. You have a resource before you
that you can use to take care of your family."

"Are you mad? This place will be a death trap. What do I know about
being a farmer? And we both know that the solar energy available at this
latitude doesn't begin to cover this building's power requirement. How
many planning meetings did I sit and listen to you drone on about the Four
Imperatives: power density, energy density, cost, and scale? And now you
pretend that the reality will magically sustain me in this place?"

Daniel Ryder took a step back like he had been hit with a bat. "You've
known all along that this building was never going to work?"

"Of course," Richard said with a shit-for-brains face. "I can do the math
as well as anyone. As long as the masses believe it is a magical fix and
the greedy capitalists are made to pay more for their energy consumption,
everyone gets what they want. Besides, it wasn't a total loss. The solar
production was net-metered back to the energy company. Plus, we got
enormous tax breaks. And we were able to negotiate a direct connect to the
Beaver Valley nuclear facility so that our carbon footprint was effectively
zero. It made great press. What was her name, Sherry Jameson? She loved
the idea of paying us to make solar power and telling her constituents that
we were providing carbon offsets. It was a brilliant deal."

Daniel stumbled back to his chair and slouched into the leather, suddenly looking very old and very tired. "All those arguments . . ." He shook
his head as if to rid himself of a bad memory. "And I almost came to respect
your commitment to your ideals. Of course, even that was a lie. How many
lies can I tolerate?" Daniel said mostly to himself. For a moment, no one
spoke. "Well, it doesn't matter now. What matters now is one of you can go,
or you can both stay here."

"But what of Rachel?"

"Hey!" Rachel said.

"That is not my problem," Daniel said. "You have used me for the last
time. That is a problem of your own creation. You will have to fix it with
your resources."

"Resources?" Richard exploded. "Are you mad? You are taking out your
hatred of me, on her! Tell me the truth. You have always hated me more
than your money. Your hate for me is making you condemn her. You can
do something."

Contempt washed over Daniel's face. "Yes, son, right now I do hate
you. For the first time in my life, I look at the man before me and I know
that I hold this person in contempt. It breaks my heart to say it. But
it is true. In this moment you have succeeded in making your greatest
fear come to life. I hold your actions and attitude in contempt. I hate
your unrelenting presumption that you should get what you want merely
because you believe I have it to give. You will lie, steal, and cheat to get
from a person who has willingly given you most everything he has. And

you do this in the name of self-righteous ideology. So, yes, this man that stands before me, I hate this man."

Daniel rose out of his chair with slow commanding deliberation. "If you were any other person, if I had not brought you into this world, I would have ended our relationship long ago. You want the truth? You demand and demand and demand. . . ." Daniel's voice hitched as the tears started to flow down his check, a liquid expression of his grief and outrage. "Since you demanded the truth from me . . . there you have it."

Daniel made eye contact with everyone in the room. "I apologize to everyone that this is a public fight. I am sure you think me a monster, but the demand was for truth. And this is also the truth. There is no more room."

"You already know that I have no resources," Richard said, his own desperation turning to sweat on his face and neck. "I dumped so much money into this building. The rest of my assets are all but confiscated. The announcement has not been made yet, but the President is going to nationalize everything. Martial Law is going to be declared later today or tomorrow morning. Can you believe it? I called the President to make sure that my assets would be exempt. And you know what that motherfucker did?"

Daniel didn't respond.

"He didn't even have the courtesy to pick up the phone. So what fucking resource do I have?"

Daniel shrugged. "Again, that is not my problem. I will no longer make up for your lack of forethought and planning. I made a plan for a day just like this, and a decade ago we started our plan. And now we are executing our plan. That fact that you failed to make similar plans for your own family is your own fault."

"But I am your family. She is my family. Kick out someone who isn't family."

"Each person invited to the ark is going because I chose to make the offer."

"And what could he have," Richard demanded, pointing at Ryan, "that you would pick him over the mother of my child?"

"Richard, I don't have to justify anything. I am free to pay for my judgments as I see fit because I paid for them. And you continue to make me the villain when you have the wherewithal to save the very woman you say you love." Daniel raised his hands expansively.

Richard sneered. "I suppose Raphael is your ideal of someone important for survival. He was a traitor to his people. And his treacherous bitch of a wife? Are they your idea of self-reliant?"

Daniel took four quick strides out and delivered a flurry of blows to Richard's face and stomach, and then with a sweep, he took him to the ground and held him by the throat. They were punches that came from a man who looked familiar with throwing them. Richard curled into a ball. Breathing heavy, Daniel said, "If I ever hear you speak of Raphael and Leona like that again—"

"You'd pick them over me? You'd beat me for calling a traitor a traitor?"

"I beat you for calling one of the finest women I've ever met a bitch. And I beat you so that Raphael would not kill you."

Raphael stood by the door, his face hard set, leaning against the doorframe, still studying his fingernails. "*Gran coño puto.* Speak of her again like that and I forget I respect your father." The soft assurance underneath the words spoke volumes of menace.

Richard lay on the floor shaking from fear. He righted himself and wiped the blood from his mouth. "I met Gaspar José de Francia. He was a great visionary. I was there. I saw how he transformed his country for the People's America."

Raphael moved off the wall and knelt, looking Richard hard in the eyes. "You saw nothing. You heard nothing. And you know nothing." Loathing filled his words. Then he rose and strode out of the office.

Richard acted indifferent, but he shook until Raphael was gone. He pushed himself off the floor. "So let me call your Noah's Ark friends. Let me try to use my influence, my *resources.*"

Daniel tossed up his hands, exasperated. He jabbed the phone face to dial a number. "You can use *my* satellite phone to call *my* friends to save your ass." As it rang, he said, "The difference between you and I, Richard, is that I don't lie." Into the phone he said, "Clark, it's Daniel. Yes. It is crazy, but this is what we planned for. Right? Yeah? No, I hadn't heard. No, I hadn't heard that either. You are all tucked in I take? You have gotten word from the other sites? How is the evacuation and relocation going in Dubai? Good. And Brazil? Outstanding. Anyway, I have a situation here. My son . . ." In a minute Daniel summarized the issue, then handed the phone to Richard. "See what you can do."

"Hey, Clark. Yeah, this is Richard! I was wondering what it would take—" A loud voice on the other end of the phone cut him off.

Daniel motioned for Ryan to move away from the desk with him. "I do apologize. Not the best impression, I am sure."

"*But you don't understand. This is Richard Ryder. Certainly, there is something we can work out?*" Richard countered into the phone.

Daniel motioned Ryan to the far side of the office. "Using my name and my reputation till the end," he said with a sigh. "I really don't understand how we went wrong. I know *when* we did. He went off to Harvard, and he came back after his freshman year angry and hateful, spouting Trotsky like it was the Gospel of John. By his sophomore year, Richard was almost lost to us. Many years later, I was to find out that they had targeted him for recruitment. They went after him just like the old Soviet empire used to recruit spies. They thought it a great victory to turn an industrialist's oldest son to the communist ideology. I had no idea how hard they worked. They succeeded."

Ryan finally screwed up the courage to ask the question that was drumming in his mind. "I must admit, I am concerned you will send me away.

I have a place I could go. For the last couple of days, I've been fortifying a place to stay." Voicing his fear brought a stabbing pain in his gut that felt like an ice pick stirring about. "If I had to go back to where I was, I could. Maybe that is what I should do. I think I have some unfinished business. And then there is that girl I've seen. Maybe I could help her . . ." Ryan's voice faded, and he tried to put on a brave smile. But he didn't feel brave.

"But what if I gave you all of my European holdings? That is a lot. That has to be worth something—"

"I wondered what you have been doing for the last few days," Daniel said." I assumed you stayed in Firouz's grocery. We called and called but got no answer."

"Long story, but the short version I was working with the building supervisor for the rentals above the minimart and sub shop to secure the building. The building is sealed, and I have supplies in Firouz's grocery. So I could go back. But I won't lie. I am concerned that you will tell me to leave, but I understand if you do. I would be okay, maybe even for the best."

"No," Daniel said. "This is an old fight that has festered for a very long time, but my resolve is firm. As far as I am concerned, that spot in my ark is yours. The fact that you have spent your last few days forging a way to survive only confirms my judgment."

"Look, Clark. I know people. What if I let it leak where you are—"

". . . STOP WASTING MY TIME!"

"That was loud," Ryan said, taking a quick look at Richard. His face was white, his hands trembling. Richard pulled Rachel into him. She was sobbing, begging him not to leave her.

"I don't even have the energy to beat him for threatening my friend," Daniel said, moving farther away into his own private misery. He pinched the inside of his nose.

Ryan turned his back to give the couple some privacy. "I think he loves her."

Daniel nodded. "Yes, but he loves all his wome—NO!"

The roar of the gun slammed against the word. Three shots cracked in the room, and for a moment the world did not make sense. Ryan was looking at the wall in front of him and the three holes that sprouted in the drywall. Then Ryan realized those bullet holes were roughly where his head and shoulders were. Then he heard the clicks of a dry-fired weapon.

Then he heard the screams.

34

Global Infection: ≤ 27.6984%

*The Marxians love of democratic institutions was a strat-
agem only, a pious fraud for the deception of the masses.
Within a socialist community there is no room left for
freedom.*

—LUDWIG VON MISES

The room was a cauldron of screams and shouts. The security team flooded into the office. Raphael lead the charge through Mora's office, Mora and the aides pressing into Daniel's office behind.

"Fuck!" Richard shouted as he wrestled a small, silver revolver in his hand, desperately pushing the cylinder release trying to empty the casings. Frantic, he dug into his pocket for loose bullets.

A seasoned shooter doesn't need to reload because he hits his target. But if he does need to reload, the seasoned shooter does it in seconds. Richard failed on all counts. From just over twenty feet away, Richard had missed Ryan, who had been standing with his back broad and exposed.

Rick was drawn down on Richard from the left. Raphael was drawn down on Richard from the right. "Drop it! Drop it!" They shouted in unison.

Daniel lunged at Raphael. "Raphael! Don't shoot! Don't shoot!"

The doorway jammed with family.

An older lady, pretty in the way of older ladies, forced her way through the crowd shouting, "Richard?! Richard?! What are you doing?"

Then Ryan realized that Richard was pointing the gun at him.

"Mom," Richard pleaded, "Your husband told me to solve my own problems. That is what I'm doing." The gun continued to quake in his fist.

"I shoot you," Raphael said. "Put it down!"

Daniel pushed his body into Raphael, fouling his shot. "He's my son."

"I thought you hated me. Isn't this what you wanted? Me dead?"

"So your solution is to murder?" Daniel snarled back. "Or are you really trying to commit suicide but don't have the courage to do it yourself."

"But I love her . . ."

Raphael pushed Daniel out of the way, but Daniel would not give. "I won't let you kill him. Raphael! Stop! Rick, hold your fire."

Ryan was armed, but he did not draw the Glock. Walking toward Richard with slow, purposeful strides, he stopped at the edge of the desk, thinking. His slow deliberation brought the room to a halt.

Maybe it was the pent-up rage that had brewed since he started reading the documents. Or maybe it was the weariness that seemed to come from every pore of his body so he just didn't give a shit. Or maybe it was an unwillingness to be bullied or threatened. Or maybe it was the adrenaline high coursing through his blood. Or maybe it was all of the above. Ryan said, "Isn't this just like a Marxist. When his moralizing does not work, he resorts to bribery. When his bribery does not work, he resorts to extortion. When his extortion does not work, he resorts to violence." His words were a jarring contrast to the pandemonium. "For all the sanctimony about brotherly love and human equality, Socialists are the first to kill so they can take what they want."

The gun shook in Richard's hand, tears spilling down his cheek, his desperation rolling off him like a stench. "What?"

"It isn't so easy, is it? I killed my first human just a couple days ago. He was infected. He would have killed me in a minute if I hadn't. I puked after."

Then, standing there staring down the muzzle of the gun, the idea that niggled at the back of his mind bloomed into a flash of images:

The pink coat . . .

Tess' words: "At least Bexley is doing something besides writing . . ."

The justice that must surely be visited on the political handlers that sent Tess and Georgia and Xyla to their death . . .

The reckoning that must come to unjust governments who fail to understand they only exist at the consent of the individual to defend that individual . . .

Daniel Ryder's words: ". . . but I would guess that the tower could sustain some people . . ."

His conversation with Ahou: "Much of our current crisis is directly tied to the reality that the only people talking about ideas are locked in a classroom . . ."

"I will sell you my spot," Ryan looked at Daniel, "if it really is my spot. If I really do own it, then I want to sell it."

"You don't have to do this," Daniel said. "He won't shoot."

"No, it is fine. This is a solution to a number of different problems. Or maybe I should say it is the beginning of a solution."

"You would do that?" Richard said, not comprehending. "You would give up your spot for me?"

"No, this is not altruism. I will sell my spot for everything you have, all of it—the building, all of your properties, all of your assets, and every dime you have. Even what is in your pocket, and the gun in your hand. I just heard you make that offer on the phone. I want that. I want this building and everything else in your name."

"You would be giving away your life," Daniel Ryder said. "This infection is going to kill the human race. This, all this is worthless. There is no need for you to make this sacrifice."

Ryan nodded, considering. Then he said, "No. Like I said, this is not altruism. I am not offering a sacrifice. I am using the capital of my life. I am exchanging value for value, precisely because I value life. I value my life that much. Worth and value are human ideas. And this building, every-thing we see is only valuable because we give it value. And we give it value because it advances our life.

"Before this three-river valley became the metropolis of industry, it was a vast wilderness roamed by creatures that did not know or care of our existence. This only has value to man inasmuch as man needs to shape his environment to live and thrive. If we leave, it will go back to that vast wilderness with no value to anyone." Ryan paused and then looked Richard in the eyes. "So sell it all to me."

"But that is a fortune. And I can still just kill you."

"No, Richard, you can't." Lisa Ryder said as she stepped in front of Ryan blocking a shot. "I will not let you kill him. I will not let you murder your way to safety."

"Mother, stay out of this."

"No, you do not get to treat me this way. You do not get to treat your father this way. If there were police to call, we would have already called them. We would have already given our statement that you tried to kill a man. I don't know where you got the idea that you could kill and steal and bribe to get what you wanted without consequence. But I will not stand for it one more second. Put the gun down!"

A mother's command has the power to stop the tides of the earth. Richard put the weapon on the desk. In a moment, Raphael snapped it up and put it in a tactical vest pouch staring daggers into Richard's skull. "*Grandes coño de mierda!*" he muttered. Rick frisked Richard roughly for another weapon and found nothing.

Mrs. Ryder turned to Ryan. "Doing business at the point of a gun is not busi-ness. It is extortion, and it is a crime. There may be no solution for Richard. He made his choices. You do not have to save him from what he has created." She paused and looked deep into Ryan's eyes. "But if my husband offered you that spot, it is yours. You don't have to do this. If you want to change your mind now, no one will object. It is a brave thing you propose, but you do not have to do it now or ever. Richard needs to solve this at his own expense."

Mrs. Ryder turned her mother eyes onto Richard. "And you will not abandon this lovely girl in this tower by herself."

Richard hugged Rachel tight. "No, Mother, I would not do such a thing."

Her snort spoke volumes. Mrs. Ryder walked to her husband, touched his chest, and kissed his cheek. "He is our son," she said and walked from the room.

No one spoke.

Firouz was in the room looking at the bullet holes. Raphael joined him. And then Rick joined. They all stood and started looking toward Richard's shooting position then back again, measuring.

"You were serious?" Richard asked, hopeful, but as if he fully expected to hear a retraction. "You would sell your spot for all of my assets? Most of which you will never be able to get to? I have properties all over the world—investments in companies that may never open again, in banks that have probably been looted or will be looted. And what I said was true; the administration will nationalize everything and declare martial law."

Ryan was thoughtful. Did he really want to do this? And then something he'd said to his sister many months ago broke into his thoughts like a clear spring out of the ground. *The Colonists fought tyranny in the dead of winter without shoes and barely any food. I can't stand by and watch bad things happen and pretend that it doesn't matter just to secure a little safety.*

Daniel came to the desk, his jaw working overtime to grind down whatever thought he had at the tip of his tongue.

Ryan said, "Yes, it is true. Governments always seek to take what is not theirs. I will address that in time. And yes, I may not live a week. But if man is to survive as a species, then it is here, in places like this that he will prevail, not locked behind the doors of some human vault. But for me to have a fighting chance, I need resources . . . legitimate, abundant resources. For man to survive, he must have the time to think. History shows us that barbarism is man's existence until he learns about a life that is suitable to man's thinking nature. I belong here."

Richard looked at his father. "Now I know why you picked him. Yes, I will do it. I will sell you all I have. Dad, I will need to ask you to help me put together a contract and a listing of assets. I will sign whatever you draw up." He walked out of the room.

Raphael looked Ryan up and down like it was the first time he had ever seen him. "*Es tu loco!*" he said. He moved behind the desk and looked at Firouz who was standing exactly where Ryan had been during the shooting. "*Madre Dios,*" Raphael said looking up to the heavens, "you protect this *muy loco hombre!*"

Daniel held Ryan by the shoulders. "This is insane!"

Ryan nodded. "It might be. Trading the assurance of security for the assurance of a brutal future. Yes, it does seem insane. But there is no guarantee. How do you know that your ark is not already filled with infected?"

"We have protocols—"

"I'm sure you do. I'm sure you have been very thorough. It isn't an accusation. My point is there are risks to every choice. I am willing to take the risk, just like you took the risk to do business with hostile governments all over the world. There is food. And even though the energy source would not support a whole building, it could support me and maybe a few other survivors." He shrugged, trying to wrap his mind around the gravity of his own commitment. "And maybe eventually, I can have a conversation with the people listed in that report."

"I told you that was the look of a man about to get himself killed," Daniel said. "Vengeance is a foolish motivation, considering you will most likely never see those men."

"I understand, but it is not just about those men. There is an entire structure that is behind them based in the most hideous ideological assumptions that have ever plagued man's existence. I've made my life combatting those ideas. The only thing I ask from you is that I have access to all the information that you have compiled."

Daniel was quiet for a long while as he sorted through his thoughts. Finally he said, "I hate to say it, but you are worth ten of my own son," he said, clasping his shoulder. "Thank you."

"No need to thank me. I think I just bought a fortune."

"And then some," Daniel said.

"But I guess there is some question about the RICO problem."

Daniel tilted his head thinking. "Don't worry about that. I employ world-class lawyers for such fights with the government, and I had them look into your case. And besides, rumor is that everyone's assets are going to be confiscated by the government. Now that I think about it, we are all going to have our assets RICO'd." Daniel winked at the irony.

"Well, I guess I'm at your mercy on writing up a contract for this sale. I have no clue how to proceed."

"Don't worry about that. Okay, so much to do and we only have about a day left before we all leave." He checked his watch and then turned to the room of gawkers. "If you don't have business in my office, you belong somewhere else. Mora! Tim! Get the team in here. Get Stephen's group on the phone. I need a legal conference in five." A moment later, the rest of his staff entered, bewildered but moving with his instructions without hesitation; they cast looks at Ryan that ranged from awe to scorn.

Firouz grabbed Ryan's hand. "Yes. Yes. I tell you. We seeing you before again. God is watching you over. Bang! Bang! But you are not dead." He grabbed Ryan and kissed both cheeks. "I am very hard praying." He kissed him again. Ryan couldn't decide what Firouz was happier about, that Ryan was alive or that his prayers had worked. "God is watching you over. My Ahou, she will be so happy." And then Firouz seemed to freeze in his mind. "Oh, my Ahou . . ." He turned rapidly out of the office without another word.

Daniel said, "I need your personal information."

Ryan opened an application on his smart phone, punched in the password, and sent all his personal and financial information to Daniel's computer. "All of my accounts are listed here. The app keeps track of all related information. If it is in my name, this is where it is. But I suspect all of the money accounts have been locked down by the Feds"

"Don't worry about that," Daniel said, reaching for a small square box. He plugged it into a network jack and a wall outlet, and then unlocked the top. There was a place for a man's hand. "This is a biometric encryption generator. This is the portable version of what they have at the bank. It will generate an encryption key based on blood, handprint, and eye print. This will be linked to all accounts that are currently in Richard's name. It is better than a signature. As long as you are alive and this means of authentication is available, you will be authenticated, and it is impossible to forge." Daniel made some adjustments to the machine and then said, "Place your hand in the palm reader. You will feel a small pinch as it gets a drop of blood."

Ryan placed his hand in the outline and jerked. "I thought you said small pinch?"

Daniel smirked. "We will verify this with the banks and handle all the related fees. Raphael, would you be so kind to show Mr. Sage around his new home. Give him a tour of the security systems and anything else you can think to show him before we leave."

Raphael nodded, his respect unmistakable. "*Loco*, but you have *cojones, amigo. Grande cojones*. Not many men can walk into a loaded gun."

Ryan got to thinking. This was the second gun he had faced down in a day. "I guess it comes with practice," he said. "And besides, he was a terrible shot."

That brought a brief smile, but then Raphael said, "Not so bad a shot. Those bullets went through you. The Virgin Mary, the Madre Dios, she protect you by interceding to Saint Jude of Thaddeus, he protect the lost cause."

"Lost cause, huh? That's encouraging. Well, this lost cause needs to understand how this building's electricity sources work. How to take it on and off the grid? And the security system? And the locked doors? And a thousand and one other things that I can't think of right now."

"Yes, a thousand things," Raphael said, "but the security and core systems are a good place to start."

"Is there a user's manual for this building?"

Raphael laughed. "*Muy, muy loco!* Cóme, I show you important things about your new home."

35

Global Infection: ≤ 27.7000%

Private property was the original source of freedom.
—WALTER LIPPMANN

Raphael installed the building security app on Ryan's iGlass and iPhone. It turned out that Daniel was right; they had done this before. The phone's RFID chip had to be authenticated against an encryption algorithm to access the security functions. The app required a complex login and was programed for remote wipe if it were lost. After they finished they left the penthouse and started a whirlwind tour at the elevators.

They did a brief walkthrough of the building entrance points and how each section of the building was sealed against other sections. It was assumed that the grocery and adjacent retail space would remain open the longest so that space was the most isolated. The office floors four through eight were build-to-suit, and only the fifth and sixth floors had been rented to tenants.

The eighth floor was filled with recreation rooms, indoor pool spas, weight rooms, security station, and a suite of offices. It was the main resident entrance that led out to a promenade, the running track, the mini playground, and the skywalk across First Avenue to the parking garage. The promenade and the running track were deep behind five-foot mini walls lined with Plexiglas barriers.

The residential floors started at nine and went to twenty-eight. The ninth to the twelfth floor was built out with smaller floor plans—efficiencies and lofts for small families. The fourteenth through the twenty-first were larger floor plans on par with thirty two hundred-square-foot homes. The twenty-second to the twenty-eighth floor were built to suit luxury condos. They didn't spend much time visiting the empty spaces except to explain the security and locking mechanisms. A lot of thought had gone into building security.

Raphael then took him to the primary mechanical room in the substructure. Under the tower was a massive space that spanned the distance from Boulevard of the Allies and Fort Pitt Boulevard. It allowed tractor trailers to enter underneath the parking garage, turn and unload under the tower and then exit. Receiving had ample industrial storage for staging and a large freight elevator that supplied access to the grocery above.

They walked down a long, lonely passage to the Renaissance Tower mechanical rooms. This part of the superstructure housed a full machine shop and fabrication, HVAC chillers, water main connections for city water, the well lines that fed the chillers, the electrical services room and the natural gas main.

Raphael explained the physical connections to the building; he was a patient and logical teacher. "Right now, this building *es* connected to the grid," he said, pointing to a large bank of electrical panels, "and it *es* currently net-metering. You know this term?"

"Yes."

"*Es* good." He pointed to a display above a bank of breakers and switches. "Tonight you will see this display change as it starts to bring power into the building."

"Can we stop selling the energy back right now?"

"Of course. On your pad, pull up the maintenance interface. Now the power management tab. You see there? You can control it from there. Yes, tap that. Now you no longer selling electricity, and the batteries are charging."

Ryan nodded, trying to take it all in. "How about a physical connection? Since I know nothing about this, I would feel much better if the net metering was physically off. That way I would not have to worry about hitting the wrong button."

Raphael moved to a bank of very large levers. "It *es* controlled by computer. But if you want to make sure that energy *es* no leaving the battery banks, we throw these switches. This *es* what you want to do?"

"Is there a reason I shouldn't? It doesn't prevent power from coming to the building, does it?"

"No. *Es* good idea." Raphael threw the switches and then looked at the pad. "See, now that option *es* gray."

"I see it. Can we charge the battery banks via the main power grid?"

"Yes, of course." Raphael touched the pad until he got to the right screen that showed a detailed readout of the battery banks throughout the building, with readings at charge capacity. "You see the readout for battery capacity? We have been testing the battery system for weeks. *Es* only twenty percent, yes?

Ryan nodded. "I just want to make sure I have as much power as possible."

"Yes, that is good. Touch here and here to start the charge. It *es* also good idea. If the power fails, you will have much power for yourself. And you can control power consumption down to the ampere for all systems. If you are willing to be hot and cold, you could survive for much time."

Raphael then showed Ryan the main security rooms in the first floor mezzanine and its mirror on the thirteenth floor near the security barracks.

"You saved his life," Raphael said.

"Who?"

"Daniel Ryder. He would sacrifice himself for Richard. That girl would have entered the ark, but Daniel would have killed himself to make space. He would have died. He loves that boy. Well, Richard *es* no boy, but that *es* the way of fathers, to love their sons." Raphael suddenly fought to keep the tears out of his eyes. "Always the Spanish men are so machismo," he said. "This crying. We are not supposed to do. But here *es* this crying."

"I understand that you lost one son in the war and most recently another one?"

"Yes, I have lose my first son a year ago, Marco. He die in combat in Italy fighting the Caliphate. He was assigned to a force recon battalion. His body was no recovered, so we have to close the casket for the funeral. Daniel *es* like the father I never have. I have a father, but he *es* no good man. Daniel, he cry for the death of Marco. He was like a grandchild to him. My third son, Simone, he *es* a crazy man. He ran away so he do no bite me. I look, but cannot find him," Raphael said, still trying to fight back his tears. "He *es* one of them now."

"It pains me to hear." Ryan said as they wound through the tower's hallways to the elevator.

"Yes, it *es* hard for me," Raphael said, "and it was very hard for my wife. Leona was close to Marco. She love him very much. He was conceived when we escaping Paraguay. He was a fighter like her. He want to fight the Marxist revolution in Europe, so he join the Army. He end up fighting the Islamic Marxists of the Caliphate when they invade Italy."

"I thought the Vatican was holding them off? I thought the Allied forces were keeping them at bay in North Italy."

Raphael made a sour face. "The West still do no have understanding of this enemy. They still try to fight this war by apologizing. They do no read history. They do no read military history. American foreign policy has always been impotent to fight these peoples." He shrugged. "It is only a matter of time before Italy falls and is conquered in the name of Allah."

These were all sober tidings. They fell silent, lost in their own worries until they got to the penthouse express elevator. Raphael placed his hand on the biometric scanner. "I am in the system for these scanners," he said, pulling out a small plastic card from his wallet, "but you can also use this master card until you set up the scanner."

"Actually, I think I still have the one Daniel gave me when I was cleaning up the kitchen." Ryan said, checking his wallet.

"Yes, that one *es* not a master key so you could not get through the security gates. You will need a master key card. Do not lose it or you will get locked out of your own home."

They entered the penthouse, and everyone fell silent as Ryan walked through each room in turn. The reaction was awe.

Daniel's team was feverishly drafting the agreement and working their satellite phones to finalize details. Ryan and Raphael moved into the security room where the teaching continued. They went over the fire suppression systems: halon, foam, and water. They went over the basics of the building's communications systems that would give him the ability to listen to most of the interior and exterior public spaces.

Raphael was twenty minutes into a tutorial about another system when Daniel called them into the office: Tim and Richard and Mora and Mrs. Ryder were sitting around the conference table. Tim had a video camera. Daniel held a thick set of papers. Richard stood with his bruises and a swollen face.

"Tim, are you taping this?"

Tim nodded.

"This is the agreement," Daniel said. "We have a few more things to do, but this will finalize everything. We are going to get this on tape so there can be no confusion in the coming months or years or even decades. It will have to serve as proof for all time, since many of the properties are being acquired sight unseen, and it is unknown if we will ever see each other again."

Mora swore in all parties and then for the next ten minutes, Daniel Ryder spoke to the camera, identified all witnesses, reciting legal jargon that was lost on Ryan, and holding up documents for identification. And then he said," Richard Ryder, you are here freely selling all of your assets to this man, Ryan Sage, for the sum of one seat in the transport and residence in a private location?"

"Yes, that is correct. And I do this being sound in mind and without coercion. For the record, the bruises evident on film were received in response to a personal fight that was the result of my own despicable behavior and have no bearing on the sale of the real estate and assets under discussion."

"Ryan Sage, as the rightful owner of this transportation and residence, you are selling that asset for the remunerations of all assets owned by Richard Ryder." Daniel had been fully formal until this moment, but in a quiet voice he said, "You can still choose to go if you like."

Richard flinched like he had been hit but did not speak.

"No, I'm good," Ryan said. "This is what I want to do."

"Very well." Daniel Ryder was all business again. "With these signatures and the confirming biometric validation, this contract will be ratified and completed, and all assets enumerated within will be transferred to ownership."

Richard, then Ryan, signed and confirmed the biometric validation. They shook hands. Richard left.

"Thanks, Tim," Daniel said. "Ryan, I don't know what to say. Part of me wants to hug you. Part of me wants to smack you. And all of me admires you." He left the room.

36

Global Infection: ≤ 27.7073%

> *He that has a house to put's head in has a good head-piece.*
> —WILLIAM SHAKESPEARE, *KING LEAR*

He had hardly known a minute's peace since buying the Renaissance Tower. It was awkward to walk the rooms of the penthouse with everyone staring. The initial awe had transformed into a brooding contempt that produced a bizarre mix of celebrity leprosy with all sorts of wild speculation for motive. And it was apparent that Daniel Ryder's assistants resented having to hunt him down for the thousand and one questions they needed answered.

So Ryan talked Daniel Ryder into giving him his network credentials and sequestered himself in the security room to start familiarizing himself with the tower domain structure. Of course, he should have known better than to expect Daniel Ryder to have credentials that would give access to Active Directory or any of the domain controllers. Within minutes, it became clear Ryan needed to be a domain administrator.

In the world of Information Technology, giving these credentials takes the right person less than five minutes of actual work. But in the bizarre world of Bruce and Patrick—the keepers of the gate for all things Molitor IT—it took an act of Daniel and then an act of God, plus an hour and forty-two minutes of satellite phone time.

At first, Bruce and Patrick just kept asking why the proper paperwork had not been submitted through Human Resources. The fact that HR had been sent home and all Molitor Group business functions were largely suspended didn't seem to matter. Then Bruce and Patrick could not grasp that the request was being made by THE Daniel Ryder. For the knowledge to bloom in their soul required an act of special revelation from the Divines, accompanied by the sacrificial offering of a small goat and a phone call from the CIO who was in transit to his ark in some far-flung location in the world's hinterlands. And last, they could not fathom why someone would buy the Renaissance Tower. That was a dumbass place to survive the zombie apocalypse. Everyone knows you have to find an uninhabited bunker in an abandoned military base near fresh water and lots of open arable land to plant crops after the Doritos, frozen pizza, and Mountain Dew ran out. Not that they had any idea where someone could find such a place.

They called themselves BruPtrick for reasons that only made sense if you were in junior high school, which was fitting since they both had the social skills of a fourteen-year-old. They bickered like an old married couple over the value of JavaScript versus VBScript and esoteric zombie lore manufactured by fiction writers. They seemed to agree on two things: George A. Romero was a prophet, and there was no way they could make Ryan a domain admin.

"This is not a request," said Daniel.

"But we don't know him," BruPtrick said at once through the speakerphone.

"You don't need to know him," Daniel said, consternation filling his voice.

"Corporate policy says—"

"I AM corporate policy!"

"It would take months to isolate the tower domain from the rest of the WAN," Patrick said.

"And we don't have days," said Bruce.

"He could hack our network," said Patrick, somehow missing the fact that there was no need to hack a network that one had credentials to access.

"It is MY—," Daniel started to say when Ryan raised a pausing hand. And this was the heart of the matter. All IT guys assume that users are dumbasses who defy the gods by daring to use the electronic toys.

Ryan had met hundreds of guys just like BruPtrick: they spent every waking moment lost in the arcana of the cyberworld, living on pizza and soda, and occasionally venturing beyond their server rooms to play Dungeons & Dragons with some equally socially inept people. If the employer could tolerate the interpersonal absurdity, IT guys like these were an asset like no other. They had no girlfriends, no drama, no other interests that mere mortals let invade their life. You paid them for fifty hours a week, and they gave you their life. The only thing they expected in return was that they owned all the toys. Their jealousy for all things IT guaranteed they were willing to die before letting someone hurt *their* domain. The downside was— like most ten-year-olds—if you made them mad, they would most likely fuck up the fort before letting girls with cooties enter the hallowed ground.

Twice, Daniel wanted to drop the billion-dollar hammer on their heads. He was not a man who suffered the absurdity of fools. He fully expected this detail to be checked off the list in a matter of minutes. The fact that this satellite phone call wore on had spiked his blood pressure into the coronary arrest category. But Ryan prevailed with caution. Daniel did not grasp one important fact: BruPtrick owned him in ways he could not fathom. Daniel thought they were in one of the half dozen Molitor arks that employees had been assigned to somewhere within North and South America where they could be summarily chastised upon arrival. Ryan suspected they were not, having decided to defy the zombie apocalypse in a location of their own choosing: the previously defined abandoned military base being the most likely candidate.

BruPtrick's constant rambling referenced some zombie survival manual like it was the British SAS handbook. They talked about life as if they assumed it would continue as it always had: role-playing game night, their multiplayer console game appointments, and their pro and con discussion of mace versus two-handed sword. And then there were the snide insults to bomb shelters and mountain side retreats and isolated island getaways. Whatever agreement Daniel had made with his employees, BruPtrick had chosen their own course and decided that their payment for keeping things running was a billionaire's global WAN with all the IT geek trimmings.

There was no way Ryan would be able to master the specifics of the Renaissance Tower domain in less than twenty-four hours. And if he did not get a domain level administrator account on the network, he would never have the opportunity to understand. Even with the credentials, he might get his mind around the technical details with fifty hours a week for a month. At present, he doubted he would have five minutes. Ryan was sure he would need Patrick and Bruce's benevolence as long as he could keep it.

Ryan could have explained every question they asked by referencing the OSI model and IPv6 protocols, bowed at the Linux command line altar, and sniffed out the usual IT nerd derision over Microsoft's endless effort to fuck up their own operating system, but Ryan knew he would never know enough to impress Bruce and Patrick. He would never appease their technical omniscience no matter the acronym sacrifice he offered at the altar of BruPtrick. Competing with Bruce and Patrick in the realm of domain administration was like playing a video game against a twelve-year-old. They did nothing all day but beat whoever dared enter their domain so they could talk smack. No one with a job—or a life—could ever hope to compete.

Through all their chatter and nattering and condescension and utter disdain for the zombie apocalypse—they had both long since prepared for this day, and how could anyone with a brain NOT have seen this coming?— Ryan learned the most important detail on the whole phone call.

"So did I hear you right, Patrick? You are a thirtieth level magic user? He is Lawful Good?"

The silence on the satellite phone stretched for a full minute.

So Ryan said, "I've got a twenty-six level monk that I drew from the deck of many things and got banished to the 7th plane of the Nine Hells. I need someone to come get me out." With those words, Ryan Sage was transformed from an interloping dumbass to a fellow nerd daring to defy the zombie apocalypse. Of course, he hadn't played Dungeons & Dragons since he was old enough to know that girls and multi-sided dice were mutually exclusive. Daednu—the name of the unfortunate banished monk—had taken up permanent residence on the Maladomini plane of the Nine Hells, because Ryan didn't have the stomach to deal with the drama coming from thirty-something adolescents. But he told the story of his fated character duped by a magic-using Orc.

"What? That is not possible!?"

"No way!"

"I know, right? How could an Orc use magic?"

And a Drow (rhymes with cow) sorcerer played by a bitchy ex-stripper who happened to be married to the magic-using Orc, who was also a network admin—like it was yesterday.

"Scam!"

"Fucking setup?"

"I know, right? Strippers? What are you gonna do?"

Ryan then told the tale of how he had been "forced" to draw a card from the Deck of Many Things in a conspiracy between them and the Dungeon Master.

"Dungeon Master was getting some of that stripper action?!"

"No excuse! He was supposed to be neutral."

"I know, right? They had it out for me."

Ryan speculated that maybe they wanted the Lawful Good influence of Monk Daednu gone so they could take over the quest?

"They wanted slaves!"

"Drow strippers are just like that!"

"I know, right?"

Ryan decided not to point out that Drow were fictional elf creatures and strippers were real. It was a minor detail after all, and BruPtrick's combined Lawful Good sensibilities boiled over into full-on Dungeons & Dragons outrage.

Two minutes later he got his domain account, and ten minutes later Ryan got his first e-mail from the company exchange server. They wanted to confirm that he had gotten their game group information. They would video conference with six other fellow gamers forting up for the apocalypse. Bruce and Patrick had sworn an oath to get Daednu out of the Maladomini. And oh, by the way, they elevated his credentials to enterprise admin, sent him the full WAN documentation complete with software license agreements and keys. Finally, they assured him that the zombie apocalypse would never bring it down.

Ryan pressed *end* on the satellite phone and gave Daniel a smile. "They will be my IT slaves for the rest of my life."

"I don't know what is more disturbing," Daniel said, "that my company actually employed those two or that you actually knew how to talk to them." He grabbed his pack of cigarettes and left the room.

Ryan worked his way through the documentation and began verifying an endless list of network settings. He heard the satellite phone ring and ring and ring, and for a brief moment, he thought it might be BruPtrick calling back but then saw a string of e-mail ping into his inbox: a flood of configuration and instruction for network shares and internal sites.

Patrick couldn't write an e-mail to save his life, supplying only as many letters as it would take to utter an electronic grunt. But it seemed that Bruce was as meticulous a documenter as any chief information officer could hope for. Ryan flashed off a couple of topological questions and some general banter about Daednu's plight in limbo. It was clear that their preferred method of contact to the outside world was e-mail. The phone was most certainly for Daniel. After a few minutes, the ringing faded into the background. Ryan didn't even know it had stopped ringing.

Between exploratory efforts in Windows Active Directory, the main means to navigate the functions and tools within the network structure, Ryan practiced switching security monitors to the main screen and browsing through the list of user manuals. It was the abrupt motion on one of the wall monitors that caught his eye. A young man, maybe sixteen, was jumping up and down on camera. It took Ryan a full minute to put the camera to the location on the main screen. The kid was near the corner of First and Wood at the receiving docks, across from the tenant parking garage entrance. The gate to the upper levels was locked in place. He wore a tactical vest bulging with magazines, a rifle on a sling that let it hang down his right side, and two handguns in holsters on his thighs.

Ryan moved to Daniel's office door. "I know you all are not expecting anyone else, but there is a guy on camera that is being very persist—" His voice died as he realizes they are both intent on the satellite phone.

"We are not waiting on anyone else," Daniel said, annoyance in his voice.

Ryan watched the monitor. The boy, in fluid motion, swept a pistol forward into a two-handed grip and fired—the muzzle flash seeming to blend into one beam of light—holsters the weapon, and started waving his hands again.

"This guy is armed to the teeth!" On different monitors, Ryan saw dozens of people advancing from Smithfield in the telltale awkward, trotting, shambling gate and the focused malevolent eyes and darkened muzzles.

The kid unleashed his handgun in that same two-handed grip and eight more flashes of muzzle blast. His right hand tilted, his left hand dropped to his hip, and then snapped back to the butt of the gun. The reload was a blur, and it took Ryan a minute to realize the shooter had just changed magazines. With deliberation, the kid dropped the zombies that were leading the pack, holstered his weapon, and snatched the magazine off the ground. He started waving frantically.

"God, this guy is good!" Ryan exclaimed. The kid brought a rifle to his shoulder and dashed down First Avenue toward the construction trailers.

"Hey, sorry to interrupt, but this kid has just dropped twenty in less than two minutes."

"I feel for him," Daniel said with genuine empathy, "but we are in the middle of something very important here."

Ryan nodded. "I understand. But if I wanted to let him in, how would I do that?"

"*Un momento,* Leona!" snapped Raphael. "You can no just open the doors. He may be infected."

"With shooting like that I doubt he has been bit. But he is going to die. I can help him." He held out his pad. "You guys don't have to help me bring him in. If you want, I will keep him in a different room until you are gone. Just show me the right buttons to push so I can let him in. He's all alone. I just need to try and save him. How do I do it?"

Both men turned back to the phone. Daniel looked grim. Raphael's face had turned ashen.

Ryan looked back at the monitors, and the kid had run back to the original camera. He shot left then right, dropping zombies like a video game. Then he bent down. It looked like he was writing something in big spray paint letters. D A D!

"Uh," Ryan said, "Raphael, I'm thinking you are dad, right?"

Exasperated, Raphael glanced around the security room door. He did a double take. "Simone!"

"*Raphael?*" A woman's voice asked from the phone.

"It is our boy!" he shouted. "*Gloria a Dios!* Simone! We call you back, Leona. Our boy, he is alive."

Raphael fumbled for the right button on the command console. "Simone! Simone! Can you hear me?"

Simone snapped his rifle to his shoulder followed by shots, then a reload. Then more shots at the other direction.

Raphael stabbed at another button. "Simone, can you hear me?"

Simone's head snapped around nodding and waving.

"See the loading dock, *a la derecha*? I am coming. It will take five minutes to get to the door. Pull the creatures away from the dock. Can you do that?"

Simone nodded. He dropped to a knee and fired six times, then sprinted out of camera view.

"Leona, we will call you back as soon as he is inside," Daniel said.

"*Go, go save my boy!*"

Daniel called his security team, and they all hit the penthouse door running. Minutes later, eight armed men stood at a loading dock used for small deliveries. Ryan held his shotgun. Raphael looked out the window only to see the infected trundling down First Avenue towards an unseen goal. He pushed through the door with the security team behind. They dropped to the street they cut down hobbling, dragging, trotting zombies in the space of a minute.

But even with the carnage: the chunk of flesh and bone and severing limbs, they still crawled or dragged themselves with single-minded animosity.

"*Mierda!*" Raphael exclaimed.

"Headshots!" Ryan called out. But they didn't hear.

Simone gunned the truck engine; he was farther west down First Avenue passed Wood Street. He was rocking and rolling forward and back, trying to keep the zombies from massing. But the mob gathered, clinging to any surface, falling under the trunk. Simone banged on the horn and revved the engine.

"On our six!" one of the security men shouted and opened fire east down First Avenue.

"Drive him into the VIP parking," Rick shouted.

"They might flood in," Raphael said.

Of course, Daniel and Richard Ryder and the VIPs and the premium tenants didn't park with the general populace. They had their own private space directly underneath the tower, behind a door that resembled a bank vault. The VIP parking entrance was forty feet from the loading dock, but it looked like a mile with the mob trundling forward. Ryan saw the reader and grabbed the badge out of his pocket; hugging the building he scraped past the blazing guns to swipe the card.

"Bring him in here!" Ryan shouted as the latch released from the ground and the door started to roll into the ceiling above. The door rattled and clicked and an eternity passed as the gate raised, inch by agonizing inch, the howling, moaning menace getting closer and louder. Ryan took three strides forward, paused, pointed, and pulled the trigger. A ghoul's head exploded. He fired again and again taking down the leaders of the pack.

"On point here!" Rick shouted.

The team fanned out across First Avenue, weapons barking, delivering rounds center mass.

"They just don't drop!"

Who knows how many professional shooters died in the early days of the outbreak, having drilled a lifetime of shooting center mass. Ryan fumbled shells into his Mossberg and took aim at the lead ghouls riddled with bullet holes. "Headshots!" he shouted again and pulled the trigger. The head blew apart splattering the creatures behind and the body dropped.

"Headshots!" Raphael echoed.

The weapons roared. Zombies dropping.

Ryan blasted five rounds into the mob and fell back into the VIP parking door.

Raphael waved at Simone.

Simone gunned the engine, scattered the mob, and bounced across Wood Street, tires squealing as he turned into the tower entrance and skidded to a halt.

"The door is closing," Daniel Ryder shouted.

The professionals fell back, smooth and efficient, in a choreographed dance.

Simone jammed the truck into park and bolted from the driver seat, rounded to the front bumper and fired at the infected clinging to the undercarriage.

Two security men stayed on the outside blasting away as the VIP door slowly closed. Two others dropped prone, shooting under the door until the door was almost shut. The men on the outside rolled under at the last second.

The VIP garage was silent.

And then from the passenger side, another man worked his way out of the truck, cringing and grunting against pain. When he managed to stand tall, he was bristling weapons just like Simone. His haircut and bearing was military, but his eyes faded in and out of focus against suffering. Blood oozed from under bandages that dotted his left arm, hand, and hip. He finally managed a smile.

Raphael looked between Simone and the bleeding man. He started to weep.

"Hey, Poppa," Simone said, walking to his speechless father. "Have you talked to Momma?"

37

Global Infection: ≤ 27.7301%

No battle plan ever survives contact with the enemy.
—Helmuth von Moltke the Elder

The answer to Simone's question was yes; Raphael had talked to Leona and it had been a very serious conversation: one he had to follow-up on as soon as the VIP garage gate closed.

"Steve, has the jet landed?" Daniel Ryder said into the satellite phone as the elevator stopped at the penthouse landing. Two security men remained behind to dispose of the creatures that had clung to the truck. Everyone else found a spot amongst the stone statues, remaining quiet while their boss planned.

Daniel listened and then checked his watch. "So, ETA for touchdown is in twenty-seven minutes? And how long to refuel?" He paused. "Wait, Rick can answer that better. Let me put you on speaker." Daniel tapped a button and said, "Steve wants to know how the prep is going in Wilmington?"

Rick said, "Hey Steve, they should have everything secured by 1530."

Steve said, "We were not scheduled to bug out until 1100 tomorrow."

Daniel said, "We need to move the extraction from the tower up ASAP."

"What? Is Bret even back from Florida?"

"Steve, I know he was your friend, but Bret was shot down about two hours ago. He's gon—"

"This from a reliable source?"

"Leona saw it happen," Daniel said. "The military shot down his helicopter. I'm sorry to be abrupt, but we have to move."

"Any reporting why they were shot down?"

"No, and we doubt there will be any reports, but we think the command has gone out to close American airspace. They must think they have lost control of the spread. We must go now. How long before you can start making runs to the tower?"

"I'm still an hour out of Wilmington. Fifteen to twenty minutes to refuel, if the ground crew is worth a shit."

"They are squared away," Rick said.

"Then you can do the math when I can be in the air."

Daniel heard the exhaustion in his voice. "Steve, when was the last time you slept?"

"Sleep is for pussies."

"No, you need some rack time. I know this change screwed up your schedule."

Steve sighed into the phone. "Okay, this pussy and my copilot need an hour."

"Make it two," Daniel said, "I'd rather we didn't crash. We need to get everyone at once. Thirty-one total, but thirteen of those are kids."

"Originally we planned with two Sikorskys and one trip but with only one . . ." Daniel stepped paces away.

The security team glanced at Simone, like he might suddenly go mad. They stared at the other man like he was a ghost.

Indeed, he might have been a ghost. He was supposed to be buried with honors in Arlington National Cemetery. He tottered like he might fall over if breathed on, and Raphael clung to his oldest son, Marco like he might disappear. Tears washed down his grey grim face.

Daniel paced back. "The kids probably average seventy-five pounds. How about if we leave all luggage? Does that work?

"I'm telling you, one trip is a no-go."

"Hmm . . . how about if we lose the guns? Strip it down to the barest—"

"They are already shooting us down," Steve said, exasperated, *"We have no chance unarmed."*

"Yes, good point. Okay, so it is two trips no matter what? How about the cargo? I'm guesstimating we've got an extra five hundred pounds per trip."

"If you want any speed at all we need to fly people and little else."

Daniel said, "We need the speed, we'll leave the extra. See you at 2130."

"Copy that! Out here."

Daniel scanned the men, but avoided Raphael's eyes and Raphael looked away from Daniel. The security team gathered around Raphael, a few touched his shoulder, the sign of a brotherhood that extended beyond working for the Molitor Group and way beyond building high rises.

"What is wrong, Poppa?" Simone whispered.

"Nothing is wrong if I have my sons with me." He hugged him again and squeezed Marco's shoulder. Marco tried to keep his expression stoic, but that pain rippled across his body.

One of the security men pulled Marco to the side and looked under the bandages. His face turned grave.

Rick said, "Daniel, the men and I could find another ride. Just give us the coordinates and we can get ourselves there."

Daniel shook head. "No, Rick, you will not be traveling there on foot. Listen to me, all of you. I know your skills. And you are all operators, but many of you have become my friends and family. You have all earned this. You have been all over the world for me, and I have asked a lot, but not this. I won't allow you to sacrifice yourself."

Each man gave off the barest hint of relief.

"Your families are there already and eager to have you safe. And *they* have earned that," Daniel said. "Here is what you can do. Get everyone ready to move. Get them out of civilian clothes. If this goes bad, everyone needs to be able to survive on the ground. Get them into jeans and outdoor gear. I told them to pack those things. Hopefully, they listened. Tell Lisa first. She will keep everyone in line. Let the kids keep some small things, but the grownups will have to leave it all behind."

"Any order you want people to leave in?" Rick asked.

"I have enough decisions to make. Let them sort that out. I'd prefer that Lisa went out first, but she won't leave without me and I'm the last flight off the roof. Give my staff the choice of who goes when, but I suspect they will stay till I board the helicopter. The next few hours will go fast, and I doubt Steve will take the full two hours sleep."

"Very well," Rick said.

The security man evaluating Marco's wounds said, "He needs some work."

"I'll be fine," Marco said.

The medic snorted. "You will die if I don't work on you."

"Can it wait a few minutes?" Daniel asked.

The medic nodded. "I need to organize medical supplies in the barracks on thirteen. I need him on the infirmary table."

"Give us twenty minutes and I will send him down," Daniel said.

"One more thing," the medic said, "I know you are happy to have your boys back, but we just let two men who are infected into the building. I see a bullet wound, but most of Marco's wounds are human bites. And the reason Simone ran away is because he had been bit."

And this was the elephant in the penthouse.

Raphael dropped his chin in unspoken dread.

"I'm not—," Simone started to say.

And for or the first time Marco spoke. "I know my presence here demands a lot of answers, but I can tell you now that I am not contagious and neither is Simone."

"How can you be sure?" Daniel asked.

"Because I was first infected over a year ago and did not go mad. I am immune. It is a genetic resistance."

"But how does that mean you are not contagious now?" the medic asked. "Those bites are new."

Marco started to sway under the pain. "Unless you start sucking on these wounds, no one will be infected."

Daniel looked at the medic. "Your call."

"Okay, I'll work on him," he said, and stepped into the elevator and was gone.

"Ryan, would you mind giving Raphael and me a minute, please? Wait for us in my office?"

Ryan's brow creased. It was actually his office, but habits were hard to break. With a nod, he walked into the penthouse and stood watching the chaos: each person shifting with the tide of emotion around them. A moment later, a woman's voice, strong and firm, rose above the din and brought everyone to silence. Lisa Ryder gained command of her brood and started issuing orders; she was cut from the same cloth as Daniel. And then Ryan noticed Ahou sitting in a distant room, huddled with her sister and mother and the blond man from the pictures. She was crying. Then she saw him and broke into sobs.

Ryan turned and walked to the office. Seeing the kid on the streets waving his hands, desperate to get into the tower, Ryan had felt a subtle breeze of hope that he would not weather the coming days alone. The kid on the camera represented more than guns. He had been the promise of someone to share the same space and the common bond of security. But that had vanished the second the kid said, "Hey, Poppa. Have you talked to Momma?"

Ryan worked through the security cameras studying the system like his life depended on it. He changed the remote cameras feeding images from Molitor Group properties across the globe and populated the screens with Renaissance Tower cameras. He set up a folder on a file server, logged onto his home security monitoring system account and downloaded the files into a local drive. When the monitoring service servers lost power, he would still have access to the incriminating evidence. It was better to have them and not need them, than to need them and not have them to shove up the corrupt federal ass.

Then he got out his iGlass and started his list:

> Perishable food storage
> Power management study
> Lenna and Erik verify
> Tower fortification
> Pink Coat girl??

Daniel walked into the security room directly from the penthouse, pulled the door closed and slumped into a chair beside Ryan, the stress of the day wearing through the tailored and polished CEO look. "We thought they were dead." He said without preamble. "Marco, we put in the ground a year ago."

Ryan nodded. "Did he give any explanation?"

"Not a word. He's in a lot of pain right now. I think he is barely hanging on." Daniel said, "What you did today with Richard . . . I don't think I have words to describe what that means. It is extraordinarily brave."

"But you think it foolish?"

"I don't know if foolish is the right word. It's more like I feel an over-whelming desire to protect. I have only known you for hours, but I have a clear picture that you are a very capable man. And what you have done for me and my family goes far beyond the purchase price of this tower. I called you son earlier. I am probably overstepping our relationship, but I say it with admiration and affection. That part I can't explain."

That brought a tear to Ryan's eye. It had been a long time since someone expressed such open affection, such pride in him. "Thank you."

"So please, do not be offended by what I'm about to ask. There is now space for you to come to the ark. Even with all the work we've done, I would gladly let you come, and there would never be a criticism. I think you would be an extraordinary asset."

"I see," Ryan said, the math finally starting to tally in his mind. "Simone and Marco make too many people, which means that Raphael will most likely not be going—"

Daniel finished the thought. "Which means there is at least one more spot available."

Ryan leaned back in his chair, watching the video continue its download to the folder. He worked his way through the emotions that threatened to compete with the goals that purchasing this tower represented. Fear was understandable. It was an enormous enterprise to live and take on this outbreak in a strange city, alone. But that didn't diminish his reasons for purchasing the tower in the first place. Did it? Could he achieve the same outcomes locked in an ark for decades? Could a closed society like the ark even work?

Very unlikely.

The kilobytes ticked down from the server, their transfer chronicled by a growing blue line.

Lenna and Erik verify
Tower fortification
Pink Coat girl??

He was already making plans. He was already treating this like it was his home.

Finally, Ryan said, "I understand what you are offering—"

Daniel's face fell. "I hear a *but* coming."

"But I need to stay here."

Daniel smiled as if he were pleased. "That is what I told her you would say."

38

Global Infection: ≤ 27.7398%

Nothing can stop the man with the right mental attitude from achieving his goal; nothing on earth can help the man with the wrong mental attitude.

—Thomas Jefferson

That is what I told her you would say???

Those words stuck in Ryan's mind like a splinter.

Her? Who?

But Ryan never got to ask the question. Daniel said, "Ryan, would you join us, please?" motioning for him to follow into the office. "This will concern you." He slid into the ergonomic chair and spun toward the office phone.

Something bad was about to happen, and once again Ryan felt like he was in the middle of a family fight.

Raphael grabbed Ryan's hand. "I say thank you."

"Thank me? For what?"

"You want to save my boys before you knew it was my boys. You want to save a stranger. If you had not been watching the cameras . . . if you had not . . ." Raphael bowed his head trying to hide his tears. He grabbed Simone and Marco and hugged them hard. Marco braced himself against the pain, but leaned into the affection.

A moment later, Daniel pressed the speaker button on his satellite phone and said, "Leona, Simone is here. He is safe."

And the next few minutes descended into wet declarations of love.

"Okay . . . enough of this crying," Leona said.

"Leona," Raphael said, looking at Marco.

"Yes?"

But Marco put his hand on his father's shoulder and shook his head no.

"But we must tell her," Raphael rasped.

For the first, time emotion crossed Marco's face. He dropped his head.

"Tell me what?" Leona asked.

"I am coming to get you," Raphael said. "I drive a Stryker. We meet and I pick you up."

"Oh, my love, you will do no such thing. You must go with Daniel. You must be safe."

"I will no go with Daniel! We are a family."

"I made my way through a thousand miles of jungle with many things that want to eat me, not just some mindless creatures that do not have the sense to avoid a bullet. This is a walk on the beach. Timoteo and Lucas, we are fine. You go with Daniel. I will meet you there."

"Uh . . . Leona, Raphael," Daniel said. "I don't know how to say this. But even if you could get there on foot in time, there is not enough room for your whole family."

"Not enough room? How can this be? There were three men on that flight crew. With them gone, Simone could surely have their place, yes?"

"Three you say?" asked Daniel.

"Yes, three. Bret, a copilot, and one man running security."

"Bret must have picked them up for the ride down," Daniel mused out loud. "But they were not part of the group heading to the ark."

Leona said, *"But without the three of us? Raphael, you must take him and be safe."*

"Leona, that is no happening," Raphael's voice brooked no disagreement. "I am not leaving you or my sons. We will no more argue this. *Entender?!"*

"Yes," Leona said, contrite. *"But can't Simone take Bret's place?"*

"You must tell her," said Daniel.

"What are you not telling me?" Leona's voice was strident.

"Hello, Momma," Marco said.

Silence.

"Momma?"

"Marco? But . . ." And then the math finally added up. *"Oh, Madre Dios."*

"Momma, Poppa," Marco said. "You go on with Teo, Lucas, and Simone. I will be fine."

"NO!" Leona was defiant. *"I do not understand how you are there. I buried you a year ago. I have the flag, but we are not leaving you."*

"I need to say this so that everyone understands," Daniel said. "I assume that they are shooting down all aircraft now. I fear that we have a very small window to get everyone to safety. We no longer have time to pick you up and get back to the tower in time. Unfortunately, when Bret was shot down, that signaled we had one opportunity to get you and the boys, Leona. There is no way for you to get to our location in time. We must bug out tonight. Marco, Simone, and Raphael are more than welcome to leave when we do but I can't get to you. And even if I could, someone would have to be left behind. I am sorry."

The silence lingered as everyone started to mourn the realities before them.

Daniel was first to speak. "Ryan, I have known you less than a few hours and you have already proven to me over and over the kind of man you are. The Paguero family is like my own children. Raphael is like a son to me. Leona is my daughter. Their children are like my grandchildren. I want to ask you a personal favor. Would you please take them in? Would you . . ." his voice broke, and he began to weep. It took him a minute to compose himself. "Would you please let them stay here with you and do everything in your power to keep them alive?"

The question percolated a moment before it registered. Ryan expected to be alone. That was the state of his existence for most of his adult life but now maybe he wouldn't be alone. He smiled. "Of course. I would be glad to have them."

"Thank you," Daniel said. "Raphael, Leona, listen to me. I believe this is your best chance to survive . . . for all of you to survive." For the next few minutes, he explained to Leona that Ryan had bought the tower and all of Richard's resources.

"He did this thing? Why would he do this?"

When Ryan didn't seem inclined to explain it, Daniel said, "It doesn't matter. He has done it. But this means you have a place to come. Please, Leona."

"Raphael," said Leona, *"we could go to the place in the Adirondacks. We can survive there."*

"Momma," said Marco, "we would never get there before the 2091s get into the mountains. I traveled the roads through Pennsylvania. It would be very hard to get there and I'm in no condition to travel back."

"2091s?" Leona said confused.

"RVCJ-2091 is the official name of the viral infection," Marco said. "Our unit called them 2091s."

"Leona," Raphael's voice was firm, "the camp in the mountains was made for guerilla war, not a siege. This tower, with much work, could withstand a siege."

"Raphael, you have met this man? This man who gives up safety for a building?"

"Yes, my treasure. I tell you later, but he is the reason that we have our sons."

"He is the reason? How does this man give us our sons?"

"Leona," Raphael said, "Listen to me. The Holy Mother, she intercedes for this one. He is *mucho loco*, but he is a good man."

"Ryan?" Leona's voice softened. *"What is your last name?"*

"Sage."

"Ryan Sage. Yes, this is a nice name. Are you wise? That is what sage means."

He was the one offering the place to live and he was being interviewed?

"I would like to think so, though some question my motive for buying a building when the world is ending." Ryan let the irony seep into his words.

"But, at the moment, my folly seems to offer options to people who might not have many."

Leona laughed. *"Yes, this does work out for me and my family. Do you want us there?"*

"Leona, I already said I did," Ryan said. "I will be candid. Now, the idea of living by myself as society collapses scares the shit out of me. So, having people with me, people as capable as your husband obviously is, will be much better."

"But why did you do this thing? Why did you buy a building when you could have safety?"

Whatever Leona Paguero's concerns were, her critical review bothered him. Ryan had a fair understanding of his motives, but he didn't really owe anyone a justification. He had spent his whole life developing and living out the content of his ideas. He knew what he wanted; he knew what the future meant and by what criteria he would allow people to come live with him. So, Ryan said, "Leona, here is my answer. I don't make choices based on weakness. I make choices based on value and sound judgment. My willingness to make the offer is because in the very brief time I've known your husband, I can see his implicit value, his respected professional knowledge, his restraint in the middle of conflict, and how he treats his family. If I had not already seen those things, I would have stopped Daniel before he finished his second sentence.

"Leona, Raphael, you can choose whatever course seems right to you. But I will be here. I will find others who have the qualities I listed. It is not enough for me to survive. It is my goal to thrive, to beat back this disaster and beat back the government forces that are at the root of the world's tyranny. If you and Raphael want to become part of my vision, to take back this planet for free men to live in peace, then you are certainly welcome."

Leona was quiet for a while, only the hum of the truck she was traveling in filtered into the speaker made it clear the satellite phone was still connected. Then she said, *"Daniel, is this a son you have not told us about?"*

Daniel chuckled. "You are not the first to ask."

"Yes, this is good. This is good way to think. To beat back the government forces of tyranny. That will be harder than these mindless beings wandering around now. Yes, we will join you in this vision. Very well then, it is decided. Start on the work. We will—"

"Momma, look out the back window . . ." said a male voice in the background.

"Mierda!" Leona swore.

"Que es?"

"Policia. Raphael, I will call you if I need help. You stay. Do the work that will make us all safe. We must go." The line went dead.

Amid the general buzz of people picking up their own individual conversations, Ryan noticed one person leaning quietly just inside the office door, his hands folded over his chest, his bruises livid, the swelling misshaping his features. It took a moment for Ryan to decide the content of the look on Richard Ryder's face. And then he figured it out. It was triumph.

39

Global Infection: ≤ 27.7400%

*Love is the expression of one's values, the greatest reward
you can earn for the moral qualities you have achieved in
your character and person, the emotional price paid by one
man for the joy he receives from the virtues of another.*
—AYN RAND

After the Leona phone call, Daniel's office became a wasp hive of tempers and emotion. The penthouse beyond roiled with arguments and accusations. Kids cried and parents shushed or cussed, depending on demeanor. Ryan escaped into the security office trying to get some peace of mind amidst the turmoil. He picked through his bags, idly inventorying the contents and thinking that his frantic rush out of the minimart proved irrelevant.

He loaded Ahou's duffel with his arsenal. The guns smelled like oil and gunpowder, but he dumped the rest of his clothes on top. He had added the rabbit and the one photo album. Ryan didn't want to risk ruining the smell of Ahou's pillow. It was too big to tote around, so he pulled off the case and put it in a plastic bag. The letter he had never had the nerve to read went in with it. It seemed like an extravagance to spend the time putting the pillowcase in a plastic bag with the clock ticking down to being left forever, and now Ryan had the rest of his life to go back to her room and find things that smelled like Ahou.

There was a cruel irony in the fact that now he didn't think he wanted to return to her room. Once again, the mirage was coming apart. Fiancé was the name of the cold, wet wind that blew across the shimmering oasis that revealed the harsh world of scorching sands.

Ryan hurt. He had been here before; his hope pinched off like a flickering candle. But at the moment it just hurt.

He felt someone behind him before he saw them. He flinched. Then he saw Ahou hugging the entrance to the security room.

"May I come in?" she said. He face looked puffy and drawn, the early starts of some crow's feet stood out against her light, coffee-colored skin. She was wearing another tight white T-shirt and a pair of jeans. It was a fabulous, heart-stopping look for her.

Ryan's heart leapt, but he casually zipped up the duffel and slid it onto the security desk. "Well, it looks like you are already in," he said with more heat than he intended.

"You are mad at me?"

Ryan tilted his head and gave her his best *Have you lost your ever-loving mind* look.

"I've never had a man look at me like that . . ." Ahou said, shaking her hands like she was trying to get something off.

Ryan wrinkled his brow, but said nothing.

"Yes, just like that. Like you can look through me, or maybe like you look into me."

"Yeah. Well, what can I say?"

"The great Ryan Sage at a loss for words?"

"Did you mean to be insulting? You—" Suddenly, Ryan felt very tired. "Is this a bad movie script?" he said, rubbing his forehead. "Why is it my job to magically say the perfect thing right here, right now? Ahou, whatever my greatness or my mastery of the English language might be—and it is vast—I'm not the one who needs to be talking. You have a fiancé after telling me that you don't."

"I never said tha—"

Ryan clenched his fist. "Do not parse words with me, Ahou. Do not treat me like I have the IQ of a peanut."

"Oh, I know that you don't have an IQ of a peanut," Ahou said, slyly turning on the charm and the wattage of her sex appeal, taking a rolling stride toward him, her nipples hardening under the cloth of her T-shirt.

Ryan looked at her flat and hard until she froze. "Woman, you are meowing around the wrong tree. I am *not* a boy toy who loses his mind at the flash of some nipples. Do we understand each other?"

"I . . . uh . . . I," Her face flushing. "You just did it again. You just looked through me. How do you do that?" her voice faded down to a whisper, suddenly sounding intoxicated.

"Well, then it will come as no surprise that I won't let you pretend that I somehow misunderstood. Nothing will make me lose the last of my respect faster than for you to play me like some chump."

"You are right," Ahou said, raising her hands in surrender. "I am so sorry. My words were misleading. In my mind our engagement was over. I can explain, but it's complicated."

Ryan laughed and rolled his eyes. "Of course! Telling the truth must be complicated. Why else lie?"

"Don't be like this."

"Okay, Ahou, enough of the clichés. The moral failing here is not mine. So if you have something specific to say, then I'm willing to listen. But even if I do, I'm not sure how it affects where we are."

"Ryan, didn't you feel anything the other night?"

He liked how his name sounded in her mouth, but Ryan said, "The issue here is not my emotional vulnerability. I'm not the archetypical closed-off male failing to open up."

"But what we shared was so intense. I feel like there is something here. I took off my clothes and . . ." she took a step closer, checking both doors to the security room to see if anyone was behind her. "And if you had been close . . ." Ahou let her eyes finish the rest of the sentence.

He didn't want his voice to filter into the hubbub of Daniel Ryder's office. He took a step closer. "Ahou, being naked is the easy part for both of us," Ryan said, matching her tone. "You have been naked before, right?" he said, "With the alcohol-drinking frat boys that bored you to tears?"

Ahou flushed. "You make me sound so . . ."

"Actually, no, I don't make you *sound* any specific way." Ryan felt his passion rising, which usually meant he got louder. He didn't want to embarrass her, so he made himself drop his voice. "I'm merely talking about who you said you are. My comment has nothing to do with how many times you've been naked. And you don't owe me an explanation. My point is that you are about to trivialize what you shared, reducing it to something akin to changing your clothes. That is not what you did with me. You wanted me to see all of you. The naked part was only a small part. I saw transparency on the camera. You gave me a gift. And then I felt hope." Ryan scrubbed his fingers through his hair, frustrated.

It was Ahou's turn to lean close, a smile pulling at the corner of her mouth. "You did feel something. I knew it was different."

"I never said I didn't feel anything. It is because I did feel something, because I thought I was free to feel something for you that I feel betrayed. It is the pesky detail of a fiancé that matters . . ."

"I am sorry about that. But it is over. And we . . ." Ahou bit her lip as her words stopped. She stood rooted in place, breath coming in shallow bursts. "So, do you . . . so . . . so what do you want?"

"What do *I* want?" Ryan's focus was deep into her eyes. And then he understood what she was asking. "You have it in your mind that I will make some everlasting declaration of love, and you will stay with me here to brave the apocalypse together?"

Ahou almost melted. "How do you do this? How do you see into me so?"

Ryan's chin dropped to his chest. He slumped back against the desk. "Ahou . . . as much as I might like to get caught up in the connection that we seem to share, a flash of transparency is not the substance of a relationship. Certainly not one that can transcend leaving out details like you have a fiancé."

"I just hadn't told my parents. It was my mother—"

"Ahou, he is *here!*"

"Daniel Ryder should never have brought him here."

"But Ahou, even your fiancé was unaware that it was over. He wouldn't have come just because. I doubt Daniel Ryder told him the whole story over the phone. So the only reason he is here is because he believed it was to be with you . . . forever."

Ahou's head dropped. Tears started down her cheeks.

"Look, here is how my thinking goes. If a grown woman does not have the ability to tell a man that their engagement is over . . . if a grown woman does not have the courage to tell her own parents about the substance of her own mind . . . if a grown woman does not have the conviction of her own self-appointment . . . if a grown woman does not have the will to suffer the consequence of her choices . . ." Ryan paused until Ahou's eyes met his. "Then how in the *hell* will she have the courage to prevail in the apocalypse?"

"You are rejecting me because I lied to you this one time?"

Ryan looked to the sky, his frustration percolating to the surface.

"What? What is wrong?"

"Have you not been listening? My point is your lie, this whole interaction with me, is a symptom of a much, much bigger problem. You don't want the responsibility of *your* choices. I'm a bit player in this drama. The harm done to me is trivial by comparison to everyone else. You misled me because it was your method of operation. You let people believe what they want, playing passive until someone else makes a decision for you. You tried to turn on the charm so that I might ask you to stay. But never once did you have the courage to openly tell me that you want to stay. Never once in this conversation have you taken responsibility for the course of events you set in motion. My point is that you can barely suffer the hardship of telling people who *love you* the truth. How in the hell will you accept the hardship where zombies want to eat you?"

"But I told my mother that it was over, and she refused to listen," Ahou said, shaking her hands again. "And she is the one who told Daniel Ryder to bring him to the tower."

"Ahou, you just did it again. So quit telling yourself stories. Everyone *else* acted consistent with what they believed to be true. *Everyone!* Daniel Ryder went to enormous expense to retrieve your fiancé from Washington. And your father, your mother, your fiancé acted in accord with their understanding of reality. Maybe your mother was presumptuous, but she couldn't get away with that if any of the others had known. Even you still have his pictures up in your room. If it were over, how come you made no noticeable change?"

40

Global Infection: ≤ 27.7402%

Two types of choices seem to me to have been crucial in tipping the outcomes [of the various societies' histories] towards success or failure: long-term planning and willingness to reconsider core values. On reflection we can also recognize the crucial role of these same two choices for the outcomes of our individual lives.

—JARED DIAMOND, COLLAPSE:
HOW SOCIETIES CHOOSE TO FAIL
OR SUCCEED

Her smile was back, and she looked beautiful despite the tears. "So, you went to our house." She took a step closer. "And you went to my room?" She was standing right beside Ryan.

Ryan let the warmth of her press against his thigh and shoulder. He didn't move. "Yes, of course. Did you forget that it is technically my house and my room?"

Ahou looked deep into Ryan's eyes. "I like that you are tall."

"I like that you are, too."

Ahou's fingers brushed against his cheek. "You have lost weight. You look good."

"That is what five days of manual labor will do for an old man, and you have lost weight too."

"That is what three days of worry will do to a silly Persian girl," Ahou said. "And don't say that."

"Say what?"

"That you are an old man."

"Okay, I won't."

Ahou bit her lip. She touched his cheek again. "What do you have in my bag that you don't want me to see?"

"Nothing much," he said, feeling exposed. He noticed the bruises around her wrists. It looked like someone had grabbed her hard.

"I saw you zip up the bag when you saw me at the door. And now I can see that it is the one from my, well, *your* room," she said with a wink. "You are not the only one who can be perceptive. You took something from my room. May I see, please? May I see what was important to you?"

Ryan shrugged and nodded toward the bag. Absently, his finger went to touch her wrist.

Ahou let his finger trace around the bruise, but she offered no explanation. She unzipped it and pulled the items out one by one. "My rabbit?!" she said as a tear slowly traced down her right cheek. "I thought I'd lost this forever." Then she pulled out the photo album and flipped through the pages. "You made your own collection of me," she said as she held the rabbit gently to her face and leafed through the album. She blushed slightly when she saw the pictures of her stretching. She flipped the page quickly. "I always hated these pictures," she said. "They make my face look ridiculous."

"Those are my favorite ones. You are totally unaware. It is just you."

Ahou brushed the hair from the side of her face with a girlish smile. "You like that?"

Ryan just watched her and Ahou let him. She finished the album and looked into the bag. "My pillowcase?" she said, puzzled. "And my letter?" She opened the plastic bag and touched the fabric. "You didn't open the letter?"

"I have been pretty busy with trying to survive," Ryan said, and then added, "and I haven't had the nerve to read it."

"How come?"

Ryan shrugged.

"Why these things?" she said to herself. "You took the rabbit because you knew it meant something to me. You chose pictures that are spontaneous." Ahou leaned against his shoulder intimately, familiar, relaxed. "But why this pillowcase? I almost thought I would find some panties," she said with a sly smile and a subtle jab.

A smile tweaked at the corner of Ryan's mouth, but he could barely talk. He was intoxicated with how good she smelled. He wanted to bury his face in her neck. He was treading fast down a path that was doomed before it started. He bent slightly and breathed deep, feeling a heady rush, and his heart threatened to explode.

And then Ahou understood. "This smelled of me. This was all you had left of me."

"Yes."

"I want to kiss you now."

Ryan wanted to kiss her too. Rarely did a woman divine his thoughts. Rarely did women even try to understand. He found the experience exhilarating, but shook his head. Ryan found himself caressing the bruise on her wrist. "I don't kiss women who are drunk, stoned, or high. I don't kiss women that have fiancés or husbands."

She bit her lip trying to suppress the emotions. "Who do you kiss?"

"That is easy. Women who don't want to hide anything from me. Women who are honest with themselves. Women who have the resolution to commit to their own desires and lives. Women who love the principles of life."

Ahou put her hand on his chest like she was trying to hold on to a lifeline and dropped her head. "Axioms," she whispered.

"What?"

"Axioms," she repeated. "Everything has axioms, foundation principles that can only be ignored. And if you ignore them long enough, eventually reality imposes a consequence."

"You were listening."

"To every word. How did you say it? A man who chooses to act consistent with life knows he must keep making the same choice? That man's integrity saves him from choices that bring death?"

Ryan smiled. "You just said it better than I did."

"I heard your words and they frightened me.

"I don't understand."

"The *woman* who breaks axioms for expedience has two problems. *She* has not found principles, or *she* is not a woman of integrity." Ahou finished, biting her lip. "You didn't know it, but you were talking to me. And that is what I was writing down. You were talking about me. And now the last part has come to pass. I was destined to suffer the consequence of my bad choices."

"That is impressive," Ryan said.

"I'm not impressive. I'm a silly Persian girl. I am smart. And yes, I know I am beautiful and that men desire me. And I've been able to manipulate those around me to get what I think I want. And now I realize why that has been so unsatisfying. Standing next to you, I realize how little my beauty matters. I think I see how my ability to manipulate has betrayed me. I think I see the bigger picture."

"That is some very inspiring introspection. Not many people can do that for themselves."

Ahou nodded. "And most important, I know what kind of man you are. When I heard you bought the tower, I cried because I thought we would have a chance to be together in the ark. I even begged Daniel to ask you again to come to the ark."

That is what I told her you would say . . .

Ahou had just plucked the splinter of those words from his mind. He nodded. Daniel had known the answer before he even sat down to ask.

"But then I realized that for you it could be no other way," Ahou continued. "You said that ideas belonged on the street, not locked away in some room. Of course, you would choose to remain because that is you. That is a challenge worthy of the kind of man you are."

"Ahou, I can't get over how much you have really paid attention." His urge to hold her, to be connected to her made him shake.

"It was because I had been listening that I wept. Because I knew I was not that person. I thought maybe I could be. I wanted to be. I hoped you would talk me into something, but only because I have not talked myself into it."

All Ryan could manage was a nod. Ahou spoke the truth. That was the reality of her character. No matter how he wished she were someone different, at the core, she had diagnosed herself correctly. And that was why any relationship with her now was doomed from the start.

"That is what you are waiting on, isn't it? A woman that already has that part figured out?"

"Something like that."

She leaned her head on his shoulder lightly. Ryan stroked her hair feeling its smooth thickness between his fingers for a long, lingering moment.

Then Ahou stood and looked Ryan in the eyes. "What if I—"

The lawyer looked through the outer security room door just then and did a double take. "Ahou? What are you doing here? I have been looking everywhere for you." His eyes studied their closeness like it was the solution for every question on the bar exam.

"Sven, this is Ryan," Ahou said, taking a small step back. "Ryan, this is Sven, my fiancé."

Ryan extended his hand. "Nice to meet you."

Sven looked at the hand like Ryan had just pulled it out of his pants. "What is going on here? What were you doing with my fiancée?"

Ryan placed himself on the desk in front of the pictures and the rabbit and the pillow case and letter. There was no way he was getting dragged into the middle of a lovers' quarrel. He looked pointedly at Ahou.

Ahou steeled herself and then turned full to Sven. "He wasn't doing anything. It was me who was being inappropriate. I—"

"What did he do to you, Ahou?" Sven said, grabbing her by the shoulders. "Why are you protecting him?"

"Sven!" Ahou said, grabbing his hand. "I am tired of you ignoring me. I meant what I said. I was the one being inappropriate."

"I'm not leaving here until I understand what was going on." Sven was breaking down under the pain of betrayal. "You two looked like you were kissing."

Ahou's head dropped. "Axioms," she whispered.

"What? What did you just say?" Sven's voice rose with the mystery. "Did you say axioms?"

"I'm sorry. It is something I heard recently. It made me think. Sven, please . . ." She put her hand on his chest, also familiar but this time restraining. "We will talk, but not here. Not now."

Sven shot Ryan a look filled with malice. "You are not going to say anything?"

Dozens of comments whirled in Ryan's mind, but all of them would add fuel to the fire. He saw the aggression that Sven used with Ahou. He wondered if the bruises came from Sven. Ryan had been where Sven stood now, at the threshold of betrayal, looking into a room that was ugly with intimacy that had nothing to do with him. There was no rejection quite like that. It took a man's bowels and pulled them out through his spine. No consolation would anesthetize the open-heart surgery going on in Sven's soul right now. "No," Ryan said, "I'm not going to say anything."

"I see what is going on. You are the idiot that bought this tower, right? You know she just wants your money."

Ahou fidgeted, shrugging her shoulder like she wanted to disappear. "Sven! Please!"

"No, I want him to know what he is really getting in the package deal," Sven said, stepping near Ryan. "What did she do? Offer you her body? She's good at that. She does that a lot!"

"Sven!" Ahou's eyes were wide, horrified.

Ryan worked to bite his words back behind clenched teeth. There was something particularly low about destroying someone you loved in public. But in the heat of this moment, Ryan was almost sympathetic—he had been there too. But he was not sympathetic to Sven's catastrophic misunderstanding. The boy had no clue. Sven didn't know what inspired the woman he had asked to marry him. And this is, of course, why Ahou knew there was something missing: *she* was missing.

Sven took Ryan's silence as defiance. "You are just a perverted old man who can't get a woman without money."

And doesn't it suck that she wants me and not you, anyway? What does that tell you?

That is the thought that popped to the tip of his tongue. But then it was better to let this kid die his own slow relational death. So Ryan nodded and said, "You are correct. That is exactly my problem."

Sven expected a fight but was caught flatfooted with concession. Finally, he said to Ahou, "See?! See?! He admits that all he has is money."

Ahou started to retort but saw Ryan's subtle shake of the head.

Ryan dropped his hands to readjust himself on the desk. If Sven saw the pictures and the rabbit, this would get uglier fast. Sven's head snapped back to Ryan. The movement drew Sven's eyes to Ryan's hip. And for the first time, Sven noticed the Glock in the holster.

"If . . . if . . ." he said, wagging his finger. "If you didn't have that gun, I'd kick your ass!" Sven stormed out of the security office.

"I'm so, so sorry," Ahou said. "What he said about the money . . ." She looked hard into Ryan's eyes, imploring. "It's not true."

Ryan stood, and took her hand. "Ahou, I know it isn't true."

"You do?" she said, squeezing his fingers.

"Of course," Ryan said. "Money doesn't interest you. And more important, I know that has nothing to do with your interest in me."

Relief flooded through her face and rolled down her body. "Thank you," Ahou said. "What you must think of me. The other stuff he said . . . it is . . . uh . . . it's not—" Her voice froze in her throat.

Ryan just looked, just took in her reaction.

"I was going to lie to you, but . . ." her voice hitched, "I won't lie to you anymore."

"The truth is always best with me."

"Even the ugly parts?"

"Well, I'm not sure what you are calling ugly, but even those. If I know who you are, then maybe I can find myself in you."

"*Maybe* you could find yourself in me?"

"Maybe."

Ahou nodded, her breath hitching in her throat. "I won't be here for a while to tell you about me. Promise me you will read my letter. Then promise me you will go back to my room and learn more," she kissed his cheek, and the cold, damp, wind blew the last of the mirage away as she walked out of the security office.

41

Global Infection: ≤ 27.8000%

"My daughter is wanting you to having this for her," Firouz said, pressing the stuffed rabbit back into Ryan's hands.

Ahou stood on the far side of the roof, looking into the darkened sky, stealing glances back at Ryan when she thought Sven wasn't looking. But Sven was always looking, his glare promising mayhem that Ryan tried not to notice. Her face was puffy and wet, her dark eyes deep wells of pain, but she stood, shoulders held high like she was determined to face the future with courage.

"But this meant so much to her," Ryan said. "She must take it."

"It is to you for a gift," Firouz said and then turned toward the sounds of rotors chopping through the air. Daniel Ryder's remaining Black Hawk was coming from the west over the mountains. It looked like any one of a dozen military Black Hawks shuttling in and out of the Three Rivers Valley.

"You having my blessing for Ahou. For she to be coming back to here. It is God's will. He is watching you over. He is watching her over. She does not believe that yet. But she telling me that she has much to be growing. This I know. She is my daughter. But I am to be giving my blessing to you for her. She will be seeing you before again."

Ryan could not seem to make sense of Firouz's thoughts. Giving his blessing for what? And how would she be coming back? Did he not understand that they were going to a vault that would be locked against the world for decades? So Ryan said, "Thank you, Firouz. Thank you for your blessing. Thank you for your kindness. Ahou is a wonderful woman. I'm sure she and Sven will make a great life together."

Firouz got the same sly smile that Ahou often wore. "Sven is a good boy, but he is not being for her. She is not being ready for her man." He opened his arms wide and gave Ryan a big hug. "You having my blessing for Ahou. Seeing you before again," he said and kissed his cheek and turned away.

And that was when Ryan remembered Ahou's notebook. The helicopter was still minutes from landing on the Renaissance tower's helipad; he sprinted off the roof.

The quiet confines of the Renaissance Tower penthouse were an eerie contrast to the pandemonium that reigned for the hours that elapsed until everyone filed to the helipad to wait for their ride out of Pittsburgh. Daniel barked orders and organized resources, and his secretary and staff chronicled his wishes and burned up their satellite phones and computers to achieve his outcomes.

Some of the Ryder clan hovered around the television or radio, consuming the federal broadcast. News reports focused on the dangers of air flight and the unreliability of pilots, the unexplained rash of aircraft crashes most likely caused by nonunion service contracts and the air traffic controllers' strike. The narrative was set and it could only mean martial law was a formality and the news template meant that government powers didn't think they had the ability to dominate the skies. They were trying to terrify people from crawling on an aircraft.

Word spread about Marco's resurrection, and people wanted answers. His parents, his brothers, Daniel and Lisa Ryder had gone to the closed-casket funeral and received the tri-folded American flag complete with the posthumous Bronze Star. The official report said that Marco Paguero saved a platoon from destruction against the Caliphate's forces in a small town called San Felice in Italy. The official report also said he had been killed in action. Marco was vague about why he wasn't in Arlington National Cemetery. Twice someone probed for details; Marco's eyes slid into the deep distance and he started to shake. His left arm and leg were covered with bite marks; his left hand was missing the pinky finger down to the second knuckle. There was a bullet wound that grazed his right shoulder, and his chest was full of small bruises. Some wounds were healing, but most lacerations were healing badly from popped stitches and infection.

The medic worked on Marco, cleaning the wounds, repairing stitches, applying combat gel and every other medical treatment he could perform before he had to leave. The medic's last demand was that Marco complete an IV antibiotics regimen. After the regimen he was to take two doses of Maksimov Therapy—if it could be found—to help regenerate the large amount of decaying flesh. If he did as prescribed, Marco might survive, but if he failed the prescriptions, the best outcome was amputation of his left arm. The worst and the most likely result was that he would find a resting place in an unmarked grave.

Of course, since he wasn't dead, others wanted to know why Marco wasn't with his unit. Someone whispered AWOL, but not in Raphael's presence. Others said it was good that he was not with his unit, because he found Simone. Simone was exhausted from his weeks of lonely vigilance. At first, he had feared he would turn into one of the infected and didn't want to sleep. Then it became clear he was not going mad and didn't want to sleep because he feared someone would find him, which is exactly what happened. Marco found his brother curled up in his sleeping bag, deep in the corner of an old, abandoned industrial building.

Ryan was lost when they started talking about streets and roads and empty industrial locations within the Greater Pittsburgh area. But he did understand that Simone had survived by retreating to where the four Paguero brothers practiced three-gun shooting. Three-gun shooting was a competition under time constraints built around handguns, shotguns, and carbines that required the shooters to navigate combat environment style courses filled with targets.

Deep in the bowels of an old manufacturing plant, they had set up a shooting range and hidden an arsenal. It turned out that there was large prize money in three-gun competitions. Because it was deemed a sport, participants could petition the government to own carbines. Lots of people flooded into the sport so they could qualify.

Before heading into the Army, Marco was good enough to get a sponsorship. And when Timoteo—the next brother in the Paguero lineage—followed in his brother's footsteps and then exceeded him in skill. The boys abused their ammunition sponsors and reloading suppliers to fill up their stockpile.

Ryan vaguely remembered catching a television show years ago called *Three-Gun Universe* that covered professional international shooting matches. It was like watching football with shaky cameras and flashy photography, listening to men invent drama like old wives, having never seeing a play from scrimmage. Ryan got so disgusted with never being able to see the shooting that he stopped watching.

Someone demanded to know how adolescent boys could afford such an appalling hobby. Raphael wasn't inclined to explain, so Richard Ryder took the opportunity to deride Leona Paguero for planning an armed revolt against the American government. According to Richard, since the U.S. government had placed a maximum on the purchase of ammunition, the revolt planning extended to teaching her boys how to deal on the black market. Raphael corrected the record to reflect "Marxist revolution."

Long before Marco shipped out for basic training, the Paguero boys spliced in power to the deep recesses of the manufacturing plant, then added lights, a heater and a refrigerator where they stockpiled food. Simone forted himself inside the old building and waited for his doom. But the bite mark healed and then late yesterday afternoon, Simone woke to his brother's prodding. Marco had come from the empty, ransacked Paguero house in the Pittsburgh suburbs. He went to their shooting range looking for weapons and food and found his brother. Simone didn't know where else to look, but the Renaissance tower, so they loaded all the magazines they had, packed the truck with as much of the as they could fit in it, strapped on their tactical gear and fought their way into downtown.

After the phone call with his mother and eating enough food to feed six men, Simone fell asleep in the master penthouse suite. Marco sat in a chair doped to the eyeballs from pain killers with an IV stand beside him and stared at a romantic comedy streaming from the penthouse entertainment system.

Ryan ran past Marco on his path to the security room. He grabbed the notebook out of his computer bag and retraced his steps through the endless checkpoints that made up rooftop security, through the rooftop door that looked like a bunker, down the winding stone path and steps at the foot of the raised helipad.

The helicopter's blades churned the air like a thoroughbred impatiently pawing at the ground.

Ahou was already on the chopper. The last few people piled into the Black Hawk. This wasn't a passenger aircraft, and people were trying to wedge in any way they could. Ahou wasn't getting out.

"Ryan Sage," Lisa Ryder said above the roar, "we never really had an opportunity to talk, but I owe you a great debt for what you did."

"Well, I did get quite a lot from the purchase."

"Yes, what you have done with Richard is good too. But what you are doing for the Pagueros . . ." Lisa's voice broke. "They are like my grandchildren. Marco and Timoteo are wonderful boys. Simone is my little pill, but he is a good boy at heart. And Lucas . . . you have not met him yet, but he is the sweetest thing. I watched him and held him in my arms when he was a baby." She descended into sobs. Slowly, she reached out and took Ryan's hand. "I will miss him. Please take care of him for me." Lisa held Ryan's gaze deep into his eyes. "Please, promise me to take care of them."

Ryan had seen those eyes before: blue and fierce. They reminded him of his mother. Lisa Ryder did not let him go, expecting an answer. "Yes, ma'am. I will do my best to take care of them."

She hugged him tight. "Oh, I am not ma'am. Call me mom, please. You have my family. Now you are part of mine."

"Yes, Mom. Thank you."

She nodded and smiled, collected herself, and climbed the stairs.

Daniel watched her go as he tried to master his own emotion. Finally, he said, "Son, I thought we were going to miss you. Where did you go?" he said. And even though he was no longer in a designer suit, now dressed BDUs, Daniel Ryder was still an imposing presence.

"I had to go find something for Ahou."

"Are you sure you want to let her go?"

"I don't think I really had her. I'm not sure what is between us, but this is all far too serious for her to be here with me on a whim in the face of the end of the world. And not least of which, she has a fiancé."

"That will never last."

Ryan nodded. "I suspect you are right. That relationship is doomed. It was doomed long before she met me, but I can't be what prompts Ahou to take the right action. I won't be the motivating force of a woman's life. That is a bad standard to set. She needs to do that for herself," he said. "Anyway, this is her notebook. It was important to her. She needs to have it."

Daniel took it in hand. "I understand. But you know they had to restrain her to get her to come to the tower?"

"What do you mean?"

"When she found out that they were going to leave you behind, they had to restrain her to keep her in the vehicle. My men had to pack a bag for her."

That explained the bruises and why she had not been able to take keepsakes. That was why they took some notebooks but not the one she had been writing in. Ahou had told them to get her notebook, and they had grabbed a handful and knocked the one she wanted on the floor. "I'm not sure what to say to that."

"Maybe nothing to say," Daniel said. "Maybe nothing to do. Maybe just the wrong time. Maybe it isn't meant to be. But I thought you should know." He held up the notebook. "I will make sure she gets—"

Suddenly, there was an explosion high in the sky to the south. They saw the brief flash of a fireball and a plane crumbled out of the sky.

People in the helicopter screamed. Steve, in the pilot seat, twirled his index finger, insistent, his face drawn tight with concentration and the implacability of military training. The message was very clear: "We've *got* to go."

Daniel watched the people slither into available space. His son stood at the door, the last one to board. "You have no idea what you have done for me today," he had said right into Ryan's ear to be heard above the din.

Ryan nodded. He saw Richard. He remembered the look of triumph. "Dad . . . do you mind if I call you dad?"

Daniel's eyes watered. He grabbed Ryan in a bear hug. "Of course, son."

"Then Dad, you must listen to me. I know he is your son. I know you love Richard. That is the way of parents, I suppose. But you must know I haven't done you any favors. Nothing has changed in his mind. He is a true believer who is committed to the ideology of Marxist destruction. He's poison. It won't stop just because he gets safety. He will always believe that what you represent is evil. You need to know that he hates you in principle. There is no compromise between you because you differ at the root."

Daniel held Ryan's shoulder. "Yes, I know who he is. But I am still grateful for the opportunity to have him with me. Do not worry." He grabbed Ryan by the neck and wept softly into his shoulder. Finally, he broke the embrace. "Of course, we already went over the location for all of the important information. My team is still working on finalizing all the details, but we have not abandoned you here. We will be in constant communication until we can't talk anymore. But this envelope is from me. You will need what is in here in the days to come." He slid a thick envelope into Ryan's hand. "A gift from me."

Then Daniel Ryder climbed the stairs and piled into the last available space in the helicopter that lifted into the air. And for the first time since Daniel Ryder sat down at the sub shop table, he didn't have a phone to his ear. The faintest rim of light coming off the western sky backlit the Black Hawks, making it look like a line of fleas jumping from the back of a drowning dog.

Ryan walked to the helipad and stood in the middle of a big blue R, illuminated only by the soft glow of solar cell lights ringing the outer edge. He could feel the cold breeze and hear the soft whip of the three-wind turbines that generated power on the roof. He could smell the cloying smoke that drifted high along the air current from the fiery basin below. He looked down at the streets running to the east. He saw the buildings thrust up out of the ground like defiant fingers washed in the color of embers from along the Monongahela shoreline. The last time he had seen this kind of setting it had been in Washington, D.C., standing in a suite in the Four Seasons hotel looking down at the city. At the time he was speaking in metaphors, but today the fingers were washed with the deep reds from the fires burning across the valley.

He felt Raphael at his side. "It is on fire," Ryan said.

"*Si*," Raphael said. "But we are safe here."

"Safe," Ryan said. "My sister wanted me to be safe and keep my mouth shut. I told her that George Washington was rolling in his grave over the endless list of constitutional violations. Maybe he really is trying to crawl out of the ground. Maybe this plague will bring him back to life."

"What *es* this you say?"

"I'm sorry, Raphael. I'm remembering something I said to my sister many months ago. I told her then that America was on fire, but you just couldn't see the flames yet."

"She *es* dead in these fires down there?"

"She is one of them, Raphael. She is one of them."

Ryan took a step forward and looked into the night, remembering. "And now Tess, I guess I really do speak for the dead. I told you, Tess. Government is not reason; it is not eloquence—it is force! Like fire, it is a dangerous servant and a fearful master. Never for a moment should it be left to irresponsible action."

Ryan paused, letting the anger build inside.

"Damn it, Tess, I told you! This is the end of the path!" he shouted like maybe she could hear him. "Government is fire, and the flames consume everything they touch!" his voice echoed dimly off the distant valley.

"And I will make sure that every living soul is dead certain what burned everything down."

We Didn't Start the Fire

Harry Truman, Doris Day, Red China, Johnnie Ray
South Pacific, Walter Winchell, Joe DiMaggio

Joe McCarthy, Richard Nixon, Studebaker, television
North Korea, South Korea, Marilyn Monroe

Rosenbergs, H-Bomb, Sugar Ray, Panmunjom
Brando, "The King and I," and "The Catcher in the Rye"

Eisenhower, vaccine, England's got a new queen
Marciano, Liberace, Santayana goodbye

CHORUS

We didn't start the fire
It was always burning
Since the world's been turning
We didn't start the fire
No, we didn't light it
But we tried to fight it

Billy Joel

Author's Note

A pocalyptic scenarios are fascinating. It is fun to ponder how a person survives in the face of full societal breakdown, and a zombie infestation is a wonderfully entertaining end of the world scenario. Of course, I'm not the first to offer this vision of the future and most likely not the last. To be sure, grim, barbaric, savage, death-worshiping Mad Max milieus are standard fare.

But what if the guiding outlook for the future wasn't nihilism and the artistic vision wasn't merely the slaughtering rehash of Saw sequel 987?

The answer to this question began to take shape on a long solitary late night car ride coming from a dance in Columbus, Ohio. As I contemplated the nature of my protagonist, I decided to further stand convention on its ear: what emerged was a philosopher-businessman, a man who knew exactly what he was doing, and why. I imagined a man who was willing to take a risk, to acquire his own prosperity at his own expense, even in the face of total disaster.

By now, dear reader, you've read the story and know why the philosopher part matters, but the businessman part is equally important, if for no other reason that you are confronted with a hero that people struggle to see as heroic. And there is good reason that readers will trip over this portrayal. The reason is simple: you have almost never seen a businessman as a hero in American entertainment.

Notice that a businessman—or the offshoot of business, corporations—is most likely the villain in modern American entertainment. This is a troublesome reality on its face, but exponentially more troublesome when considering that serial killers are the runner-up villain.

Art is the tip of the leaf on the very end of the philosophical tree, reflecting back to a culture, a specific affirmation of its most deeply held values. The fact that the businessman is an archetype of evil is a profound testimony to our cultural expectations. That we have a moral equivalency between John Wayne Gacy and Charles Kettering, Dexter and Steve Jobs,

Ted Bundy and Gordon Gekko screams from the housetops our true sense of bankrupt virtues, which is the fact that western culture presumes that the "businessman," the "rich" man, is a creature more sub-human than a psychopath, bespeaks a profound cultural malady.

The serial killer motif is past worn out and it is time for the real historical villains be brought into full relief. The world's greatest monsters have always been—and will always be—those holding the reins of government power. On the short-list of mass murderers, there are numerous government leaders who make Jeffrey Dahmer look like a vegetarian preschool teacher. For example, most of you, dear readers, can rattle off the answer to this Jeopardy question in seconds.

Who was the painter who became *der Fuhrer*?

Easy to answer, right?

But I would make a small wager that most people cannot name the top five on the list of genocidal despots list. And here is the punch line to the ignorance: good old Adolph was a piker when compared to those people. The collective ignorance in western culture is tragic considering that the mechanics and outcomes of tyranny are profoundly, maddeningly, obviously consistent.

The outcome of my many musings—this work you now hold in your hands—is a cross between George Orwell's *1984* and George A. Romero's *Dawn of the Dead*.

Now that you have a glimpse into the method behind the madness, I want talk about Pittsburgh. I was about 80 percent through the first draft and I hadn't picked a city. My story editor is like, "So where the heck is this happening?" And I'm like, "Uh, I don't know."

I vaguely, kinda, sorta, generally knew that it was going to be in the Midwest-ish area, but I couldn't seem to land on a firm location. Growing up near Dayton meant I was inclined to consider that city first, but after decades of punitive socialist public policy, the city planners have managed to tax just about every world-class business out of its narrow limits and turn downtown into a ghost town with tumbleweeds and everything. I did get the idea for the Renaissance Tower while attending a Christmas party in Kettering Tower, so there are some vague-ish mental pictures that ended up in the novel. I also used the underground loading dock concept of the old Rikes building. Back in Dayton's heyday, when NCR, Delco, Frigidaire, Elders, Dayton Press, General Motors, etc. were the economic backbone of the Gem City, Rikes Department Store was *the* place to go shopping. I remember my grandmother getting dressed up in her Sunday best to take a trip into downtown just to go to Rikes. The means to bring product into the building was by a vast underground loading dock that let semi-trailers pull in and do a full turn. The underside of the Renaissance Tower is basically that concept.

Cincinnati was among the considerations. I love old inner city architecture that emerged during the late nineteenth century and persisted well into the 1950s. And I've spent lots of hours just walking the streets looking at how builders from a hundred years ago created structures that touched the sky, wondering at their original use and pondering why they sit empty. I want to play like an adventurer and go spelunk in those old buildings, but that usually gets a brief stay in jail.

Cincinnati had the added value of being a populous city. People live there, and I thought the conflict of a large-ish zombie infected population was a more interesting problem to overcome than the standard rural outpost for civilization. However, Cincinnati posed some geographical problems: its specific topology and its location in relationship to the rest of the country didn't seem to fit well with my overall vision of unfolding events. I had similar problems with using Lexington and Louisville. Cleveland will probably have a role later in the storyline, but it wasn't where I wanted to start. Indianapolis is a beautiful city, but its topography is flat and wide open. So it doesn't lend itself to a very high creepy factor. And there isn't really a high population city until St. Louis, and that was too far west with what I wanted to do.

So the spot that fit the bill, at least from pictures and form aerial footage on Monday Night Football, was Pittsburgh. But from that last sentence, you can guess at my problem. I had never been there in my life, and you can only learn so much from Google Earth. So late in September of 2012, I packed up my SUV with my bike (one you pedal) and spent two days riding around downtown: up streets and down avenues using my iPhone to take videos like I was my own location scout. I'm dressed like I'm racing the Tour de France and I'm talking to myself. I got really interesting looks.

Anyway, Pittsburgh is perfect for the zombie apocalypse, particularly the downtown area and the wedge of land that runs between the Allegany and Monongahela rivers. The streets are narrow, and the buildings are tall. Additionally, the tunnels are dark, and the little enclave neighborhoods are packed tight and the city is full of people, which means lots of zombies. And once I started looking the city over, I realized I'd written scenes in my head that were spooky similar to the actual locations—too freaking fun.

Without the trip, I would never have really grasped the environment, or how that would impact authentic character reactions. (Oh my God, the hills!) I had a great time chatting up anyone who would talk to me about the city. (One waitress in the Hard Rock Café was very helpful while she did her side work before going home for the night.)

There was only one problem: the buildings I created in my head—Firouz Hoagies and Minimart at Our Way and Pride and The Renaissance Tower sitting at the corner of First Avenue and Smithfield—don't exist. So for you Pittsburgh natives, you will be quick to point out that Firouz's retail stores and Builder Bob's apartments are really (as of the time of this writing) a gravel parking lot. To build the Renaissance Tower (my environmentally friendly engineering feat), I think I wiped everything from Boulevard of the Allies to Fort Pitt Boulevard. This means that Pittsburgh is out (at the time of this writing) a couple office buildings, a college, an adult bookstore, some apartments, a couple hole-in-the-wall restaurants, a fire station and a government building. I figure losing a government building isn't a great loss. (And in the story, the city tyrants are making the Molitor group build it gratis just like real city tyrants extort business men in the "free market.") In the event that you are offended . . . sorry for screwing up your city but I did it for the greater good.

And for you, dear readers, who go to Pittsburgh looking for actual locations, my liberty is called *literary license*. If nothing else, you can just pretend I'm NBC cutting and pasting the George Zimmerman tape together to make it say whatever they want. Great fiction advancing a political agenda is still great fiction, right?

J. Lorin 2013

www.ingramcontent.com/pod-product-compliance
Lightning Source LLC
Chambersburg PA
CBHW032211030726
47494CB00020B/956